Reconciled again draw[...] their precarious unfol[...] struggles to right an o[...] like pure golden threa[...] [s]criptural prayers exploding in Technicolor. As the characters intuitively pray for wisdom and protection, the story unfolds in surprisingly complex and unusually delightful scenarios of reconciliation. Only criticism: I want more, more, more!

—Shirley Harness, former Governor
of the Canadian Bible Society, Vancouver, BC

Sheilah has done it again with another compelling novel that will stir you to believe for the will of the Father to come to pass in our generation. Once you start, you will find it hard to put down, as each passage deepens with excitement!

—Dave Mathieu, Dean of Students
at Victory Training Centre, Barrie, ON

The captivating saga of Kaye and Max catapults one into the midst of suspense, romance, and intrigue. As the plot twists, there are surprises around each corner, and one's promise to "stop at the end of this chapter" will be futile! Satisfaction will come as all is reconciled with the conclusion. The story is a testimony to God's promise that *"all that happens to us is working for our good if we love Him and are fitting into his plans"* (Romans 1:28, TLB). Completely engaging!

—Ruth E. McGuire,
Teacher and avid reader, Chesley, ON

Sheilah Fletch is a special writer who always wants you to believe that Jesus is for real. Another great book that keeps your attention right to the end. Very compelling. Well done.

—Cathy Wellwood, Chief Development Officer,
Good Shepherd Centres, Hamilton, ON

SHEILAH FLETCH

RECONCILED

RECONCILED
Copyright © 2014 by Sheilah Fletch

Scripture quotations marked (NIV) taken from THE HOLY BIBLE, NEW INTERNATIONAL VERSION®, NIV® Copyright © 1973, 1978, 1984, 2011 by Biblica, Inc.® Used by permission. All rights reserved worldwide. Scripture quotations marked (TLB) are taken from The Living Bible copyright © 1971. Used by permission of Tyndale House Publishers, Inc., Carol Stream, Illinois 60188. All rights reserved.

Printed in Canada

ISBN: 978-1-4866-0537-8

Word Alive Press
131 Cordite Road, Winnipeg, MB R3W 1S1
www.wordalivepress.ca

Cataloguing in Publication information may be obtained through Library and Archives Canada.

dedication

I dedicate *Reconciled* in loving memory of three special sisters in Christ—Linda L. Bursack of Minnesota, Brenda A. Leroux of Ontario, and Ann Miller of Pennsylvania. Each one was a living letter from God who significantly impacted my Christian walk in their own unique way. Your love for Jesus, your trust in the Scriptures, and your heart to pray for others, even in the midst of your own personal health adversities, truly inspired me. You knew Christ reconciled you to God and you willingly picked up His ministry of reconciliation. You were His ambassadors and most definitely wives of noble character, models for our time!

acknowledgements

Thanks to the following:

My husband, Dr. Andy Fletch. Your prayers, encouragement, proofreading, electronic expertise, prodding, consoling, and just always being there helped me persevere to birth *Reconciled*.

My four teenage grandchildren, Codie, Bryce, Mitchell, and Faith. Your active imaginations and interest in reading rekindled my own imagination and love of storytelling from days gone by.

Mary Golem, for the back cover's photograph of me and continuous words of encouragement.

James Culligan, Gwen Smithers- Kiar, and Eleanor Pauling, for your artistic comments regarding the cover and your publicity help.

Donna Hatten and Liz Pulley, former parishioners, who were the first to scrutinize my rough draft. Your encouragement prompted me to continue.

Word Alive Publishing Consultant Marie Luhmert and Publishing Assistant Kylee Unrau, who carefully guided me through the publishing maze to make *Reconciled* a reality.

The many spiritual renewal teachers in Canada and the United States, who deepened my own relationship with the Holy Spirit. Especially Pastors Glen Carlson of Alberta and Wes Campbell of Be A Hero Ministries, British Columbia, both of whom encouraged me through their writing and teaching to pray Scriptures, particularly the Psalms.

The many authors of faith-based novels, such as Randy Alcorn, Frank Peretti, and Francine Rivers. Through your storytelling, you opened my imagination to better ponder specific Biblical Kingdom of God realities like heaven; the ancient Nicene Creed's invisible realm of creation; and the first-century Christians' life experiences as they engaged their culture.

And of course, the premier storyteller, Jesus Christ, who told parables—earthly stories with heavenly meanings—to stimulate our imaginations to better grasp Kingdom of God truths.

author's introduction

Parables are earthly stories that hold a heavenly meaning or truth. When Jesus told a parable, He would later explain its heavenly meaning to His followers. Today, Jesus reigns in heaven, but as He told His disciples in John 16:14 regarding the Holy Spirit's work, *"He will bring glory to me by taking from what is mine and making it known to you"* (NIV).

Faith-based Christian novels can be viewed as modern parables. Indeed, they are earthly stories which can be read solely for entertainment. However, for the discerning reader, beneath the surface a heavenly nugget can often be found just waiting to be mined.

My previous novel *Forgiven*, and now the sequel *Reconciled*, were written with that purpose in mind. I crafted the stories hoping to challenge the reader's imagination to explore how God, including the Holy Spirit, is portrayed interacting with ordinary people who simply choose, by faith, to step out and pray Scripture into their circumstances. As they do so, Jesus comes alive within them.

To this end, I use quotation marks whenever characters in the novel pray to God, either silently or spoken. This is to emphasize that Christian prayer is meant to be a living conversation between Christ and His followers. It is a dialogue, not a monologue! Although this is a simple truth, it is one which eluded me for thirty-seven years of my life, even though during that time I would have identified myself as Christian. Then the Holy Spirit opened my eyes to God's reality and faith exploded, transforming my life!

By including this type of prayer in my novels, I hope those who practice it may be encouraged in their faith journey. For individuals who are like I was, unaware that God really desires a living relationship with you, I pray that my personal experience may become yours.

prologue

Previously, in the novel *Forgiven*, Max Carron, on his release from prison, rather than heading home to his family in Chicago, secretly set out to confront the judge who convicted him. Unwittingly, he ended up in Pennsylvania, not in the judge's home but in that of his neighbor, Kaye McDonald!

Kaye was CEO of Kayleen Enterprises, a highly successful multinational corporation. She inherited her position following the untimely tragic death of her parents. Despite both youth and gender handicaps, she not only solidified her control of the company but also propelled the organization into a respected global entity.

Aside from her astute business sense, Kaye possessed a keen ability to bring out the best in others and had an infectious laughter that could immediately diffuse even the most intense boardroom situation. A stunningly beautiful woman with striking red hair and sparkling green eyes, she was also a woman of deep faith.

The accidental and highly volatile collision of these two lives immediately immersed them in a dramatic game of cat and mouse with a serial sexual predator intent on making Kaye his next victim. However, before collaborating with one another, they needed first to forgive the offense each had committed against the other. In Max's case, he also needed to learn to forgive himself. With God's help, they eventually released their forgiveness and tentatively began to trust each other while formulating a plan to transform their predator into their prey.

Unfortunately, this process took longer than Max planned and his absence soon became a concern not only for his Sicilian family but also for law officials who were friends of Judge Jack Walters.

A further complication was the fact that after her parents' death, Kaye became family to her two neighboring households—Sue and Dave Davidson and Jack and Marnie Walters. They and their children literally adopted Kaye into their lives.

In addition, Jack was the judge who not only convicted Max but also handed down an unduly harsh sentence for a supposedly first-time offender, the reason for which was known only to him. Prior to accepting his appointment to the Supreme Court, he had promised Marnie that he would reserve two months to take a long-promised vacation with her and their daughters to the Holy Land. Two weeks before the trip was scheduled to begin, the judge scheduled to hear Max's case died of a heart attack. Jack was then asked by two older justices, as a favor, before his Supreme Court responsibilities began, to preside at Max's case. Initially he denied their request, knowing it would be unfair to his wife. However, the two older men pleaded that they were too overloaded to take the case themselves. Eventually, they persuaded him that it was simply another Sicilian mob caper, a chance for Jack to show that he was a no-nonsense judge. He decided to throw the book at the young tough, believing the mob would appeal anyway. He did just that, then, went on with his vacation and his life, giving the matter no more thought.

No more thought, that is, until his friend, FBI Special Agent Bernie Epstein, informed him of Carron's release and the Bureau's concern that an attempt at vengeance could be in the offing.

In the meantime, unknown to everyone else, right next door Max and Kaye realized that her predator was indeed a dangerous serial killer who would soon strike! They were involved in a life and death struggle. Equally significant was the fact that forgiveness had opened the door for them to develop a Godly relationship with each other.

As the narrative in *Forgiven* drew to a close, Max barely survived his deadly conflict with the killer. His left leg severely shattered, he lay immobilized in a hospital bed. Exposed was the budding romance between him and Kaye, a relationship that was highly problematic for her two neighbors... Judge Jack Walters and Chief of Police Dave Davidson.

Jack was now convinced that he had been guilty of not exercising professional due diligence in Max's trial. In addition, he had to admit that Max's presence had unquestionably saved the life of his family's dearly loved neighbor and friend. Furthermore, both he and Dave knew Kaye was intent on marrying this man, and their wives were wholeheartedly behind seeing this happen. Unfortunately, neither Sue nor Marnie knew Max's true identity and the difficulty Max's Sicilian ancestry and possible mob connections could pose to their husbands.

Another enigma was that neither Jack nor Dave knew what actually had happened in the drug case in which Max had been charged, even though both now believed he was innocent.

Further complicating matters, Max requested that his whereabouts be kept secret to avoid his domineering father from interfering with his plans to marry Kaye. So Jack Walters, the very person Max's family would consider their enemy, found himself involved in concealing their son from them.

Consequently, Jack Walters was left wrestling with the path that his faith in Christ now dictated he must follow. For him, forgiveness had ushered in the daunting challenge of orchestrating reconciliation. Could all these opposing factions ever be reconciled?

chapter one

J ack Walters perched on the edge of his desk, staring out the window. His blue eyes seemed transformed by the drizzly sky into sharp, steel slits. He pondered the droplets of rain beating mercilessly against the glass panes and slowly exhaled.

Good God, what have I gotten myself into?

Was that a prayer, or merely his frustration escaping like a volcano on the verge of eruption? Jack really didn't know. All he knew was that his well-crafted world had been smashed into oblivion by the events of the past month.

With a sigh, he stood, hands on hips, and glanced yet again out his expansive sixth-floor window. Even on a dreary day, this view of Washington D.C.'s vast parkland was spectacular. It offered a refuge from the weighty, daily issues he faced as a Supreme Court justice.

But not today!

At six-foot-two, Jack's stature afforded respect, even without his title. In his early fifties, he still followed a daily exercise routine. He had maintained the same dedication to physical fitness that had allowed him to become a star quarterback during his college days.

His college gridiron exploits seemed irrelevant to his current dilemma. He let out a low grunt and sank into his oversized leather chair. Even that failed to provide the comfort it normally afforded.

Jack spun the chair around, planted his elbows on the desk and cradled his head in his hands. Up until a month ago, Jack would have labeled his life, private and professional, as perfect. He and his wife Marnie had been one of the first to purchase a lot in a new subdivision in Summerside, a moderate-sized Pennsylvania city and a great place to raise their two daughters. Also, it offered a feasible commute by car or rail to Washington and the small condo he maintained for work-related stays. They had custom-designed their home. Marnie had even been able to find a job as principal at one of Summerside's prestigious schools. Their girls were now off on their own career paths; the youngest had just completed her freshman year of college, while her sister was well into her post-doctorate program on the West Coast.

Jack allowed a faint smile to flit across his face as he thought of his neighborhood. Dave Davidson, on his appointment as Summerside's chief of police, had also bought a home in their subdivision. The developer's only daughter, Kaye McDonald, purchased the third lot. Kaye was a strong-willed, no-nonsense gal. But…

A small laugh escaped from Jack's lips. Indeed, she was strong-willed and no-nonsense, but also extremely beautiful, with the emphasis on *extremely*. She had also been blessed with infectious laughter that could crack a grin on even the dourest face. Jack had surmised correctly that Kaye's father, R.K. McDonald, had caved in to his only child's demand to live independently. However, the man had then carefully orchestrated who her next door neighbors would be.

Jack's eyes misted over. Kaye had definitely become family to both the Walters and the Davidsons after R.K. and his wife were killed in a tragic plane crash. Kaye, now in her mid-thirties, was like a kid sister to him. She had inherited her father's multinational corporation, Kayleen Enterprises. In the gene pool, she had certainly gotten his aptitude for business and keen intuition for what made people tick. Despite age and gender handicaps, she had propelled herself into an astute businesswoman, well capable of being Kayleen's CEO.

Nonetheless, with R.K.'s death the subdivision's development had ground to a halt. This had left all three property owners an idyllic private green belt in which to enjoy nature. Not only had the three households bonded as neighbors, all worshipped at Summerside's large Community Church, where Jack served as a lay pastor.

And you blew it.

Jack winced, knowing exactly which memory these words evoked. Over six and a half years ago, just before he had assumed his Supreme Court justice appointment, as a favor to two older justices he had agreed to hear a drug case. As a result, he had sentenced a young American Sicilian, Massimiliano Carron, to six years in federal prison for drug trafficking. It had been a rush trial, because earlier he'd promised that before beginning his Supreme Court duties, he would take Marnie and the girls for a month-long cruise, culminating in a trip to the Holy Land. Jack had negotiated a two-month grace period before assuming his role as a Supreme Court justice, but all that evaporated pretty quickly when the judge assigned to the Carron trial suddenly suffered a massive heart attack and died.

Jack slammed his fist on the desk. In making his decision to hear that case, he had ignored the needs of the three most important people in his life. Marnie, for the first time in their married life, had been absolutely furious with him. With good justification.

So what did you do, Jack? You took the advice of those two older justices, presumed Carron's guilt, expedited the trial, delivered the verdict and sentence, appeased your wife and daughters, and enjoyed your vacation.

He'd assumed the young Carron belonged to the mob, would appeal the sentence and receive a slap on the wrist and soon be free. The bonus? The mob would have a healthy respect for Justice Jack Walters.

However, it was only a few months ago that he had discovered there'd been no appeal. Carron had served his full term. To make matters worse, Jack's long-time friend Art Brown, now a highly esteemed Harvard law professor, believed Carron innocent. In all Jack's legal career, he had sought to be a hundred percent aboveboard. He'd carved out a reputation for being hard but fair.

Jack sighed. *"Here I am, Jesus, having to face the fact that I may have very well blown it in the Carron trial."*

Another thought, firm but gentle, penetrated his gloom. *"Really? Who then would have been there to protect Kaye from that vicious killer?"*

Jack frowned. *"But Lord, the man could be connected to the mob. If Carron is innocent, what did go on in that motel room that they never appealed?"*

Immediately, Jack recalled the scripture he'd read in his morning devotion: *"Ask and you will receive, seek and you will find, knock and the door will open for you."* He sat back in his chair, preparing to ponder this, when he was interrupted by a knock at his office door.

He cleared his throat. "Please, come in, Mrs. Stuart."

His secretary, a graying, middle-aged woman, entered. However, Jack carefully concealed from her the inner struggle that raged within him.

"Sorry to interrupt you, Your Honor, but you said you needed to catch the early commuter train to Summerside," she said. "You wanted to make your evening meeting there."

Jack glanced at his watch and grimaced. He'd totally lost track of the time.

"Thank you for reminding me." He smiled lamely. "Have a good weekend. I'll see you on Monday."

He grabbed his briefcase, stuffing it with the large pile of papers that adorned the corner of his desk, and made a mad dash to hail a cab.

chapter two

J ack sank into his seat on the commuter train, perspiring. He had barely made the connection. His earlier thoughts had fled in the rush to get here, but as soon as the train began to wind its way through the countryside, his angst returned.

He stared out the window, listening to the clickety-clack of the wheels, remembering that Kaye had been the brunt of a brutal killer's fantasy. Carron had unexpectedly shown up in their neighborhood to confront Jack, but he'd gone to Kaye's house instead—in time to save her from Henry Glaxton, who had broken into her house. If not for that mistake of Max's, Kaye likely would have died.

Jack was grateful for Carron's intervention. That only problem was that Kaye had never given a member of the opposite sex a passing glance until then. Now she professed to be head over heels in love with Carron. Even worse, the attraction seemed mutual!

Massimiliano—or Max, as he insisted everyone call him—was now in Summerside's hospital with a mangled leg. No one was to be notified of his whereabouts. This gave he and Kaye opportunity to sort out their emotions for each other

Keeping him incognito was no small feat. Jack's Bureau friend, Special Agent Bernard Epstein, had warned them that Carron's father and the rest of his Italian friends were on the prowl for the missing offspring.

Jack laid his head back against the seat and sighed. Along with his neighbor Dave, he'd concocted a plan to ensure that Max would never be left alone in his hospital room. Someone from the neighborhood would always be with him.

On the surface, this plan appeared sound, but it had two serious flaws. The first was that they all had important career commitments. The second was that, except for Kaye, Dave, and Jack, no one else knew Carron's true identity. They had chosen to identify him in the hospital as Maxwell Kerr. This had meant lying to their families. Marnie and Dave's wife Sue were excited about the vigil because Kaye was so smitten with him. Indeed, Sue and Marnie held out real hope that their Kaye would soon settle into matrimonial bliss.

For Jack, however, this "Max vigil," as they called it, was very taxing on his schedule. Perhaps that's why he dozed off and nearly missed the Summerside stop.

Glancing at his watch, he was horrified to see it was 6:30 p.m. He snatched his briefcase and overnight bag, poised to dash the moment the train stopped.

Of all nights for this train to run late, he thought with a groan. *I was on deck to babysit Max at 6:00 so Sue could make her 7:00 meeting.*

The moment his feet touched the platform, he raced for the parking lot. Not very dignified for someone of his age and position to jostle through the crowds, but given the circumstances there wasn't much else to do.

That's when he spied the car waiting for him. He started to laugh. The chief of police also had the premier parking spots.

He threw his bags into the back seat of Dave's police cruiser and hopped into the passenger side. "Hi Dave. The train was running late. So sorry!"

Jack sank into the seat gasping for breath.

"Tad out of shape, are we?" Dave grinned. "Jack, my man, you need to set aside time to get back to the gym. But now that I've given you my fitness lecture, hold on to your hat. We can be at the hospital in ten minutes."

"Yeah, right. It's a good twenty to twenty five minutes away, and rush hour traffic isn't finished."

"Just watch."

As Dave pulled into traffic, up went the flashing lights, on went the siren. Cars pulled over everywhere in sight. Ten minutes later, Dave pulled up to the hospital's rear door.

Sue had been watching their approach from the fourth-floor window. She turned to Max, who was just finishing his supper.

"My relief has arrived, sir, so I shall be off." She crossed the room, giving the man an affectionate kiss on the forehead. "Your recovery is amazing, obviously the benefit of being so physically fit."

"Do you think I'll really get out of this confounded sling tomorrow?" Max asked.

"According to the docs, it looks promising." Her encouraging words prompted a big grin from her patient. "But hey, before you start celebrating, remember the next step: lose the sling but gain a steel brace! You won't be any more mobile than you are now. The only difference is you won't be tied to this bed any longer."

"At least it's the next step. Each leg of the journey is a step forward, and I intend to celebrate each step!"

"Max, if anyone deserves celebrating, you sure do. See you tomorrow evening."

Squeezing his hand, she headed for the door.

"Sue, when does Kaye get back?" he called to her.

"I think she's back in town tomorrow. I expect you'll see her by evening." Sue wheeled around and blew a kiss. "Good bye, lover. Be patient!"

With that, she disappeared down the corridor.

Max heard the elevator open and Jack's muffled apology for being late. Then he heard the judge's footsteps heading toward his room. Jack burst into the room breathless.

"You know, Your Honor, you really should pay more attention to exercise. You're really huffing."

Jack stood ramrod straight, dropped his bags by his side, and placed his hands on his hips. "Thank you for your unsolicited advice. Do I need to point out that for the past four weeks every spare moment I have has been devoted to this hospital room?"

"Wow, you're touchy tonight. I might remind you that it was your call to ensure that I not be left alone. I never asked for it."

Jack nodded curtly. "You're right. I apologize for snapping. The trains are usually excellent, unless the commuter is trying to meet a deadline. I was upset about making Sue late, but Dave assured me he'd have her there with ten minutes to spare." He smiled. "Did you hear the siren?"

"Yeah." Max shrugged. "But in here I'm always hearing sirens."

"Well, the Chief of Police was my cabbie."

"In his cruiser," Max asked in surprise.

Jack nodded. "You bet."

"He can do that?"

"Apparently."

"Neat! That would be real cool. Maybe when my leg heals, he'll give me a ride. I never rode in a cruiser before."

Jack looked at him dumbfounded. "Never?"

Max stared at Jack like he had two heads. "Of course not. I never had any cop friends, and I wasn't doing the kind of stuff they give people rides for."

"What about that night, seven years ago, when you were charged?"

"I rode in an ambulance. I was knocked out, had a bad concussion, saw double for three days. Didn't you even read my trial transcripts?"

Jack pursed his lips. "Yeah, I did. Must have forgotten."

"When?"

"When what?"

Max clenched his jaw. "When did you read it?"

"Well, if you want the truth—"

"That would be a good place to start."

Jack pulled up a chair beside Max's bed. "It was a few days ago."

"You didn't read it when you presided at my trial?"

"No, Max, I didn't."

Max just stared at him, jaw dropped. Jack figured it probably was a good thing Max's leg was in a sling attached to the bar above his bed. Otherwise Max would have decked him; at worst, he might have strangled him.

"I told you before about the personal reasons for me wanting your trial to end quickly. I confessed the biased information which I was given, information I wrongly chose to follow." Jack's voice was genuinely apologetic.

"Sure, but I figured you would have at least read the evidence."

Jack studied Max. It seemed as if the man was registering the effect Jack's choices had had on him. Did Jack detect a little moisture in Max's eyes?

Max swallowed hard. "What's done is done. I guess if you had read it, maybe you wouldn't have sent me down for six years and I wouldn't have come looking for you. Then I would never have ended up at Kaye's house and been in a position to stop that psychopath from making Kaye his twenty-third victim." Max inhaled deeply. "I ended his murderous rampage. He may have shattered my leg, but hey, Your Honor, both you and I are glad Kaye came out unharmed, right?"

"True, Max, but a major injustice was done. I really screwed up. You know why, but the why doesn't make it right. Furthermore, both of us know why the prosecutor stayed mum."

"Personal advancement." Max snorted. "If he would have revealed the evidence supporting my innocence, he would have lost."

"So why did your defense choose not to reveal the truth?"

Max's eyes suddenly grew hard. "That, Your Honor, is personal!"

"Well, I told you my personal stuff."

"Well, I'm not telling you mine."

"Max, if you're in trouble with the mob—"

"You think I'm not talking because to do so would mean squealing on someone?"

"Maybe. If that's the case, we could help you."

Max started to laugh. "Well, Your Honor, that is not the case. I think I'm finished discussing this."

Jack shrugged. "Have it your way, Mr. Massimiliano Carron. Or rather, Mr. Kerr!"

He stood and smiled amicably at the man in the bed, but to himself added, *Max, old boy, I'll know the answer eventually. Even if you don't care, that conviction is going to be overturned. For yours and Kaye's sake!*

Jack turned to his briefcase and pulled out a large binder. Out of the corner of his eye, he saw that it had the effect he had desired. Max's curiosity had been piqued.

"What's that?"

"Work to occupy your time, Mr. Kerr."

"What kind of work?"

Jack screwed up his face. "Files. Myriads of files of various business infractions. You should read them, study them, memorize them, then study them some more, looking for legal precedents. Thought you might be interested in perusing these, being as Kaye's in big business. The info you gain might help her make better and wiser decisions."

"Really?"

"Yes. Do you want me to leave it with you?"

"It's not confidential or nothing?"

"Nope, Max, they're just old cases that wannabe lawyers need to familiarize themselves with to prepare for the bar."

"I can't go to the bar, though. Because of my conviction."

"True, but you can still train yourself to be of use as a personal counselor to Kaye. After all, as a CEO she has to traverse a legal minefield on a national and global scale."

He could see Max's curiosity getting the better of him.

"Okay, I'll do it," Max finally volunteered. "I actually enjoyed those law courses I took in prison."

The two bantered back and forth, all the while watching the Phillies beat the Cards. Then, while Jack was helping Max get ready for the night, Max began to share his really big news.

"I almost forgot," he said. "Dr. Chandrah—you know, my orthopedic surgeon—was in today. She said they'd X-ray my leg tomorrow. If all goes well, she expects they'll take me out of this bed sling and put me on the metal frame support."

"Great, Max. Will that allow you to be mobile?"

"Not just yet, apparently." Max sighed. "She said it would be pretty cumbersome. At least I won't be attached to the bed. They can move me into a chair, so I could be pushed around. As I understand, my leg is still going to be pretty much perpendicular to my body."

Trust would not be an easy thing to establish, Jack thought as they fell off to sleep. Their relationship could at best be described as cautious, intertwined here and there with skepticism. The chasm between convicted felon and judge was vast.

Jack had to admit that his motivation in handing Max these legal cases stemmed in part from his college rivalry with his old roommate. Brownie had started a new program in Max's penitentiary to encourage deserving inmates to take the time to upgrade their education. For some, it meant working on a high school diploma; for others, taking college courses. In Max's case, he already possessed a B.A., so Brownie had enrolled him in law. Max proved so competent that he actually secured all his course requirements, and did so with flying colors. Brownie had even declared Max to have "the best legal mind he'd ever witnessed." Considering Brownie's reputation, this was high praise indeed!

Jack was determined to assess the validity of Brownie's accolades regarding Max's legal aptitudes—accolades Jack was sure would prove overinflated.

Max, on the other hand, deeply missed male companionship. He also sensed Jack had answers to the many spiritual questions he yearned to know. But Jack represented a legal system that had been ever so hostile toward him. He had spent six years constructing a wall to guard his vulnerability. It wouldn't be dismantled overnight.

* * *

Morning arrived, and with it Jimmy, Max's nurse, to bathe and prepare him for X-rays. There'd be no breakfast, just in case Dr. Chandrah decided to apply the metal traction; anesthesia could be a possibility.

"Lucky you," Jack said as he prepared to head home. "But don't worry. I'll eat an extra pancake just for you."

Jimmy laughed. "It's great to have such caring Buds."

For Max's part, nothing anyone could say or do would upset him today. He turned to Jimmy. "It may not seem like much, but after being bedridden for four weeks, the prospect of getting into a wheelchair is pretty exciting! For me, it's one giant hurdle towards a full recovery."

Dr. Chandrah was delighted with the new bone growth that the radiographs demonstrated.

"Yes!" Max said when informed of the good news, pumping his arm in triumph.

Chandrah laughed. "In truth, Max, I think you've achieved a far greater victory in your healing process than any athlete could claim, regardless of their sport." She elected to use a short-acting anesthesia to ensure total relaxation while positioning Max's leg in the steel frame.

Consequently, it was mid-morning before he finally awoke.

Despite feeling a little groggy, he was elated to find himself out of bed and in a wheelchair. The chair itself didn't resemble the other wheelchairs Max had seen; in fact, it looked like an oversized lounge chair. He sat upright, his legs at right angles to his body. His left leg in the "cage," as Jimmy called it.

"High five, my man!" Jimmy slapped Max's hand. "You're mobile again!"

Jimmy began wheeling him down the corridor, chatting all the way. Had he seen the Phillies' game? Wasn't that a spectacular catch?

Max suddenly realized they were heading outdoors. It looked to him like it was the back entrance to the hospital. The mere thought of getting outside exhilarated him.

The doors opened and Max found himself squinting in the bright sunlight.

"Thanks, Jimmy, this is great!" He was so preoccupied with being outdoors that he missed the black van that suddenly drew abreast of them and stopped. The door opened, a wheelchair ramp came down, and a driver emerged. He wasn't dressed like a hospital attendant at all. He was dressed in a black suit.

"Thanks, Jimmy! I'll get you in here, Mr. Kerr. Get your chair strapped down."

"Whoa, wait! No one said anything about leaving the hospital!"

"I know, man, but after the X-ray it was decided you were healed enough to go to rehab. Great news, huh?" Jimmy was acting very enthusiastic. Too enthused, Max thought. He began to feel very uneasy.

An orderly appeared with Max's stuff. Amongst it all, he saw the binder Jack had given him last night. Everything was placed behind him in the van.

Max had never felt so helpless. He was strapped in a chair, unable to move, and the chair itself was belted into the van. He swore under his breath. What bothered him the most was that neither Sue nor Jack had said anything about a move.

As the door closed, he yelled to Jimmy, "What about my... uh... my family?"

"Oh, the hospital will let them know, man. No worries. It's all looked after!"

The door slammed shut, the driver hopped in, and they were off. To his horror, Max suddenly realized that all the windows of the van were heavily tinted. Alarm bells rang in his head.

"Where are we going?" he called to the driver, trying his best to sound unconcerned.

His driver was a man of few words. "I can't tell you our destination, sir. What I can say is that we are not to arrive until 2:00 p.m."

Max's mouth went dry. He watched where the van was heading. It seemed to be moving southeast, onto the freeway. Toward New Jersey. Why?

"Can't you talk?" Max asked, trying to bait him.

"Sorry, sir, my instructions are to make sure we aren't followed."

Oh, that's comforting. Just what I want to hear. The next thing Max knew, they were turning off the interstate. *What the hell is he doing? Now we're heading west.* He threw his head back in frustration. *I'm the biggest sitting duck there is. I'm doubly strapped in.*

"Lord Jesus, I'm helpless. There's nothing I can do. If ever I needed a miracle, it sure is now!"

Kaye popped into his mind and the terror in her eyes when she had thought he was going to die.

"Lord, for her sake, please don't let me disappoint her. Please look after her. Keep her safe." He paused, a funny thought crossing his mind. *"One good thing about my non-communicative friend is that I can focus on you, Jesus. We can talk freely!"*

Max looked in the rear view mirror, which seemed a bit askew. The way it was positioned, he had a good angle on the driver—at least the lower half of his face and his chest.

His heart froze. The driver was packing a gun!

Max closed his eyes. *Oh God, no!*

His mind now left Kaye. Left Summerside even. He was back in New York State, seven years ago, in that motel. Someone had wanted to kill his sister's boyfriend, Tony Marconi, and that same someone had framed him. Suddenly the "who" and the "why" appeared more relevant than he had previously considered.

The van turned after a while and headed down a gravel road. There was nothing, absolutely nothing, he could do. He was trapped.

chapter three

Kaye had sequestered herself at the McDonald mansion in Lakeland for a three-day retreat with her Kayleen Enterprises board of directors.

M.K., as she was professionally known, was always energized by these meetings, and today proved no exception. The company had enjoyed an exceedingly profitable first-half to the fiscal year. Projections indicated that the next quarter would likewise prove excellent.

There was, however, even more reason for the atmosphere of jubilation. Everyone had seen the media coverage following Henry Glaxton's horrific attack on M.K.'s life. She had appeared visibly shaken and exhausted from her ordeal. Now, barely four weeks later, both her staff and the board members saw her fully rejuvenated. In fact, if anything, her old exuberance and fire had intensified. Some even commented that she appeared to have a new glow about her.

Indeed, my lady, Kaye mused to herself. *There is a new glow in your life, and his name is Max!*

Publicly, however, the story was that Mr. Maxwell Kerr, a private investigator from Indiana and the man she had hired to apprehend her stalker, had survived his life-threatening injuries in the attack and was recuperating at an undisclosed location.

"No, I haven't seen Mr. Kerr recently," she said to the board, choosing her words carefully. "The doctors have said they're pleased with his recovery thus far but it will be awhile before he's able to bear any weight on the shattered leg. They anticipate several months of physiotherapy for him to regain normal usage." She then added, "When his medical condition warrants it, he'll appear publicly with me."

As the third day of the meeting wound to a close, Kaye cloistered herself with her senior management staff and the board's executive to summarize the discussions that had emerged from their strategy sessions.

The key item, in Kaye's assessment, was the unanimous decision to acquire new company offices. She hadn't been surprised by this decision, and had in fact encouraged it. Kayleen's exponential growth had certainly outstripped the building established by her late father. It was time to move on. The question for some time hadn't been whether the company should relocate but when and where.

"I'd really like to leave the decision concerning location in the hands of Clarin and Omar." She turned to the two men. "Would you be willing to set up a working committee to look at our options? Clarin, you can pull from our management resources while Omar accesses the board's assets."

The decision was applauded by all since both men were highly respected. Not surprisingly, the two asked if she wanted to chair the committee, since the committee's final recommendation would certainly have long-range implications for Kayleen.

"That's not necessary," she said, flashing her most winsome smile. "I trust the abilities of our staff and board." She lowered her voice and added softly, "Although my strength and stamina are returning quicker than anticipated, the past four months, especially the first three when Mr. Kerr and I were trying to lure my stalker into the open, proved difficult for me. Quite frankly, I need some space and time to rest, reflect, and re-energize."

In unison, everyone murmured their approval and understanding.

Then Kaye let loose that disarming laugh which was one of her greatest assets. "Besides, if we choose a place and it belly flops, I won't be the scapegoat!" She paused, cocking her head. "More importantly, I like surprises, intrigue, and excitement. I can't wait to see what your committee recommends."

Her housekeeper, Flora, and her butler, Jackson, then proceeded to usher everyone into the opulent dining room. Kaye's father had had the foresight to include the spacious room when constructing his Lakeland mansion. One thing that had always impressed Kaye about her father was the ease with which he had blended business and family. Now it appeared she might be provided the same opportunity. Had he deposited those same skills in her?

I certainly hope so, she thought with a sigh.

It was nearly 7:00 p.m. before the last of Kayleen's staff and board departed. Those with international destinations had left mid-afternoon, at the completion of the general meeting. Others had remained for the meal and special task-oriented meetings.

Kaye, for her part, was astonished at how exhausted she felt. *M.K., old girl, these past four months have taken more out of you than you realized.*

She retired to her personal apartment to gather what she wanted to take home to her house.

She wondered which locations the committee would suggest. The West Coast? East Coast? Houston? Miami? Maybe even Canada? She understood Montreal had European flavor. She might finally be able to use her French.

Unconsciously she began humming, instantly recognizing the hymn… *Amazing Grace*. Her attention abruptly zeroed in on one person: Max. When would he get out of his sling? Sue had said there wouldn't be much real change in the short-term. He would still be immobile.

Her mind flitted back to the fateful day of the attack. For nearly three months, Max had been secretly sequestered in her home. He had silently listened in on those late-night sinister phone calls, mapping a strategy to secure the caller's confession of previous crimes. Eventually he succeeded in luring the killer into the open to expose his true identity.

The actual day had begun so wonderfully. A faint smile crossed her lips as she remembered Max's "dance date." They had both looked so elegant all dressed up. In the privacy of her downstairs recreation room, they had danced non-stop for two hours. He was such a good dancer, and he injected passion into every move.

A tear trickled down her cheek. *"Oh, Jesus, please heal his leg so that once again Max can dance."*

She laughed as she thought of him in the dance competition he had described with his fourteen-year-old sister, Sophia. He had blown their chance at winning the cup when, in the most sensuous moment of the tango, he'd glimpsed the braces in his sister's mouth and burst out laughing. Winning the cup had been his sister's dream.

Max, that's what endears me to you—your frank honesty. You have no qualms about telling stories that paint you in a bad light.

Glancing at her watch, she realized it was now just a little past 8:00. With luck, she could make Summerside before 9:30. The hospital's visiting hours would be over, but they usually allowed her and the others to come and go as needed in order to maintain the "Max vigil."

The closer she got to Summerside, the more she longed to be with him. She had gotten through most of the week's meetings without a thought of Max. Business as usual. But when business was done, she couldn't wait to see him.

She pulled into the parking lot at the rear of the hospital. She'd been given a temporary key pass allowing her access to the wing that held his room. She bustled down the corridor to the elevator, waited impatiently for it to arrive at his floor, then jogged to his room.

The door was shut, which was a bit unusual for the early hour. He usually didn't turn out the lights until after 10:00.

As Kaye pushed open the door, she got a real surprise. No, the shock of her life. Asleep in the sole bed was an elderly gentleman.

She let out a startled yelp, then covered her mouth. The patient didn't stir; the reason was evident on the night table: two hearing aids.

Kaye backed out of the room and tore off to the nursing station, only to encounter yet another surprise she didn't like. She hadn't seen this nurse once in the nearly four weeks of hospital visits.

"I'm sorry, ma'am, visiting hours ended an hour and a half ago. You'll need to leave."

"You don't understand," Kaye stammered. "Mr. Kerr is supposed to be in Room 4206!"

"The patient in Room 4206 is not a Mr. Kerr, ma'am."

Even though she knew the woman was just doing her job, Kaye wanted to throttle her. She paused and took a deep breath, desperately trying to remain calm.

"I know that man isn't Mr. Kerr," she said. "I want to know where Mr. Kerr is. My family and I, with full hospital approval, have kept a twenty-four-hour vigil in his room for the past four weeks. I wasn't told that he would be moved!"

The nurse checked her charts. "I'm sorry. We have no Mr. Kerr on this floor."

"Then please, call the switchboard and ask them where he is!" By now, she wasn't only irritated, she was beginning to panic.

The nurse rolled her eyes, dialed the switchboard, and handed the phone to Kaye.

"Yes, I want to know where Maxwell Kerr is," Kaye said. "He was in Room 4206, but he isn't there now. Where have you put him?"

"I'm sorry, ma'am," the voice on the other end of the line said. "Mr. Kerr was discharged around noon today. I have no record of where he went."

Click.

Kaye gave the receiver back to the nurse, turned, and in a daze retraced her steps to her car.

Getting into the vehicle, she began to tremble. Tears flooded from her uncontrollably.

"Oh God, no! He's gone back to his family. Or worse, they found him and took him home."

She started the motor and slowly drove home, the windshield wipers ineffective against the tears clouding her vision.

chapter four

Max struggled hard not to let mounting panic become visible to the driver. It appeared they were driving in circles, but why? He breathed a sigh of relief when the vehicle finally turned onto a more traveled road. Glancing at his watch, Max realized they'd been on the road over an hour. It was now 12:30. According to the driver, in another hour and a half he'd discover his destination and who lay behind this abduction.

What on earth have I done? Has Pop done something to upset someone? He didn't want to entertain such a thought. *How is that possible? He's always super cautious, or at least he used to be.*

His father had the reputation for smoothing over turbulent waters rather than generating storms. The more Max sought to make sense of his predicament, the more confused he became.

He sucked in his breath, deciding it would be more profitable to focus on the *where* rather than the *why.* He could see they were approaching what looked like another small city. Just as the van drew close enough for him to read the upcoming city sign, a transport truck parked on the side of the road began to move, blocking his view.

Irritation welled up inside him.

Keep control, Max.

"Got enough gas to drive until 2:00 p.m.?" he asked nonchalantly. "There's lots of places to stop here."

"We have enough," the driver replied. "Good barbeque up ahead, though. Excellent chicken on a bun. What would you like to drink?"

Max was shocked to hear him speak after being subjected to the silent treatment.

"Root beer, please." Max sounded amiable, but inwardly he was hatching a plan. When the driver handed him the meal, Max would grab him and take his gun. With a gun aimed at his head, he'd be much more willing to drive him back to Jack's.

The meal was ordered through a squawk box, leaving Max no opportunity to call for help. To his chagrin, each meal came in its own disposable tray.

"Here," was all the fellow said as he pushed the tray onto the seat beside Max's legs.

"Can you hand it to me?"

"Nope." He drove the van into an isolated area of the parking lot, conveniently away from all the other vehicles.

Max thought about tipping his tray onto the floor in spite, but it smelled too good. Besides, he hadn't eaten breakfast. He wasn't into missing lunch, too!

If this is to be my last meal so be it. Then he remembered watching a CSI episode where they had tracked down a murderer based on the food found in the corpse's stomach. *Personally I'd rather be alive when they find me.*

He had to admit it was the tastiest chicken on a bun he'd ever eaten. He had just about forgotten his situation when the driver barked at him. "Here, Kerr, your nurse sent along your medication. He said the injection you received when they changed your sling would wear off before we arrived."

Again he placed the capsule beside Max's legs, just where Max could reach it but not grab him. This guy wasn't leaving any room for error.

"Your nurse said you're to take it with food in your stomach." With that, he started the van and they were off again.

Max stared glumly at the medicine. It seemed different from what he'd received in the past. If they were going to kill him, why would they bother to dope him up? His leg had just begun to throb, however, so he popped the capsule in his mouth and swished it down with a slurp of root beer.

He fought sleep for as long as he could hoping to take note of where he was being taken. The motion of the van coupled with the medication soon won out, however. The last thing he remembered was checking his watch at 1:30.

He awoke later to the sound of someone calling his name.

"Max! Max! Wake up."

Someone shook his shoulder, and in a flash he grabbed the offending arm in a vice grip.

"What the heck are you doing?" the person asked, annoyed. "Wake up!"

Max opened his eyes, shocked to discover that the arm he held belonged to none other than Jack Walters. Max's demeanor changed from that of a snarly pit bull to a little puppy. He blinked and released his grip.

"Sheesh, Jack, I'm sorry. I just had a terrible dream. More like a nightmare. Maybe I am supposed to tell you a bit about what happened six years ago. That is, tell you like a priest, not as a judge."

"Why the sudden change of heart?" Jack asked, puzzled.

"Well, Jimmy got me ready to have them switch my sling to that metal brace. They gave me something strong, which I guess caused me to doze off and dream. The sling is removed, isn't it?"

"Yeah, it's switched. So what did you dream?"

"Well, Jimmy put me in this new wheelchair, took me outside, and a black van drove up. He loaded me into the van with this creepy driver. I mean, I was helpless! I was strapped in the chair and the chair was strapped in the van, my leg in this metal vice. I was a sitting duck. Even worse, the creep was packing a rod. You know those damn dreams where you try and figure out how you can escape but nothing works? That dream has got me thinking again about that New York motel room and who framed me and tried to kill Tony, my sister's boyfriend. "

Jack nodded, a faint smile creeping across his face.

"Anyway, back to the dream, the guy stops for food. I figured if I could trick him into handing me the food, I could grab him and get his gun, make him take me to you. If not, I could kill him before he killed me. I guess that's what I was dreaming when you shook me." Max suddenly noticed the smile on Jack's face. "What's so funny?"

"You weren't dreaming."

"What do you mean?"

"Where do you think you are?"

Max slowly looked around, confused. It wasn't his hospital room. He was inside a house, but a house he'd never seen before. His eyes locked on Jack's, which by now twinkled in amusement.

"What the hell is going on?" Max demanded. "Where am I?"

"Everything you described actually happened, Max. It's a good thing your so-called creep was smart enough not to give you a chance to get your hand on his gun." Jack's smile had evaporated. "I can assure you, the man was not connected to the scenario that got you arrested over six years ago. It just so happens that your creep is a sergeant on Summerside's police force. You remember Tom? He was there the night you nailed Glaxton, so he knows both your agility and ability with a gun."

Max was anything but amused. His dark brown eyes flashed angrily. "How could you do that to me? What a stupid, sick joke. Damn you, Jack! I just start to trust you and you screw me over. You set me up." He paused to catch his breath.

"You knew I'd think somebody was trying to kill me. I could've hurt myself or that cop. That's no practical joke. That's cruel!"

"Whoa, just one minute. No one set you up. When I left you, I had no idea they'd need to move you today. My friend in the FBI caught wind that *The Enquirer* was blitzing all the hospitals in a hundred mile radius of Lakeland to find Mr. Kerr. He needed to move you quickly. No one could know what was happening, in part so they couldn't identify where you went. Epi got the unmarked van and asked Dave to supply one of his officers to drive it, ensuring that no one followed. Tom volunteered, which was a good thing because he knew exactly what you're capable of."

"Epi?"

"Yeah, remember Special Agent Bernard Epstein, from the Bureau? When I was in Washington, he called to ask when I would be home to receive you— the package, as he put it. I knew I couldn't get back until two o'clock." Jack paused, suddenly aware that someone with Max's background might not view Epi's secretive transfer positively. He looked Max square in the eye. "Max, I'm sorry. The transfer probably felt very threatening. Believe me when I say we didn't mean to frighten or scare you."

"I wasn't scared," Max snapped.

Right, Jack thought to himself. *Wrong choice of words.*

"I know, Max, but you were upset and I'm sorry. You really don't need any more stress in your life."

"You didn't do this as a joke?"

"Definitely not. You wouldn't do something like that as a joke, would you, Max?"

"No, but I know guys who would."

"Trust me, bud, none of us would intentionally do anything to hurt you, after all you did for Kaye. We respect you too much."

Max looked bewildered. "You mean that?"

"Most definitely! You self-sacrificed and denied yourself to help others. That's a very decent thing to do."

The tone of Jack's voice left no doubt as to his sincerity. His words had a profound calming effect on Max.

"So, where exactly are we?" Max asked.

Jack sighed. "In our dining room. Marnie insisted we turn it into a rehab room for you."

"You okay with that?"

"I am now."

Max raised his eyebrows. "But you weren't initially?"

"Truthfully, no. You have to remember that neither Sue nor Marnie know your real identity."

"Why don't you tell them?"

"I thought it better to wait and let them get to know you and—"

"And what?"

"And for you to get to know them," Jack finished. "After all, you, Massimiliano Carron, are a marked man."

Max registered surprise. "Marked for what?"

"Marriage, old boy. Marriage!" said Jack, laughing. "Our wives have you earmarked for Kaye. They've been on the prowl for years, hunting down a mate for her."

"So what stopped them in the past?"

"Kaye's disinterest. She lived unisex before the word was invented! For her, relational interactions—men or women—were all the same. You, my friend, are the first one of the male species to awaken in her the reality that she is a *she* and you are a *he*, the reality that God created men and women radically different, yet intended for them to fall in love and learn to live as one, using their differences to work together for each other's benefit."

"Jack, I already asked Kaye to marry me, when I thought I was dying."

"And she said?"

"Yes."

"Well, sport, can I give you a word of advice?"

"What?"

"Let the ladies figure it was their idea."

"That's not dishonest?"

"Not at all, Max. When they get through with you, you may even agree it really was their idea all along." Jack laughed. "Anyway, I let you sleep a long time. How about supper? Are you game for an omelet?"

Just before supper, Jack helped maneuver Max into his chair. Dave and his son Matt came over after the meal and they all played cards until nightfall. Afterward, the guys all helped get Max ready for bed.

Jack was cleaning up the kitchen when he heard a car drive up. He glanced out and recognized that it was Kaye's.

Kaye burst through the door as distraught as the night of the attack on her life. She flew into his arms, sobbing uncontrollably.

"Kaye, what on earth is wrong?"

It took him several moments to understand what she was saying. He tried repeating each phrase to ensure he got it right. "You went to the hospital, to Max's room, but another patient was in the bed."

Kaye, still sobbing, nodded yes.

"Then you went to the nurse's station, but found a nurse there who you'd never seen before…" At last he grasped the reason for her distress. Max had left and she hadn't even been given the opportunity to say goodbye.

He held her tightly, consoling her. But when he turned her tear-streaked face toward him, he grinned. "Then, why don't you go into the dining room and say hello?"

"What?" Kaye looked at him in disbelief as she walked hesitantly to the dining room.

Marnie's most prized and elegant room was in total disarray. The furniture had all been shoved against the wall and in the center stood a hospital bed—and in the bed was the one for whom she'd been weeping.

"Kaye, what's wrong?" Max asked, his voice conveying genuine alarm. He was astonished to see her standing before him with makeup smeared and eyes red from crying.

Damn, nothing makes me more upset than seeing this woman cry. I've never felt this way before. He furrowed his brow. *Then again, maybe I have.*

He thought back to Sophia. Whenever his kid sister turned on the tears, he would be pumped to respond, unless of course she had turned on the tears to get her way with Pop! Then he'd just duck. The memory brought a smile to his face.

Unfortunately, that smile only served to fuel Kaye's Irish temper. Her green eyes flashed. "So, you two think this is one big joke!"

Fortune smiled on Max, for the nearest thing Kaye could find was the extra pillow sitting on his wheelchair. She strode across the room, snatched the pillow, and slammed it over his head.

Jack entered the room to intervene, but before he could do anything she swung around and smashed him with it. The pillow ripped, deluging all three with a torrent of goose feathers.

The two men stared at her, their mouths agape.

"This is not funny!" She stomped her foot as a new flood of tears poured forth. "I cared for you, Mr. Carron, and for you, Judge Walters, and I thought you cared for me. I don't know what possessed either of you to play such a cruel joke on me."

The two men marveled at the fact that she didn't even need to stop and catch her breath. The words just spewed out.

"For your information, I drove from the hospital so upset that I could have caused an accident." She paused long enough to put her hands on her hips. "And if I did, I would have made sure the two of you took the blame!"

Max looked at Jack. Jack looked at Max. Neither quite knew who should speak, or even what could be said to diffuse the bomb.

Finally, Jack cleared his throat. "Kaye, please listen to me. This isn't a joke. Epi…"

She snapped her head around and glared at him. "Don't you go blaming Epi to weasel out of this, Jack Walters."

Max formed a 'T' with his hands, signaling a timeout.

"What?" she asked.

"Please listen to what Jack has to say."

"Fine!" She sat down on the nearest chair, folding both her arms and legs. "Speak!"

Jack explained again how Epi had quickly orchestrated the move to avoid the media uncovering both Max's whereabouts and his true identity. There hadn't been time to reveal the details to her and Max; she had been sequestered in board meetings and Max had been anesthetized.

"I, too, thought it was a joke," Max chimed in. "A bad joke. But what Jack's saying really is the truth. They were doing it to protect us. When I was still in the hospital, Marnie suggested to Jack that I come here when it was time for me to go to rehab, so it would be easier for you and me… you know, to be together." He looked to Jack, his eyes pleading for agreement.

Jack nodded his head.

"Now you're blaming Marnie?" she demanded.

But not nearly as sharply as before, Max thought. Maybe there was even a playful lilt to her voice?

"No." Jack said with a sigh. "It's just that it was her suggestion to use our place until Max got rid of the steel brace. So when Epi said we needed to move Max today, I told him to come here. Marnie and Sue had already set up the dining room beforehand. I didn't call you because you said you'd be back late. I didn't expect you to go to the hospital first."

It was Max's turn to register concern. "Wait. Why were you expecting her here, Jack?"

Oh Lord, Jack thought, *how can I cope with these Irish and Italian temperaments under my roof for even one night, never mind a month or so?*

"Because someone bled all over Kaye's house, if you'll remember."

"So it gave me a chance to redecorate and remodel," Kaye interjected.

"Thus Marnie invited her to stay here while she's remodeling it," Jack said.

Max looked at Kaye. "You're living here?"

"Yes!"

"Upstairs," added Jack.

"Wow! That's great. Marnie sure is a good organizer." Max grinned. "So Kaye, now that you know I didn't run out on you, maybe you could give me two kisses?"

"Two?" Kaye and Jack asked in unison.

"Yeah, the hello kiss Jack suggested earlier, and the good night kiss. It's midnight, after all."

Jack laughed as he headed for the stairs. "Good night to both of you. And no, Max, I'm not kissing you!"

chapter five

"Well, well, so how is our gentleman landlord coping?" Art Brown gave Jack a hearty slap on the back as he sat down at the table in Edward's Steakhouse. He reached across the table and shook hands with Jack's two companions, Epi and Dave. "How are you managing to survive, Jack?"

"If you must know, Brownie, I'm surviving just fine," Jack said. "I'm enjoying it, and Marnie, for her part, is thriving. She has a captive audience upon which to practice all her gourmet recipes." He paused, raising his eyebrows. "By the way, I don't think I mentioned it to any of you, but she's writing a cookbook."

Dave grinned. "Is she going to dedicate it to Ms. M.K. McDonald and Mr. Maxwell Kerr, or should I say Max Carron, who courageously tested all her fares?"

"Maybe. And you never know, Dave, you and Sue could get an honorable mention," Jack said with a laugh. "But seriously, Max never ceases to amaze me. You were right, Brownie; he does have an excellent legal mind. He has unbelievable recall. He devours the annals I take home, accurately nailing and cataloguing the precedents."

"Which ones does he seem most interested in?" Epi asked.

"White collar crime and international trade cases."

Epi looked surprised. "Really? That amazes me."

"Why?" asked Jack.

"Well, I would have thought he'd pour over the organized crime cases, given his Sicilian connections."

"I don't think our Mr. Carron is really interested in such involvement," Brownie said.

"No," said Jack. "He's pretty fixated on one individual, which gets me to the reason I wanted to meet with you three."

"You mean it's not our charming camaraderie?" Brownie laughed.

Dave smiled. "Personally I thought it was the Eagles and Skins game tonight."

"Yeah, well I know Jack well enough to figure out that when he volunteers to pay for dinner, he has more than charity in mind." Epi sighed. "So, Your Honor, to what do we owe this auspicious gathering?"

"Well, Chief Justice Douglas said he revered your opinions on legal aptitude, Brownie," Jack said. "Since you thought Max had a superior legal mind, Douglas felt it might be better to have him on our side rather than crime's. He commissioned Epi and me to try and orchestrate the best happily-ever-after scenario possible for Kaye and Max."

"So Judge Walters' hospitality does have an end to its means," ventured Brownie.

Jack smiled, "Very perceptive, Professor Charlie Chan."

"And the brains of a Supreme Court justice and special agent of the Bureau are, I take it, insufficient for this task?" Brownie asked. "Thus you need the minds of a very humble law professor and a simple uniformed cop? See, Dave, it's really us ordinary guys in the trenches that move our justice system." He flipped his ears forward with his forefingers. "So, dear Jack, what is your problem? I'm all ears!"

"Now do you see what I was stuck with for six years as Brownie's roomie?" Jack sighed. "And humility was his best character trait!"

Everyone roared with laughter. Almost in response, the waiter appeared out of nowhere to take their order.

"I guess he figures that if we can get that rowdy on water, he'd better hustle us out before the more well-heeled clientele arrives," Jack quipped. "At least it sets us up to be at the game in time for the opening kickoff."

Over the meal, Jack began to share his dilemma.

"As you know, I convicted Max of drug trafficking nearly seven years ago," he began. "He'd been found in that motel room unconscious, presumably from a blow to the head, drug paraphernalia scattered all around. It was assumed that a drug deal had gone afoul. The bed's pillows had been arranged beneath the sheets to suggest someone was sleeping in it. A shot had been fired into what would have been the sleeper's head. Police later found the bullet in the wall behind the bed.

"Max's statement to the police was that he had come to the motel room to meet some other college students and work on a collaborative term paper. When the others didn't show, he sat on the chair and fell asleep. He was awakened by what he later realized was a gun being fired beside his head toward the 'figure' in the bed. Startled, he let out a yell and promptly felt the butt of a gun hit his head. He lost consciousness, but as he did he heard a voice saying, 'Shit, it's Carron!'

"The ballistic report corroborated Max's statement that the gun could have been fired from that open door. Unfortunately, Max couldn't or wouldn't name the students he was there to meet. In addition, it was discovered that he hadn't been working on any term paper. Therefore, given his background, it was decided to press drug trafficking charges.

"Even though the offense took place in New York State, his defense lobbied to have him tried in Illinois. The New York D.A. agreed, since this would remove any taint of organized crime that could tarnish the college's reputation due to unfavorable press.

"The defense opted for trial by judge. I entered the scene, as a favor to old colleagues, because the judge assigned to the case died prior to the trial beginning. To my chagrin, I was less concerned with detail and more concerned with expediency, given the fact that it had been agreed that I wouldn't assume my Supreme Court appointment for two more months. I had scheduled that time to wind up my other professional commitments and take my promised vacation with Marnie and the girls. So I yielded to the Sicilian bias, choosing not to do my own study of the data but foolishly depending solely on the presentation of defense and prosecutor."

"Which would have been sufficient if both attorneys had been doing what they ought to, I might add," Brownie said.

"Yes, but in fact neither did so." Jack shook his head sadly. "So the justice system badly failed Max. The prosecutor's motives are clear—career advancement. If he had dealt fairly with the evidence, he would have lost. The defense's ineptitude was surprising, though. Scallion was Frank Carron's personal solicitor, and he just doesn't lose. Yet his defense of Max was abysmal. But why? That's the million dollar question."

"True," Dave chipped in. "It makes one highly suspicious that organized crime is covering something up."

"Up until now, Max has steadfastly refused to discuss the issue," Jack said. "Which further implied that something criminal was going on."

Dave nodded. "When Epi orchestrated Max's surprise move from the hospital, it frightened him. Max began to have second thoughts about his silence."

"That's right," Jack said. "And the truth is that Max is in love with Kaye. He knows she loves him, and he's painfully aware of how his death would have devastated her. He must have reflected that maybe it was important to know what did happen in that motel room. Consequently, he finally confided to me the defense's reason for not appealing Max's conviction, or for that matter, failing to strenuously defend him in the first place.

"Apparently Max's father, and his brother-in-law's father, were rivals from way back. Why? Max hasn't a clue. However, when Tony and Sophia fell in love, the two men were faced with a serious dilemma. Both knew someone had tried to kill Tony, since it was he who had been supposed to meet the students to complete a term paper. Max had simply agreed to go to the motel to pick up Tony's assignment, allowing Tony and Sophia to go to a dance. But since Max's father was unaware of his daughter's romance with Tony, the senior Marconi accepted that Frank hadn't been involved in the attempt on Tony's life. As Max put it, the two older men didn't want a Romeo and Juliet scenario for their kids. Thus, they decided to bury the hatchet and let sleeping dogs lie, so to speak."

"This meant Max would simply have to take the fall for the drug setup," stated Dave. "They agreed not to contest the charges or the decision of the court. This way, the authorities wouldn't come snooping and uncover a perpetrator with loyalties to either Carron or Marconi. Doing so could force the two older men again into antagonistic roles."

Brownie gave a low whistle, "They obviously were relying on Max's lack of previous criminal charges to produce a light sentence. A year, maybe a year and a half at most. It could have even been probation."

"Enter prick Justice Jack Walters—"

"Thanks, Dave, I love you, too," muttered Jack. "Anyway, I sentenced Max for six years. Thanks to Professor Brown, when he was released Max came to challenge me about what I did!"

"However, boy gets diverted. Boy meets girl, and they fall in love," said Epi, finishing the story. "Only problem is that the girl is a high-profile business executive."

"Who travels internationally, often attending state dinners which require her to be escorted," Dave said. "But a boy with a criminal record can't get a passport, let alone clearance at those dinners."

Brownie nodded. "Which is indeed a very big dilemma, especially given the boy's Sicilian heritage. I dare say he wouldn't be thrilled about another man publicly escorting Kaye around. So His Honor seeks to undo the mess his shabby bench work created."

Jack hung his head ruefully. "Yep, that's it in a nutshell, Brownie. Doing so in court makes such a course of action easy, but it throws bad light on judge, prosecutor, and defense. As for justice, the first two deserve it—one was sloppy, the other power hungry. But the third is the one who has already suffered."

"Do you think, if the evidence was reviewed with you, a clue may exist to throw light on the person who fired that shot?" Brownie asked.

"Personally, my gut instinct is an overwhelming yes," Jack said

"So why don't you review the evidence?"

"Max won't go there."

Brownie raised his eyebrows. "Why?"

"Perhaps it's a family code of silence," Epi suggested.

"A mob family code?"

Epi nodded. "Yep. The elders decree, the underlings obey!"

Brownie frowned. "But I didn't think there was evidence linking the two older men to the mafia."

"There isn't any legal evidence," Jack said. "But there is genetics. And sometimes, old world ways spill over to life in America."

"Does either Max or Kaye know the consequence of all this to their relationship?" Brownie asked.

As one, the three men sighed and shook their heads.

"I really don't want to share that with them at this point," Jack said. "I was rather hoping we might strategize some plan to uncover the culprits without involving Max."

Brownie locked eyes with his old friend. "Knowing you, Jack old boy, now that you're certain of an injustice, you won't rest until justice does happen, one way or another!"

Jack smiled. "You know me all too well, my friend."

"The key would seem to lie in the data collected regarding that early conviction," Brownie said. The other three nodded their agreement. "I would judge the three key players to be Max, Sophia, and Tony. Their fathers wouldn't have access to all that took place at the college. Correct?"

"That's our assessment, too," Epi concurred.

Brownie scratched his head. "Max won't talk, and knowing Max and his principles, when he says no, he means no."

"Right again, Brownie," Jack said.

"So that leaves Tony and Sophia," Brownie said. "What do you think? Would Tony cooperate? He must have some guilt, knowing Max wasn't even supposed to be there. He was just going to get Tony's term paper. Or do you think there never was a term paper? Maybe Tony was, in fact, involved in a drug deal? You're shaking your head, Epi. Explain."

"Tony is clean as far as we can determine, both with drugs and with the mob," Epi said. "However, in New York's Little Italy, he's known as one dude you shouldn't mess with. Legally, he packs a glock. Even physically he's a much more threatening presence than Max. I'd also have to say, from the data we have on his family, that his father has a stronger old-world mentality than Max's dad."

"What about Sophia?" Brownie asked. "The few times I worked with Max in the prison, her name surfaced. It seems to me she was studying for a law degree."

Epi nodded. "That's correct. She's a pretty smart lady. Along with birthing twin girls and later a little boy, she obtained her Bachelor of Law from Columbia."

"That doesn't sound like she's very old world. Most Italian mammas I know aren't into professional careers," Brownie offered. "Maybe she'd look at your case files with you, Jack."

Epi started to laugh.

"Something I said amused you, Agent Epstein?" Brownie retorted coolly.

"Jack could never talk to Sophia alone!"

"Why not?"

"You'd have to take her with her husband."

"Take?" Jack asked. "Take her where? I don't want to take either one of them anywhere!"

"Fine, Jack, but we're brainstorming here," Epi replied bluntly. "Max is your ace, and the fact that his family is searching for him. Sophia just might be willing to go with you to see him."

"But we don't…" Dave trailed off. "No! Max doesn't want his family brought into the picture until after he marries Kaye."

Brownie shrugged. "So you let him marry her, then discover later that their family values are totally incompatible?"

"Well, Brownie, now you grasp our dilemma." Jack sighed. "If only you could see those two. They're very much in love, and at their age it isn't puppy love. Especially after what they went through—and are still going through, as Max recovers from his wounds. I really do want to work behind the scenes to make it work out for them."

"To give them, as best we can, Chief Justice Douglas' happy-ever-after option," added Epi.

"You know," Dave said. "I've been thinking."

"Well, Chief Davidson, you've been unduly silent for most of this discussion," Jack said. "I'm relieved to discover you've actually been listening, and not daydreaming about the Eagles clobbering the Skins."

"Very funny, Jack." Dave glared at the three. "If you don't want my thoughts, I'll keep them to myself."

Brownie shook his head. "We're the four Musketeers, Dave. All for one, one for all! Please share."

"I think the key is Sophia and Tony. The bait is Max. If there was some way we could get the two of them alone in Summerside? Maybe even let them meet Max? What if we could get them there on the pretense of seeing Max—say, a few hours before he and Kaye marry. They could even watch the wedding. I agree, when it comes to reviewing the evidence, Tony's stance is likely to be the same as Max's. However, on the basis of what Max has shared about Sophia, she seems to be pretty headstrong." He chuckled. "Mafia collegiality is pretty much that of a male chauvinistic pig. Even if there are family connections to the mob, I doubt Sophia will be under any code of conduct."

Brownie looked up at his friends. "Supposing you do get the two of them to Summerside and Sophia looks at the trial transcripts and evidence, what happens if there's no link, gentleman? What if your gut instincts were wrong, Jack?"

"We should cross that bridge when we get to it," Epi said. "In the meantime, we need to eke out some sort of game plan, to see if what Dave suggested is even plausible. Based on my sources, I don't think you could call up the Marconis and invite them to an evening in Summerside."

"Couldn't you just bring them in for questioning, then take them to Summerside?" suggested Brownie.

"You know how astute Max is," Epi said to him. "Even if his sister is only half as good, do you honestly think we could get them into a police precinct, much less get them to Summerside without them squealing foul play and bringing in their legal battery? I assure you, it would be anything but quiet. Furthermore, it would attract the media. For Kaye and Max's sake, not only do we want to keep the media at bay for their wedding, but they'll need at least a few weeks of marital bliss before their nuptials are made public."

Jack nodded. "True. Max wants to marry as soon as that steel brace is off, but he'll need time to learn to maneuver with the crutches so as not to undo the healing that has already occurred."

"For Dave's plan to work, you'll indeed require very, very, very good strategy," murmured Brownie, placing increasing emphasis with each *very*.

"That's for sure," Epi said. "Getting Sophia and Tony out of New York is going to be as hard as a bear trying to steal honey from a beehive without getting stung!"

Jack smiled. "Well, gentlemen, this has been a most profitable meal! I don't mind paying for it, either. For the first time, I sense there might be a solution to my dilemma that needn't involve the courts."

"Jack, you're joking, right?" Epi said "Didn't you hear what I just said about stealing honey from bees?"

"Certainly! Therefore, you carefully plan your attack on the hive, making certain you're wearing protective netting and thick clothing! I do believe that Sophia and Tony, perhaps unwittingly—at least I hope it is unwittingly—hold the key to unraveling our mystery."

With the other three eying him skeptically, Jack rose to pay the bill. He turned, and this time it was he who slapped Brownie on the back.

"Strategizing, old man, is why I was the quarterback and you were the defensive end," Jack said. "Time for us to go, fellows, if we're going to catch the kickoff!"

chapter six

"Top of the morning to you, Stephanie." Kaye beamed as she greeted her receptionist. "You're in early today. How's life in the fast lane?"

The young woman laughed. "I'm sure it's not as fast as yours, Ms. McDonald."

"Steph, I need to tell you that I'm really, really proud of you. I've talked to different counselors, and your progress, in the face of what you've experienced, is nothing short of phenomenal! Here you are, back at work in less than two months."

Stephanie Baxter lowered her eyes and blushed. "That's very kind of you, Ms. McDonald, but you and Kayleen have had a lot to do with that. I mean, you were there for me that awful night, when I had to face the truth about why Henry Glaxton courted me." A tear trickled down the young woman's cheek. "He didn't love me at all. He just used me to stalk you, fully intending to brutally murder you." She bit her lip and sniffled. "Despite all you endured that night, you came to Lakeland to support me. Your behavior really inspired me!"

"It did?" Kaye leaned on the receptionist's counter, genuinely intrigued.

"Oh yes, Ms. McDonald, the fact that you were there for me, when you could have accused me. You supported my parents, too. Both of them were so grateful that you stepped up to the plate, as Daddy says, to declare me a victim of Glaxton's deviant behavior, just as much as you were. I believe your stance truly helped me face the truth of how Henry used me."

Kaye's chin rested lightly on her hand. "I really meant what I said, Steph. It was such a shock when the police removed his balaclava to expose his face. My first response was disbelief that I actually knew this person. It took a few moments for me to process that this was the one who had threatened to torture and murder me, like those other poor women he boasted of killing. As I looked at him, I was so shocked and repulsed, but then there followed a far greater shockwave." She uttered a low hollow laugh. "You know, Steph, how a little tremor can precede a major earthquake? Well, that's what I felt I was experiencing psychologically. I suddenly realized that this man had preyed on Kayleen—not just me, and not just you. He invaded the lives of people you and I care about. He worked with them, joked with them, all just to set you up, so he could get to me… to kill me. And for what? His own perverted pleasure! I have to tell you, Steph, at that moment great anger flooded through me."

"Wow, Ms. McDonald, that sort of matches my experience, though my feelings didn't flow as quickly as yours. But all those feelings were there, especially my denial that this perfect young man could have been making those distressing calls to you. Initially I had no knowledge of them. Then, as Agent Epstein talked with my parents and me, he shared snippets of the gruesome murders Henry had revealed. Agent Epstein told us how Henry broke into your home, about the weapons he had, and how he would have succeeded had you not had that private investigator to help you. I think that's when the truth of who Henry Glaxton really was seeped in. When you came into the room and I saw how distraught you were, I knew everything I was being told had to be true. I began to feel so used and, Ms. McDonald, just so dirty! So filthy! Your words seemed to cut like a knife through those dark cords that were attempting to entangle and entrap me."

Kaye stood up and went behind the receptionist's desk to embrace Stephanie. Both women wept quietly.

Stephanie sniffled and reached for a Kleenex. "When you said I was a victim, like you, those words managed to penetrate my heart. They severed those dark cords of self-loathing. I thought, *Ms. McDonald said I was a victim like her. This means she's with me. I am not alone. I will be able to get through this.*"

Kaye gently rocked the young woman. "Stephanie, what you're sharing now is so precious and encouraging to me."

"Oh, Ms. McDonald, your offer for my parents and me to get away was so great! So very great! We were able to get away from prying eyes. On that island retreat, no one knew us. The sun, the warmth, just being quiet, watching the water… it revived and restored our souls. In fact, those were the actual words my mom used to describe what transpired." Stephanie's eyes now fastened onto Kaye's. "But Ms. McDonald, what about you? Did you get any opportunity to rest, to have your soul revived?"

Kaye gave the young woman an affectionate hug. "I did, Steph. Believing that you and Mr. Kerr could both heal revitalized me." She sat opposite Stephanie in the other chair behind the receptionist's desk. "I guess the other thing that's helping my own healing is knowing that the families of Glaxton's other victims can have some closure. They can know that the one who harmed their loved ones won't harm anyone else."

"My counselors shared with me information they received from the FBI about Henry…" Stephanie gave a hollow laugh. "I say Henry, but he used at least six other aliases. Anyway, my counselor said Henry used other people to help him get to his victims, just like he used me to try and hurt you. My counselor suggested that maybe, depending on how you and I felt, we might be able to help some of those people deal with their emotions, when they face their own duplicity in his crimes."

"Really? Your counselor suggested that?"

Stephanie nodded. "Yes. In fact, she said the FBI would even be willing to organize it."

"No kidding?" Kaye registered both shock and surprise. "Would you like to do that? Or I guess I should say, would you be *willing* to do that?"

"I would, if I was doing it with you, and if it would help others heal. Really I would." She hung her head, staring at the clasped hands that rested in her lap. "I'm not sure how useful I would be, but, if it could help someone else, even a little, I'd be willing to try."

Kaye gazed lovingly at this self-effacing young woman. "Well, Steph, I agree we should try and help. However, I do think it would be wise to wait until after Christmas. We still have more healing to do ourselves."

"Oh yes, definitely. The counselor continues to help me recognize how naïve I was. Her suggestions are making me feel more competent in other relationships."

"That's wonderful, Steph!"

"Can I share one funny thing? Well, not ha-ha funny, but a peculiar thing? Do you have time?"

"Most definitely, Steph. Your insights help me, too."

"Well, remember the time you met… we'll call him Henry?"

"Yes, I do."

"Do you remember how he said all those nice things about me?"

"Indeed."

"Well, he was constantly doing that, but then the counselor asked me about how I felt when he kissed me, I just looked at her stunned. I realized that he never did. He never hugged me or put his arm around me. Occasionally he'd reach out and hold my hand, but only briefly."

"Wow! That is peculiar."

"Yes! Definitely not normal, my counselor said. It should have been my red flag. I just attributed it to his shyness. I guess his words disarmed me. The counselor said I was looking to others to give me self-worth rather than believing that all people, including me, are valuable in God's eyes."

"That's a very good insight, Stephanie," Kaye ventured.

Stephanie giggled. "My counselor is teaching me to be more aware of nonverbal communication. It's obviously helping, because I could tell by your body language that you really did want to talk with me and were interested in what I had to say."

Kaye laughed. "That, Stephanie, is wonderful, and you know it really is true."

"What is?"

"In the Bible, one of my favorite life verses says that God will work all things to the good. For me, that is such an important truth. That verse gives me hope, even in very bad circumstances, that God is there, able and willing to ensure that good will eventually triumph" Kaye reached over and gave her receptionist's hand a gentle squeeze. "As bleak as that Glaxton situation was for us, here you and I are, only a few months later, beginning to glimpse new life out of the ashes."

Kaye stood up just as the elevator door opened. "Looks like others are finally starting to arrive."

A tall, gangly lad with a large portfolio stepped in front of the receptionist's desk. Kaye wheeled around to face him.

"Excuse me, miss," the young man said. He fidgeted from one foot to another. Each time he shifted his stance, a shaggy lock of blonde hair floated across his face. This would prompt him to flick his head sideways, thus temporarily clearing his vision.

Kaye bit her lip, struggling not to smile, as an image of her childhood pony Dubbe flooded her mind. No matter how carefully she had tried to groom her pet, his shaggy forelock always found a way to flop over his eyes. Each time it did, Dubbe would jerk his head. Initially the constant bobbing had bothered Kaye, but over time she had managed to adjust to his idiosyncrasies. In fact, the two of them had gone on to secure their Pony Club's top award for the year.

"Could… could I please… please see, Ms. McDonald?" the young man stammered, obviously mistaking her for the receptionist.

Kaye's eyes twinkled. With her hand behind her back, she motioned Stephanie not to intervene. "What is your name, sir?"

"Roland. Roland Verquzzi."

"Why do you wish to see Ms. McDonald?"

The young man chewed his lip nervously. He cleared his throat and motioned to his portfolio. "I, uh… design women's clothes."

Kaye raised her eyebrows. "Yes?"

"Well, I need a partner, you know… like a business partner to help establish my business. I was hoping that maybe she, I mean her company, might consider it."

"Do you have an appointment, sir?" Kaye asked, pretending to look for an appointment book, all the while observing the young man's meek demeanor.

"No," came his soft reply. "I—I was hoping maybe I could make one."

Kaye glanced at the clock. Her board's luncheon meeting was another three hours away. *"Do unto others as you would have them do unto you"* popped into head.

"Yes, Lord," she said silently to herself. *"Thank you."*

Cocking her head and leaning across the receptionist's desk toward the young man, she said crisply, "Well, Roland, this is your lucky day!"

"It is?" he gulped.

"You bet!" Turning towards Stephanie, she smiled sweetly. "Stephanie here is Ms. McDonald's personal assistant." She turned to face Stephanie, whose eyes were like gigantic saucers. "Ms. McDonald isn't expected in for a couple of hours, is she, Stephanie?"

Stephanie's tongue had apparently frozen. All she could do was nod in agreement.

Kaye continued, "Perhaps Mr. Verquzzi could display his designs on the table in Ms. McDonald's office. That way, she could see them when she comes in."

"Yes," Stephanie responded haltingly. "That would be a good idea, M—"

Kaye reacted quickly. "Oh how ignorant of me, Mr. Verquzzi! I forgot to introduce myself. I'm Mary."

She reached across the desk to shake his hand. Stephanie discreetly rolled her eyes heavenward and turned to open the door with the big brass monogram "M.K."

Kaye, for her part, continued her personal dialogue with the Lord. *"Well, it's not really a lie, is it? Mary is my first name."*

As Roland set about proudly displaying his portfolio, Kaye couldn't help but notice how shabbily dressed he was. In fact, he looked half-starved.

But then she let out a startled gasp. His sketches were absolutely stunning! She stepped forward to admire them. Stephanie joined her at the table, equally impressed.

Before their eyes, this lanky young man was suddenly transformed. He came alive as he passionately described, with sweeping gestures, the flow of each garment, its texture, fabric, and form.

Amazed, Kaye couldn't help but think, *This kid not only has innate talent, he's got the passion to carry it! Kayleen's never invested in fashion before, but this guy could actually set the fashion world on fire.*

"Roland?" she said.

"Yes, Mary?"

Mary? Oh for heaven's sake, Kaye, that's you! No wonder we should always tell the truth. It's too easy to get caught in a lie.

She cleared her throat to camouflage the tardiness in her response. "Are you an American?" she asked.

"Yes."

"I mean, born in America?"

"Yes, in California, why? Is that a problem?"

"No, absolutely not!" She smiled inwardly. *Absolutely not, dear boy. You are exhibiting talent usually seen only in European designers.* She felt like she had just encountered the Leprechaun's pot o' gold at the end of the rainbow. "Roland, can I ask you another question?"

"Yes, of course."

"Stephanie and I are of different ages, different coloring, and different body shapes."

The young man nodded.

"Could you show us how you would design outfits for the same type of event… what event would that be, Stephanie?" She looked to the young woman for direction.

"For a dinner date," Stephanie offered.

"Like to a good restaurant," Roland ventured. "But not one requiring formal attire, as a nightclub might?"

"Yes," the women murmured in unison.

To their amazement, Roland pulled out a sketchpad and began to draw furiously. No longer the hesitant youth, he became the take-charge man of the hour.

Stephanie stood in the doorway, nervously eying the empty receptionist's desk. *Whatever am I to do if someone comes?* she thought.

In less than half an hour, Roland proudly displayed his sketches. He had created two radically different outfits… different design, different material, different color. Then he began to expound their value to each woman, flattering the attributes of both.

Kaye was both astonished at her find and challenged. Beyond a shadow of a doubt, this young man was worthy to be sponsored. She'd do it herself if need be, but she really wanted her board to sanction the endeavor. The big but was Roland himself.

She decided to square with him. Much to Stephanie's relief, because someone was now approaching the receptionist's desk. Stephanie hustled to take care of the business she felt competent to manage.

"Roland," Kaye said. "I have to be honest with you. People around here don't really call me Mary. I'm M.K. McDonald."

Roland, for his part, sat in a nearby chair, awestruck to be in the presence of *the* M.K. McDonald! Not only that, but she thought his work was okay.

The mere thought brought a smile to his face. Roland felt like he was living a dream. He truly hoped no one would pinch him to wake him.

A few minutes past ten o'clock, a tall and thin man, impeccably dressed, swished into Kaye's office. Roland looked up, startled.

"Philippe, let me introduce you to Roland," Kaye said, beaming. "Roland, Philippe is my personal assistant." She grinned and added, "My real one!"

Roland shook his hand. Philippe looked at the shabbily dressed man, feeling that shaking his hand might not be safe—sanitary-wise, that is. Nonetheless, eventually he extended his hand for a polite, brief shake. The two men sat down on opposite sides of the expansive coffee table that graced Kaye's office.

Kaye wasted no time in laying out her agenda. "Philippe, I'm convinced Roland has the capability to become one of the world's most prominent fashion designers. Furthermore, I'm certain this will occur in the not-too-distant future."

The look on Philippe's face revealed that he suspected his employer must be suffering from some sort of post-traumatic stress disorder. He raised his eyebrows in total disbelief.

Roland, for his part, read Philippe's rejection and looked like a scared rabbit.

Kaye sat back. "Your reactions clearly illustrate the problem."

The two men looked at her blankly.

Kaye turned to Roland. "I believe the real Roland, the true Roland, is the take-charge Roland, the one who passionately described his portfolio to Stephanie and myself. The Roland who instantaneously and, I dare say brilliantly, took on the exercise to appropriately design an outfit for each of us to wear, an outfit that would complement us both." Next, she turned to Philippe. "As for you, Philippe, you heard every word I spoke and then wondered where in this room was such a person."

She smiled at Roland. "You see, Roland, we need to help you with your image, so you can help American women with ours. That is what I think Kayleen can do for you. You need not only a financial partner. You need a confidence builder."

Roland was obviously struggling over her words, perplexed as to exactly what she meant.

She crossed the room and knelt before him. Looking into his eyes, she clasped his hands in hers, praying he could receive her genuine concern for his success, personally and professionally.

"Roland, you have great talent. You are a man of humility too. But somewhere along the way, someone knocked to smithereens all the confidence you ever had in the goodness of yourself. We need to put those pieces of your heart back together again."

As she spoke, tears filled Roland's eyes. He simply nodded ascent.

"Whatever you want me to do, I'll do it," he whispered.

Kaye stood and turned back to Philippe. "Can you take Roland to Bluhmdale's Menswear and get him properly outfitted? If any adjustments are necessary, tell them we need them done immediately." She stood back and sized up the young man. "I'm sorry, but we'll also need to do something with your mane. Philippe will take you to our hairstylist. If you have no particular preference, Philippe can advise." Turning back to her assistant, she added, "Get him shaved, showered, and dressed in our apartment here. I want him to meet the board. Preferably by one."

She took another long look at the young fashion designer before her.

"Roland?" she said.

"Yes, ma'am?"

"When did you eat last?"

"Yesterday morning."

"So feed him," Philippe interjected.

Kaye smiled. "That's right! You'll discover, Roland, that Philippe is a great person for detail. And one more thing before you go. When you come before the board, don't worry about being perfect. In presenting yourself and your portfolio, you can stumble. Confidence in presentation is a learned skill. You'll have ample time to work on that. Just tell them about your dreams."

Roland grinned like the Cheshire cat. "Thanks! Thanks ever so much!"

He shook her hand and waved goodbye, exiting in a daze. If the truth be known, he was half-afraid the morning's events would prove a mere figment of his imagination.

Kaye's day had begun on a surprising note. She had made a chance discovery of someone who appeared to be a true fashion prodigy. Through him, there existed the potential for yet another profitable business venture for Kayleen Enterprises.

Her board meeting went well. Very well, in fact! The board also saw the genius in young Roland and endorsed her decision to back him. Not only that, but the board and he liked her suggestion to designate the new company Rolando Fashions.

The real surprise—more to the point, the real shock—occurred when the relocation committee revealed the three possible sites for Kayleen's new corporate headquarters. They had analyzed the potential in each site and identified the preferred options. The board listened attentively to the pros and cons of each. The committee began with the third option, then the second. When they revealed their number one choice, Kaye's jaw dropped.

chapter seven

Chicago! Kaye tried her best to appear attentive, to listen to all the positives and digest the negatives. *I don't want to go anywhere near Chicago, for fear I run into Max's parents.*

She had never seen the board so quick to unify, so fully enthused about a project. Normally there would be some oohs, some aahs, some raised eyebrows, some scratching of heads, some "I need to study this further," some "I don't know." Not this time! A hundred percent excitement, a hundred percent "Let's contact the city planners immediately." Full site agreement. On and on it went. The board wanted to engage the current owners of the properties at the proposed site to determine the dollar value of securing the land.

Kaye tried to appear neutral, to maintain her focus so no one could detect her personal bias. She smiled. She nodded her head at just the right times and in the appropriate directions. The one thing that should have been a dead giveaway that something in her world wasn't quite right was the fact that she never opened her mouth. Since everyone was so enthusiastically vocal, that small detail eluded the others. So began Kayleen's Chicago Project.

Everyone's focus quickly became doing whatever they could to facilitate the move. Everyone, that is, except the CEO. Kaye's solitary focus became the prayer of her heart: *"Dear Lord, please do not let me encounter Francesco and Josephine Carron!"*

It wasn't that she feared them. The truth was that she felt guilty about harboring their son without their knowledge, knowing they would be yearning to welcome him home after his six-year absence. She wondered what they would think of her when the truth came out. Yet she wanted to honor Max's wish not to involve his family until they were married, especially given all he had done for her.

She sat brooding at her desk long after the board had adjourned. She was exhausted! She worried how Max would receive the news. Would he believe her that she had nothing to do with the decision, or would he suspect her of meddling?

"Ms. McDonald?"

Startled, she looked up to see Lewis, her chauffer.

"Ms. McDonald, I'm taking Alice and Philippe to their respective Lakeland apartments. Would you like to ride with us, and then proceed to Summerside?"

The alternative, she quickly surmised, was that she drive home by herself. Quite frankly, she knew she lacked the energy to do so.

She looked at Lewis and sighed. "You know, I think your offer is the best I've heard all day. When do you plan on leaving?"

"Philippe and Alice said they'll be ready in a half-hour. That would be 5:30, ma'am."

"5:30 it is then. I'll gather my stuff and meet you in the parking garage."

"You won't need your own car this weekend?" Lewis asked.

"No. If I need a vehicle, there's several at Independence Drive that I could borrow," Kaye smiled gamely. She actually relished the hour-long ride with Philippe and Alice. It would give her time to catch up with her two special assistants. The stress of the past few months—the attempt on her life, Max's injuries—had interfered with the close working relationship she usually had with these two.

Her two aides were delighted to have their chief join them. Philippe apprised her of all he had secured for young Mr. Verquzzi. He admitted that he had changed his opinion of the young man. "At first I doubted him. He seemed so shabby. Then again, we shouldn't judge a book by its cover, should we? I do believe that financing his business will prove a sound investment for Kayleen."

"I think you'll be a big asset to him, Philippe, until he gets on his feet. Please take that as a personal assignment from me." Kaye smiled warmly at her aide. "By the way, where is he staying?"

"Thought you'd never ask! Well, I recalled that Stephanie's mom was a skilled seamstress, that she might be helpful to Roland. With Stephanie's approval, I gave her a call. Mrs. Baxter got just as excited as we did over Roland's potential, particularly after Stephanie described how he'd designed those outfits for the two of you. As a result, she absolutely insisted he stay with them. She volunteered to contact other dressmakers to help Rolando Fashions spring to life."

Kaye burst out laughing. "Philippe, you do indeed have an eye for detail! You've taken care of everything. Please keep me informed of Roland's activities. I can't help but feel this venture is going to explode."

On arrival at the Lakeland estate, Lewis drove straight into the parking garage. Alice and Philippe both gave Kaye an affectionate hug as they departed.

"It's great to have you back, M.K.," Alice whispered in her ear.

"Good to be back."

Lewis had taken her briefcase and overnight bag, depositing them in the silver SUV with tinted windows. Kaye crawled into the back seat, grabbing the pillow and blanket. She was asleep before Lewis left Lakeland. In fact, the next thing she remembered was Lewis announcing their arrival at the Walters' house.

"What time is it?" Kaye mumbled.

"8:00 p.m., ma'am."

She grinned. "You made good time."

"Indeed, I did. When do you wish to be picked up?"

"I plan to work at home for a few days, Lewis. I'll call the office on Monday to give you a specific day and time. Have a great weekend!"

With that, she sprinted to the Walters' door. The moment she opened it, she felt revived. The aroma of freshly baked bread wafted down the hall. Looking into the kitchen, she spied Marnie's crockpot sitting on the counter.

"Grab yourself some stew," Marnie sang out cheerfully. "Jack just got home. He's in the rehab room."

Kaye quickly changed into her lounge pajamas and entered the rehab room, stew and bread in hand. Setting her food on the table, she hopped up on the edge of Max's bed and gave him a hug and a kiss.

"Missed you," he whispered.

"And I you."

Jack and Marnie sat on the loveseat. Jack, like Kaye, was finally getting a chance to eat after a long day.

"Hey everybody, where are you?" a booming voice hollered from the front door.

Jack shouted, "In the rehab room!"

"Food's in the kitchen, if you haven't eaten," Marnie added.

Dave and Sue took Marnie up on her supper offer. Soon all three couples were sharing their day's activities. Everyone marveled at how Marnie could prepare such a meal given her demands as a school principal.

"My secret," she said with a laugh, "is that I have a guest who can cook. All

I had to do was bring home the Italian port wine, and Max did the rest. It gives the stew some zest, don't you think?"

Everyone agreed.

While the silence of the normally gregarious M.K. McDonald had escaped Kayleen's usually astute Board, it didn't go unnoticed by her five close confidantes.

"So, Kaye, we've been yapping for over an hour and you've scarcely said boo," Dave observed. "What's up?"

Ten eyes suddenly riveted on her.

"Just because I haven't said anything doesn't mean something's up," Kaye snapped.

Max laughed. "Maybe not, but the two S's definitely do!"

Kaye furrowed her brow. "Whatever do you mean by two S's?"

"Silence followed by a snap," he said with a smile.

Everyone except Kaye burst into laughter. She grabbed a pillow and bopped him on the head.

"So, what's bugging you, Ms. McDonald?" Jack asked.

"Well, if you must know, the board tabled its proposed locations for Kayleen's new corporate home."

"Really," Sue said. "So soon?"

"Yep, and they did a really thorough job. Not only is my board uniformly enthusiastic, but they're a hundred percent united."

"What about you, Kaye?" Marnie asked softly.

"I have mixed emotions."

"So where is it?" Jack said. "Don't keep us in suspense."

"Chicago!"

There were three quiet "oh's" from the men, and from the two women a not so quiet "Does this mean you'll move?"

"Definitely not!" Kaye stated emphatically. "In fact, of the three geographical choices, Chicago is the closest to Summerside. It's just that—"

"Chicago takes a little getting used to," interjected Max.

Dave eyed her. "Yeah, I can see your mixed emotions, Kaye."

"Well, Marnie," Jack said, quickly changing the subject, "now that we know Kaye needs a pick-me-up, this is probably a good time for your chocolate mousse!" He rose and headed for the kitchen, carrying the dirty dishes.

Jack's timing was perfect. Marnie's exquisite dessert soon had their minds off the day's events. For his part, Max was beginning to realize just how included he was in this close-knit surrogate family of Kaye's. He had to admit it felt good!

Sue challenged everyone to a Scrabble contest. They decided to play couples teams. With their diverse backgrounds, all three teams were pretty evenly matched.

At eleven o'clock, the Davidsons went home. Jack helped Max toilet for the night. Afterward, Jack headed upstairs to bed. He passed Kaye on her way back down to talk with Max.

"Chicago," he muttered to her.

"Exactly. Chicago!"

Kaye returned to the rehab room and climbed up onto Max's bed.

He pursed his lips. "Chicago!"

Crossing her legs, she replied, "In the long term, Max, it may be good for us. It's the short term I worry about."

"Exactly!"

"Well, how big is Chicago anyway? Don't you think it's feasible that I could go there and see neither your mother nor father?"

He scowled. "There's an excellent chance you won't meet Mama. A 99.9% chance you'll encounter Pop."

"Really?" she said. "Why?"

"Kayleen moving its corporate headquarters means construction, and that translates into the potential to make money. Wherever that potentiality exists, you will find my father!"

"Maybe we should contact them. Your parents, I mean."

"No."

"Max, I know we've been through this before, but please be patient with me. I don't understand your Italian culture. I feel so guilty. It's been nearly six months since your release from prison. You say they love you. I love you. If I was expecting you home and you didn't show up, I'd be beside myself. I just feel so very, very sorry for them."

He brushed his hand up against her face, gently pushing back her hair. "I know, Kaye, and I do too, but I really love you. I want to marry you, and I want to do it when I can consummate the marriage. That, darling, isn't feasible until this iron albatross of a cage is removed from my leg!"

She looked at him, her eyes twinkling. "If memory serves, we could say it was nearly consummated four months ago. I've forgiven your break and entry and attempted act of passion, which could have succeeded if Glaxton's phone call hadn't interrupted." She feigned a pout. "However, Mr. Carron, I have not forgotten!"

He peered over his glasses. "No! That doesn't count."

"I know." She giggled, nuzzling up against him. "But Max, you're a grown man. Your father wouldn't bodily take you out of here, would he?"

"Yes, he would."

"Well, if he'd do that now, why won't he do it after we're married?"

"Kaye, there are two things about my old-world Catholic culture you should know. No matter all your wonderful personal attributes, you aren't Catholic. And you aren't Italian."

"But I know many couples who are happily married despite being from different cultures. Including Italians."

"Well, the problem for the parents isn't what happens after, it's the before," he said. She looked confused by this, so he explained. "I'm like a sitting duck with this iron brace on my leg right now. I can't move. I can't do a darn thing on my own."

"You can verbally argue your point."

"Right. And when Pop sees he's not winning or making any headway, his solution will simply be to remove Junior from the equation. Kaye, I don't want to be removed, but I can't and won't charge Pop with kidnapping if it happens."

"Okay, but I still don't understand. How come the person who's deemed unkosher *before* the marriage suddenly becomes kosher after it?" Kaye queried.

"That's simple. They're married! My parents are Catholic, and they believe marriage is for life. So they'll grin and bear it. That's why Sophia and Tony married before they told their parents. It was their only hope!"

Kaye was truly stupefied. "But both of them were Italian and Catholic. Why did they have a problem?"

"The two families were feuding. If Tony had gone to Pop and asked for Sophia's hand, he would have been lucky to escape with his life."

Kaye breathed deeply. "So the earliest we can marry would be towards the end of October?"

"Yep, but don't you think it would be nice if we had maybe two weeks to ourselves? When will your house be ready for us to move back into?"

"Probably the same time we can marry." She snuggled up against him. "So if I go to Chicago in October, I've got to avoid your father. Otherwise he might ask about Mr. Kerr and my reaction could cause him to be suspicious."

"Kaye, it's not necessary to avoid him. Trust me, if he meets you, your brush with death won't be on his mind. Business will be... so when you run into him, simply put on your best CEO demeanor and confront him."

"Confront him?"

Max grinned. "Yep. He may go head to head with you, but at least he won't become suspicious that you're hiding something personal from him."

He gave her a quick peck on the cheek.

"Oh no, Mr. Carron, no go. I want a *nice* kiss!"

"This is torture," he said. "When I kiss you, I get turned on and can't do anything about it." He frowned. "What are you doing?"

Kaye wore a very sad face and was rubbing her thumb and forefinger together. "Why, Mr. Carron, this is the world's smallest violin, playing a sad song for you!"

"Very funny."

She grinned, then leaned in to give him a passionate kiss. "I think so."

"Kaye, just don't underestimate Pop, that's all I'm asking. Be wary!"

"Just like I was with you?" Looking pensive, she put her forefinger to her lips. "Well, I suppose I do still have my briefcase. It slowed you down when you ran into it!"

"You're impossible! Good night, Ms. McDonald."

chapter eight

J osephine Carron snuggled up against her husband and felt him respond to her touch. She kissed him gently, smiling softly to herself. *It never fails. In thirty-eight years of marriage, intimacy with Frank never ends with sex. Most men roll over and go to sleep after, but you, my dear, never do. This is where your heart becomes mine.*

At this point, Frank allowed himself to be vulnerable, willing to honestly talk with her. Over the years, they had shared their joys, fears, pain, sadness, hopes, and dreams. Often she would start the conversation, but other times he would. The topics of conversation varied, but they were never abstract concepts, only those things that related to family and friends. Naturally, he would be discrete about business matters, which she respected, but he would always alert her to changing situations. For example, "Things are good, Josie" or "My work's causing me to be a little irritated, Jo." She appreciated his sensitivity towards her feelings. She never had to worry if he was upset with her. She was his lady, his most precious possession, and that was exactly how he treated her.

I may have stayed home and not gone out into the workforce like so many young women do today, Josephine thought, *but I read, listen, and now through television I can keep abreast of just about anything.*

Not that she'd watch talk shows or soaps. Frank was very intelligent. He had an active, inquisitive mind. She knew from the beginning that if their marriage was to be more than a certificate, she would need to keep herself informed. So that's exactly what she did. Many immigrant Italian women never bothered to become fluent in English. Not Josephine. She set about to learn the language. True, she still had a slight accent, but her vocabulary was extensive.

Yes, she ran the household, and yes, she had the major role in rearing her children, but always Josephine kept her eyes open to the interpersonal dynamics that swirled about her, including interaction with the Family. Relationally, she was very astute. In fact, over the years Frank had come to regard his wife as his most accurate barometer of the emotional swings of the Italian community.

Josephine's hand slid over Frank's chest—over his heart. Just feeling the rhythmic beat of his presence brought her peace.

He reached over took her hand in his. "Jo?"

"Mmm?"

"Remember a couple of months ago when you were so upset about Massimiliano?"

"You mean when I awoke in a cold sweat, terrified that he was dying?" Fear rose in her as she wondered what could have prompted Frank's question in this, their time of deep sharing.

Frank leaned up on his elbow and gazed into her eyes. Even in the dim light, he couldn't mistake the fear his question elicited.

"Why do you ask, Frank? Do you know something I don't?"

"No, Jo. I didn't mean to scare you." He gently stroked her hair. "It's just that sometimes you're so perceptive. In spiritual things, you often get things I can't even imagine. Like the night of the attack on that McDonald broad. Remember, you woke up, beside yourself with fear. We had a house full of overnight guests, so we went to my study, but nothing I said or did took away your fear that Massimiliano was dying. Then your nephew George, who's on Kayleen's board and was with us that night, got the phone call from McDonald about the attack. He saw the light on in my study and came to check. We shared your fear and George said that sometimes God can wake his people up to pray for people or situations they know nothing about. He told us that McDonald's private eye, whose name was Max, had been critically wounded. George suggested maybe that's who you were praying for, not our son. After this, you had total peace about it, where seconds before you had been encased in fear." Frank paused, lying back down beside her. "So I was wondering, do you still have that peace? Or have you had any more moments of fear?"

Josephine turned on her side to face him. "Funny. Until you mentioned it, I hadn't thought about that night. Now I realize that I have had a total peace since then. You know what else?

"Reading your mind is one aptitude I've never been able to master."

She laughed and kissed him. "Well, as long as I can keep ahead of you, our marriage is likely secure. Truthfully, though, since that night I haven't thought that much about Massimiliano."

"I can't believe that!"

"No, no, I don't mean that I haven't thought of him. Rather it's *how* I've thought of him. Before that night, I was so worried, wondering why he hadn't come home. What trouble he was into. Whether I'd ever see him alive again. Those type of thoughts."

"And you haven't had them since that night?"

"Right. My thoughts seem to focus on what he looks like now. I mean, he's thirty-four years old!"

"Do you wonder whether we'll be able to relate to him at all?"

"No, I don't think that will be a problem, dear."

"You don't? Why not?"

"Because Massimiliano loved to read. He could do that in prison. I'm sure he could watch world news on TV. He has an active mind like you and I have."

Frank chuckled. "Jo, you always bring things into a broader perspective."

"Don't forget, Massimiliano was good with children. He loved them. Micki and Jo and little Rici have been our delight. When the time comes, I'm sure they'll wrap their uncle around their little fingers too!" She giggled at the thought of that reunion.

Her laughter eased the tension Frank had been feeling over the past few weeks. *Funny*, he thought. *She stopped worrying and I started. Fortunately, she's the intuitive one. I shall follow her lead.*

"When do you think he'll come home, Frank?" Now she was the one to raise herself up to lean on his chest and look into his eyes.

"I haven't got a clue!" Her question caught him totally off-guard. "What do you think?"

Josephine furrowed her brow. "Frank, I have no reason to say this, but intuitively I sense it could be sometime around Thanksgiving or Christmas."

"Is that really intuition, or just wishful thinking?"

She laughed and laid her head on his chest. "That, dear, I am totally unable to answer. One thing I intend to do is ensure that both our house and his are decorated for Christmas."

He kissed the top of her head, giving her a hug. "Said with all the determination of the Josephine I know. I'm sure you'll make it happen."

"Why do I sense that there's one more thing troubling you, Frank?"

Now it was his turn to feel unsettled. "Jo, I guess what's troubling me is whether he…"

Frank cleared his throat, searching for the right words to adequately express his heart while not divulging the one and only secret he had ever hidden from her.

"Whether he what, Frank?"

"Whether Massimiliano hates us." There it was. He had blurted out his deep-seated fear.

"What?" Josephine recoiled in shock at the suggestion. "Why? Whatever would make you think that?"

"He was sentenced to prison for six years. It isn't a fun place."

"Frank, you never did drugs. You never involved him in that, did you?"

"No, of course not."

"Well, our son chose that route for himself. Just like he chose not to think when he hit the baseball through the cathedral window at school. There were consequences to that choice, and there were consequences to what he chose to do in that motel room. Massimiliano faced the baseball consequences in a responsible manner. After that, we never had any more problems from him, nor did he resent us. I'm confident he will do the same in this situation."

Frank's jaw dropped in amazement at his wife's assessment of their son's sentence. *Good thing she never became a judge,* he thought. *She and Max's judge would probably see eye to eye.*

He gave her a playful squeeze. "You have this unique ability to always set my heart at ease."

"All of which means you want me to blow out the candle so you can get to sleep." Even this part Josephine loved, for Frank never turned away from her; he always fell asleep embracing her.

As Frank held his wife in his arms and felt the rhythmic breathing that told him she was fast asleep, he once more kissed her gently.

My beloved, you don't know what I do and what our son knows. Frank sighed. *Massimiliano never did drugs! We should have appealed his sentence and got a mistrial. But we didn't because the Marconi and Carron families made a covenant not to expose whoever was behind the attempt to kill Tony, and who then set up our son. So, Massimiliano ended up the Family's sacrificial lamb.*

Those were the details Frank had withheld from his wife, the secret he reluctantly held in his heart, praying—yes, praying—that God, in his mercy, would never reveal the truth to Josephine. If she found out, would she ever trust him again? Even worse, would she hate him? Thankfully, sleep soon numbed those thoughts.

chapter nine

When Frank awoke, Josephine was already dressing. He quickly showered and grinned as he saw his clothes all neatly laid out for him. "Good thing we both have the same tastes," he said, giving her a peck on the cheek.

They headed for the dining room, where Gus and Angel D'Amato were already at the table.

"Have you heard the news?" Angel gushed.

The D'Amatos were Frank and Josephine's most trusted friends. People laughingly referred to Gus as Frank's lieutenant, and he really was. Gus would often troubleshoot for Frank. If Frank had a business confidant, it was Gus.

Frank eyed his friend. Gus looked the epitome of Hollywood's tough-looking, tough-talking Italian mobster.

Gus could have coached Marlon Brando in his portrayal of the Godfather, Frank mused to himself. Angel, on the other hand, had been a bleached blonde for as long as Frank could remember. *And you, Angel, could have coached every actress in dumb blonde roles.*

"How could we have heard any news?" Frank said, laughing. "We just got up. It's barely eight o'clock!"

Angel proceeded to ignore Frank and zero in on Josephine. "You know that nice, young, smart businesswoman," she emphasized *smart* and *business* for the men's benefit, "who that wretched man tried to torture and kill a few months back?"

"M.K. McDonald?" Josephine said, her hand covering her mouth in alarm. "Did that poor private eye of hers die?"

"No, no! That's not the news. The news is that she's coming to Chicago to live."

"That's not quite it, either, sweetheart," Gus interrupted her good-naturedly. "Kayleen Enterprises will be relocating their corporate headquarters here."

"Which is precisely what I said," Angel replied emphatically.

Gus and Frank exchanged smiles.

"Why are they interested in Chicago?" Frank pondered out loud.

Angel took a bite from her muffin. "Frank, for someone who's supposed to be an astute businessman, you're sometimes just so dense! Illinois is right next to Indiana, and Chicago is just a short drive."

This allowed Frank a moment to consider his response. He looked desperately at his wife in hopes of a clue. What did Indiana have to do with anything?

"Oh," he said diplomatically.

"Don't you think that's so romantic, Josie?" Angel rushed on. "Poor dear, remember how dreadful she looked that morning? That episode probably got her thinking. Why, goodness, she's what—thirty-four, isn't it? Time she should marry. Any girl needs a man to protect her, particularly one as famous as she is, and just think of her responsibilities!"

"So Kayleen wants to relocate to Chicago so M.K. McDonald can be closer to this Max Kerr fellow, her investigator?" Frank ventured, putting the pieces together. As he recalled, Kerr was from Indiana.

"Most assuredly!"

"Well, that's wonderful news, Angel." Josephine beamed enthusiastically at her friend. "Did you make these muffins and the blueberry jam? You are so talented in the kitchen."

Angel blushed at the compliment and remarked on how she loved to cook and bake for her family and friends.

Frank knew that at that point he should have kept his mouth shut, but he admitted later to Gus that he just couldn't help himself. Trying to appear sincerely interested in Angel's speculations, Frank decided to play the devil's advocate. "Well, that's an interesting theory, Angel," Frank said. "But what happens if this Kerr character is married already?"

"Honestly, Frank Carron, you are thick! Then she'll be able to find a good man in Illinois." She paused and stared at the men. "But you two are ineligible!"

"Well, of course," blurted Josephine. "For one thing, they're a lot older than Ms. McDonald."

Frank raised his eyebrows. "I think, dear, she was referring to our marital status."

Angel clucked. "But guess who isn't ineligible?"

"Who?" they spoke in three-part harmony.

"Massimiliano!"

Josephine's eyes bulged in horror. "Massimiliano? No, Angel, I'm certain Ms. McDonald is neither Catholic nor Italian."

"Even more problematic, Massimiliano isn't here," Frank reminded them. "Will you allow Gus and me to retreat to my office—with our coffee and a couple more muffins, of course—while the two of you plan Ms. McDonald's future matrimony?"

As they entered Frank's study, Gus said, "Isn't it incredible how different our brains work?"

"You mean yours and Angel's?"

"No! I mean guys and dolls. Like the first thing Angel thinks of is that this McDonald doll is in love."

"And the first thing Gus thinks?" asked Frank.

"The same thing you thought, my friend," retorted Gus with a grin. "Which is… I wonder where they're thinking of building? Do we own any land there? Even if we don't, there will be construction contracts."

Frank started to laugh—a real deep, belly laugh—and tears began to flow down his cheeks. Gus soon joined him. At last, Frank finally managed to say, "That guy was dead-on when he said men are from Mars and women are from Venus."

When they finally stopped laughing, Gus said, "Okay, so what's up? You have something on your mind."

"Well, talking with Josie last night helped clarify my thoughts."

"Which are?"

"Massimiliano was released from prison in mid-April."

"So?"

"So, in a few days it'll be mid-October."

"Six months since his release," murmured Gus. "You don't think he's lying low to go after Judge Walters, do you? Massimiliano knows the cops usually let down their guard when nothing happens after six months. Usually cooler rationale prevails. Unless, of course, he has premeditated an attack."

"I don't know, but if he has, Josie would be devastated. She has it in her head that he'll be home before Christmas."

"Josie's destruction would have a domino effect," added Gus. "It would probably bring down the whole deck, so to speak… the house of Carron and the house of Marconi." He tented his hands, resting his chin on his fingers. "So, my friend, what are you thinking?"

"I'm thinking we need to find my son before he does something we would all regret. I don't want him or anyone else touching that judge. At least not now!"

The phone rang, bringing their conversation to an abrupt halt. Frank picked up the receiver. "Scally? No kidding! Yeah, Gus and I can come down right away!"

"Did they find Mass?" Gus asked hopefully.

"No," Frank said grinning, "but we do own some of the property Kayleen wants."

chapter ten

Philippe knocked tentatively on his boss's office door. "M.K., we need to discuss something with you."

Glancing up from her desk, Kaye called out a cheerful invitation for her two aides to enter. "I just need to sign these few letters. Have a seat. I'll be with you in seconds." Setting down her pen, she smiled. "Okay, so what is on your mind?"

Alice hesitated. "I've delayed mentioning it before, because of your personal trauma."

Kaye looked at her assistant. *Horrors! She's about to tell me I've forgotten something major. For the life of me, I can't imagine what it is.*

Alice was personally responsible for Kaye's schedule. Philippe would fine-tune the details, but it was Alice who kept Kayleen Enterprises on track. This allowed Kaye to devote her attention to the specific task at hand.

Throwing her hands up in resignation, she said, "Sorry, Alice, I can see by the look on your face that I promised to do something." She screwed up her face. "But try as I might, I can't recall. How bad is it?"

She hoped that whatever it was, it wouldn't necessitate her being away from Summerside. *"Lord, please help me! Max needs me to be there for him. It will be different when he's mobile."*

Alice sighed. "M.K., do you remember last fall when Mayor Turiano asked if you would be the keynote speaker at New York's civic dinner?"

Kaye slapped her hand to her forehead and slumped into her chair. "Oh God, no!" And she really did mean that as a prayer. "No, no, no... oh no! When is it?"

"Not this Friday, but next," Alice murmured, trying to sound positive. She could tell that her boss was on the verge of tears. "I thought that with all you've been through, it might have slipped your mind. I took the liberty of asking Sim and Kenzie if they could assemble the data you need. I also asked Nelson and Raj to ghost a speech. They have done so." Alice caught her breath. "Both Philippe and I think they've done an excellent job. I also gave it to public relations, and they feel it is accurate."

Alice studied Kaye, hoping her words would ease the woman's initial panic.

"Really, M.K., I think the speech is doable. You may wish to edit it and insert one or two of your own anecdotes, perhaps even a joke."

For her part, Kaye buried her head in her hands, moaning almost imperceptibly. Philippe unobtrusively set his handkerchief on her lap. He and Alice looked anxiously at each other, wondering which might come first—the end of the world or their boss's response.

At last, Kaye looked up. She dabbed her eyes with Philippe's hanky. Alice thought she had never seen Kaye so drained, so tired.

She'll never be able to do this, Alice thought.

Kaye exhaled deeply and spoke from the heart. "Guys, thank you for all the effort you and your team have gone to. It's just that this is one mammoth event. City politicians, senior public officials, leading business executives, not to mention the Wall Street bigwigs and media… everyone will be there! What on earth did I agree to speak about, anyway?"

Philippe cleared his throat. "The subject of give and take."

"How multinational corporations have an obligation to nurture the communities in which they reside," chimed in Alice. "You said that there needs to be much giving, not simply taking. You were going to cite some of the initiatives Kayleen has begun to explore."

Kaye bit her lip. "That topic is as dear to my heart as when I first agreed to it, but while I know this is the topic the mayor agreed to, it's not what everyone will have on their minds." She paused, tears welling up in her eyes. "Truthfully, I simply cannot speak about what they want to hear. Not yet, anyway. I just can't!"

"M.K., that's what we thought, too," Alice spoke softly. "When we spoke with public relations, they agreed that it's too early. They felt, and so do we, that Kayleen should be very forthright about that."

"Yes," Philippe added. "It would be good for people to see you and hear you making a typical business speech. That would signal that your recovery is progressing well. You could let the public know that in the not too distant future, when okayed by doctors, you'll share about your traumatic experience."

Kaye sat for a few moments, feeling pensive. "Is it possible to speak with Vice-President Smithers today and the public relations department? I'd like to meet with them. If they're all unified in the approach you've outlined, I'll take the speech home and peruse it."

* * *

Kaye arrived back in Summerside with a mandate to speak as originally agreed. Coincidentally, Special Agent Epstein had dropped in to visit Dave and he'd been invited along with the Davidsons for supper at Jack's. So she was able to discuss the situation with all the residents of Independence Drive and Epi. Everyone gave her the same green light to proceed with the speaking engagement.

"It's akin to climbing back on a horse when you've had a tumble," ventured Jack. "The sooner you do it, the better off you'll be. The longer you leave it, the harder it'll be."

"Yes, but you must be adequately protected," Sue added. "You don't want to get dragged into answering media questions about the Glaxton affair. I know you're not ready for that!"

That's when Epi stepped in. "Not only should you have Kayleen security, Kaye, but I'll be there with Brian and two other agents. If needed, we'll intervene to remove you."

With Epi's pronouncement, Kaye felt as if a lead weight had been removed from her shoulders. Agent Brian had been on duty that fateful night and was fully in the loop regarding Max. Her biggest fear was being trapped into speaking about Glaxton.

"I know it's way too early to talk about it." She dropped her eyes. "But there is another issue. Max, you stayed around for me. Now, while you're immobilized, I want to be here beside you. I don't want to be away."

"Yeah, but Jack is right," Max said. "It's important for you to step out into the public light again. This New York engagement will provide you an excellent venue to do so. You'll gain the confidence you need to realize that you can be in control of what you wish to share about the Glaxton ordeal."

As Max spoke, Marnie went up behind him and gave him a playful poke. "And we promise to keep His Highness occupied."

So it was agreed. Kaye would keep the New York engagement. Her staff had done an excellent job in ghosting the speech. It was relatively easy for her to personalize the text.

Thus, she arrived in New York with her entourage—and with a carefully crafted statement alerting everyone to the fact that she wouldn't be addressing the trauma she had endured. It was acknowledged that at some point those details would be shared. However, both she and Kayleen had been advised that now was not the time.

Kaye and her staff occupied the top floor of the convention hotel. She had met earlier with Mayor Turiano, who expressed delight that she was able to attend. He had pledged that the city would do all it could to protect her and ensure that only the agreed-topic would be discussed.

As the various guests began to arrive, Tony and Sophia stepped out of a black limousine with his parents in tow. Tony bore a striking resemblance to his mother, Lena, who was most enthused about attending the dinner. In fact, she was trying her best to rub off some of that enthusiasm onto her husband. The man was much smaller in stature than she. It also didn't appear that anyone or anything could soften his countenance.

"I don't care what you say, Pepi," Lena said to him. "I'm interested in seeing this young woman. I think she has to be made of pretty good stuff to be able to fulfill a speaking engagement so soon after enduring that terrible attack."

Lena was a large woman, but not dumpy. She carried herself regally and dressed in a fashion flattering to her size. Her son, the younger man, was ruggedly handsome.

"Mamma," Tony said. "Undoubtedly you have your autograph book poised to get Ms. McDonald's autograph."

His father's face brightened. "Get it on a cheque, Lena! Get it on a cheque!"

Lena was set to berate him when Sophia's cell phone rang.

"Sophia, are they calling you from work?" Tony said, scowling. "Don't any of the other interns ever work?"

"This isn't work, Tony. It's Pop's number. I'll answer him and catch up with you in the banquet hall." She gave him a peck and stepped aside from the flow of people to respond to the call.

Sophia answered and was startled to hear her mother's voice. She couldn't recall her mother ever using her father's cell phone. Furthermore, her mother was clearly distraught. When she first heard the words *heart attack*, she was seized with fear thinking it to be her father. Eventually she was able to calm her mother and uncover the reason for the older woman's despair. The speaker for the upcoming Our Lady of Mercies Hospital fundraiser banquet had suffered the heart attack and couldn't fulfill his speaking engagement. Desperate to help the hospital, her mother was hoping Sophia could offer suggestions for a substitute speaker.

Sophia was about to tell her mother no when she noticed M.K. McDonald, accompanied by several staff, slip into a private lounge beside the banquet hall.

"Mamma, I have an idea for a speaker, but I'll have to get back to you, okay? Love ya, bye!"

She smiled to herself as she shut off her phone. *What luck! I know that room well. The city's legal aid department held a seminar there last week. It has another entrance off the back corridor.* She opened her purse, eyes sparkling. *Eureka! And here's my New York City Legal Aid photo ID badge.*

She pinned it on and slipped down the corridor, heart pounding. Normally she'd never be this bold, but Mamma was so broken up over the possibility of having to cancel the hospital fundraiser. Our Lady of Mercies had been Mamma's passion for years. They needed a substitute speaker like Ms. McDonald.

Sophia gritted her teeth. *That fundraiser is Mamma's lifeline to health and sanity as she waits for that darn brother of mine to show up. If I could only convince Ms. McDonald to speak, it would be an unprecedented success for the hospital.*

Suddenly, fear and trepidation gripped her heart. Who was she to ask? Her next thought was more encouraging. Pop had said that Kayleen was thinking about relocating to Chicago. Perhaps Ms. McDonald wished to make an impression on Chicago. Offering charity to a hospital could do that for her.

Arriving at the room's back entrance, Sophia shot an arrow prayer. *"Please, Mary, Mother of Jesus, grant me success."*

She crossed herself and opened the door. To her surprise, she found herself standing in the room with only three people—Ms. McDonald, a man, and another woman.

He who hesitates is lost, she said to herself boldly as she walked quickly to the trio.

Abruptly they became aware of Sophia's presence.

"Who are you?" demanded the tall man, stepping protectively between Sophia and Ms. McDonald.

"Excuse me, Ms. McDonald," Sophia said, trying hard to disguise her nervousness, "I'm Sophia Marconi. I'm from New York's Legal Aid Department."

Kaye couldn't believe what she had just heard. Alice stepped forward to usher Ms. Marconi from the room.

"No, Alice, Philippe, please!" Kaye studied the young woman's features. There was no doubt that this was Max's sister. "What can we do for you?"

Sophia was too nervous, and Philippe and Alice were too stunned to notice how startled Kaye appeared.

Trying hard not to reveal her emotions, Kaye quietly asked again, "Is there something I can do for you?"

Sophia found her voice and spoke calmly, rationally. "Ms. McDonald, my mother just called from Chicago. Our Lady of Mercies is one of Chicago's oldest hospitals and it serves many poor families. It holds a large fundraiser every year. My mother's passion, aside from her family, is this hospital. This year's keynote speaker just had a heart attack. The dinner is only a month away."

"That's too bad," Philippe started to say.

Alice added patronizingly, "I don't know how Kayleen could help, dear."

Sophia bit her lip and plunged ahead. "Well, Ms. McDonald, I understand Kayleen is looking at Chicago as a possible place to relocate. If you would be willing to speak at the hospital's dinner, it might make a favorable impression."

There, she'd spat it out. Now it was up to God.

Alice was just about to dismiss this brash young woman when Kaye asked, "What is the date?"

"Friday, November 16," stammered Sophia.

"Alice, check my calendar. See if anything is scheduled for that day."

"Oh I will, Ms. McDonald. I suspect something is on your schedule, but Ms. Marconi, if I can have your card, I'll notify you."

"No!" Kaye stood. "Alice, if I do have something on that day, we will reschedule. It's a good idea to do a work of charity in Chicago. In fact, it fits right into the topic I'm addressing tonight."

"It does?" replied Sophia in amazement.

Philippe and Alice looked totally bewildered.

"Do you have a card, Ms. Marconi?" Kaye asked.

"Oh, yes." Sophia handed her a card, and for good measure offered one each to Philippe and Alice.

"Philippe, give Ms. Marconi our card." Kaye extended her hand to Sophia. "When you call, please instruct the receptionist to refer the call directly to myself, Philippe, or Alice. One of us will speak with you. Thank you for thinking of me. I do hope our participation in the fundraiser will be a financial benefit to the hospital." She smiled demurely. "And that the publicity will foster good relationships between Kayleen and Chicago. Ms. Marconi, before you leave, I'd like Alice to take a photo of us on my cell phone. She'll send it to you as confirmation of our agreement."

Afterward, Sophia floated to the Marconis' table. Her mother-in-law, however, was the only one who received her news positively.

Tony was downright skeptical. "She just told you that to get rid of you."

"I agree," echoed Pepi. "How much is her speaker fee, Sophia?"

"I don't know. We didn't discuss it."

Pepi shook his head. "You honestly think someone of her caliber took you seriously? I don't think so!"

Soon other friends of the Marconis filled the ten seats around their table. Conversation touched on every topic but the one on Sophia's mind.

Have I just been snowed, or is she sincere about coming? She groaned inwardly. *Pepi's right. I never did ask her the fee. It's probably exorbitant!*

As the meal progressed, Kaye spied on the Marconis' table, managing to unobtrusively steal sideways glances at it. *Finally, I get to see his family,* she thought. To say she was excited by this turn of events would have been an understatement. Yet she kept reminding herself to stay focused. *I need to give tonight's talk, and do it well!*

There was a brief interlude before she was to speak. It allowed Kaye time to visit the ladies room. On her way back, Mayor Turiano intercepted her to introduce her to a congressman and the district attorney.

Kaye was being gracious to those at the mayor's table when Tony Marconi pushed his way into her presence.

"Excuse me, Ms. McDonald!" Tony's voice was stern, but so was Mayor Turiano's response.

"Mr. Marconi, I'm afraid Ms. McDonald has a speech to give shortly. If you need a private conversation with her, it must wait."

"No, Mr. Mayor, it can't wait! My wife asked Ms. McDonald to speak at a hospital benefit in Chicago next month. My wife believes you agreed, Ms. McDonald." He flashed a charming smile. "I know that sometimes it's convenient to say yes when no is really meant, but I need to know the truth. My wife's mother is a very passionate supporter of the hospital. I don't want her having false hopes."

Kaye smiled sweetly. "I appreciate your concern, Mr. Marconi. My response may seem…" She paused, searching for the right words. "May seem a little unusual. However, I assure you it's all a matter of timing. Her invitation to speak at a hospital fundraiser, especially one that serves less privileged people and children, is a wonderful charity for me to be involved in." Kaye became very animated as she spoke. "In fact, it's a living example of tonight's topic. If you'll let me head to the podium, I'll be able to elucidate my point."

Tony's mouth dropped. "So your yes...is yes?"

"My yes is always yes, Mr. Marconi, and my no, a no!"

"What is your fee?"

Now it was Kaye's turn to look amazed. "It's a charity, Mr. Marconi. My fee is zero! Your wife has contact information with my aides for further inquiries. Mayor Turiano, here is my cell phone. Would you please take a photo of myself and Mr. Marconi?" She smiled at Tony and added, "I'll send you a copy as confirmation of what we've just discussed. Now, please excuse me. I need to speak."

Tony headed for his own table in a state of shock.

"Ha ha!" said his mother triumphantly. "She did say yes. Way to go, Sophia!" The older woman high-fived her daughter-in-law, raising the questioning eyebrows of her fellow table guests.

In sharp contrast, her husband simply scowled. "There's got to be a catch," Pepi grunted. "Nothing is that easy!"

As for the rest of the evening, Kaye skillfully tied her new speaking engagement into her speech. It was an opportunity for her to give to the new community that Kayleen was considering relocating to.

Then came the bombshell that would be sure to stop all media queries. "I apologize," Kaye said. "I know that people, well-meaning people, wish to know more about the tragic incident I was involved in earlier this year. Sadly, it's just too soon for me to comment at this time. By working with my counselor, I hope that in a month's time I may be able to at least share something at the hospital fundraiser." She hesitated. "Depending on his recovery, it may even be possible for Mr. Kerr to be present."

With that, she blew the audience a kiss and left amid a standing ovation, thus missing the Marconis' response to her announcement.

Lena turned abruptly to her daughter-in-law. "See to it that your mother reserves four tickets for us at that banquet!" Smiling sweetly, she tilted her head toward her husband and son. "The Marconis will *all* be visiting your parents, Sophia! With Ms. McDonald speaking at that fundraiser, it will be a big social event, and I'm not about to miss it." She poked her husband and laughed. "Get your wallet out, Pepi. It's time to be generous! Like you said, nothing's that easy! You have to go to Chicago with me."

chapter eleven

Kaye tiptoed across the dining room floor toward the hospital bed. As she bent over the sleeping man, she whispered sweetly, "Max, Max, are you awake?" Not waiting for a response, she planted a kiss on his lips.

"I am now," he replied groggily. "What time is it?"

"Almost 3:30," she said, lowering the bed's guardrails.

"3:30 in the morning?"

"Of course, silly! It's dark outside. Can't be afternoon."

"What are you doing here? I thought you were in New York addressing the civic club?"

"I'm back already." By now, Kaye was so excited that she was bouncing like a hyperactive preschooler.

Jack entered the room and flipped on the overhead light, eliciting a string of profanities from Max.

He glowered at them. "What's with the two of you? That chandelier is over six hundred watts! You're both lucky I'm bound in this metal brace!"

"What am I doing, Mr. Grump? I'm checking on your safety. I thought I heard the door open, and obviously it did." Jack glared at Kaye. "What are you doing, sneaking in at this hour? You told us you'd be staying in New York."

"What endears me to the two of you is your unflappable cheerful disposition," Kaye said, rolling her eyes. "I rush home to share my fabulous news and all you can do is whine about the interruption to your beauty sleep."

"Your exciting 3:30 a.m. good news?" Max said.

"With emphasis on the 3:30," added Jack.

Max raised his bed to a sitting position while Jack straddled a chair.

Kaye started to laugh.

"What's so funny?" the two queried in unison.

"Well, just look at the two of you."

"Trust me, Kaye, when I'm awakened from a sound sleep in the middle of the night, nothing is going to look funny!" Max snapped.

"My sentiments exactly," Jack groused.

"Au contraire, mes amis." Kaye looked at herself in the mirror, then twirled around to face them. "There you sit in your pjs, unshaven. Max, your hair is tousled, and Jack, even your bald spot has its two hairs twisted. In contrast, I am eloquently dressed in formal dinner attire. We are indeed mismatched!"

Jack rubbed the back of his neck. "Whatever, Kaye. What is your exciting news? My bed is beckoning me. But wait!" He abruptly sat ramrod straight. "Did you chicken out and not speak tonight? If so, your news is neither good nor exciting."

"Excuse me, my doubting Thomas, Not only did I speak, I got a standing ovation. So there!" She held up her hand like a traffic cop. "Trust me. My news is both good and exciting. But first, I shall answer *how* I arrived here. So exciting and good was my news that I couldn't sleep. I tried to unwind. No success! I thought I'd burst if I couldn't share it. I finally decided to call Lewis and sneak out of New York when no one would expect it."

Max's jaw dropped. "You called your chauffer at midnight and asked him to take you here?"

"Yes. I've done it before when I can't sleep." Almost as an afterthought, she added, "I make sure he hasn't had a drink. I'd never have him drive then. Lewis says he doesn't mind."

"That's all very reassuring, Kaye," Jack replied with a raised eyebrow. He sounded sarcastic.

"I get your concern, but you should note that he gets paid time and a half and then two days off."

Max gasped. "With pay?"

"Of course!"

"Need another chauffer?" he bantered.

"I will ignore your remark, Mr. Carron, because my good, exciting news is more important than continuing this trivial chatter."

"Puh-lease, Kaye," moaned Jack. "Do get on with it. Sleep beckons!"

"Okay, I will." With that, she pulled out her cell phone.

"Kaye, you got a new cell phone." Max sighed. "Is that your good news?"

"Men! You're all alike!" Her eyes flashed. "Good, exciting news for you is up-dated technology! Not so for us women. What's important to us are relationships!"

"Relationships?" The tenor and baritone responded in two-part harmony.

"Yes," Kaye said, warming to the task of full disclosure. "A young woman approached me with a crisis. Her mother is organizing a hospital charity dinner, but the slated guest speaker has had a heart attack. The dinner is scheduled for Friday evening, November 16." Kaye paused to catch her breath. "Obviously, this is very short notice, but the charity hasn't been able to book a replacement."

"So you volunteered yourself," ventured Max.

"Right. Since my speech tonight focused on the need for corporations to seek ways to better serve the communities in which their office resides, I couldn't very well decline."

"This woman was offering a 'show and tell' for your address," quipped Jack. "How convenient!"

"I thought so, too, particularly since it allowed me to make a very personal statement."

Max nodded. "The one for which you got a standing ovation."

Kaye beamed at them. "You two are obviously waking up. However, none of that is what was good or exciting."

"Kaye, it's nearly 4:00 a.m. What exactly is your news?" Max asked, exasperation clearly evident in his tone.

Kaye triumphantly snapped open her phone and hopped beside Max on the bed.

"You took a picture of the young woman on your cell phone?" Jack asked.

"Oh, indeed I did!" she said, handing the phone to Max.

The color drained from Max's face and tears welled up in his eyes. "Sophia," he said softly. "It's Sophia!"

"Your sister?" Jack leaped up to peer over Max's shoulder. "That's your sister?"

Max just nodded, a faint smile appearing on his lips. "Wow! I haven't seen her for more than six years."

"Here, give me my phone," Kaye said. "There's more."

The next shot was of Kaye and Tony.

"Tony!" Max fairly shouted, his eyes glistening. "They look great, just like I remember them." Then he added, "Well, maybe five pounds heavier."

Jack grabbed the phone for a closer look. "He's a really big man," he exclaimed. To himself he thought, *Maybe my plan isn't so brilliant after all!*

He handed the phone back to Kaye, who was busy expounding on how she had gotten the pictures. "I agreed with Sophia to be the dinner speaker, but that was before the meal. The others at Sophia's table didn't believe her, so Tony confronted me as I returned to my table. I assured him that my offer was valid, and in fact that the timing was perfect. I had Mayor Turiano take my picture with Tony, like Alice had done with Sophia. I told them that I'd send a copy of the pictures as proof of our agreement."

Max started to chuckle. "It's amazing that he agreed to a photo. Sometimes guys like him are cautious about being photographed."

"Kaye, how does doing a charity engagement for Sophia in New York tie in with your talk?" Jack asked, puzzled. "Kayleen's headquarters aren't in New York."

"Oh, sorry. Didn't I say? The hospital fundraiser isn't in New York. It's in Chicago."

"Chicago? You're speaking in Chicago," blurted Max. "When?"

"I told you. November 16."

"This year?"

Kaye threw up her hands in mock despair. "Of course, Max, this year!"

Max frowned. "But that's a little less than four weeks away."

"Your math is good, honey," Kaye replied, arms folded across her chest. "I'm led to believe you'll be losing your tin-lizzy leg next week, right?"

"That's our hope, Kaye," Jack said.

Max scowled. "But there's no guarantee, Kaye. I might have to wait longer."

"No, you won't," Kaye said. "You, Mr. Carron, are slated to begin your most strenuous rehab. You're going to slowly strengthen that leg, regaining your lost muscle mass and joint movement." She furrowed her brow. "Max, I know that you don't believe it now, but when you look back you'll see that your bed confinement was the easiest part of your return to health. Trust me! Nonetheless, you won't have to do it alone. I'll be beside you all the way, cheering you on."

"I don't doubt your support, Kaye, but when will the remodeling be completed in your house?"

"Right on schedule, love. Just like you wanted. Off comes your metal cage splint, then we get married. We can honeymoon in *our* new home, and on November 16, Chicago gets to know the true identity of Mr. Maxwell Kerr!"

"What?" Max asked, genuinely shocked.

"Oh, I forgot to tell you that part. It's why I got the standing ovation. Everyone understood I wasn't able to share about Glaxton, but people are curious to know about it. Quite frankly, I don't blame them. The more high-profile a person is, it's only natural to expect them to be more accountable to the public."

"Where are you going with this, Kaye?" Jack inquired.

"I'm not sure I want to know," Max said glumly.

"Well, I shared that my counselor advised that I should wait a few more weeks before talking about my experience. That's when I mentioned the hospital fundraiser in Chicago, and how by choosing to accept it, I was in essence practicing what I preached. I added that perhaps I might be strong enough to share a little about my ordeal." She hesitated. "I also suggested that Mr. Kerr might even be well enough to accompany me."

Max's eyes glazed over. All he managed to squeak was "Oh no!"

Kaye was oblivious to the reaction. She was recalling the audience's enthusiastic response. "So, I guess you can appreciate now why I was so excited to get home and share my news with you!"

She squeezed Max's hand and turned to give him a big hug and kiss.

"I love you so much," she whispered in his ear. She then reached over and grabbed Jack's hand. "I'm so glad you heard me and came downstairs. It was perfect to be able to share this with the two of you at the same time. I've had friends plan marriages. They were so giddy and happy. I know they had some anxious moments, but overall they were just so excited! I have to confess that I thought, 'Big deal! What's all the fuss?' Well, now I know!" She gave Max another hug. "Truthfully, Max, when I marry you, it will be the most important day of my life! And you know what?"

Max blinked. For the past few minutes, his mouth had remained open. In answer to her question, all he managed to do was shake his head. He hadn't a clue what she could possibly be thinking. The only thought bouncing around his cranium was, *"This must be what a guy feels like when he's whitewater rafting; the river takes a bend and he realizes he's at the brow of Niagara Falls."*

"Well," Kaye continued unabated, "when you suggested getting quietly married the first night you got here, I have to admit I was a little disappointed. But now I know it's the best choice! Jack, Max is very wise. We need some private time together to regain our equilibrium after our ordeal. I want to say thanks to both of you for making everything happen so very beautifully." She gave each one another big hug. "If neither of you mind, I'm truly exhausted. I'll go to bed and leave the two of you to work out the details." She flashed them a big smile. "If that brace comes off on Wednesday, then Thursday's our big day!"

Kaye actually glowed as she turned to traipse up the stairs.

As for the two men, the lights were on but no one was home. Max stared at the corner of the ceiling. Just when it appeared he was about to speak, he looked to the opposite corner. Still no sound erupted from his mouth.

At last, they looked back at each other.

"Kaye seems really... umm, really..."

"Happy," Jack inserted.

"You think?"

"Yes, definitely!"

"So, Jack, what do I do? I mean, what do we need to do to make this happen?"

"I suppose Dave or I can get you the marriage license. Sue could initiate the blood tests. It's feasible we could have the license by Monday."

"What about the rings?" Max queried.

"The rings? Why don't you get them after? Or maybe buy two plain gold bands for the ceremony."

"I don't want to do that," Max protested. "I want to give Kaye a nice ring. A special ring. That's just the way we do it."

"The way we do it?" Jack rolled his eyes. "I'm assuming you mean that's your Italian custom. Well, reality check: between now and next Wednesday, bud, the only way you can make it to a jewelry store is in your wheelchair, and that's not inconspicuous. It will attract attention you don't want."

"Couldn't you or Dave arrange a private viewing, like through the back door or something? Or you could take pictures of some rings, then bring those pictures here. I could choose the ones I'd most like to see in person. The jeweler could bring them here... he'd trust you two, wouldn't he? Can't you set something like that up for me, Jack? Please!"

Jack smiled to himself. Max constantly surprised him. He had coldly calculated how to outwit a deadly killer, yet here he was scared silly over a marriage. For all his many attributes, Max was entirely clueless when it came to matters of the opposite sex. Nonetheless, he genuinely wanted to do things the right way, for Kaye's sake.

"Okay, Max. Step one: how much do you want to spend on the ring?"

Max hesitated. "I just want it to be a special ring. I don't know what they cost."

"Let me rephrase the question. How much can you afford?"

Max rubbed the bridge of his nose. "Well, my credit card limit is fifty thousand."

"Dollars?" croaked Jack.

"Uh-huh." His tone seemed to indicate he thought everyone had this much credit.

"How can you have that much credit?" Jack asked dumbfounded.

"Well, in case Your Honor has forgotten, I had free room and board for six years, thanks to you." Max smiled triumphantly. "Interest rates were good and my outside expenses minimal. I had to pay taxes and utilities on my house, but Lou and Bill, my staff, looked after the place in exchange for living rent-free. I made some good real estate deals and invested well." Max paused. "Guess what, Jack? I invested a lot in Kayleen, but when I first met Kaye, I nearly blew everything. I didn't know who she was. I told her I'd invested in Kayleen stocks because I'd read up on R.K. McDonald and was impressed with the guy."

"Why would that put you in a negative light?" Jack asked, puzzled. "Kaye adored her father."

"Oh, it wasn't that. It's what I said after." Max laughed heartily. "I was really derogatory about R.K.'s spoiled brat daughter. I told Kaye I was sure my investments would drop badly with that broad as company head."

"You really said that?"

Max winced. "Unfortunately, yes."

"Well, Max, all I can say is you have a unique way of getting into people's bad books only to emerge as the one everyone wants to love!" By now Jack himself was laughing. "Okay, I'll talk to the jeweler about rings for Kaye and see what we can set up for you. What about your own ring?"

"Don't need one. I have my family ring. I just switch hands and wear it on my wedding finger."

Jack gave Max a playful jab. "Well, old man, I sentenced you to six years. Now, you realize, you're setting yourself up for a life sentence. Think you can cope?"

"Compared with the six you gave me, life with Kaye should be a breeze." A long yawn followed this quick retort.

"I'll take that as a sign that you're tired, not that your life with Kaye will be boring." Jack winked, checking his watch. He let out a groan. "Wow, it's almost five o'clock! How about I close the drapes so you can sleep in, like I intend to do?"

Max nodded. "Good night. At least what's left of it. And Jack, thanks for being my friend. I really appreciate it!"

Jack looked the younger man square in the eye, then reached out and grasped his hand. "I assure you, it's my privilege to count you as my friend."

Max swallowed hard. Somehow, with Jack and Dave—and yes, even Epi— he had encountered the elusive respect for which he had yearned and sought all his life. He felt warm inside, and suddenly very tired. He lowered the head of his bed while Jack raised the guardrail, with an admonition that falling out of bed to rebreak the leg wouldn't let him out of the marriage trap.

Jack turned out the light and headed up the stairs. His head was spinning. All he could see was Max's hulking big brother-in-law, Tony. Now he knew what Epi had meant when he'd said that if you wanted Sophia, you had to take Tony, too.

"You can say that again," Jack muttered to himself as he crawled back into bed. "Even more problematic is how to rendezvous with those two before the wedding."

chapter twelve

It had been a long time, an awfully long time, since Jack Walters had slept until noon. Marnie made a mental note to quiz him about his workload. For that matter, she had heard Kaye showering only fifteen minutes ago. Peeping into the rehab room, she was surprised to find Max still out cold.

She frowned. *I thought Sue said they were decreasing his pain meds, not increasing them.*

Marnie tried to be as quiet as she could in the kitchen. Unfortunately, her plan was to try a new recipe for her cookbook. She had to get the meat marinating.

It's time the rehab patient stirs anyway, she reasoned. *After all, Kaye will soon emerge and expect her captive audience to be attentive.*

No sooner had the thought crossed Marnie's mind than Kaye dragged herself into the kitchen. "Marn, by any chance do you have a strong cup of brew available?"

"What on earth, Kaye? I heard the shower and expected you to come bounding in. Instead you look like death warmed over." Marnie offered her friend a strong *cup a*, as she was found of calling it. "By the way, when did you get home? We were expecting you later today."

Kaye yawned. "Exactly, but I couldn't sleep. Lewis drove me down in the night. Everything went great with my talk and—" She paused, remembering Marnie's limited knowledge of Max. "I just wanted to share it."

The look on Marnie's face seemed to say, *So?*

"When I arrived, I woke up Max," Kaye continued. "Apparently Jack heard me come in and the three of us talked for an hour. At least that's when I bade adieu. I was out cold until a few minutes ago, when I got up to shower."

"When did Jack and Max turn out the lights?"

"Absolutely no idea at all, Marnie."

Marnie started to laugh. "I guess that explains all my sleepyheads. Here I thought you and Jack were working too hard while Max's meds were too strong!"

The phone rang and Marnie answered it, still chuckling.

"This is the chief of police," Dave said on the other end of the phone. "I hear the reports concerning excess frivolities at 168 Independence Drive are accurate."

"Not so, sir. I awoke to find everyone but me comatose. Kaye has just begun to move, but as we speak the other two are out for the count. Apparently Kaye arrived at 3:30, waking everyone but me."

"Well, Marn, I'm afraid I have to ask you to wake up your sleeping prince. Epi's passing through town and asked to meet with Jack and me. I suggested the golf club, but he insists on my office."

"Oh my. It sounds serious. In that case, I'll run upstairs and get His Honor to take your call there."

"No need. Just have him up and dressed. I'll pick him up at your place at 12:30."

Before Marnie could respond the phone went dead.

"What's up?" Kaye asked.

Marnie shrugged. "I have no idea. Epi has arrived and wants to speak with Dave and Jack at the station. Excuse me while I awaken my love and please make sure this pot doesn't boil over."

* * *

Jack exited the house coffee cup in hand, looking slightly worse for wear. Dave's honking horn had caused Max to stir. This left Kaye and Marnie to attend to Max's needs. By now, practicality had long won out over modesty. Max accepted help from any and all.

As Dave drove to the station, Jack filled him in on Kaye's early morning news, including how imposing Max's brother-in-law Tony looked.

Dave grinned. "So I take it we'll be scrapping your plan, Your Honor, to kidnap Sophia and Tony?"

"Fraid so," came the quick reply.

Epi was sitting in Dave's chair when the two entered the office.

"Well, Special Agent Epstein, you are bright eyed and bushy-tailed this morning, unlike my slow-moving neighbor." Dave jested.

"That's because he got a normal night's sleep," grumped Jack.

Epi's voice registered genuine concern. "Something wrong with Max?"

"Nothing wrong with Max. You let Kaye escape and drive home last night. Consequently, Max and I were awakened to hear about her profitable night in the big apple."

"I see," said Epi, cocking one eyebrow. "Well, gentlemen, I'm here on account of Kaye's news. When is Max's metal brace scheduled to be removed?"

"Wednesday." Jack said with a yawn. "Provided, of course, there are no complications."

Epi sighed softly. "Let's assume there will be none. I suggest the two of you pay a visit Wednesday to New York's Twelfth Precinct."

"I'm not sure I can break free that day," Dave said.

"Me neither," Jack said. "Why that particular precinct?"

"Because the captain is a straight shooter. He's a hundred percent aboveboard. Most importantly, Tony Marconi knows him. He can command Tony's attention," stated Epi bluntly.

Jack croaked in disbelief. "You want Dave and me to go to New York, pick up Tony and Sophia, and bring them back here?"

"That was your game plan, I believe," Epi said.

Jack frowned. "Yes, but—"

"But what?" Epi said with a smile.

"Very funny, Epi! You were there with Kaye. You saw Marconi."

"I already knew what he looked like. Apparently now, so do you."

"Darn right," Jack said. "Kaye had her picture taken with him. He's got to be over six feet and two hundred and thirty pounds! He looks like a defensive back."

"Six-foot-two and two hundred and thirty five pounds, to be precise," Epi laughed. "And oh yes, I have it on good authority he does work out. Has the quarterback lost his nerve? Come on, Jack, you've faced bigger guys in your college days."

"Yes, on the football field, but they weren't said to have ties to the mob. Furthermore, I'm the guy who sent his brother-in-law to prison for six years. When I first suggested this, you said the idea was a little loopy. Why would you give it a green light now?"

Dave started to chuckle. "Epi, you caught us both off-guard, exposed our angst. You win!"

"I'm not joking." Epi's jaw tightened. "I've thought a lot about your options. Quite frankly, Jack, your only non-court option is to try and reel in Tony and Sophia. Gain their cooperation. I'm not sure your plan will work, but you'll never know until you try it!"

Jack was unconvinced. "What happens if he freaks and—"

"And?"

"And takes us out! That would be a supreme disaster not only for the Carrons and Marconis, Max and Kaye, but also for the Walters and Davidsons," Jack protested. "It's way too dangerous, and not worth the risk!"

Epi folded his arms across his chest. "I don't agree, Jack,"

"Really? Why am I not surprised? Let me see. I don't recall mentioning the Epstein family in that list—"

"Hold on a minute, Jack," Dave interrupted, "Epi would stand to lose his credibility as a law officer if he were wrong. Knowing Epi as I do, I don't think that's something he would risk. So Epi, regardless of how intimidating Tony Marconi may look, I gather you think he's neither a common thug nor a hothead."

"Yeah, Dave, you've read me right. Also his relationship with Sophia seems very balanced. I suspect Sophia will insist on seeing her brother and that Tony would cooperate to help her do so. The big challenge is to convince Tony that you're not a threat to his wife's safety. My professional read of Marconi is that he won't stand idly by and see his wife harmed."

"We have no intention of hurting her," Jack said, surprised that a threat to her safety was even being mentioned.

"True," Epi continued, "but don't lose sight of their ethnic background."

"Remember Max's thoughts when we moved him secretly from the hospital?" inserted Dave. "His first thought was that someone was out to rub him out."

"Absolutely, Dave, their world is different than ours," agreed Epi.

"So, how do you suggest we soothe Tony's fears?" Jack asked, plunking himself down dejectedly in the office chair.

His resignation to the task at hand began the trio's strategizing for Mission N.Y.S.—namely, the New York to Summerside pickup."

When Dave and Jack had said goodbye to Epi and headed home, Jack confided glumly, "Now I know why I chose to be a judge and not a cop. This clandestine stuff plays havoc with my digestive system! If I had to do this often, I'm sure I'd have an ulcer. Or a coronary. Or a stroke."

Dave's eyes twinkled. "Don't look so depressed, Eeyore. You might actually find you enjoy it!"

Sue met them when they entered the Walters house.

"What did I tell you?" she asked good-naturedly, turning to Kaye. "I knew we could count on these two showing up within a half-hour of supper."

"What did Epi want?" Kaye asked.

"Not a whole lot," Dave said nonchalantly. "He simply asked Jack and me to gather some background data for him concerning an antitrust case."

"Really?" Max commented, eyes quite wide.

"Not so clandestine, I'm afraid," Jack volunteered. "We simply need to go over some files for him in the Pittsburgh area."

Dave nodded. "The only problem is that we have to do so this Wednesday."

"Wednesday?" the rest of the room reverberated.

"That's when Max is scheduled to get his tin leg removed," Kaye pointed out. "I have to go to Chicago on Tuesday and won't get back until Thursday morning. You promised you'd marry us, Jack!"

"And I will, Kaye," Jack reassured her. "I'll be home late Wednesday night. Your wedding will happen as per the schedule."

Sue let out a moan. "Dave, Wednesday is a very bad day for you two to be away. Have you forgotten that I have that inner-city health luncheon in Philly on Wednesday? I can't get back to Summerside until early evening. Can't you ask Epi to reschedule?"

"Gee, Dad," added Matt, walking into the kitchen, "I overheard what you just said and unfortunately I can't help out either. I'll be in Scranton Tuesday and Wednesday for a two-day seminar on internet fraud. I'll try to leave early Thursday morning to get here in time for the wedding, but I can't be of any assistance in getting Max to the doctor."

"Look guys, we're really sorry," Dave chimed in.

"Max, we'll help you get washed, shaved, dressed, and into the van before we go," Jack said. "Marnie, Wednesdays are your light days. Couldn't you take Max to the hospital?"

Marnie went over and gave Max a big hug. "Max, I'll arrange to spend the day with you. I have paperwork to complete. When you get that brace off, you'll be mobile enough to get in and out of the van using your crutches."

Max gave her a grin. "Dependable Marnie. Even if everyone else deserts me, you never will! But I have two questions. First, what happens if the docs decide they can't remove the brace on Wednesday?"

"Tough!" the three women echoed in unison.

Sue feigned a scowl, and with hands on hips declared firmly, "Tin Lizzy or not, you marry on Thursday. The stage is set."

Max laughed. "Hey, I'm not bailing! I just meant that if I don't lose that brace, how can I get back home?"

"Should that eventuality happen, we'll ensure Jimmy is there to get you in the van and here to help you out," Dave replied. "So what, sir, is the second question?"

"I've never used crutches before. I'm not supposed to bear weight on my leg. What if I screw up?"

"Good point, Charlie Brown," Sue said. "I'll make sure you have a session with the occupational therapist before you and Marnie leave the hospital."

Marnie smiled demurely. "Well, now that we have next Wednesday all planned out, do you think we might undertake supper?"

Everyone raved over Marnie's exotic Thai spread. However, Matt commented that he was glad she had deviated from her Thai theme when it came to dessert. "Your cheesecakes are the best," he said. "Especially the pumpkin!"

The men volunteered to clean up the dishes. When they were finished, everyone gathered in the family room for an evening of games. One thing could be said about the Independence Drive residents—their natures aptly suited the name of their street! All except perhaps one; as the evening progressed, Marnie became quiet and pensive. Champions rose and fell, and so focused were the rest on winning that no one paid any attention to her.

At last, in the midst of a pause between a victor's shout and the group's enthusiasm for a new game to begin, in a soft yet firm voice Marnie said, "Jack, you, Dave, and Matt are planning on being away next Wednesday. Does that include the evening?"

Jack peered over his glasses at his wife, oblivious to the seriousness in her voice. "Sweetheart, I've been away before for several days in a row."

"Gosh, Marnie, I've stayed at your house when Jack's been away," Matt said. "You said that I was like a son to you. Max is the same, isn't he?"

The men were laughing, all except Max, who was trying to grasp why Marnie would be upset at being alone with him in the house. Kaye, too, was puzzled by Marnie's concern, but not Sue.

"It has nothing to do with Marnie or Max," Sue said. "The Bible says we Christians are to live our lives beyond reproach. Marn, when you and Max get home from the hospital, will you let our dog Ruf out? You can take him to your house. Then I'll come directly to your house and stay overnight with the two of you."

Marnie stared in disbelief at the others. When the rest finally took the time to look at her, they all knew a serious error had been made. Jack's diminutive wife leapt into the middle of the room, hands at her sides, fists clenched. All five-feet-two inches of her conveyed, *I have had enough!* "It seems to me that you've all forgotten a rather significant piece of information you handed out over five months ago."

The room went quiet. Jack tried furiously to recall what on earth his wife could mean.

"Jack," she continued, "throughout Kaye's ordeal with those threatening phone calls, you, Dave, and Epi warned about how criminals often bide their time, until their prey forgets all about the threat. You kept quoting six months. In fact, that's what Glaxton did with you, Kaye, isn't it? He resumed his calls after six months. Correct?"

Kaye furrowed her brow and nodded, still at a loss to grasp where Marnie was going with this.

"Well, Jack, you showed us a mug shot of some fellow named Carron," snapped Marnie. "It's been nearly seven months since he was released. At the time of that man's release, Epi expressed concerned for your safety. However, ever since Max killed Glaxton, I haven't heard a peep about Carron. Is he or is he not still a threat?"

A barely audible whisper escaped the others in the room.

All eyes riveted on Jack, who desperately searched for the appropriate words to diffuse what was now a decidedly volatile situation. He looked pleadingly first at Dave, then to Kaye, and then to Max. All chose to remain mute.

"Well?" said Marnie in a tone that clearly implied, *Don't mess with me!*

At last, Jack sighed. "Dear, why don't you ask Carron himself if he's a threat?"

Tears welled up in Marnie eyes. "Jack Walters, this is the most callous thing you've ever said to me! Why are you mocking me concerning that threat to our family? I took it very seriously. Obviously you don't!"

She would have stormed from the room had Jack not leapt up to block her path. "Marnie, I'm not mocking you. I'm being serious. Only Mr. Carron can answer your question. He needs to answer for himself. In fact, he's here in the room with us. You were sitting next to him."

Before Jack could duck, Marnie smacked his face. "Sitting next to me?" She wheeled around and pointed at Max. "He was sitting next to me!"

Max had an instant flashback to Kaye's reaction upon learning his true identity. The memory was anything but comforting!

"Max, are you Jack's mafia drug dealer?" Marnie's eyes bore right through him.

Max tried to clear his throat. His mouth went dry. It seemed his voice had vacated his body. He finally managed to sputter, "Sort of. I mean sort of yes, and sort of no."

"What type of answer is that?" demanded Sue.

Mercifully, Dave intervened. "Max isn't a drug trafficker. He isn't mafia either, but he *is* the one Jack sent to jail. He's the person Epi was concerned about."

The room was suddenly silent and still.

chapter thirteen

It was still dark as Kaye climbed into her car to head to Summerside's airport. She couldn't help smiling to herself. She had given a groggy Max a goodbye kiss accompanied with a wish that tomorrow he'd see the last of Tin Lizzy. She had then added mischievously, "Next time I see you, darling, will be to say I do!"

Without a doubt, that remark awoke my sleeping prince, she mused. Come to think of it, she had to admit that both of them, for all their bravado in other areas of their lives, had been shy around the opposite sex. She sighed. So now they found themselves totally fixated on each other, knowing full well that their relationship was problematic for the people around them.

She gripped the steering wheel and slowed, suddenly aware of the dense fog that covered the road. *Funny. Emotionally, I feel as if I'm living in a fog.*

It was good for the truth about Max's identity to come out on Saturday night. She didn't blame Marnie, Sue, and Matt for being upset and hurt that they hadn't been told about him.

She bit her lip and brushed away the little tear traversing her cheek. "Dear Lord, You know how much they all mean to me. You gave the Walters and Davidsons to keep me afloat in the aftermath of the horrid plane crash that killed Mummy and Daddy. They became my only family, and in You, Jesus, they are my brothers and sisters. I am truly thankful for them. I felt awful when Marnie burst into tears and said that we obviously hadn't trusted her."

Rivulets of tears cascaded down her own face, but then she remembered how Max had tried to be the peacemaker. A little giggle erupted. He really had felt bad that he was the cause of the tiff between Marnie and Jack. Max had been so comical in how he'd attempted to handle that emotionally charged situation. *It was like how he tried to placate me when I discovered his true identity.*

With that thought, Kaye's tears of sorrow were replaced by those of hilarity. Max told Marnie how she had ordered him to leave, and he had actually tried to go! Then he said, "But the Holy Spirit, through that severe storm, ensured that I remain."

At the mention of the Holy Spirit, they all saw Marnie soften. No one was more Spirit-led than Marnie.

As she pulled her car into the airport car park, Kaye reached over for a tissue, glad that at 6:00 a.m. the garage was pretty empty. No one was present to witness her crying and laughing simultaneously. She wiped her tear-stained face, blew her nose, and reapplied her make up.

She had to admit it had been pretty amusing to see Max apologize to Marnie for being in her dining room. After all, it had been Marnie who invited him there in the first place! He had then told her that he knew she didn't want him there, that he didn't want her to be upset—because he really liked her. Then he had asked for Marnie to forgive him.

Kaye started to laugh again. *Here was Marnie's terrible criminal, so sweetly and innocently trying to make things better for her.*

At that moment, everyone in the room had seen the real Max, the one who had endeared himself to me. Jack had summed it all up when he said, "Like I told you before, Max, you have such a talent at getting into everyone's bad books only to emerge as the one everyone wants to love."

As Kaye composed herself and prepared to leave the car, she thought how true that remark was. All of them adored Max now. By the end of the weekend, Matt, Sue, and Marnie were back aboard the marriage train. Everyone was excited about the new mobility Max would have with the crutches. The wedding would take place Thursday; she and Max would move back to her house, allowing Jack and Marnie's home to at last return to normal.

She headed into the terminal, briefcase and overnight bag in tow, recalling how animated Matt had become when he offered to help Max with his leg strengthening exercises. The indoor pool was going to be a hit with all the residents of Independence Drive.

"Ms. McDonald, please let me take your bags," Lewis said, his solicitous voice slicing into Kaye's thoughts. She had forgotten that Lewis had been asked to meet her at the airport, to accompany her to Chicago in case they needed his services there. Kaye abruptly switched into full Kayleen mode.

"Lewis, why thank you. Has our company plane arrived yet?"

"It just came in, ma'am. Everyone else is on board."

As the plane taxied down the runway, all thoughts of home quickly faded.

In the air, the board and staff members flying with her excitedly brought Kaye up to speed on the day's agenda. When they arrived in Chicago, they would rendezvous at the hotel with those flying by commercial airliner. All would have breakfast together at 9:00 a.m., after which limousines would take them to the proposed site. There, they'd meet representatives of the architectural and construction teams. They would assess the retail value of the prospective properties and then return to the hotel for a one o'clock lunch to weigh the options. In the evening, Kayleen representatives would cloister to review the data. They anticipated Kayleen would be in a position to submit their offers to purchase various properties by then. Mere formalities, she was told.

On Wednesday morning, Kayleen would host a breakfast brunch for the mayor, members of the city council, and city planners. Kayleen's board would meet over a late lunch and assess all that had transpired. It was hoped that by 3:00 p.m., they could have an open meeting with the property owners, allowing for questions, answers, and frank discussion. At 7:00 p.m., Kaye would gather for dinner with her senior management staff and board to further discuss and finalize the terms of the various purchase proposals.

"A very ambitious and busy schedule, M.K.," Alice ventured.

"Indeed, but I have one other item I personally need inserted."

Philippe groaned. "Not something more! M.K., the schedule is full already."

"I need to pay a visit to Our Lady of Mercies Hospital."

Public Relations V.P. Martin Smithers jumped at her request. "Excellent, excellent! A wonderful strategy! We should have thought of that. After all, we want to demonstrate Kayleen's interest in contributing to the city's overall well-being. I'll arrange the details."

He then commented on the excitement that the corporation's relocation was generating in the markets. Kayleen's stocks had enjoyed a five-dollar per share increase.

"I think Chicago will prove to be a wise choice," intoned one of Kayleen's oldest board members.

As the aircraft began its descent, Kaye launched into a quiet dialogue with the Lord. *"You promise that if we commit all our ways to You, You will direct our path. That's what Daddy always did, and he taught me to do the same. I certainly vouch for how You honor Your word. Well, You've seen the agenda I've been given. Please, grant me the wisdom to see the path You want this company to take, and give me the courage and strength to follow it."* She had just breathed a silent "Amen" when the plane touched down.

Everyone was literally off and running as soon as the aircraft docked. Kayleen's breakfast meeting, as always, seemed to focus the day; good food energized people, and Philippe had a knack for ensuring that its presentation was perfect. The meeting room overlooked Lake Michigan, and even in late fall the water sparkled under the sun's rays.

As usual, Kaye flitted around the room engaging others in conversation. Like her father, she possessed the unique ability to make others feel like they were the only people in the room with her. Also like her father, she possessed a near telephoto memory. She could recall not only who each person was, but exactly the reason they had been invited to the meeting in the first place. Thus, no conversation with her was inconsequential.

As the limos conveyed the entourage to the proposed site, Kaye found herself next to Philippe. Always the encourager, she leaned towards her aide and signaled a thumb's up. "Great job! Well done!"

"Better reserve your accolades until all is completed," he said with a sigh.

She winked. "Knowing you and your abilities, I can do so now. But tell me, any news on Roland?"

Philippe beamed. "I thought you'd never ask. With Mrs. Baxter's help, we've established a little seamstress shop. A dozen of his designs are now a reality, and we've hired three young models—very attractive young women—who show considerable promise given the poise and movement they exhibit."

"I can see by the twinkle in your eye that there's a little more." Kaye's lilting laughter filled the car.

"Indeed, M.K., indeed! The Valencio Fashion House is holding a pre-Christmas show. Their premier designer is a personal friend of mine."

"So?"

"So I've secured an opening spot for Rolando Fashions in the show."

"Really?" Kaye asked in amazement. "You've done all this in just a few weeks?"

"Yes, ma'am. I've always found the fashion world exciting, but I never thought I'd have the opportunity to dabble in it. Thanks to you, Roland, and Mrs. Baxter, I now have that opportunity."

"My, my. Personal confessions from my trusted aide," purred Kaye. "That's great news. So far the day is going well. I trust it's going well for Roland as well. Personally, I mean."

"He's rooming with the Baxters, and basking in their love." Philippe raised his eyebrows. "By the way, Stephanie has a new beau."

"You mean Roland?" Kaye asked incredulously.

"No, no. Those two are like brother and sister. No, it's one of our chartered accountants. Young fellow, I think his name is Dario."

Kaye frowned. "I hope this guy is on the level."

Until now, Alice had remained silent. She could contain herself no longer. "Oh, M.K., I think this is a good thing for our Stephanie. She has such a wonderful heart. She's an attractive young woman, but she most certainly lacks the movie star figure. As for Dario, he's a pleasant lad. He doesn't have the physique of a Greek god, but he seems to have a good work ethic and is kind-hearted." She looked at Philippe and giggled. "Their first date involved Dario buying Steph lunch in our cafeteria."

Philippe chuckled. "A week later, we saw them heading to a movie hand in hand. Everyone in the office is teasing both, all in good nature. Trust me, everyone has been most sensitive to Stephanie's trauma with Glaxton."

Kaye eyed her two aides. "Then you're informing me that our Stephanie's heart is healing?"

"Most definitely," the two spoke in unison as the limo stopped.

Clarin and Omar were waiting for her as she got out of the car. They were beaming.

"M.K., here's the site," Clarin said. He held the door open for her.

"We have to walk down this short street. It ends at the ridge. We're a few miles west of the lake, but the rise allows us a glimpse of the water," offered Omar. "Depending on how many stories our building has, the view from the top should be stunning."

Kaye thought the area seemed a bit rundown. Old warehouses stood all around them. In their heyday, some may have been factories. Their paint had long ago peeled, a few were boarded shut, and others had broken windows. Some were occupied with miscellaneous small enterprises. One, she noted, had been spruced up. It was identified as home for a community church.

The walk was brisk. Although the sun was shining, Chicago lived up to its reputation as the windy city. Wherever possible, the entourage was allowed to examine the interior of the buildings. On one occasion, Kaye asked a business owner about his lease.

"Lady, there is no lease. These buildings have long had their day. Most are firetraps. None meet the building codes."

"Then they could be sold and demolished. However," Kaye persisted, "if that happened, would you be able to relocate your business?"

The man looked at her as though she came from another universe. "Lady, there's lots of these broken-down dinosaurs in this area, and all for rent. Hey, are you with that Kayleen group that's talking of comin' here?"

Kaye nodded and asked what he thought of the area.

The man laughed. "Now, doll, I'm your competitor for this space. You trust me to give you an honest answer?"

"Actually, I do. You seem to know Chicago well." She laughed and winked. "And you have an honest face."

"Yeah, I've lived in Chicago all my life. The area's good but pretty rundown. The problem with new development is that it changes the landscape. Often makes it impossible for people who lived here all their lives to stay."

"How so?" Kaye asked, genuinely interested.

"With every new development, taxes get jerked up, making it rough for folks on fixed incomes."

"So if Kayleen came in here, do you think it would be beneficial for the existing community?"

The man spat on the ground. "Doll, you really think Kayleen or any other corporation gives a damn about the little people?"

Her green eyes twinkled. "As a matter of fact, Mr.—"

"Angelo," the burly man replied.

"Well, as a matter of fact, Mr. Angelo, I do. No company is a god, but it can and should make an effort to work with the community to make the place better than when it arrived."

Mr. Angelo received that same winning smile which had endeared so many to its bearer. "Well, little lady, if ever you run for office, I'll give you my vote. You have the makings of a good politician."

She grinned. "And you, sir, seem to know Chicago well and could be useful to me. Do you have a business card?"

Mr. Angelo gave a self-conscious shrug, pulled out his wallet, and produced a card which read:

ROCCO ANGELO

Landscaping, snow removal, household repairs.

The hand that gave it to her, she noted, was obviously used to manual labor.

"You want to see my place?" he offered.

"Delighted." She laughed inwardly at Alice and Philippe's horrified expressions.

By now, the rest of the group had moved on. Mr. Angelo unlocked the padlock and escorted them into a largely vacant and derelict warehouse. Here he kept his modest equipment—an ancient dozer, flatbed, tractor mower, and plough for a truck.

"How much square footage do you need for your business?" Philippe questioned nervously.

"Aww, just an extra-large garage that's secure. You know, this old building has history."

"I can bet that," whispered Philippe, tugging on Kaye's sleeve like a little boy anxious to escape.

Kaye was having none of it. "What type of history?"

"Rumor has it that at one time Capone owned it. Used it for bootlegging. Some suggest that if someone dug it up, you might find human remains."

"Really?" said Alice, her eyes as wide as saucers.

"So who owns the building now, Mr. Angelo?" Kaye asked, her curiosity piqued.

"Vesuvias Enterprises. Which, when translated, means Mr. C."

"Mr. C?" Philippe queried.

"Yeah. Frank Carron."

At the mention of Max's father, Kaye blanched

Philippe merely asked, "Who's Frank Carron?"

"Who's Carron?" Mr. Angelo huffed. "Better not come to Chicago if you don't know him. He's Mr. Italy."

At that moment, Clarin came busting through the door. "Good heavens, M.K., we thought we lost you! Are you all right?" He gave Mr. Angelo a suspicious glance.

"Quite all right, Clarin. I've learned a lot about the area from Mr. Angelo." She glanced at her watch. "My goodness, it's time to leave."

"Do you want to see the rest, M.K.?"

"I don't think it's necessary, Clarin. I'm sure we'll have a good overview of the site when everyone meets together later."

"I'm sure we will," murmured Alice under her breath. "Bodies and all!"

Mr. Angelo stopped them as they were about to leave. "Wait a minute!" he said, looking rather threatening.

"Yes?" Kaye replied softly.

"I told you who I was, little lady. I even gave you my card. You never said who you was."

Clarin was ready to rebuke him, but Kaye intervened quickly. "You're absolutely right! I'm so sorry. I was just about to give you my card when we were interrupted."

She pulled a green, gold-embossed card from her coat. It said simply "KAYLEEN ENTERPRISES, M.K. McDONALD" and listed her personal office extension number. "Please feel free to call me if ever I can do something for you. I take it I can do the same with you?"

"Yeah, of course, doll," he said, glowering. "M.K. McDonald, hmm. This is the boss of Kayleen, isn't it?"

Clarin rolled his eyes. "It is indeed, sir."

"So who are you?" Angelo jabbed his forefinger at Kaye.

"M.K., Mr. Angelo, and indeed it has been a pleasure to meet you. Thank you for taking the time to talk with us."

She reached forward and took the surprised man's hand in hers, warmly shaking it. With that, she headed for the limo with Clarin, Philippe, and Alice. The others had already departed.

On the trip back to the hotel, Clarin gushed about the site and the excitement of the architectural engineers. The other three listened without comment. Each entrenched in their own thoughts.

Bodies? Dead Bodies? Alice thought. *Are we building on the same ground men were murdered on? Heaven forbid!*

Philippe had questions of his own: *Mr. Italy? Did he mean like a mafia godfather?*

As for Kaye, she wished she was alone in a padded room. All she wanted to do was close her eyes and scream, *No, no, no! Now I'm going to have to meet Max's father. You've got less than forty-eight hours to your wedding. Don't blow Max's cover!*

Don't blow his cover? Don't blow mine! I want to marry his son and I'm neither Italian nor Catholic!

chapter fourteen

"You are the most grumpy, gloomy companion I have ever driven with!" Dave said, a dour pronouncement timed just as he exited the interstate and headed towards the New York's Twelfth Precinct.

"Well, sorry!" came Jack's unapologetic response. "I'm not used to all this cloak-and-dagger stuff. I don't enjoy it one bit."

"And you think I'm used to it and enjoy it?"

"You're a cop."

"Cop?" Dave said. "It would be more respectful to say 'police officer,' thank you."

"Sheesh, you're right. I'm really unnerved, Dave. How's Marconi going to respond? I can't even begin to guess. He could go ballistic. Then what? The very families we're trying to help could get screwed!" Jack flopped his head back against the headrest. "That felt good."

"What?"

"Banging my head against the headrest. What I feel like doing is banging my head against a brick wall."

Dave started to laugh. "Get over yourself, Jack. Not only are you a judge, you're also a lay preacher. It's time to pull up your faith. We've asked everyone we know to pray for us."

"True, but none of them really knows what we're up to."

"Our Savior and Lord knows everything about us," Dave reminded him. "He cares about us and the ones we're going to meet. You know as well as I that before a thought hits our peanut-sized brains, He knows it. Our mission is one of reconciliation, making things right for the Carrons, and especially for Max. In my books, Christ was and is the Master Reconciler. Seriously, we need to get our thoughts off our meeting with Tony and Sophia and onto Him!"

Jack sighed. "You're right, Dave. I really am sorry I snapped at you. Please forgive me."

"I do, bud, so why don't you read the twenty-third psalm to help refocus? My Bible's in the glove compartment. Then let's heed Paul's advice and lift all our concerns to Him, trusting Christ's love, compassion, and care—not just for us, but for Max and his family."

"Chief Dave, I am duly impressed. You keep your Bible in your car!" Jack pulled out the Bible and began to read: "The Lord is my shepherd. I shall not want…"

A perceptible peace settled not only in the hearts of the two men, but in the car itself. By the time Jack finished reading the passage and placed the Bible back into the glove compartment, both men had refocused. The Holy Spirit was breathing life into their prayers.

Dave pulled into a spot designated "visiting chief" in the precinct's underground parking garage. As they exited the car, a uniformed cop yelled, "Can't you yoyos read? That spot is designated!"

"Only in New York," Jack muttered under his breath.

Dave pulled out his ID and showed it to the young officer.

"Sorry, sir," the officer said. "Every day in this city, people ignore the signs and do as they please."

"No harm, officer," Dave replied. "Can you direct us to Captain Burrows' office?"

"Take the elevator to the third floor. Captain's office is to your left."

As the two approached the elevator, with Jack in the lead, Dave sidled up to him and said quietly, "Your Honor?"

Jack made eye contact. "Yeah."

"I'm the chief, so the officers expect me to lead."

"Really?" Jack laughed. "I'm learning new protocol all the time."

Now it was Dave's turn to be a grump. "You think it's funny? It's no funnier than everyone standing when you enter the courtroom."

Jack looked at his friend. "You're right! We do have some pretty pretentious hang-ups, don't we?"

"Problem is, Jack, that all were instituted to generate respect and honor for the office." Dave shook his head sadly. "Doesn't take much for us humans to corrupt something and switch the honor and respect from the office onto ourselves."

"Well, with that humbling thought, let's meet Captain Burrows and hope he has arranged our quarry," Jack replied as they exited the elevator and headed towards the captain's office.

Dave showed his I.D. to the receptionist, and shortly after they were greeted by a portly balding man in his early forties. He led them down a hall and ushered them into a much smaller room. Burrows indicated that the two should sit in the two chairs opposite him.

"I've known Special Agent Epstein for some time," Burrows said. "He's a square shooter, and that's why I agreed to help."

"He said the same about you, sir," Dave said.

"Then you should know that's the same reputation I have with Tony Marconi. Tony may harbor unease, even resentment, against the NYPD. In some cases, those sentiments are justified. Corrupt cops exist everywhere. One bad apple unfortunately taints the barrel. What I'm getting at, gentlemen, is that your dealings with Tony had better be legitimate. I've risked my reputation with him over this, and through him my reputation with a large segment of the Italian community. Do you get my drift?"

"We do, sir." Dave nodded. "Agent Epstein knows the whereabouts of Mrs. Marconi's brother. We were sent to bring her to him. I assure you, everything is aboveboard. To help allay the Marconis' fears, neither I nor my partner are armed, nor are there weapons in our vehicle."

Burrows squinted. "Will it bother you if Tony's armed?"

"We anticipate that he will be, sir. We hope that will provide him the security he needs for him and his wife to agree to travel with us."

"I'm sure Mrs. Marconi will be relieved to meet her brother." Burrows stood up. "Street scuttle indicates that many have been searching for him, and a growing number believe he may already be dead."

"Captain Burrows, her brother is very much alive." Jack smiled broadly as he extended his hand to the captain. "Thank you for helping us to meet with the Marconis."

Burrows nodded curtly. "Good day, gentlemen. I expect they will be here shortly."

The captain shook their hands and departed.

"Jack," whispered Dave. "This room is likely bugged or videotaped. Let's be guarded."

Fifteen minutes passed as the two men sat silently waiting. Then thirty.

"If they don't come soon, we'll be stuck in New York's rush hour," Dave groaned.

Just then, the door opened and a very big man stepped through the door. He glowered at the two of them, studied the room, and then motioned for a pert and pretty young woman to join him.

Dave and Jack exchanged glances. Neither needed to speak; both knew the thoughts of the other: *Thank you for the photos, Kaye.* They had no doubts. This was Tony and Sophia Marconi.

Before either could say a word, Sophia addressed them. "Captain Burrows said you know where my brother is. So where is he?"

"Actually, we were sent to bring you to him," Dave said softly.

"No one told us anything about going anywhere with nobody," Tony snapped.

Jack put his briefcase up on the table, motioning for them to be seated. Neither moved.

"What are you doing?" Tony demanded.

Jack was caught off-guard. *Nobody talks to me like that! I'm a Supreme Court Justice.* A smile crossed his lips. It was a good thing he and Dave had talked earlier about respect.

"What's so funny?" Tony growled.

"Pardon?" Jack said, totally confused.

"You smiled."

"Sorry. It's probably nerves. Uniting families with missing relatives isn't something I do every day," Jack said apologetically. "What I'd like to show, Mrs. Marconi, are pictures of her brother. We hope that you will both come with us to him."

Sophia's jaw dropped. "You want us to just up and leave?" Before either Jack or Dave could reply, she continued, "We can't do that. We have three small children!"

Dave closed his eyes. *Oh crap, they do! We forgot all about them. A mother's concern for her kids will outweigh concern for siblings any day. We're doomed!*

"Is there no one who could mind them tonight?" Dave asked, keeping his voice calm. "Maybe even tomorrow night, at the maximum. Like grandparents, uncles, aunts?" To himself, he added, *Surely there's somebody. Italians are supposed to have big families.*

"Show me the pictures," Sophia said, her voice cutting through his thoughts.

Tony carefully positioned Sophia behind him. "Open it slowly, and keep your hands on top of the case."

"Dear God, help," Jack prayed as he opened the case. Inside were the photographs he had brought with him. Aside from that, the case was empty. On

top was the framed picture Kaye had snapped of Max as he'd wired her house for added security.

Sophia's expression softened the moment she saw the photo. She picked it up lovingly, tears flooding her eyes. "Tony, it is Max. It really is! He's alive then?"

"Very much, ma'am," Dave said. Jack thought he sounded as good as any TV cop he'd ever heard.

"Why can't you bring him to us?" Tony asked.

"Or to my parents, in Chicago?" Sophia added.

Dave shook his head. "Unfortunately, he can't be moved yet."

Sophia stifled a scream. "He's in jail again?"

"No, no!" said Jack, "He was in an accident and was injured. He can't be moved." He was trying to ease her anguish, but realized too late that he'd intensified it.

"Tony, that's why he never contacted us," she said. "He must have been unconscious, or had amnesia or something like that, but now he remembers who he is and wants us. Oh Tony, I've got to go to him!"

Tony pointed at a photo of Max smiling. "He doesn't look very unconscious there."

"That was before the accident," Dave volunteered.

"This is the after." Jack pulled out a picture of Max in intensive care, immobilized and unconscious, his leg in a sling.

Sophia was now sobbing. "Tony, we've got to go to him. Please, ask Pepi and Lena to look after the children. They can pick them up from the day care center. Please!"

Tony put his arm around his wife. "How far away is he?"

"It took us about five and a half hours to get here," Dave said. "We ran into some construction and traffic, but if we leave now, even if we stop for supper, we should get there before midnight." Dave emphasized the *leave now* part, hoping it would prod the Marconis into action. It worked.

"Put your hands on the wall," Tony ordered.

Jack started to question why, but Dave stopped him.

"Just do it," Dave interceded. "He's checking us for weapons."

After Tony checked and realized they weren't armed, Tony stepped back, satisfied. "So where's your car?"

"In the parking garage," Dave ventured.

The four rode the elevator in silence, then stepped into the lot and headed for Dave's car.

"How come you're in the visiting chief's spot?" Tony asked, sounding suspicious.

"Dear Lord, this guy misses nothing. Help us get to my house with all of us intact," Jack silently pleaded.

"Sorry," Dave replied. "I never noticed the designation."

"Open the trunk!"

Dave and Jack looked at each other.

"What? Why?" asked Jack.

"Cause I want to see who or what you got in it!" Tony's hand had slipped into his coat.

Dave complied.

"Golf clubs? Dave, you brought your golf clubs?" Jack blurted.

"I always carry them," Dave responded defensively.

"Why?"

"To play baseball! Why else?"

Sophia rolled her eyes. "Boys and their toys!" She opened the car door. "Enough already! Get in and let's get going. Tony, you need to phone your parents to go get the children. We're running out of time."

Fortunately, they had timed their exit just before the rush hour began. Tony pulled out his cell and managed to reach his mother. "Hi, Mamma, it's Tone. Can I ask a big favor of you and Pop? Sophia got two days off from her firm and we just need a few days to ourselves. Would you pick the kids up from daycare and look after them for us?" The grin on his face indicated his request had been favorably received. "Gee, thanks, Mom. Sophia says thanks, too." He let out a little chuckle. "Aww, come on, Mamma, we already have three."

In the rearview mirror, Dave saw Tony roll his eyes. It was all he could do to stifle a smile when he heard Tony's next words.

"Yeah, I know, sometimes what you don't plan happens. You go right ahead and pray for that. Give Jo and Micki a hug, and be sure and read to them and tell them and Rici that their Mommy loves them very much." Tony let out a sigh. "Yeah, of course I love them, too! I was telling you what Sophia asked me to say. Okay, bye. We'll call tomorrow. Love ya!"

Jack and Dave exchanged glances. Talking to his mother Tony's voice and demeanor had totally changed. He actually sounded human!

"Man, Italian mammas take the cake!" Tony said with a scowl as he shut off the phone. "She's already got three grandkids now."

Sophia started to laugh and snuggled up to her husband. "So, she wants just one more, Tone? Is that it? Well, you'll have to be nice to me. Better be careful about saying disparaging things about Italian mammas. Remember, I am one."

Tony looked at her in disbelief and jerked his head toward the front seat. "Sophia, think of what you're saying! We don't even know these guys. By the way, you'd better call your work and let them know you won't be in for the next two days." He paused. "You even forgot your job, didn't you? You're so fixated on Max!"

Sophia screwed up her nose and sat back. "You're right, hon." She bit her lip. "When I saw his picture and saw that he was alive, I forgot about everything."

She took the phone in her hand and waited patiently for the receptionist at her work to answer. "Hi, Gail, it's Sophia. I won't be in the rest of the week. I need the time off. We just got word that my brother Max has been hurt. Tony and I are driving to the hospital now. Yeah, thanks, I'm glad he's alive, too! Apparently he was in a coma for a while, and that's why we couldn't locate him. Thanks again, Gail, and yep, I'll keep the office updated. Oh, Gail, should Tony's Mom or Pop phone, we just told them I had a couple of days off. We didn't want to alarm them until we saw Max. Yeah, thanks Gail, you're a real friend!"

Sophia smiled as she shut off her cell. "Of everybody in the office, Gail is the one good egg. I'm so glad it was her who picked up."

"Where do you work?" Jack asked, though he already knew the answer.

"In the D.A.'s office. Well, not really. Just affiliated. I'm connected to the city's legal aid department. I'm articling for the bar."

"What did you mean when you said the one you were talking to on the phone was the one good egg?" Jack asked.

"She's the only one who will be straight with me. Everybody else sends me on wild goose chases."

Through the rear-view mirror, Jack noticed tears in her eyes. "You mean you're the intern victim for the year?" He smiled, remembering some of the harassment he had experienced the year he articled.

"No." Sophia shook her head. "There's a bunch of us who are articling. Sure, everybody gets teased, but only one is fed misleading information, and unfortunately that's me."

"Why? Because you're a girl?"

"No, smart ass, because her last name is Marconi and her maiden name was Carron!" Tony said. "Nobody wanted to give her a position to article, but they had to because she topped Columbia's graduating class."

Jack turned to Sophia. "So you had to work doubly hard just to qualify."

"Nope, triple or quadruple," Sophia said. "And that, sir, is the truth. I'll get severely chastised for taking this time off."

No, you won't! Jack thought.

Jack, Tony, and Sophia dozed on and off for the next hour. At about 7:00 p.m., Dave roused them all. "Folks, we are now going for dinner. Whether anyone else agrees or not, your driver is exhausted."

Jack leaned forward to open the glove compartment.

"Woah!" exclaimed Tony. "No smart stuff. What are you doing?"

Jack sighed. "Simply getting another photo album for Sophia to see."

"You have more pictures of Max?" Sophia was suddenly animated again.

They found a booth in the truck stop diner. "Dinner's on us," Jack said. Dave glared at him. "Well then, dinner's on me. I'm having the steak. What about the rest of you?"

The other two men followed suit. Sophia elected chicken with rice and a salad.

Jack studied the couple across from him *Maybe she's just like her brother, with a tremendous aptitude to get into people's bad books only to emerge as one everybody wants to love.* He found himself smiling again.

"What's so funny?" Tony was anything but amused.

"I was just thinking that you might like to know more about your brother and us," Jack said.

"Of course we would, stupid. That's why we're here."

Sophia wasn't amused, either, Jack saw. He sat back in the booth, looking at them over his horn-rimmed glasses.

Dave watched the three of them, choosing not to smile. He thought that *His Honor* Jack Walters had just re-emerged. *Somehow Jack is about to take control, and when he does, I think the rest of our drive home will be a little less tense.* He glanced around the restaurant. It was reasonably crowded and too loud for others to eavesdrop on their table's conversation. It was also crowded enough that Tony would behave himself.

The waiter brought their food and then disappeared back to the kitchen.

"Please say grace, Jack," asked Dave as he bowed his head. Out of the corner of his eye, he glimpsed Tony and Sophia doing likewise.

Jack offered a very pastoral prayer and Dave saw surprise register on the faces of both Tony and Sophia.

"Are you a priest?" Sophia asked Jack.

"I'm a lay pastor."

Tony rested his fork on his plate. "What does that mean?"

"Our church is referred to as nondenominational," Dave said. "We take the Bible seriously, meaning it's important for a person to believe that Jesus is the Savior and that on the cross He gave His life as a sacrifice to pay for our sin. But to prove that this was a God thing, not a human thing, on the third day Jesus rose from the dead. Such belief allows us to accept Jesus as our Lord and trust that Christ has a plan for our lives. A plan He desires to help us fulfill."

"This means everyone is called to some ministry role in the body of Christ," Jack added. "We pay some people to do ministry full-time. Others have jobs in the world but still minister in the church in specific capacities. For me, that means serving on the pastoral team, both preaching and teaching."

"So, are you married?" Tony questioned, obviously intrigued.

"Yes, I am."

"In our church, priests can't marry, and they have to be specifically ordained," Sophia ventured.

"Yes," Dave said. "The Bible says that some Christians serve celibate while others marry."

"Would you like to see the pictures now?" Jack hoped the previous dialogue might have served to soften up his two guests, allowing them to digest not only their meal but also the truth he was about to reveal.

Sophia accepted the album as if she were cradling the crown jewels. She studied the photos of Max in the hospital. "What happened to him?"

"He was shot," Dave replied.

"Shot?" The two jerked their heads up simultaneously. "Where?"

"In southern Pennsylvania."

"Pennsylvania?" Sophia looked at Tony. "Max's men, Lou and Bill, told us that from Cleveland, Max headed south."

"He doubled back," Jack said dryly.

Tony's eyes went as black as coal. "He was going to that blockheaded judge."

"The judge shot Max?" Sophia barely whispered.

Now it was Dave and Jack's turn to speak in duet. "No!"

Dave eyed Tony sternly. "Your so-called blockheaded judge saved Max's life by stopping the bleeding."

"Max was doing nothing wrong," Jack added. "In fact, he risked his life to save another. Look at these pictures."

"He looks unconscious in this one," Sophia offered.

Tony looked genuinely hurt. "But why didn't he contact us?"

"Certainly not because he didn't love you," Jack replied softly. "He cares for you very much. That's why we're taking you to him, so he can answer all your questions."

Sophia flipped through the album. Her brow furrowed. "He doesn't look like he's in the hospital anymore in these shots. Look, Tony, his leg isn't in a sling."

"It's in a very uncomfortable metal brace," Dave commented as he pointed to Max's left leg. "There can be no weight-bearing or movement. Hopefully, his healing has progressed sufficiently so that the brace can be removed today. Then he'll be given crutches and be a little more mobile."

"But when did all this take place?" Tony asked.

"Approximately three months ago," Jack replied.

"Three months ago!" Sophia cried. "But he was released from prison well over six months ago!"

Jack reached across the table and gently touched her hand. "Sophia, look at those pictures closely. Does Max look upset in any of them?"

She shook her head.

"So where are you taking us?" Tony sighed resignedly.

"To Summerside, Pennsylvania. Judge Walters' house," Dave volunteered. He had to call upon all his reserves not to crack a smile at the Marconis' reaction.

It's a worn cliché, Dave thought, *but gosh, the man truly does look like a deer caught in headlights.*

Almost in despair, Tony blurted, "To that blockheaded judge's house?"

"Tony." Jack established eye contact with the man. "I am your blockheaded judge!" With that, he stood and went to the register to pay the bill.

chapter fifteen

Max found it hard to get to sleep. In many ways, he felt more imprisoned by this metal brace than when he had been locked in a jail cell. He grinned to himself. *One thing I know for certain... revenge isn't sweeter than love!*

It was true. Max's sole focus on his release had been to confront Jack Walters, to learn the man's motivation for imposing such a harsh sentence on him. After all, even if he had been guilty, he'd also been a first-time offender. Indeed, revenge had driven him then. Now he was consumed by the prospect of once again sleeping beside Kaye, only this time with no imaginary dividing line, no bulky pajamas, and no need for cold showers!

He winced at the thought of the time he'd spent sequestered in her house trying to expose the identity of her vulgar late-night caller. He didn't know how he had managed to endure sleeping beside her for nearly three months platonically. Once he realized the perp was a serial killer, he had been scared of the alternative. Had Kaye and Max been intimate and Glaxton been able to overpower him like he had his earlier victims, he'd have made it look like Max had killed her and then himself. He let out a low whistle. "Sicilian trash" would have been his posthumous label.

Mamma would have been devastated!

A wave of remorse swept over him as he remembered how he'd first entered her home—a break and entry, ending up accidentally in her room, falling asleep in her closet. A deep sigh escaped his lips as he recalled how she had come home completely unaware of his presence and innocently undressed in front of him. He grimaced at the memory of his attack on Kaye.

If it hadn't been for Glaxton's call, Max would have succeeded in raping her!

Most people fail to grasp the power our sinful nature has over us—that is, until we commit an act we never thought we'd be capable of, he mused.

"When we do, that's when we finally recognize our deep need of you, Jesus! As painful as it was for me to face that truth about myself, Lord, I'm so grateful. In that moment, I personally understood that I was a sinner and that You died for me!"

His thoughts returned to prison and the remorse he'd seen in so many men. Outwardly they'd have on their macho, bravado masks, but if a guy got their trust, then would come the honest sharing. The nature of their offense didn't matter—brutal assault, thievery to pay for drugs, booze, gambling, even murder. He sighed. Or rape.

Max ran his hand through his hair as he spoke to the Holy Spirit. "The one real blessing for me was taking the Alpha Course with those guys." He chuckled "Okay, I admit I didn't think so in the beginning."

He really had been skeptical, but as the teachings progressed each week, everyone began to relax and open up. When the guys saw that no question was stupid, and that nobody would laugh at them or hold what they said against them, their true feelings emerged. In his mind, he could see their faces again, and he began to realize the debt he owed each one. To the world, those guys were nobodies, but God had used them to draw him closer to Him and His living reality.

Eventually, the men had shared their first awareness that Jesus had indeed died for their sins, and that through Him they knew God had forgiven them. That's when they knew they needed to forgive themselves.

Max drew his hand across his mouth. It was only because of those guys that he could face what he'd tried to do to Kaye and learn to forgive himself and others.

He thumped his head on his pillow.

"Rape."

He spat out the word. He never thought he'd ever try that! His real fear, after he learned to use his gun, was that he might tip over the line, lose control, and plug someone just for the heck of it.

"I guess it's not what we expect that slams us, Lord. It's the unexpected."

Max sighed. The Bible warns that the devil prowls about like a roaring lion, seeking whom he can devour. Well, he knew the devil couldn't make him do things. The devil didn't have that power, but Satan was pretty clever at blindsiding people to their own frailties.

We don't even know they exist—until bam! He pounded his right fist into the palm of his left hand. *We've fallen!*

Big John's face suddenly loomed before him. He'd killed his wife in a drunken stupor. Even now, Max could see the tears streaming down the man's face, hear him share about how he loathed himself. He had wanted the death penalty, but instead he'd gotten life.

"Life," Big John had laughed. "It weren't no life! It was a living hell of self-hatred. No hope. Then one day I opened the Bible that the chaplain had given me. It fell open at Mark 2. Jesus was at a party with no good sinners."

A smile crept across Max's face as he recalled the big man's excitement.

"Those big shot respectable dudes criticized Jesus for being with those sinner guys," Big John had said. "But Jesus told them that healthy guys don't need doctors, only sick folk. Jesus said he wasn't calling people who think they're righteous, just them that know they're sinners!" Big John had looked up, a huge smile pasted across his face from ear to ear. "That's when I knew Jesus was calling me to Him, cause I knew I was a sinner!"

Max bit his lip at the remembrance of the words that followed from this lifer: "It's not until a man sees and accepts the filth in him that he'll run to Jesus for His love."

He clasped his hands behind his head and stared at the ceiling. *Big John, for all the masses I attended, it wasn't until I had to face myself and admit the filth in me that I could fully understand what you were saying about Jesus.* He sniffed. *It sure isn't with the head that Jesus becomes our friend, but with the heart!*

Max reached for a Kleenex and blew his nose. God's love was amazing. When people accepted it for themselves, that's when real life could begin.

His mind drifted back to when Kaye had told him that she had forgiven him and challenged him to forgive himself. He thought about his near-death confession to Jack Walters. It really had been surreal—there he had been, confessing to the guy who for six years he'd carefully cultivated his heart to hate. Yet when Walters pronounced those words—"Jesus forgives you"—he had been released from the worst prison ever: the prison of self-loathing. It had set him free to love Kaye, and yes, even Jack, Marnie, the Davidsons, and himself. Life was indeed becoming much more abundant.

Around 6:00 a.m., Jack and Dave entered his room and ended his time of self-reflection. Jack got breakfast while Dave helped Max use the toilet, shave, and dress. An hour later, they bundled him into the van and left on their mission for Epi.

Once again, Max was left alone with his thoughts. No big deal. Jack's garage was heated. Even though it was late October, everyone was anticipating a pleasant fall day. But truthfully all he could think about was that soon this cumbersome metal brace would be gone and he'd be able to navigate independently once more.

The moment the word *independent* crossed his mind, he started to laugh.

Then again maybe not so independently. The brace will be gone, but it'll be replaced by a ring on my left hand. I can't believe I actually proposed to a woman and she said yes.

Another memory danced across his mind. Aunt Louisa! He had all but forgotten her. A sly smile stole across his features as he let out a whoop. Not all revenge was bad. At least that one sure didn't feel bad.

He began laughing so hard that tears rolled down his cheeks.

"Aren't we a cheery one today?" His reverie was cut short as Marnie entered the van. "Don't be too jubilant. Sue warned me that you'll have many hard days of physio, as you stretch those ligaments and muscles and mobilize your joints into activity again."

"Marnie, do you ever let go of your strict principal role?" he joked. "I actually wasn't thinking about my leg. I was thinking about my Aunt Louisa." He knew Marnie well enough by now to know how much oblique comments piqued her curiosity.

"So, who is Aunt Louisa that she has you laughing so hard?" she asked as she started the van.

"She's the only woman the whole population of single male Sicilians absolutely fears."

Marnie turned and looked at him in utter disbelief. "The mafia fears a woman?"

"Mafia and non-mafia. Everyone. And she's not just a woman, she's a very *old* woman."

"Okay, I bite," Marnie said, eyes twinkling. "Do tell."

So Max began to relate how this ninety-plus-year-old woman had seen it as her personal mission—Max suggested the right word might even be vendetta—to ensure all single Sicilian men, if they hadn't escaped to a seminary, got married. In her eyes, it was their duty to procreate and ensure the perpetual survival of the Sicilian people. He went on to describe in detail her matchmaking parties and dinners, how she'd even coerce men's parents into collaborating.

By the time they arrived at the hospital, Marnie was in stitches. "Am I to understand, Mr. Carron, that tomorrow you will be escaping Aunt Louisa's perilous clutches?"

"Indeed I will be, Mrs. Walters. Indeed I will!"

Marnie pulled up to the hospital's back door, where Jimmy stood waiting to help unload him.

Max entered the hospital at nine o'clock. The hospital staff conducted multiple tests and x-rays, all indicating that the healing was progressing favorably. The new bone growth was excellent. Then came the actual removal of the steel brace. Dr. Chandra ordered mild sedation to minimize Max's distress and to allow for better assessment of his current mobility, as the previously rigid joints were once again forced to move. Later Max was fitted for crutches and instructed on their use.

"Absolutely no weight-bearing!" the doctor told him.

Dr. Chandra ordered a half-hour session in the pool to coax the inactive muscles and ligaments to once more flex and extend. Max was shocked to discover the muscle loss in his left leg and equally surprised at both the rigidity and pain he experienced as he tried moving the leg.

The physiotherapist gave both him and Marnie a copy of the mild exercises they wanted Max to begin doing two or three times daily in his home pool.

"Home pool?" Max queried.

"Don't you have one?" asked the physiotherapist.

"No."

"It was supposed to be a surprise," Marnie said. She gave Max a poke. "He knew we talked of building one, but he didn't know it was a fait accompli. Just act surprised when Kaye tells you."

It was 3:30 p.m. by the time they arrived back at Independence Drive. They went directly to Dave's, where a very grateful Rufie greeted them. When Rufie had relieved himself, they took him to the doggie park. Few other dogs were there, so Rufie amused himself chasing the frisbee Max cheerfully tossed for him.

"It really feels great, Marnie, just to be able to maneuver myself at last. If anyone would have told me I'd see crutches as a blessing, I would have said they were nuts. But man, these crutches have given me a new lease on life."

Marnie smiled, took his hand, and gave him a peck on the cheek. "Max, we're all so very, very happy with and for you. You know something else?" He stared at her with a blank expression. "Kaye's right."

"About what?"

"You are a very special person, Max. A true gentleman."

Her compliment caught him off-guard. "You really mean that?"

"Absolutely, absolutely!" She reached over and gave his hand a squeeze as Rufie bounded to the van and leapt inside. "I think Rufus is telling us that it's time to go home for supper."

She started the van and headed home. Max rode in silence to the Walters' house, a very warm feeling of acceptance flooding his soul like soothing sunlight.

All three entered the house with specific agendas. For Rufie, it was a full bowl of food and big drink of water. Marnie's goal was to fix supper. Max was bent on achieving his dream for the past three months… to finally take a nice warm shower. Marnie went upstairs and set out the towels, insisting he use their en suite since it had a walk-in shower.

Max selected the clothes he wanted to wear, delighted that he could at last discard the ones designed specifically to accommodate the brace. Marnie had carried them to her bedroom and set them on the bed. By this time, Max had navigated the stairs and managed to get himself upright. He was genuinely pleased with how well he was mastering the crutches.

Then it hit him—this was the first time he'd actually seen the upstairs of the Walters' house. For six years—six very long years—Jack Walters had been public enemy number one in Max's books. Now here he was, in Jack's house as his friend!

"Wow, God, you really do move mountains!"

"Max," Marnie said in her school principal voice. It succeeded in drawing him away from his private thoughts. "Look at me!"

He obeyed.

"Be very careful in the shower, and be sure to take your crutches into the shower for support. The shower has a no-slip finish, but take no chances! Just don't—"

"Put any weight on that leg," Max finished, grinning. "Don't worry, Marnie. I'll be careful!"

"Right. I'll fix dinner. By the way, Mr. Carron, silk boxers—very nice!" She laughed as she closed the door behind her.

Max stood still for a few moments, overcome with emotions and trying to sort out the reasons for them. On the one hand, he stood in the bedroom of the man who had sent him to prison. Never in his wildest imagination could he have envisioned doing so. Yet he was also overcome with gratitude at all Jack had done for him. He had saved his life by stopping the hemorrhaging vein caused by Glaxton's gunshot, stayed with him through surgery, had been there over these past twelve weeks when he couldn't fend for himself. Now, in Jack's bathroom, he was about to enjoy, all by himself, his first shower since his injury. It may just have been a shower, but to him it was anything but ordinary!

How we take the ordinary for granted until it's no longer there, he mused. *But when it returns, do we ever recognize the blessing! Man, do I recognize it!*

The moment the warm water flowed over him, Max began to sing. His deep tenor voice rang out in Italian and English. He just couldn't stop singing. "Thank you, Lord, for the gift of music and for giving me a voice to sing, and thank you, thank you, thank you that I'm mobile once more! Amen!"

By the time he emerged from the shower, it was after five and daylight was starting to fade.

He was so elated by the day's events—and by the prospect of being able to dress himself—that he almost failed to notice it. He backed away and went to the door.

"Marnie! Marnie! Please come quick!"

She came bounding up the stairs. "Can't get your socks on?"

He grabbed her hand and pulled her towards him, away from the window. Hoarsely he inquired, "Did Jack make an enemy of anyone else?"

She looked at him in astonishment. "No! In all his years as a lawyer, on the bench and as a Supreme Court justice, you were the only one whose name he ever mentioned." She started to laugh. "You're just teasing."

"No, Marn, I'm not. Somebody—or somebodies, plural—are in that car on the side of the street. They're observing this place. It wasn't there when we came in. Must have just gotten here. I'm sure it wasn't there when I went into the shower."

"Max, what should we do? Should I call the police?"

"Not yet. They're just watching. Let's not let them know we've noticed. You close the blinds at the front of the house. Should they know Jack's away, we won't let them know I'm here. Even if they know I am, they won't know I'm mobile." He looked her in the eye. "Marnie, you said I was a gentleman. Do you trust me enough to let me put on my gun?"

She leaned against him. "Of course I trust you."

"Jack, put it in the downstairs closet, top shelf. Will you get it for me, please?"

Marnie shuddered as she closed the drapes.

Max tackled the stairs on his bottom, pushing the crutches ahead. He had to admit that it felt good to once again strap on his holster. He affectionately fingered his gun—he'd named it "J.D."—then popped it into the holster.

Marnie bit her lip. It wasn't that guns never entered her house—Dave and Matt often came in uniform—but this… this wasn't a police officer. She glanced at the clock as she put the meal on the table. It was now six o'clock and dark outside. Maybe Jack and Dave would be home by ten. She certainly hoped so, for dread had gripped her heart.

As for Max, Marnie's food had captivated his attention. He appeared to have even forgotten the vehicle outside as he peppered Marnie with all sorts of questions about weddings. It was clear his focus was still on Kaye. After desert, however, he hobbled into Jack's darkened office and peered cautiously into the street.

"It's still there," he whispered as he came back to the kitchen. "When do you expect Sue to arrive?"

"She thought around eight. I told her I'd keep a plate ready to heat in the microwave."

"Do you have her cell phone number?"

"Of course."

"Give her a call. Find out how soon she expects to be here. Tell her about the car on the street and instruct her to act as if she doesn't notice it. Make sure she pulls in on the left-hand side of the driveway. That way, Jack can get directly into the garage. Let her know I'll be watching out for her. Make sure she doesn't move suspiciously, but do tell her to waste no time getting into the house. Oh yeah. And don't forget to tell her Ruf's here with us."

A half-hour later, a breathless Sue entered through the front door. "There's someone in that car!"

"We know," Marnie replied.

"Who?" And then, "You're wearing a gun!"

Max raised an eyebrow. "Sue, would you rather it be in the closet?"

"No, but maybe they're police."

Max frowned. "Perhaps, but don't you think Dave would have told us if he was assigning surveillance to the house?"

All were at a total loss as to who could be in that car. They entertained the thought that perhaps it could be media. But hopefully none, beside themselves, knew of tomorrow's planned nuptials.

Marnie busied herself getting Sue's supper.

Suddenly, Max's new mobility registered with Sue. "You got it off!" she squealed. "How does it feel?"

"Absolutely great!"

In no time, thoughts of the car disappeared as the trio began to plan the following day's festivities.

Sue initiated the conversation. "Max, we both want you to know how happy we are for the two of you. Thank you so much for saving Kaye's life!" A Cheshire cat smile appeared on her face. "You, sir, are a great addition to our family. Welcome."

With that, Sue leapt behind Max and dropped a huge ice cube down his back.

Instinctively, he started to rise.

"Max, no weight-bearing!" Marnie admonished, giggling.

"I've waited a long time to initiate you," Sue said with a laugh. "But I figured that in fairness you should have some mobility before I did."

Max squinted at them. "Mrs. Davidson, be forewarned that I have a little black book."

"In which you record all the naughties committed against you?" laughed Marnie.

"Exactly!"

Sue yawned. "Well, family, I've been on the go all day long, as I'm sure the two of you have. It's 10:30. Tomorrow will be a huge day. I suggest we turn in. I'm sure our two gallant men can get themselves safely into the garage."

Marnie put Rufie on the rope and let him out the back door. Soon he was back, signaling that he, too, was ready for bed. She put the security lock on the door.

Max checked the front door lock, then hopped back into the kitchen.

"Ladies, thanks for the great bachelor party," he said. "You two guard the upstairs. Have no fear, Hopalong Carron and his faithful dog Rufus will secure the downstairs."

The two women looked at each other. "Not!" was their only reply.

"What?"

"Excuse us," Marnie said. "When Kaye was being stalked, you insisted on staying in the same room as her. You said that if the perp came into the house and you were asleep in another room, he might kill her. And you wouldn't even hear him."

Max was stunned. "Those were entirely different circumstances!"

"What do you mean?" demanded Sue.

"Well, for starters, sexual predators don't go around in groups setting up visible surveillance." Max laughed. "You girls are joking, right?"

"Wrong," Marnie said. "We'll sleep here."

"In my bed?" Max squeaked. "Three of us can't get into that bed!"

Marnie smiled. "You're absolutely right, Max. I'll blow up the air mattress and fix you and Rufie up on the kitchen floor. It's a Queen, it'll give you both plenty of room," she added.

"Besides," added Sue mischievously, "now that you have your mobility, you'll naturally want to exercise it. It'll be much more challenging going to bed on the floor than in a regular bed." She laughed as she cupped the big Bouvier's head in her hands, "Ruf, you get to have a stag night with the groom. Don't keep him up too late."

"Gee, thanks," murmured Max.

In a few minutes, Marnie had the bed ready. He lowered himself ever so gingerly onto the air mattress, then felt the dog lie down beside him.

"Just you and me bud," he said as he reached out and stroked his furry companion, who kindly rewarded him with a slurpy kiss.

chapter sixteen

Wednesday morning in Chicago found Kaye humming quietly to herself as she dressed for her second day of whirlwind meetings. "This is the day that the Lord hath made, we will rejoice and be glad in it! Yes, this is the day Max's Tin Lizzy comes off and he gets some mobility back." She smiled. "Well, sir, your newfound freedom will be but temporary." A little giggle broke out as she checked her watch. "In less than twenty-six hours, you will be tied to me!"

Kaye sighed. *"Oh, dear Lord, I really do need You to help me remain focused today."*

She stood and looked out the window of her suite. It offered a panoramic view of the Chicago waterfront. Overall, she had to admit she had been impressed not only with the selected building site but with the proposed architectural designs and projected relocation costs. She had been even more pleased that both Kayleen's board and its management had unanimously approved her demand for a uniform purchase price for the various properties—based of course on square footage, finished or unfinished space, and current usage.

After what I discovered yesterday about the owner of one of the properties, we can't be seen to be offering him more money than anyone else. Most definitely not! She pursed her lips. *Most definitely not!*

There was a knock on the door and a cheery voice called, "M.K., are you ready?"

Alice poked her head into the room.

Kaye sprinted to the door. "Absolutely, my dear Alice. Let's be off."

Alice kept step with her boss, quickly briefing her on the names of all the council members, their jurisdictions, and of course the mayor.

"You'll like the mayor, M.K.," Alice gushed. "She's their first female black mayor. She has a very keen wit. The type you like."

Alice then began to outline the particular passions of the current city politicians. Kaye had of course already perused the personal and political profiles of the individuals she was about to meet.

True to Alice's prediction, Kaye and the mayor did hit it off extremely well. The breakfast meeting resulted in a mutual admiration society between the city and Kayleen.

Following that meeting, Kaye decided to arrive at Our Lady of Mercies Hospital just before lunch. She planned to meet with the Chief of Staff and senior hospital administrators, then hopefully tour the hospital before returning to her hotel around 2:00 p.m. This would allow time for her to be debriefed concerning the various property owners' initial responses to Kayleen's offers to purchase. It would also provide Kaye, her board, and management team at least an hour for in-house deliberation before actually meeting with the owners.

Kaye had to acknowledge that of all the activities scheduled for her, the impromptu hospital visit was the one she looked forward to most. Largely, this was because she had a personal agenda. Either there or on the way back to the hotel, she intended a side trip down Maple Grove Drive.

Philippe, ever faithful Philippe, would soon accompany her to the hospital. Alice remained behind to fine-tune everyone else's agendas. Philippe had some last-minute details to oversee concerning the evening's banquet, and thus Kaye found herself briefly alone with their driver.

She began chatting him up. "How long have you lived in Chicago?" she asked.

"All my life, ma'am."

"I understand Maple Grove Drive is a rather unique residential area. Is it near Our Lady of Mercies Hospital?" she asked, knowing full well that it was.

"Oh yes, ma'am," he replied politely. "Would you like to see it?"

"Yes, provided it isn't out of our way."

Philippe quickly arrived and they started off.

"I'll take you to the hospital through Maple Grove Drive, ma'am," the driver announced.

"Why Maple Grove Drive?" Philippe demanded.

"Oh, it's a historic part of Chicago," the driver explained, letting Kaye off the hook. "Initially the region was settled by Italians. Some are still there but there is a significant black community in the area now."

"Big deal," Philippe muttered under his breath.

The driver continued. "The neat thing about Maple Grove Drive is the trees.

It has a treed boulevard in the center and beautiful trees line each side of the drive.

This description interested Philippe. As the car turned onto the drive, both sightseers gasped. It was indeed beautiful. Many of the trees still held their fall colors. The houses had been built in the early 1900s, their architecture complementing the builders of that era.

The driver started to laugh. "The other reason people like to see Maple Grove Drive is for its historical connection to the mob in Chicago's infamous prohibition days. Many of the houses have secret passages."

"Really?" said Philippe.

Kaye was preoccupied with the house numbers. One number in particular was of interest to her. Early on, she had ascertained that it would be on her side.

The road wound gently around a bend, and then she saw it. A large red brick edifice set back from the road, fenced in with a five-foot brick wall, and ornamental wrought iron gates. The driver had slowed and she could see that the circular drive went up to the front door. White Roman columns supported the portico. Despite herself, Kaye let out a little gasp.

"Magnificent, isn't it?" the driver commented. "Mr. Carron lived there for twenty-five years. Some call him Mr. Italy, especially in the Italian community. He and his wife built a large estate in the burbs, and sold this one to his son. Young buck must've got his money from drugs, for he got busted and received a stiff sentence. He was supposed to be out this past spring, but so far he hasn't showed up."

"What happened to him?" asked Philippe.

"Rumor has it he's likely dead, but nobody knows. I do mean nobody!"

"Well, this is a lovely street!" Philippe said. "Maybe the property will come up for sale. Or does Mr. Carron Jr. have a family?"

Kaye looked at Philippe in disbelief.

"Nah," replied the driver. "Never married. Rumor was that he was gay. That don't go over too well in those Italian communities, if you know what I mean. You folks ever see those TV episodes of *The Sopranos?*"

Both Kaye and Philippe indicated that they hadn't. She looked at Philippe and saw him become rather subdued. She chuckled to herself.

I can understand now why Max was surprised at my house. He grew up in a virtual fortress. Well, rumor mill, Mr. Carron is neither dead nor gay. She smiled sweetly. *And I have no need to buy this property. By this time tomorrow, half will be mine.*

Arriving at the hospital, Kaye warmly thanked the driver for taking the time to show them a beautiful part of Chicago.

Everyone was there to greet Kaye—the press, the hospital chief of staff, the senior administrators, and several nursing sisters. Even Bishop Masseroti would be joining them shortly. Kaye had taken care to note that while some parts of the area were affluent, like Maple Grove Drive, most of the region serviced by the hospital appeared poor. The hospital itself was old. Yet there was warmth, compassion, and concern emanating from each person she met; those feelings seemed even to pervade the bricks and mortar of the building. She was glad she had agreed to speak at their fundraising dinner.

"The bishop has been detained," an out of breath nursing sister explained as she padded up to Kaye's group. "He so wanted to meet you. Would you be able to stay a few minutes longer?"

Her request gave Kaye the out for which she'd been praying. She screwed up her nerve to ask permission for what she had wanted to do all along. "While I wait, would it be possible for me to tour some of the wards? I'm particularly interested in the children's and women's wards."

Yes! Philippe thought. *You just know how to wind everyone's heart around your finger. Way to go, girl!*

Philippe had most decidedly read everyone's emotional response. One sister, named Sister Madeline, just beamed. "Oh Ms. McDonald, I'd be honored to escort you!"

With that, the two women were off. Philippe was squeamish about hospitals in general, and touring the women's and children's wards was even more intimidating. Consequently, he opted to stay behind and talk with those organizing the fundraiser.

Sister Madeline proved a most helpful tour guide. However, when they arrived at one of the children's wards, another nursing sister spied her and rushed over to ask advice on a particular case. Kaye told her to go ahead, but then requested permission to simply wander through the ward.

"Is it appropriate for me to talk to the children, family members, or staff?" Kaye asked.

"By all means!" Sister Madeline said.

That's how Kaye ended up in a room with an older woman comforting a tiny child. Kaye guessed the child to be two or three years old. She assumed the rather attractive woman was the child's grandmother. Her hair was cut short, a lot like Kaye's, except hers was a beautiful silvery grey and had much more curl to it.

The woman sat in a rocker, cuddling the tot on her lap. She sang ever so softly as she rocked gently back and forth. Kaye thought the language sounded Italian. What struck her most was the profound love the woman exhibited toward this little one. Clearly, the child was the only one in the room for the woman.

Kaye stood silently observing this precious moment. Soon the wee one was sleeping peacefully. It was then that the older woman looked up, startled to see Kaye in the doorway.

"I'm sorry," Kaye said. "Sister Madeline is taking me on a tour of some of the wards, but she was detained for a few moments. The staff said I could look around and observe. I heard the child cry, so I came to see if I might help." She paused, having spoken softly so as not to awaken the sleeping child. "You have such a gentle way of comforting."

The woman responded with a blush. "I'm sure anyone could have done what I did. It's so heartbreaking to see little ones diagnosed with cancer." She brushed the child's hair gently with her hand. "The doctors had to take bone marrow. It's painful, but to a toddler it's also terrifying."

The woman had tears in her eyes.

"Oh my," Kaye said, shocked at the child's diagnosis. She was also surprised the woman had such an excellent command of English. There was only a hint of an accent. Her beautiful smile was oh so gentle.

Kaye walked over and knelt by the rocker, looking up at the older woman. "As a grandparent, this must be awful for you."

This brought a smile to the woman's face. "Well, dear, I am a grandmother, but not of this little one."

"You're not? But you held the child so lovingly." Kaye fought for the right word, "As tenderly as if it was your own."

"Well, I do love children. All children. That's why I volunteer here at Our Lady of Mercies Hospital. I guess every little bit helps. There's so much need, and it seems so little help. Are you considering volunteering, dear? I can assure you it is very rewarding." She leaned forward and whispered, "You know, I do believe Jesus' Mother gives us her compassion to love those who need it."

Kaye couldn't help but return the woman's smile. Something about her seemed oddly familiar, but she couldn't place what it was.

A nursing sister swished into the room. "Oh, Josephine, you've done it again! You certainly have the touch of our Lord's Mother." She took the sleeping child from the older woman, allowing her to stand.

Leaving the child with the sister, the older lady motioned for Kaye to follow her into the hall. Turning to Kaye, she said encouragingly, "Really, dear, anyone can do it."

Kaye shook her head. "Let me assure you, everyone can't do what you just did. I for one would be terrified."

Sister Madeline burst into the hall, nearly colliding with the two women. Initially, she appeared astonished that the two would be conversing together. Her amazement quickly gave way to fervent enthusiasm. "Isn't that just like our wonderful God? He always does what we can't!"

Kaye and Josephine looked at her and then at each other in total bewilderment.

"I knew this was your day to volunteer, Josephine. When Ms. McDonald made a surprise visit to our hospital, I thought, *Wouldn't it be wonderful if the two could meet?* After all, it was on account of your Sophia that Ms. McDonald agreed to speak at our charity dinner."

"Ms. McDonald is in the hospital?" The older woman sounded incredulous.

Sister Madeline looked shocked. "Oh, you didn't formally meet?"

Kaye, on the other hand, was simultaneously shocked, incredulous, and feeling like she might faint. *Oh my gosh! This is Max's mother, and I've stolen her baby.* She tried to slow her racing brainwaves. *Well, he's not her baby. But oh my gosh, how she must miss him and I've hoarded him. She's bound to hate me forever!*

Fortunately for Kaye, her boardroom mask was securely in place. She pasted a smile on her face, hoping no one could see behind her façade.

Josephine was obviously very embarrassed. "My dear, I'm so very, very sorry. I thought you were looking to volunteer at the hospital. Instead you're the one who is going to speak at the fundraiser. That is such an important job!"

Kaye instinctively reached out and clasped Josephine's two hands in hers. Looking the older woman directly in the eye, she said, "Mrs. Carron, I need to tell you something. This is the truth. Maybe you don't think you could get up and speak like me, and maybe you think what I'm doing is important, but let me tell you, I could never comfort and quiet that child like you did." She paused to allow her words to register not only with Mrs. Carron but the nursing sisters and other staff and volunteers, all of whom were now listening attentively. "If a hospital fails to provide comfort through its staff and volunteers, as you did that wee patient, no amount of fundraising can ever justify its existence." She reached out and embraced the older woman.

Kaye stood back, tears in her eyes. "What I have seen in that room with Mrs. Carron and the child, I am seeing throughout this hospital. This is why I needed to visit. I had to come and *feel* the heart of Our Lady of Mercies Hospital. Thus, when I do get up and speak on your behalf, I can do so with the passion that all of you have for this place!"

Kaye had totally captivated her listeners. In fact, Sister Madeline's face beamed as she announced that she'd just been informed that the bishop had arrived. With that, she shepherded both women back to the hospital's administrative wing. Formalities were exchanged, and soon a very emotionally drained M.K. was heading back to her hotel.

Philippe was wearing his mouse-with-big-piece-of-cheese expression when Kaye joined him in the limo. "Looking at you, M.K., I gather you got the emotional connection you desired?"

She smiled and nodded. "And you?"

"I got exactly what we need for that fundraising night, including the full approval of the bishop and the hospital board."

Unfortunately, bad news was soon to follow. Once they returned to the hotel, they learned that Frank Carron, Mr. Italy himself, was demanding $100,000 more for his property than the agreed fair trade value.

"Just give it to him," several board members said to her. "It's routine business for Chicago."

She reminded them that they had all agreed on a uniform purchase formula based on established criteria. What she knew, which no one else knew, was that should she capitulate, the "Chicago way" would open both of them up to suspicion of insider trading.

She had no choice but to say no to Mr. Carron's demands, and with this declaration came the potential to veto Kayleen's move to Chicago.

She met Frank Carron for the first time late Wednesday afternoon. She was shocked at how closely Max resembled his father. Both were strikingly handsome men. Though only in his early sixties, Frank's hair was pure white. Coupled with his olive skin, it made him look very distinguished.

But unlike your son, you possess not one pliable fiber in your body, of that I am certain!

In fact, that was everyone's fear. Kayleen had been warned that Carron wouldn't change his mind once it had been set. Thus, if Kayleen didn't capitulate, its corporate move would have to be scuttled. One look at the man and Kaye had to agree with this assessment.

"M.K.," Clarin said, breaking into her thoughts, "this is Mr. Carron's lawyer."

Let me guess, Kaye fumed to herself. *His name is Mr. Scallion.*

The man extended his hand graciously to her. "My name is Scallion."

She extended hers and brusquely replied, "Mine, sir, is McDonald."

Clarin simply closed his eyes and prayed, *"God, I don't even know if You exist, but if You do, a little help here would be nice!"*

chapter seventeen

Tony's and Sophia's jaws dropped, stunned by Jack's revelation of his true identity. They stared in disbelief at one another, then at Jack, who by now was at the cashier paying their bill.

Dave folded his hands on the table, lips pursed. Sophia's eyes started to mist up; over what, Dave couldn't fathom.

Finally she choked out, "Why are you doing this to us?"

"What?"

"Why are you messing with us like this?"

Dave spoke softly. "Sophia, we're not messing with you. We're telling you the truth and trying to take you safely to Max."

"What do you mean *safely*?" snarled Tony.

"Tony, you have a gun. We allowed it so you could feel secure."

The couple looked at each other and slowly nodded. "So we're... I mean, *I'm* the danger?" Tony asked, almost meekly.

Now it was Dave's turn to nod. "Let's just say you have the potential to be the danger. Because of the situation."

"What situation?" Sophia questioned anxiously.

"Jack sent your brother to prison for a crime he never committed," Dave said. "Something you knew then, and we know now. Also, the sentence was harsh for a first-time offender, even if he had been guilty. Jack Walters brought a lot of pain to your family." Sophia laid her head against her husband's shoulder and wept softly as Dave continued. "So us coming to take you to Max had the potential to be very explosive."

"*Had* the potential?" Tony asked.

"You alone can affirm that, Tony. At least we're now communicating the truth to you and I view that as a good thing."

Out of the corner of his eye, Jack observed Dave talking to the Marconis. After paying the bill, he slipped into the men's room. A few minutes later, he returned to the table.

Dave noted that Tony's hands were on the table. *The guy's at least trying, I'll give him that.*

Tony rubbed the back of his hand across his mouth. "You're really Jack Walters?"

Jack sighed and reached into his breast pocket. Fortunately, the move didn't threaten Tony. Jack pulled out his ID and gave it to the two, who studied it intently.

Sophia bit her lip. "I guess I shouldn't have said what I did about the D.A.'s office."

"Why not?" Jack said. "If it's true, it's true."

She nodded, then pointed at Dave. "So who are you?"

Dave handed his identification to the two.

"You're a cop," Tony exclaimed, frowning. "The chief of police at Summerside."

"Why wouldn't Max want us to know he was hurt before now?" Sophia moaned. "I can't understand why he'd reach out to you and not to us."

"Can I ask a question?" Jack asked. "Did you two go to your parents before or after you got married?"

"After," they both replied.

"Why?"

"If we'd gone to our parents before, they would have yanked us apart," Sophia said.

Tony nodded. "Frank would have killed me!"

The two looked at each other and back to Jack and Dave, putting the pieces together.

"Max has a girlfriend?" Sophia squeaked in disbelief.

Both Dave and Jack smiled and nodded.

"Wait a minute," Tony snapped. "Clarification: he has a *girl*friend?"

Sophia shot daggers at her husband. "Tony!"

"Look, babe, anything's possible. Last I heard, the pen isn't co-ed."

Jack and Dave covered their mouths to block laughter escaping. It wouldn't be wise to be frivolous.

"So, Max's girlfriend came to you because you're a minister, not just a judge." Sophia was clearly grabbing desperately for any silver lining she could find.

"That's sort of it," Jack said. "They're marrying tomorrow morning."

Sophia's whole demeanor changed. "Oh, and we can be there because Max knows we wouldn't interfere."

"*Couldn't* interfere, more like," snorted Tony. "I mean, after what he did for us."

"Do you have her picture?" Sophia asked excitedly.

For the first time that day, Jack actually laughed. "Sorry, no. That's for him to share."

Dave held up his hand. "Can we continue this discussion in the car? The sooner we get on our way, the sooner we'll get there and the sooner you'll get all your answers. But before we leave, I suggest we all take a bathroom break."

"I already did," Jack volunteered. "I'm going to get some water. Anybody else want something?"

"Water for me," Dave said.

"Me too," added Sophia.

"Get me a beer, judge!"

Jack stared at Tony.

"Just seeing if you were on your toes, Your Honor. I'll have water too!"

The atmosphere in the vehicle had definitely altered. Sophia was beside herself at the thought of not only seeing her brother but seeing him get married. Her cross-examination continued the moment the car began to move. "Surely you can tell us some things?"

"Is she a shrink?" Tony asked. "After all, what other type of woman could he meet in prison?"

"No," Jack said. "That's a good guess, though. But they didn't meet in prison."

"He knew her before he went to prison?" Sophia asked, wide-eyed. Dave and Jack didn't say anything. "That means he met her after he got out."

"Right, Mrs. Marconi," Jack said.

This seemed to horrify her. "He's only known her for six months!"

Jack looked in the rear-view mirror. "How many months did you and Tony know each other?"

Tony grinned and eyed his wife. "Less than three months."

"Is she Sicilian?" Sophia asked.

Jack shook his head. "Definitely not!"

"Italian?"

"Nope!"

"Catholic?" Sophia's voice now sounded almost pleading.

"Sorry."

"They have nothing in common," she wailed.

"Yes, they have," whispered Jack

"What?" Sophia crossed her arms in front of her, and the tone of her voice was as defiant as her posture.

Dave looked at Jack. "One, two, three…" and in unison, they said, "Love!"

Tony burst out laughing and was rewarded with a swat.

"That's not funny, Tony!" Sophia pouted. "You know Max never even looked at a girl before."

"Maybe so, sweetheart, but after staring at guys for six years, perhaps he finally figured out there had to be something better on the planet."

His remark got everyone laughing, even Sophia, and before they realized it they were at the Summerside exit. It was 11:30 p.m.

"Hey, can we get a cup of coffee somewhere?" Tony begged.

"That's a great idea for us all," Jack said. "We can get some for Max and the girls."

"What girls?" Sophia asked, hopeful that Max's future wife would be there.

"Our wives," Dave replied nonchalantly. He turned towards the back seat. "We can stop for coffee, sure, but not with the gun."

"What do you mean?" Tony asked.

"I'm chief of police. My men frequent the coffee shop. They know me. They know Jack. They could come to us, like ants to honey. You, sir, have a gun. Are my concerns registering with you?"

Tony reached into his holster and pulled out his gun. "Here, put it into the glove compartment."

Dave did so, thanking him.

Coffees were obtained. Other cops did come to chat. To Tony's and Sophia's amazement, when they were introduced as Max's sister and brother-in-law, everybody warmly accepted them.

Everything was going great until they turned onto Independence Drive.

Tony was the first to spot the car parked out front. Alarm bells began to go off within him. "Keep driving," he said to Jack. "Go back to the corner store and get some milk. Do as I say!"

"What are you trying to pull?" Jack asked.

Tony was visibly angry. "That car was doing surveillance. Or are you trying to tell me Max was in the vehicle making out with his sweetie," he said sarcastically. "I'm not stupid! What are *you* guys trying to pull on us?!"

"Dave, did you ask for surveillance when we were away?" Jack questioned, alarmed himself. "Tony's right. There was a guy in the driver's side."

Jack continued down the street to a nearby convenience store. They stopped and he went in to buy milk.

"I'm sorry, Tony, I really wasn't paying attention," Dave said apologetically. "I was simply thinking of getting home."

"Look," Jack said. "I have an automatic door opener for the garage. We can drive in, shut the door, and get out."

"Give me my gun back."

"Fine, Tony, here it is." Dave handed it back. "But do us a favor. Keep the safety on."

"Now, you do what I tell you," Tony ordered. "We'll drive in like you said, but as you approach the house Sophia and I will duck down. When you get into the garage, before you close the door behind you, flip your trunk open. Dave will get out and make a point of taking out the golf clubs."

"Why in heaven's name would we do all that?" Dave asked.

"Cause if the buddy in the car is after His Honor, he'll know that he's home now but not alone. It'll seem like it's been a nice late fall day, two guys out getting in their thirty-six holes or whatever else before winter hits."

Jack looked at Dave. "Not a bad strategy, Chief. Not bad at all."

Tony's instructions were followed to a T, except Dave also carried a milk bag to offer prying eyes an explanation as to why the car had driven off the first time. At last, the garage door closed.

The house door opened a crack.

"Jack? Jack, is that you?" came a low whisper.

"Yeah, it's me," Jack said. It was too dark to see who the voice belonged to

"Did you see the car on the street?"

"Yeah."

"Whose is it?"

"Why are you whispering?" Sophia loudly proclaimed. "The car is in the street. You're in a closed garage. I've had enough of this." She strode to the partly open door. "Turn the light on now, Jack!"

He obeyed and she yanked at the house door. To her surprise, she found her brother lying on the floor, with a gun pointed directly at her.

"Max!" Sophia said. "What are you doing?"

"Watch his leg! Be careful," Jack cried out as he raced to Max's defense.

"Would the two of you please put away your guns?" Dave said.

Tony, Sophia, and Max looked at each other, stunned.

"Why were you whispering?" Sophia repeated like a broken record.

"So as not to wake Marnie and Sue," Max stammered.

"Where are they?"

"In my bed."

"Their wives are in your bed? Where?" Sophia was now the sister Max remembered—in full command! Instinctively, he responded by pointing to the dining room.

Sophia snorted and charged into the room, hitting the light switch as she did. Sure enough, in the bed were two startled women.

"Oh," Sophia said apologetically. Emotionally overwhelmed at discovering Max alive and in the home of a man she had hated for the past six years, Sophia lost it. She wheeled around and started to bawl.

Max was standing between Dave and Jack, balancing himself with his crutches.

"I don't believe a word you've been feeding me this whole trip! It's all a pack of lies!" Sophia tore back to Max, sobbing. "And I don't believe you were hurt at all!"

In one yank, she pulled down his pajama pants just as Marnie and Sue entered the room. Tony blinked, in utter disbelief at his wife's behavior. The other five and Rufie just stood there frozen. Fortunately for Max, he'd worn his briefs under his pjs. Sophia collapsed in front of her brother, staring at the big ugly scar that extended from his groin region to below his left knee. The marked muscle loss of that leg was evident to all.

Her tears commenced to flow like Niagara Falls. "Oh Max! Oh no! I'm so sorry. I'm so very, very sorry!"

It took everyone's efforts to finally calm her. Even Rufie decided it inappropriate to either growl or bark. He simply lay down, nose between his paws, and watched the human antics.

Dave stepped back and uttered a silent prayer. *Dear Jesus, thank you that she didn't have the gun!"*

Marnie offered Sophia some warm milk. Everyone agreed that Sophia didn't need caffeine, but they most certainly did.

Sue helped Marnie bring out some fruit, veggies, and sandwiches. By now, Sophia had quieted down. She sat on the sofa between Tony and Max, snuggling into her brother.

Tony grinned. "Yep! She's a purebred Sicilian, a very sensitive and expressive person."

That's when Jack chose to go into his office. He returned with a large manila folder. "Okay, confession time. I need to explain why Dave and I went to New York to bring the two of you here."

"You mean Max didn't ask you?" Sophia exclaimed.

"I was going to, right after I got married," Max clarified. "If memory serves, I don't recall either of you seeking my permission when *you* married."

"That's true, Soph," Tony reminded his wife, hoping to avoid any further outburst.

"Sophia, when Max was in prison, he qualified to participate in an innovative educational program," Jack said. "Because of his undergraduate honors degree, he was allowed to take some law courses from Harvard. Bottom line: Max aced each one. One opportunity led to another and he ended up with enough credits for an LLB."

Sophia's eyes sparkled. "Really? You did that, Max? I'm so proud of you!" She leaned over and gave him a kiss.

"Let me cut to the chase. You both know Max didn't do what he was accused of." Jack held up his file. "The evidence on the case supports this. The trial judge—me—messed up. The prosecutor and defense both ignored the evidence, and neither did their jobs at trial."

Tony was about to respond, but Jack held up his hand, stopping him. "I know, Tony, the only one with even a remotely good motivation was the defense."

Marnie frowned at Tony. "But why would your family have let the defense perform so poorly, thus letting someone you knew was innocent go to prison?"

"Someone tried to kill Tony," Dave explained. "Tony's and Sophia's fathers were feuding at the time, but they wanted to bury the hatchet. So they pledged not to pursue the real culprit, in case the answer opened old wounds."

"And I followed an old justice's very ethnically biased advice, in order to rush the case through the system," Jack said. "As a result, I threw the book at Max and arrived back home in time for our family vacation. Like I had promised you, Marnie."

"When Jack took the Supreme Court appointment, Sophia, he was promised that he needn't start for two months," Max explained to his sister. "He and Marnie had planned an extended vacation with their daughters. Jack also thought for sure that we'd appeal the sentence."

"Our prosecutor," Jack said, "was obviously interested in personal advancement, regardless of the cost to anyone else."

Max scowled. "Jack wants us to look at the case to see if the evidence points to who *did* try and kill Tony. I already told him I won't, because I promised Pop

I wouldn't." He looked sternly at Tony. "Neither can you, Tone! You promised your Pop and mine the same."

Sophia suddenly stood up. "Well, I'm not bound by any of your archaic male rules! I'll look." She bounced over and squeezed into the easy chair with Jack.

He looked at her and smiled. "I thought you just might."

Sophia began flipping through the transcripts, one page after another. Suddenly she stopped, her entire facial features changed.

"Bingo," Dave whispered.

She went livid, then began to wail and pound the papers. "No! Oh God, no!"

Max and Tony stared at her, noticeably afraid to ask who might be involved.

"It's not us! You went to jail for no reason, Max. Absolutely, no reason!" She slumped back into the chair, dejected.

Tony came to his feet and stared at his wife. "What do you mean, Soph?"

"They weren't Sicilian at all, not even Italian! It was those creepy brothers."

"Who?" Jack asked.

Sophia was in tears again. "I know I was a horrible flirt, Max. I did it to tease you. You always ticked me off. Everywhere I went, you were there—my own personal secret service!" She stood, hands on hips, toe-tapping and looked around the room. "Don't you remember those two creepy brothers? They were fondling that blonde cheerleader. Probably got her pregnant, because she left campus three weeks into the semester." She stomped her foot. "Don't you remember, Max? That's when they started making passes at me, but since you were always there, they cooled it. By then I'd met Tony and only had eyes for him."

Dave watched Tony and Max carefully. He could tell both men were starting to recall who Sophia was describing.

"Yeah, I remember," Max said. "Thickset, sort of ugly guys, light-colored hair."

"Like in a crewcut," Tony added.

Max shook his head. "I can't recall their names."

"You don't have to," said Jack. "It's all here."

Sophia bit her lip. "It's Leuzecki... Jon and Alex Leuzecki!"

Now it was Dave's turn to leap across the room. "What did you say?"

"You're not sitting on my lap." Jack peered at his friend over his horn-rimmed glasses and laughed as he showed Dave the names.

Dave scanned the page, "Oh, Wow!"

"Do you know these guys?" Jack asked.

"I think I may. At least, I know of that name. The ones I know are in New Jersey, Newark area. The same area as the Bastaldi family."

"Lou," Sophia interjected.

"Is that family of yours?" Jack asked.

Max nodded. "Distant cousins, Jack."

"Are they connected to the Leuzecki brothers?"

"Not by love," Dave ventured. He stopped abruptly and weighed what he should reveal. He decided it was time to clear the air. "It's suspected that the Leuzeckis are responsible for the murder of a Newark police officer and an FBI agent. It's also suspected that the Leuzeckis are trying to lure Bastaldi into a mob war."

"Why do you say that?" Max asked.

Dave looked around the room. "This is classified. If I tell you, it can't leave this room."

"Meaning you can't share it with Pop, Pepi, or Lou," Max said, glaring at Sophia and Tony. They nodded.

"Lou Bastaldi likely already knows," said Dave. "I'm sure of it. I'm also sure he's biding his time."

"Why do you say that?" Jack asked. "What are the Leuzeckis suspected of doing?"

"Bastaldi's father, or maybe his uncle, was in a nursing home. Gunmen burst into the home, killing him and another old fellow. Two or three bystanders were injured."

"Uncle Tommy!" Sophia said in horror.

Dave nodded. "Yep. Tomaso Bastaldi was the old man's name."

"But our family hasn't been informed of Uncle Tommy's death," Sophia mused.

"Likely because Lou plans on handling it himself," Max said quietly.

Dave stood and stretched. "Well, Your Honor, things don't look as hopeless as before."

"What do you mean?" Sophia asked.

"Jack knows an injustice has occurred and he'll take steps to right it," Dave said. "There are two ways to acquit Max. One is through the courts. The other is to have those responsible for the crime confess."

"The court route could be problematic for my father," Sophia commented.

Jack nodded. "Very true, counselor, very true."

"But if an old case has new implications, there's a greater likelihood of finding a solution outside the courts," Dave said. "It seems to me that the Leuzeckis may have stirred up too many hornets."

"Including the police, the Bureau, and the mob," Jack said. "We may have some unusual allies to help us right a six-year wrong."

Marnie stood up, interrupting them. "Folks, I hate to poop on all this strategizing, but it's now two in the morning, and our bride will be arriving by eight, which means we need to be up by six to get breakfast ready, decorate the dining room, and dress!"

"So, Sergeant Major, if we want any sleep, it's now or never," Jack said. "I suggest that Dave and Sue sleep here to appease whoever's outside. Tony and Sophia, we've got a room for you. Max can have his bed back, and Rufie, you get the queen-size all to yourself."

"Jack, can I say a prayer of thanksgiving before we go to bed?" Max asked.

"By all means!"

So he did—a beautiful one at that!

Wow, has he changed, Sophia thought as she gave her brother a goodnight hug and headed up the stairs.

chapter eighteen

An annoying buzz resounded in Jack's ear seemingly seconds after going to bed. Before his mind was able to even connect sound with source, Marnie reached over and turned off the alarm clock. Rolling over, she threw her arms around him.

"I'm so excited and happy for Kaye and Max, aren't you?" She planted a kiss on the nape of his neck.

Happy and excited weren't the adjectives that popped into his mind, the clock having so rudely awakened him after only four hours sleep. Nonetheless, he had to chuckle to himself. He'd learned over the years that if Marnie was happy and excited, it wasn't long before the whole household was equally so.

Marnie was already out of bed, declaring that she would shower first.

The wedding day had at last arrived! Soon Marnie had the house in a beehive of activity—and yes, happy and excited! Max's bed was relegated to Jack's study and Marnie's elegant dining room resurrected.

"How long did you live in their dining room?" Sophia whispered.

"A little over two months," Max replied. "Boy, is it ever great to be mobile again!"

"Well, move yourself upstairs," Sue said. "It'll soon be time to dress. It won't be too long before Kaye arrives."

"Kaye? Is that her name?" Sophia quizzed. "It's a pretty name. Is it short for—"

"Kathleen." Max grinned, tweaking her nose. "And you aren't going to weasel anything more out of me!"

Sophia feigned a pout. "Not even when the wedding takes place?"

"As soon as the bride arrives," Dave said with a laugh.

"Is it kosher to ask if you're having a honeymoon, and the when and where?" Tony queried.

"Immediately after the ceremony," Max replied, his finger pointing in the direction of Kaye's house.

"You're leaving immediately?" wailed Sophia. Her face clouded over. "Where are you pointing?"

"To Kaye's house," Jack said. "It's the one you passed when we came in last night."

Sophia's eyes widened. "You're taking your new wife to her own house for her honeymoon?" Her tone clearly registering disapproval.

"Max can't travel any distance for a few more weeks," Marnie said. "Doctor's orders."

Dave spoke reassuringly. "Don't worry, Sophia. They'll be back for supper at six. You'll have the opportunity then to get better acquainted with your new sister-in-law."

"But why don't they just stay here so we can visit? They could go home after supper," Sophia objected, perplexed at her brother's most unusual wedding plans.

Tony rolled his eyes, then cocked his head at his wife and grinned. "Because, dear, they obviously want to get some sleep!"

"So can we," Marnie added. "When they leave, we can go back to bed. But Max, don't forget your water exercises."

"Water exercises?" Tony was all ears. "Is this some new-fangled postnuptial stuff?"

Jack began to laugh. "Nope, Max needs to exercise his leg. Water offers the best physio, since he can't bear any weight on it. Kaye installed a new indoor pool. Afterwards we'll take you to the mall. You can pick up some suits for yourself, and tomorrow we'll all go swimming with them."

Suddenly the room erupted with the sound of Rossini's William Tell Overture. Sophia looked frantically for her purse. "Oops, Pop's phone!"

"Pop's phone?" Max glared at his sister.

"Uh-huh," Tony said. "He bought her a private phone that only he could use. Charger included. God help us if we let it run down or don't answer it."

"That's Pop?" Max was visibly alarmed. He mouthed, "Don't you dare say anything about me," accompanied by hand motions that indicated he'd strangle her if she did.

"I won't!" was mouthed back.

"It's 7:30 a.m. here, which means it's 6:30 in Chicago," Jack said incredulously. "He calls this early?"

"Only if he has concerns that I could be abusing his princess," Tony replied glumly.

Max grinned. "Nothing's changed!"

"Why would he think there'd be trouble?" Sue asked, puzzled.

"It means he called our house late last night. Our housekeeper would have said we were away, with the kids at my parents. So he'd have called them. He probably got Mom, who'd have gushed about us going on a romantic date and warned him not to dare call until morning."

Jack nodded to Max. "Interesting family."

"Don't laugh!" Max said, glowering. Sophia turned off the phone and joined the conversation again. "Sophia, so help me, you had better not have said anything about me." He clearly wasn't kidding.

"Don't worry, I didn't. But why don't you want him to know about you?"

"Because I want two weeks alone with Kaye, living in our house. I figure I've earned two weeks!"

"How come your Pop didn't want to speak to me? He could have given me his 'be a good husband, even though I know she's a handful' lecture'," Tony quipped.

Sophia started to scowl but instead began to laugh. "Because for the first time I can remember, he's really in a quandary."

"About what?" Max asked.

Sophia looked around the room, "Okay, I guess since Kaye's family will soon be ours, I can tell you. But like Chief Dave made us promise earlier, no one can say anything! Promise?"

Everyone agreed to the promise—except Dave and Jack, who just looked at one another. Sophia paused, waiting for their response.

"What you're about to tell us isn't criminal, is it?" Dave asked.

"Of course not!" It was Sophia's turn to roll her eyes. Once she'd gotten promises from everyone, she continued. "It has to do with M.K. McDonald."

Under the table, Jack kicked Max's good leg. Max glowered. Their antics were totally missed by the others.

"What about her?" Tony asked.

"Her company has chosen to relocate to Chicago. It seems Pop has property at the particular site they'd like. Apparently Ms. McDonald got the company to agree that there would be a uniform price to all, based on square footage, amount of land, state of building completion, etc. All the offers were based on that, and everyone was pleased."

"Except your father," Tony said.

"Right. Pop's lawyer requested an additional $100,000."

Dave raised his eyebrows. "Why would they expect that?"

"Respect," replied Tony, as if the question were a no-brainer.

"That's not the way Kayleen operates. Everyone is treated fairly and equally," Jack stated bluntly.

Max sighed. "So, that's his problem. Not much has changed in six and a half years."

"That's not it," Sophia said. "If that were all, you know Pop, he'd just hunker down, dig in his heels, and it'd be either deal or no deal."

"So there's more?" Tony asked.

"Much, much more." By now Sophia was grinning broadly. "Last week, I asked Ms. McDonald to be the speaker at the annual Our Lady of Mercies Hospital fundraiser. It's in Chicago. She agreed and the dinner is only a few weeks away."

Everyone was nodding their heads.

"You know about this?" Sophia asked, surprised.

"No," Jack lied. "How would we know? We were just nodding in agreement. Letting you know we were listening."

"Oh, right." So Sophia continued. "Pop knows I asked a favor of M.K. McDonald and she agreed. Ms. McDonald asked to visit the hospital and fitted it into her busy schedule. While there, Ms. McDonald was allowed to wander through the wards. She met—"

"Let me guess," Max interrupted. "Mamma!"

"Right, only she didn't know it was Mamma," Sophia said, gesturing with her hands. "You see... Mamma volunteers there. She loves helping in the children's ward. She was comforting a child when Ms. McDonald walked into the room. Apparently, Mamma's ability to sooth the little one really impressed Ms. McDonald. She complimented Mamma and the whole staff on the love and compassion she saw in the hospital. It was very special to Mamma!"

"So, everyone at Our Lady of Mercies Hospital, including your mother, loves Ms. McDonald?" Jack said.

"Why does that not surprise us?" whispered Sue discreetly to Marnie.

"Pop should just take Kayleen's offer and be done with it!" Max said emphatically.

"He can't do that, Max," Tony said. "It's not respectful!"

"Trust me, Tone," Max said. "It'll be a lot more disrespectful if he takes more.

I don't want to be a prude but I'm thinking of my marriage, not Pop's dilemma. It's moments away. Is everything ready? Dave, you got the ring?"

"Affirmative. How about I give it to Tony? He can be your best man."

One look at Tony and everyone knew this would be a big honor for him... a huge sign of respect.

Max grinned. "Great idea! Will you do that for me, Tony?"

"Honored."

"I have the paperwork right here," Jack stated.

"We've got the room decorated," the girls announced as Marnie opened the French doors into the living room. It looked beautiful. Everywhere they looked, they saw rose-colored bows and white tulle with sequins that glittered in the light. Two large vases with a dozen long stem roses graced the mantle.

"Wow, great job! I'm impressed," Max said. "Thanks so much for doing this for Kaye and me."

Marnie smiled. "And we have your boutonniere and Kaye's corsage. Note the use of burgundy and green."

Max bit his lip. "Yeah, those are her favorites."

In short order, everyone reappeared dressed and polished—men in the living room and ladies in the dining room. Five minutes after eight, a car drove up and the bride breezed through the front door to be met in the vestibule by Dave. He had been assigned the role of father of the bride.

"Dave, there's a car out there with people in it," Kaye said. "Who are they? Are they press?"

"Don't know, Kaye, but don't worry. You and Max can leave in my car. Max can lie down on the back seat."

An objection rose from the living room. "What?" Max said.

"Max, we don't want press, be a sport!" a woman's voice pleaded from the hall.

"Say okay and get used to it," was the best man's advice.

"Okay, whatever you want, love." Max laughed. "Let's just do this before I run away."

"You got the brace off! Well done, Mr. Carron!" Kaye replied. "I just saw Matt run into his house. He should be here in five minutes. We need to wait for him."

"We'll honor the bride's request," Jack replied.

"While we're waiting, do you want to hear the latest news from Chicago?" Kaye asked.

"M.K. McDonald and Frank Carron are squaring off," chortled Max.

"Don't even go there," she said. "I refuse to even think about that today."

"So, Kaye, tell us the rumors," Marnie shouted from the dining room.

"Mr. Massimiliano Carron is gay!"

"What?" said Marnie, shocked.

"Oh yeah, that's an old one," murmured Sophia.

Kaye continued. "Well, the Italian community doesn't go too much for that, as anyone who watched *The Sopranos* knows."

"See," Tony hissed to Jack and Max. "It's because of that crap that it's important to garner respect for Italians in the greater community."

"Any other rumors?" yelled Max.

"As a result of the gay rumor, Massimiliano is dead!"

Max's jaw dropped. "You're kidding!"

"Nope. Girl Guide honor. And I should also point out that my well-informed driver took me down Maple Grove Drive. Very impressive!"

"It is lovely," Sophia said softly to Sue and Marnie. "We were raised there."

"And?" Max shouted.

"My aide fell in love with Mr. Carron Jr.'s house. He thinks we should buy it." With that, Kaye burst out laughing.

Conversation ended when Matt came bursting through the back door. "Do you know there's a guy out front watching the house?"

"We know," reverberated throughout the downstairs. "And we don't know who."

"You can find out who," Max replied. "But only *after* we're married."

"Matt, you and Rufie can fight over which one of you is the flower girl and which is the ring bearer," yelled Sue.

Dave pointed to the living room. "Guys are in there."

Matt stepped into the room and gasped. "Wicked! It looks like a real wedding!"

"It *is* a real wedding, Matt," Jack said.

Matt noticed Tony. "Who's he?"

"My brother-in-law Tony. My sister Sophia is with your mom and Marnie. Can we do this now, Jack?" Max was almost pleading.

"That's only half of an intro, bro!" shouted Sophia. "You haven't told us who he is."

"This is Matt Davidson," Max replied testily. "Sue and Dave's son."

Matt waved to Sophia and shook hands with Tony. "Pleased to meet you."

Sequestered in the hall, the bride exchanged a shocked look with Dave. "Do they know about me?"

"Not exactly," Dave said with a smile. "They know you're female, non-Italian, Protestant, and named Kaye."

Some sharp claps of the hand interrupted their conversation. "Okay, everybody, listen up!" Marnie said, jumping into wedding coordinator mode. "Matt will start the CD. As the music plays, we girls will join the men in the living room. Wait a few moments, Dave, then escort Kaye in to join Max and the rest of us. When we're all together, shut off the player, Matt."

The music began. Sophia started to cry, then Marnie, and then Sue.

When Dave and Kaye entered the room, it was amazing that nobody fainted. Max stood in shock, absolutely mesmerized. He had never seen Kaye so radiant. Indeed, she glowed. As for Tony and Sophia, the words *shocked, stunned,* and *speechless* didn't come close to encompassing their emotions. Massimiliano Carron would momentarily be saying "I do" to M.K. McDonald herself!

Following the service, Matt drove Kaye's car to his house, went in only to exit the back door, and scamper back to Jack's. His return was out of sight of the surveillance car's prying eyes.

Kaye had put one of Jack's wind breaker's over her wedding dress and wore one of Marnie's caps. She hoped whoever was in the car wouldn't recognize her true identity. She backed Dave's car out of the garage and drove down Independence Drive to her house. Matt had retrieved the automatic door opener from her car. Consequently, she was able to enter and close the door before either she or her hidden passenger exited the vehicle.

None of these movements escaped the eyes that silently watched from the parked car. Yet it remained stationary, keeping its vigil of the Walters' house.

chapter nineteen

K aye and Max had barely left the Walters' driveway when Sophia turned on Jack. "You never told us he was marrying M.K. McDonald!" she sputtered.

"You never asked," Jack responded with a smile.

"Kaye's a wonderful person," Marnie offered. "Really."

Tony's big arm went around Sophia's shoulders, pulling her close. "It's not that. It's just…" He hesitated, "It's just that Max is a real okay guy, who happens to be Sicilian, and—"

"You think Kaye's attraction to him might be our culture's current fascination with the mob?" Jack said softly.

"No. Well, maybe." Sophia sighed. "I mean, M.K. McDonald could have had any guy on the planet. Someone richer, more powerful, more prestigious. Why Max?"

"Why did you marry Tony and nobody else?" Dave asked.

"Because I loved him, but this is different."

"Is it really?" asked Jack. "Sure, the two of you were of the same ethnic and Christian background, but your attraction for one another was equally problematic."

"True," Tony said, sitting down on the sofa. "But I guess what Sophia's trying to say is that we were both of the same social status. Putting it bluntly, Kaye, as you call her, is the CEO of a powerful corporation."

Sophia bit her lip. "And Max is an ex-con."

"That's part of the reason Dave and I risked bringing you here. Your brother may be an ex-con, but that doesn't define him. Sophia, you aced your exams at Columbia. Max aced Harvard's. Professor Brown has said that in all his years of teaching, Max possesses the best legal mind he's ever seen."

Sophia sat up eyes wide. "*The* Professor Arthur Brown of Harvard?"

Jack laughed. "Max has the potential for a brilliant legal career. Our justice system is most anxious that it occur on our side of the fence. Do you read me?"

"Clear so far," Tony said, "but with a criminal record, Max can't go to the bar."

"Correct," said Jack, his eyes locking on Tony's.

"That's why you want his conviction over turned?"

"That's part of it, Tony."

"And the other part?" Sophia asked in astonishment.

"Let's face it. While he's been recuperating, Max has focused on international law—more precisely, international corporate law. In that capacity, he can be of great assistance to Kayleen, whether or not he ever goes to the bar." Jack looked directly at Tony. "So here is my main reason for insisting his conviction be overturned. Even a cursory look at the evidence reveals a travesty of justice. That in and of itself demands the conviction be overturned. However, Tony, pretend for a moment that you are Max and Sophia is Kaye. Sophia's work means she has to travel internationally and appear at many state functions, several of which demand she have an escort. Your felony conviction prevents you from ever obtaining a passport."

"So I can't accompany her?" Tony's eyes darkened. "No way is another guy going to take my wife out, even if he's a crotchety old geezer!"

"Exactly," Jack said.

Sophia gasped. "Surely they both thought of this?"

"Did the two of you think of your fathers' feud when you fell in love?" Jack demanded.

They shook their heads.

"There's another point that needs to be factored into this discussion," said Dave. "They lived platonically, in very close proximity, for nearly three months."

Sue nodded. "Shared the same bed even."

"Yes," Jack said. "For nearly three months, they faced a traumatic and life-threatening situation every day."

Sophia frowned. "So where was this Mr. Kerr guy in all of this?"

Jack chuckled. "There was no Mr. Kerr."

"But the media all said there was. In fact, so did that Bureau guy!"

"Sophia, your brother was Mr. Kerr." Jack's voice was now very firm. "It was he who was critically wounded by Henry Glaxton, when Glaxton tried to make Kaye his twenty-third victim. Max needed time to recover, and the two of them had to sort out their emotions for one another. Agent Epstein, Dave, and I felt it expedient to give them that time. You have a correct read on our culture's fascination with the mob. Even if Max isn't involved, his Sicilian ancestry, M.K.'s high profile, and their role in the demise of a serial killer would have had the media clamoring for photos and stories."

"Not to mention your father arriving to whisk him back to Chicago," murmured Tony.

"Absolutely," Jack affirmed.

"You're telling me that my brother slept next to her for three and a half months and they never—"

"Were intimate," Jack said. "Yes."

Sophia looked askance. "Are you naive? What type of freak do you think my brother is?"

"I'm neither naïve nor do I think Max is a freak. Max has a brilliant legal mind and strong self-control, which I might add is a fruit of Holy Spirit's indwelling presence in Max. And he is a very rational man. Perhaps equally significant, Max is committed to upholding the honor of his family and the Sicilian community."

"Meaning what?" Tony asked.

"If they had been sexually intimate and Glaxton had succeeded in killing them, DNA tests would have revealed that Kaye and Max had had intercourse. Given Max's record and the fact that I live next door, one doesn't need a crystal ball to see that the crime would have been laid on Max's doorstep. By the way, that was the exact scenario in one of Glaxton's previous murders. A fact of which, both Max and Kaye were aware."

"We had no idea," Tony said softly.

"At one point, both Kaye and Max wrote letters to their respective families, just in case they didn't survive the attack. The letters were sealed and dated four weeks before Glaxton made his move. Kaye put them in her personal safe at Kayleen, and they also hid copies in the house. They wanted the killer stopped at all costs, even if it meant sacrificing their own lives. We've read the letter Kaye wrote to us. Your brother's letter we have kept for your parents, Sophia. I tell you, their letters are a wonderful exposé of their hearts!" Tears welled up in Jack's eyes. "They are a very special couple!"

Tony ran his hand through his thick black hair. "No wonder he was so focused on getting married and out the door."

"Mmhmm," Sue said. "And don't forget that he spent another three months immobilized by that broken leg."

Dave entered the room. No one had noticed him leave earlier. "Anyone interested in what I've gleaned about our peeping Toms?"

"You know who they are?" Jack asked.

"Yes and no."

Sue shook her head. "That's a lot of help, dear."

"The two cars are rented."

"By who, Dad?" Matt asked.

Dave groaned. "A nonexistent company, at a nonexistent address. I'm going to ask Tom, when he reports in later, to pick them up and see if we can get anything out of them."

"What's the company and address?" Tony asked.

"Lacentia Holding Company, 63 Via Grove St., Queens."

Both Tony and Sophia burst out laughing.

"It's Gus," Sophia said. "Please, don't have anyone pick them up."

"Who's Gus?" Dave demanded.

"Augustus D'Amato." Sophia giggled. "That's 'Uncle Gus's to Max and me. He's Pop's right-hand man."

Marnie reacted in alarm. "Your father is stalking our house?"

"Don't worry, Marnie," Tony said. "Why he's stalking you, I have no idea, but I can assure you it won't be to harm you or Jack."

Dave glowered. "How can you be so sure?"

"Chief, Max and Sophia's legal minds didn't pop out of thin air. It's in their genes. Trust me, if either Gus or Frank wanted to harm anyone, there would be no trace of either one."

"Lacentia is the name of the boat they traveled on to America," Sophia said. "That's where they first met. Ever since, they've been each other's trusted confidants. They would die for one another. Their wives are friends. Their kids are like a younger brother and sister to Max and me."

"So what do we do with them?" Dave asked. "They need to be gone by 4:00 p.m."

"What? Why?" Jack asked.

Dave sighed. "At four, I'm expecting Epi and some of his agents. Chief Snyder of Newark and his men will be joining us, too."

"Dave, how dare you?" Sue said with a snort. "Max and Kaye will be here at six for our wedding supper."

"Yes, dear, and this will be one of our wedding presents. I gave both Epi and the chief the information we have on the Leuzeckis. They want to meet with Tony and Sophia immediately."

"A half-dozen cops or so want to meet with Tony and me?" Sophia asked, alarmed.

"Don't worry. It's not about you. We want to see if we can collaborate and rein in these characters." Jack's eyes narrowed. "Sort of like a sting."

"Well, like you said earlier, they've angered just about everybody," Tony commented.

"Including us!" Marnie stood before them arms crossed, toe tapping, "This is supposed to be a special day for Max and Kaye!"

Over the past few moments, Sophia had grown suddenly silent. Now she burst out giggling.

"You think this is funny?" Dave growled.

"Yes, Mr. Police Chief, sir, and Your Honor." Sophia made a sweeping bow before them. "My understanding of a sting is that it doesn't consist solely of law officers."

Tony looked at his wife and started to smile. "That's right. A sting involves others not known to usually cooperate with the law. What Sophia's getting at is that the ones in the car outside your house, Your Honor, could become an asset in your effort to clear Max."

"Right on, Tone!" Sophia clapped her hands in gleeful anticipation. Marnie, could you add another five or six people to Max and Kaye's wedding party? Tony and I would gladly pay for them, won't we, Tony?" Sophia's eyes were absolutely sparkling.

"Only you have to let us bring in the collaborators our way," Tony stated.

"Meaning what?" Jack asked skeptically.

"Meaning that Marnie orders the extra food," Sophia said. "It's now 10:00 a.m. We can all get another three hours of sleep. If we get up at 1:00, I'll guarantee you the car out there will be replaced by another. Gus won't show up until the afternoon shift." She chuckled as she sat down beside Rufie, who was sprawled in the middle of the oriental rug. "You and I, boy, will take a w-a-l-k."

"Sophia, will haul out Gus and bring him here, where you," Tony pointed to Jack, "will have three empty wastepaper baskets waiting for me."

"What for?" Jack asked, completely in the dark.

"One for guns, one for knives, and one for cell phones."

"What?" Dave squawked.

"Chief, last night you wanted my gun so nobody got accidentally hurt," Tony said. "Trust me, if you want a real sting, you don't want excess weaponry floating around until everybody is on board with the plan."

"And Gus does nothing without first conferring with Pop," Sophia added. "Right now, that would infuriate Max. This will have to be Gus's coming of age party. The first time ever, I suspect, where he acts without my father's knowledge."

Dave frowned. "What makes you think Gus will cooperate with us in this matter?"

Sophia's eyes hardened. "For starters, his wife Angel is Tomaso Bastaldi's niece."

"Oh," was all Dave said.

While Jack quickly added, "We need to increase our supper guest list, dear."

In response, Marnie, the wedding organizer, stood. "Okay, I'll call Vincenzo's to increase my dinner order. I'll allow for eighteen additional meals, plus Tony and Sophia and the seven of us. Twenty-seven in all." She shrugged her shoulders and smiled. "No matter how well you plan, it seems all weddings grow bigger than anticipated." She looked at Tony. "You, sir, can help me order the appropriate wine. As for the rest of you, I'll need your help getting snacks and sandwiches ready for our late-afternoon guests. For the moment, though, I agree with Sophia: we could all use a little rest!"

chapter twenty

The moment the garage door closed, Kaye breathed a sigh of relief. "I'm glad I chose not to have those decorative windows installed in the garage door. Do you think the media has caught on to us?"

"No."

"How can you be so sure, Max?"

"Who was driving the car?"

"Me."

"So, who did the guy in the surveillance car see?"

"Oh, right. Me, of course," Kaye smiled, "And they never gave chase."

He winked. "Brilliant, Ms. McDonald. Keep it up and you might make detective someday."

"Excuse me, sir!" She laughed as she opened his car door. "I expect to be addressed by my current name."

"Which is?"

She planted herself in front of him. "The side effects of all those anesthetics and painkillers have given you short-term memory loss."

"Pardon me, Mrs. Carron!" Max grinned. "That's going to take some getting used to, hon. By the way, Kaye, your outfit is simply stunning. You looked so gorgeous I almost forgot to say 'I do.' I should have told you so earlier, I'm sorry."

Her green eyes narrowed. At first he thought he'd said something wrong. Then he noted the twinkle in her eyes.

"Hey, I paid you a compliment," he said. "What's so funny?"

In response, she leaned over and gave him a lingering kiss on the lips. He swallowed hard. Then she stepped back, allowing him to stand. "Well, I was remembering an article I once read. It said married couples begin to act alike. I just didn't figure it would take less than an hour."

Max looked bewildered. "Whatever do you mean?"

"You, a purebred Sicilian, are dishing out Irish blarney," she teased.

"No, Kaye, the compliment was real. You look gorgeous! And—"

"And?"

"It's real snuggly, too!" He said as he pulled her close.

She put her arms around his neck. "I'll be your teddy bear anytime, Mr. Carron." The banter stopped as she leaned against his cheek. "I never thought I'd see this day. My heart broke when you left in that ambulance."

"What kept me fighting, Kaye, was you. I kept thinking about how distraught you were when you spoke about your parents' death." His hand brushed her hair. "I didn't want to hurt you, so I strove to survive."

Tears filled his eyes as he spoke. He remembered how embarrassed and angry he had been the first time he cried in front of her. Then how surprised he had been when she shared that it was those tears that had allowed her to trust him.

"Max…"

Her voice jerked him back to reality. He caught the impish look in her eye and knew his moment of sensitive reflection had ended. "Yeah, Kaye?"

"We certainly have had some memorable moments in this garage."

He grinned. "If you're alluding to your bawl fest, then yes, I remember!"

"Personally, I'd rather forget that. What I was going to say is that the rest of the house is more alluring than the garage. Why don't you go in and I'll bring in our clothes?"

"Our clothes?"

"Dave and Jack put our bags in the trunk for us."

"His Honor didn't waste time booting me out the door, did he?"

"If you want the truth, I asked them to do it. In the past few weeks, I've been taking stuff over bit by bit."

Max maneuvered the two steps into the house, standing upright with his crutches the whole time.

"Very good!" she said. "You've had those crutches less than twenty-four hours and already you're taking the stairs."

He turned and flashed a mischievous grin. "It all has to do with motivation, love!" He headed down the hall to the living room, "Wow, Kaye, you even got me a leather recliner… Now that's impressive! It seems like ages since I was here."

He ran his hand pensively over the mantel.

"Don't ye dare go checking for dust, sir," she chastised good-naturedly.

He laughed as he gazed at her with his deep brown eyes. "Kaye, I never dreamt I could call this place home, but I must tell you, in the hospital… even at Jack's… I longed to be here. While I like my place in Chicago, in all my six years in prison I can't say I ever longed for it." He stood looking through the big bay window to the woods behind. "Most of the leaves are down now."

Kaye came up behind him and put her arm around his waist. "Speaking of your Maple Grove Drive residence, it looks lovely, Max."

"It's well taken care of then?"

"Indeed. I understand now why you were taken aback at this place when you learned my identity. Your place is a walled fortress."

"But I've come to really appreciate the openness of this neighborhood. If Dave discovers that car is actually stalking Jack, though…" Max frowned. "Well, you guys are going to have to rethink your security."

"I think you mean *we*, Max. You're a part of this neighborhood." She gave him a peck on the cheek. "So, dearest, are you ready to tackle the next flight of stairs?"

"Not until I check out this pool you built."

"Pool? Who told you about the pool?" She feigned a pout. "It was supposed to be a surprise!"

"Oops! The physiotherapist let it slip, but I really *was* surprised. You do realize, Kaye, that water therapy will benefit my leg greatly." He spied a door that hadn't been there before. "Is this the door to the pool?"

"Open it."

Kaye smiled as Max opened the door to reveal a spacious and empty room.

He looked at her blankly. "What's this?"

"A his-and-her office, my dear. I figured we could shop together for furniture. You need to take some ownership of the place." She laughed. "I also figured tit for tat. If I give you a say here, I get a say in refurbishing Maple Grove Drive."

"So that's it! Well, Ms. McDonald—I mean, Carron—it's no wonder Kayleen's so successful. Its CEO never stops wheeling and dealing. What's this? Are these windows? What's the view?"

One side of the room appeared to consist of a wall of blinds. He reached and tugged on one cord. The verticals parted, providing a stunning view of the pool.

Max gave a low whistle. "Wow, Kaye, that is spectacular!"

She slipped her arm around his waist. "Like it?"

"Like it? I love it. What are those two doors for?" He pointed to the doors located on the far wall of the pool area.

"Change rooms, for guys and dolls. The pool will be utilized by all the residents of Independence Drive. I had a back door installed to give easy access to the other houses. Incidentally, Matt has already volunteered to be your personal trainer." She smiled as she opened the blinds at the far end of the room. "Over here, we have our exercise room."

Max shook his head. "How on earth did you find time to plan all this?"

"I had this sick friend who slept nearly three weeks. Sitting by his bed gave me lots of time to think and plan. Nonetheless, the biggest changes have yet to be revealed."

"You're kidding."

"Nope, but you'll need to go upstairs to find them." She wiggled her nose.

"Did you install an elevator?"

"Sorry. Stairs only."

"Too bad"

"Seriously? You'd want an elevator in a house this size?"

Max cocked his head as he approached the stairs. "It's all about image, Kaye. It's pretty hard for a guy to achieve any kind of swashbuckling sexiness when he has to go upstairs on his bum!" He plopped down on the step and handed her his crutches. "But without an elevator, this will have to do. Let's go, dear, and explore all your changes."

A smile stole across her face as she watched him navigate the stairs. When he reached the top, she sat down beside him.

"Did I look that silly?" he asked in embarrassment.

She leaned her head against his shoulder. "Not at all. You did exceedingly well, but I can't help smiling. Do you realize how much you look like your father?"

"I do?"

"Absolutely, minus the white hair." She pointed to his eyes. "And those."

"Pop has brown eyes, too, I'm sure of it!"

She shook her head. "It's not just the color. It's the soul behind them," Kaye said softly. "That's definitely your mother. I met her, Max."

He grinned. "Yeah, I know."

Kaye sat up, shocked. "How could you?"

"Pop told Sophia. He apparently gave her a cell phone, just for his use."

"You're joking."

"Nope." Max laughed. "He set up the ring tone. It's Rossini's William Tell Overture. You know, the theme music for *The Lone Ranger.*"

Kaye stared at him in disbelief. "You're not serious!"

"Fraid so, Kaye," he replied, chuckling.

"He's that controlling?"

"It's not about control. It's just that he and she were always close. Somehow Sophia could connect emotionally with Pop."

"What about your mother? I mean, I was always close with Daddy, but Mummy was still his confidante."

"Well, that's how I'd describe Sophia and my parents' relationship. However, temperament wise, Sophia and Pop are very much alike."

"I can understand that, I guess," Kaye reflected. "My father and I were like two peas in a pod."

"Good way of putting it," Max said. "Anyway, Pop called early this morning to give his version of yesterday's events."

"Which was?" Kaye demanded.

Max pulled her close and kissed her. "Pop told Soph how disrespectful M.K. McDonald was to him and the Italian community by not giving him $100,000 more than everyone else's share."

Kaye's eyes narrowed to two green slits. "You've got to be kidding."

"Nope. Then he shared his real dilemma."

"There's more?" Kaye said stupefied.

"Oh, most definitely. Pop shared how 'that woman' made an impromptu visit to Our Lady of Mercies Hospital and got everybody fawning over her. Went on to say how she accidentally met Mother, but she didn't know who she was and praised her in front of everyone."

"How is that a dilemma?" Kaye asked.

"Mamma loves M.K. McDonald now," Max said, rubbing his nose against hers.

"Does Mamma know what he thinks of M.K. McDonald?"

"I'm sure she doesn't." Max chuckled. "If she did, Sophia would not have gotten the call."

"So what did Sophia tell him?"

"She suggested that there might be a compromise between Ms. McDonald and his stance. Soph knows who will have to budge and—"

"It can't be M.K. McDonald, out of respect for him," Kaye blurted. She cuddled up against her groom. "Max?"

"Uh-huh."

"Your mother is a very sweet, gentle lady. I fell in love with her."

"Apparently she did with you as well," he said quietly. "I look forward to the day they finally can meet you. I know you'll win him over, too!"

"Thank you," she said. He gingerly stood up and they began walking down the hall. "I should tell you that after Kayleen's dinner meeting yesterday, I had the opportunity to speak with George Cantaro. While I didn't tell George, I was hoping that he, as a Kayleen board member with family ties to your mother, might have an inside track to resolve the impasse between me and your father. I asked if he might convey a couple of options to the Carron camp on behalf of Kayleen."

"Does George suspect you know his connection to my family?" Max asked, concern registering in his voice.

"Don't think so. I've often bounced ideas off of George before. He's a wise man."

"What were your options? Is it kosher for me to ask?"

"Of course it's kosher. We're one now, love. At least, we soon will be. However, to demonstrate my absolute trust in you, I shall be forthright before the consummation." Her lilting laughter echoed through the house. She leaned back against the wall of the hallway and folded her arms against her chest. "Option number one: Kayleen could take the $100,000 and divide it equally among all the sellers, allotting to each one in proportion to their estimated share. Option number two: Kayleen could take the $100,000 and donate it to whatever bona fide Chicago charity that Vesuvius Enterprises would like to propose. If they want, they can select one that's beneficial to the Italian community. Surely that would indicate respect? So, Mr. Carron Jr., what do you think of those innovative compromises?"

"Not bad, M.K., not bad," he said, hobbling down the hall while stifling a laugh. "But I'm surprised you didn't send George with a third option."

"What third option?" She leapt up and darted down the hall, planting her feet in front of him. Only then did she notice the creases of mirth in the corners of his eyes. "I'm not so sure I want to hear it, but curiosity has gotten the best of me."

He leaned forward, eyeball to eyeball. "Well, you should have told George to convey to Mr. Carron Sr. that if he didn't like either of your first two options, your briefcase would be available… like it was for me, when you and I were negotiating whether or not I would remain with you to catch your perp."

He slipped quickly into the bedroom, laughing as her well-aimed swat grazed the back of his shoulders.

"That wasn't very nice," she pouted. "I told you it was totally accidental. I didn't hit you in the groin with my briefcase; you ran into it! Furthermore, I apologized and you forgave me."

"I did, I did!" He turned, still laughing, and hugged her. "But I do like how you look when, on very rare occasions, I actually pull a fast one on you."

"So?"

"So what?" Max asked, puzzled.

"How do you like it?"

He'd been so focused on her that he'd failed to notice the very major renovation. He looked around in amazement. The flower wallpaper was gone. The huge walk-in closet had been removed. In its place stood a spacious spa separated from the bedroom by a glistening wall of glass. Behind the spa, the wall was mirrored, creating an illusion of space. The bedroom walls were a very soft shade of pale green, almost to the point of being imperceptible. The plush carpet was a beautiful emerald. Earthen-shaded ceramic tile covered the floors of both bathroom and spa. The bathroom shower stall had been greatly enlarged. Twin basins had been sunken into the gold-veined marble vanity. The bedroom furniture had been replaced with ones built from a rich cherry wood. In the place of her dainty flowered duvet rested one with a green and earthen abstract pattern. For Max, everything said that a man—a real man—and his wife live here: her colors, his style! He stood mesmerized by the transformation. Nothing, absolutely nothing, of the previous room remained, except the picture of her parents.

He turned to her with tears in his eyes. "Kaye, this is wonderful! Thank you."

"I didn't have a lot of choice. Someone in a death struggle with Glaxton chose to bleed all over the old room. I do hope you noticed the absence of your 'invisible line.' The one you said existed down the center of the bed, so you had your side and I mine! A line we both agreed never to cross except to jointly listen to Glaxton's calls. I took the liberty of discarding it. I trust you will approve?" She grinned impishly. "All frivolity aside, I must point out that the spa is off-limits to you until Dr. Chandra gives her approval!"

"Yeah, the physiotherapist already lectured me on that point." Max laughed. "And I concur with your decision to discard my invisible line, even though you did so without consulting me."

Kaye walked over and pulled the cord on the vertical blinds. A soothing green pattern emerged, blending perfectly with the rest of the room.

Max sat on the edge of the bed, letting the reality of the room soak into his being. Everything old had been erased, and with it the horrific memories of those calls… his fight with Glaxton… his excruciating pain… his anguish as he struggled to cling to life… and yes, even his own shameful attack on Kaye. The old had been vanquished! The room beckoned to be filled with new, vibrant, good memories.

Kaye squatted down in front of Max and began removing his shoes.

"Gee, Kaye, I'm sorry," he started to say. "I forgot to take them off at the garage door."

She didn't reply. She simply stood and carried his crutches to the head of the bed, where she leaned them against the night table. She walked over to the dresser, lighting the large vanilla scented candle. He watched her move—so graceful, like a gazelle. She took off her flowing white angora sweater and draped it over the chair. She then returned to undo his shirt, depositing it on the chair beside her sweater.

He watched as she slipped off her floor-length skirt, letting it fall gently to the carpet. Max caught his breath as she came over and undid his belt buckle. Her eyes locked on his as she unzipped his pants. He enfolded her in his arms and fell backward onto the bed. He could feel the passion rising within him. Passion he'd felt only once before, but this time his was matched by hers.

He could feel his heart pounding as he raised her blouse. *Man, how I longed to do this,* he thought, biting his lip. Lying beside her for three months and not touching her had been sheer agony. Now his faithfulness was being rewarded.

Kaye sat up and removed her top. She looked like one of those marbled statues. Every part of her body was so beautifully sculpted; he couldn't take his eyes off her. She snuggled up close against him, her hand caressing his chest. His lips found hers.

As her bra fell away, she murmured, "I'm yours, Max. No one else's."

He couldn't stop kissing her, or she him. Soon they were one. No invisible line, no clothes, just one in embrace. His agony had at last given way to ecstasy!

chapter twenty-one

It was ten minutes to one when Marnie tiptoed downstairs to the kitchen. Jack was still asleep. She had reasoned that if the men in the surveillance car were to be brought into her home, they would surely be hungry. Making people feel at home was her specialty; it came naturally, whether in a classroom, her office, or her house.

Last night, I was afraid of those people in the car, she mused. It was interesting that when relationships were built, fear dissipated. She had felt so threatened when she first saw that mug shot of Max four and a half months ago. Now he had become one of her dearest friends.

She smiled. As for Tony, she wouldn't even need to meet him in the dark to be intimidated. However, watching him interact with his wife endeared him to her. She wondered about the strangers soon to come under their roof. Would a lasting friendship emerge with any of them?

Marnie was so immersed in her own thoughts that she would have missed Sophia's arrival had Rufie not become so animated. He bounded down the hallway, Sophia's quiet laughter intermingling with the tinkling dog tags. She entered the kitchen, roughhousing with Rufie, then stopped abruptly.

Sophia grabbed the big dog's head between her hands. "Uh-oh, maybe you're not supposed to be in the kitchen?"

Marnie laughed. "Until your brother arrived, Rufus had very defined boundaries in our house. Because Max was so immobile, we all began to joke that Rufie had become his nanny. Max got Rufie trained to bring him the paper, the mail, and when Jack wasn't around, even Rufie's pull toy. The two would engage in major tugs-of-war. In addition, Kaye stayed with us while her house was being renovated, and the dog had full access. Our boundaries got obliterated, and Rufie went everywhere, even with Jack."

Sophia grinned and blew into Rufie's face. "You've got everyone wound around your paw, you big bear!" Turning to Marnie she said, "The thing I miss most in New York is the lack of space to keep a big dog. Pop had a Rottweiler who periodically had puppies. Tony's folks never had pets. Not that I blame them; apartments aren't usually pet-friendly environments. Anyway, our children are a bit too young to be responsible with a pet right now." Sophia sighed. "When they're a little older, I hope we can get a small dog."

Marnie glanced at the pretty and vivacious young woman. "Sophia, you have the most beautiful sparkle in your eyes. Life emanates from you. Have you any pictures of your children with you?"

"I do. Do you really want to see them?" Genuine surprise registered in her voice. Then, reassured, she retreated to the living room to get her purse. Beaming widely, she returned triumphantly clutching a small photo album.

Marnie wiped her hands and sat down at the table with Sophia, who proudly displayed her brood. "The twins are five years old. Time seems to fly. This one is Michealina—she's named after Tony's Mom. We call her Micki. This is Josephine, after my mom. She gets called Jo."

"Are they active?"

"Most definitely! It's hard to tell them apart, until you've been around them a while. Micki's a little more outgoing than Jo. Actually, each one is a lot like their namesakes." She paused. "You know, Marnie, I think what freaked Pop out about M.K... or should I say Kaye?"

Marnie put her arm around Sophia. "Indeed, family privilege. We use M.K. if we're in a business setting, but truthfully sometimes I forget."

"Anyway, what Kaye said about Mom—I mean, what she publicly praised her for—that *is* my mother! Everyone in the family knows it, but none of us has ever verbalized those wonderful traits before. It obviously touched Mamma deeply, and in turn, my father's heart, to see her honored so. Yet he knows all too well what's expected of him publicly. That's why he found himself so conflicted."

Sophia turned towards Marnie and almost instinctively leaned into the older woman's embrace.

"It's really shocking how quickly Kaye sized Mamma up so accurately." She gave a little sniffle. "But knowing what I now know, maybe it's not so surprising. After all, Max does have her temperament."

Marnie tilted her head lovingly to Sophia as she turned the page and looked at another picture in the photo album. "So, who is this little go-getter?"

"That's Enrico Antonio Marconi. We call him Rici. He's a tornado on two stubby legs. You are very perceptive around children!"

"Knowing children is my job, and I do love them. I find them fascinating. I used to teach, though now I serve as principal."

Just then, Sue joined them in the kitchen. Marnie offered the photo album to her neighbor, who equally fussed over the pictures.

"As soon as you can, you must bring them to Independence Drive," Sue said, returning the album to Sophia.

Sophia nodded. "I'm a little disappointed that Max never asked me about them."

"Sophia, it was only this past weekend that we found out Max's true identity," Marnie said.

"You're kidding! How come?"

"In fairness to our husbands and Agent Epstein, they believed Max and Kaye needed the opportunity to rebound from the terrible trauma they endured. Protecting their privacy was essential for their healing. However, a situation arose on the weekend which necessitated us being told the truth. Only then did Max begin to talk about himself and his family."

"I might add very lovingly," Sue interjected.

"Yes, indeed," Marnie continued. "Max was very excited about being able to see you!"

Sue looked Sophia in the eye and lowered her voice. "For the last few weeks, Max has had only two objectives—to get mobile and get Kaye!" She burst out laughing and the other two quickly joined in.

"I understand your point precisely!" Sophia managed to say amidst her laughter.

"What's so funny?" Tony asked as he entered the kitchen, followed by Jack.

"Look who finally got up," Sue said. "It's about time, gentlemen."

Jack peered over his glasses. "Given the frivolity emanating from this kitchen, who could sleep?"

Dave walked in from the living room. "Another car has taken the place of the vehicle that was here overnight," he reported.

"Gus has arrived then." Sophia put her hands on her hips. "Time to camouflage and take a w-a-l-k with Rufie."

Dave eyed her intently. "What if the men in the car aren't your Gus?"

"If you see Rufie and I start to hightail it," Sophie said, "shoot out their tires and call for a squad car."

"I'm sure it's them," Tony replied. "But we should cover you just in case. Dave, watch by the door leading into the garage. I'll stand at the front door. Have we got those buckets ready?"

Marnie nodded. "Here are three plastic wastebaskets. Will they do?"

"Perfect," Tony said. He sniffed the air. "Hey what's cooking?"

"Oh goodness, I forgot I put the oven on automatic." Marnie pulled out a tray of strudel-like cakes. Wielding her spatula like a sword, she commanded, "Don't touch. They need to cool first."

"Wow! They're perfect, too." Tony smiled. "Just what we need to placate what will be a very cranky, crusty, enraged beast by the name of Gus... a pot of coffee to go with them would be ideal."

Sue and Marnie were assigned kitchen duty. They were ready to serve when Tony called.

"So where do you want me?" Jack queried.

Tony laughed. "Out of sight, Your Honor. Perhaps upstairs until we have Gus and his men subdued."

"Maybe you shouldn't offer coffee," Sue volunteered. "It's suggested that caffeine be avoided in stressful situations."

"Trust us, Sue." Sophia grinned. "The sooner we get coffee and food into Gus, the more amicable he'll become." She looked impishly at Jack. "Can we sit him on your throne?"

"You mean my recliner? Do whatever it takes to secure his cooperation."

"All jesting aside," Tony added, "don't give Gus an inch. He's very street-savvy and he'll object strenuously to not being in control. He'll be doing his utmost to recover that position."

"Hi," yawned a groggy voice from down the hall. "Have I missed anything?"

"Matt, dear," Sue said, "Tony's setting up his strategy to receive our guests. Perhaps you can help Marnie and me in the kitchen."

"Sure. Any way I can help Max and Kaye."

Sophia asked, "How is Rufie with agitated strangers?"

"Good point." Dave reflected a moment and added, "Matt, stay in the kitchen. Don't go out under any circumstance. Sophia, as soon as you think it appropriate to let Rufie go, Matt will call him to the kitchen and take him directly to our house. There's going to be too much activity here for Ruf."

Sophia was outfitted with a bulky sweater, a scarf flung around her face, tam on her head, and sunglasses. Rufie sat quietly, studying the transformation. Matt gave her the leash, and then the magical word was uttered: *walk*. To Sophia's delight, Rufie became an animated ball of fur. It enhanced his size and ferocity. Dave slipped to his post and Jack retreated upstairs to watch. Sue, Marnie, and Matt prayed in the kitchen, the latter oblivious to the urgency in the women's petitions.

Sophia knew all about how to manage big dogs. She had Rufus totally in control while masterfully appearing as if the dog was leading, even dragging her. She started down the road, on the side opposite the car. It appeared the dog was jerking her this way and that. As she approached the vehicle, Rufie was extremely attentive.

"Who is that, Ruf? Who are they?" she whispered.

The dog began to focus on the car. A low growl emanated from his throat.

"Good boy," she encouraged. Coming abreast of the car, she suddenly swerved into it, grabbed the handle of the back door. "Augustus D'Amatto, how dare you!"

Bingo! She had hit pay dirt. Two young men leapt out to grab her. They stopped dead in their tracks as she flung off the scarf and sunglasses.

"Sophia!" An older man sprang forward to grab her, but a threatening growl halted him midstride.

"Good boy, Ruf! Good boy!"

Rufus clearly enjoyed the compliment from his new friend and bared his teeth. This resulted in an animated and volatile conversation between Sophia and the man.

Dave watched silently from the garage door, one hand on his revolver. The only thing suggesting there might be a positive outcome was Sophia's posture. When not gesturing, her hands were placed firmly on her hips. Her toe tapped repeatedly.

I think she might be winning, he thought to himself.

To his amazement, soon Sophia was leading the three men to the house. Well, not exactly leading; it was more like herding. The two younger men walked ahead of Sophia and the one he presumed was Gus. The young bucks kept a watchful eye and appropriate distance between their rear ends and Rufie's nose.

Dave chuckled. *Wow, Ruf, Never knew you had it in you.*

Tony patiently hid behind the door to Jack's study, glock in hand.

Jack had cracked open the bedroom window, so he heard the exchange between Sophia and the older man, who was almost certainly Gus. He didn't need to speak Italian to appreciate Gus wasn't amused. Their conversation was a smorgasbord of English, Italian, and expletives. It escalated when Sophia put her hand on the doorknob to enter the house. The man's voice registered alarm, demanding to know what she was doing.

"You said Pop sent you to find Massimiliano," she said angrily. "So come get him."

"This is that frigging judge's house," Gus croaked.

"Duh! You think I don't know that?"

"You're breaking and entering."

Tony saw Gus look furtively around him, uncomfortable with the proceedings.

"I'm simply opening a door," Sophia said. "I'm not breaking anything at all. Come in, gentlemen."

"Massimiliano's here?" one of Gus's guys blurted.

Gus was clearly agitated. "Are you telling us Massimiliano's holding the judge hostage?"

"I thought Pop sent you here to bring Massimiliano home," Sophia said. "Then get inside and help us end this situation. Go!"

Finally, the men stepped into the house.

"Sophia, this is absolutely wrong," Gus protested. "I want nothing to do with this insanity!"

By this time, they had all entered the foyer of the Walters' home. Sophia closed the door quietly and locked it, positioning herself and Rufie between the men and the door.

"Put your hands on top of your heads," Tony ordered, stepping into the foyer from Jack's office. Startled, all three men obeyed. Tony kicked one plastic basket into the foyer. "Starting with you, Al, put your gun in the basket slowly and carefully. Don't try anything stupid. You're covered." Both young men complied. "Now you, Gus. All your guns. Even the little one strapped to your leg!"

"Tony!" Gus was distraught at this perceived break in their friendship. "What's going on here?"

No explanation came, only more demands. Tony instructed the one named Al to gently push the gun basket towards Tony with his foot. All of them were to keep their hands on their heads.

The first basket secured, Tony pushed out a second. "Now the knives!" As the disarmament proceeded, Gus grew even angrier. Out came a third basket. "Now put your cell phones in it."

At this indignity, Gus spun around to face Tony's glock, pointed square at his head.

"Now, Gus," Tony growled. "Now!"

He knew full well that Gus was assessing his options. However, with no other option apparent, Tony felt confident Gus's wisdom would prevail. He was no fool. For the moment, anyway, compliance was necessary. Into the third basket went their cell phones, and into Jack's office went that basket.

"Go sit in the living room like nice gentlemen," Tony demanded.

Throughout the ordeal, Rufus had sat obediently by Sophia's side, emitting low growls. Periodically she'd stroke his head, but now she bent over and whispered in his ear, "Good puppy!"

Rufie cocked his head. She was using her play voice again. The growling stopped. He crouched down in anticipation ready to leap.

"You're not going to sic him on us, are you?" whined Al.

"No. In fact, I'm removing Rufus from your presence." Sophia let go of the leash. "Go to Matt," she said to the dog.

"Rufie, come! Dinner!" Matt called to him.

"Sophia, take these baskets to Dave to stash for safekeeping," Tony directed.

She gathered them up and headed to the garage, meeting Dave on the way. He did a double take at the arsenal of weapons and quipped, "That's a few more than you and Tony had."

Gus sat glumly in the living room. Sophia knew his anger encompassed deep hurt.

"Why are you doing this?" Gus finally said. "Did Pepi put you up to it?"

Tony shook his head. "The answer is no. Now, let me ask you a question. What do you think 'this' is?"

The older man responded in Italian as Dave entered the room. The ferocity of his speech left no doubt in Dave's mind that in English the words weren't fit to be repeated.

Tony interrupted Gus's harangue. "He doesn't speak Italian," he said, jerking his head toward Dave. "It's not polite. Use English."

The next expletive Dave did understand. He also understood that if looks could kill, he would be dead.

"Fine," Gus spat. "He's your man, Tony. You translate!"

Jack had slipped downstairs unnoticed. Sophia motioned for him to join her in the dining room.

"Okay," Tony said, obviously relishing the circumstances. He nodded in the direction of Dave, and then at Jack. "Gus figures this must be a frame job… that my father decided to break the truce he and Sophia's father agreed to. See how complicated our world is?"

Jack and Dave were dumbfounded. At first they thought Tony was playing a prank on them, but one look at Gus's face convinced them otherwise.

"Knowing that Frank is worried about Massimiliano," Tony continued, "my father decides to take the judge hostage. Maybe even murder him. We bring these guys in, make it look like they're responsible, and so Frank gets blamed. Did I convey the essence of your thoughts, Gus, minus a few choice adjectives?"

Jack was stunned, in total disbelief at what Tony was disclosing.

Tony sighed and sat down. "See how complex your so-called simple non-court solution is? I rest my case."

Jack stifled a smile. The three men all had in their eyes the look of a trapped coon. He turned and coughed in an effort to compose himself. Finally, he spoke as reassuringly as he could. "Mr. D'Amato, I assure you it's nothing sinister. Tony took your—"

"Arsenal," Dave chimed in.

"Whatever," Jack continued. "He took it to protect you."

Gus's face registered unbelief. "Bull!"

Sophia stepped in, squeezing in beside Gus and leaning her head on his shoulder. "No, Gus, it's true. You just won't believe what we have to tell you. It's so unreal, yet true! We didn't want anyone overreacting and thereby getting in trouble."

"Mr. D'Amato, you haven't broken the law," Dave interjected. "You were invited into this home. Our hope is that you'll bring your men who were in the other car here too, and willingly have them surrender their weapons. We need your participation in a meeting later in the afternoon."

"With FBI agents and the Newark police," Jack said.

"The feds and cops are coming here to talk with us?" Al blurted. "Why?"

"That's why we wanted your weapons," Sophia said softly. "We can't have anyone hurt, especially you, Gus."

"Most especially you," Jack remarked. "The injustice done to their son hurt everyone involved with the Carrons. This needs to turn out very well for the Carrons."

Sophia kissed Gus on the cheek. "Which means nobody related to us must get hurt."

At that point, Sue, Marnie, and Matt brought out the food—not simply strudel and coffee, but sandwiches, too. Gus's eyes appeared to brighten. Tony's approach was apparently working.

"So where's the judge?" Gus asked skeptically, but not in as threatening a tone as before.

Jack raised his hand.

"You asking permission to speak?" Gus growled. It appeared the man was beginning to feel a little more in control. He actually smiled at the food-bearers as he sampled their wares.

That's a good sign, Sophia thought.

Everyone else looked at Jack, who for a moment was speechless. "No," he said with a frown. "I was signaling to you that I am the judge."

Mid-bite, Gus looked at him. "Bull," he said for the second time. He glared at Tony with a look that clearly communicated, *I am through being humored!*

"It might be a good idea to present an ID, Your Honor," Tony said.

Marnie began to laugh.

Gus scowled. "What's so funny?"

"Have another strudel," she said, still laughing. It was obvious that control in the room had shifted, and Marnie left no doubt that she knew who had it. Passing the plate to the younger men, she folded her arms. "I never thought Jack would ever be asked to prove his identity in his own house. Quite frankly, I find that totally hilarious!" Suddenly her voice turned stern. "However, don't you or anyone else think you can boss me around in my home."

Gus's mouth dropped in astonishment.

"Have you noted how this room is decorated?" Marnie continued.

Al piped up. "Looks like it's set up for a wedding."

"Very perceptive, young man. I'm serving notice to all of you here that at seven o'clock sharp, the wedding meal will be served. I expect each one of you to participate. If your discussions haven't been completed by then, they'll be postponed until after supper. Have I made myself clear?"

At this point, all five foot two inches of Marnie towered over them in her no-nonsense principal posture.

Tony stood ramrod straight. "Yes, ma'am, perfectly clear!" He even saluted her, whereupon everyone, even Gus, started to laugh.

"So who got married, doll?" Gus asked.

Sophia giggled. "Massimiliano. Or Max, as they call him."

"To who?" Gus asked with a gasp.

"That, Mr. D'Amato, you'll have to wait until after supper to discover," Tony said as he reached for a strudel. He took out his cell phone and handed it to Gus. "Please, connect with your off-duty crew and get them to promptly join us!"

chapter twenty-two

Gus may have been Sicilian, but in appearance he resembled an English bulldog—a bulldog with the attitude of a pit bull, highly resentful at being tethered on a very short leash. The two younger men sat on the carpet, backs against the wall, clearly expecting Gus to call the shots. Sophia had introduced them as Rocco and Al, men on her father's payroll.

Gus was struggling to grasp what on earth was happening. All he knew was that this situation was unlike any he'd been exposed to before.

Sophia, you're a little vixen, he thought, looking at the young woman curled up beside him, wrapped around his right arm, holding his hand. *You know darn well I'm right-handed. You also know I'd never harm you. You take liberties with both myself and your father that no one else would dare to take.* His countenance darkened. *And Tony knows that you're totally safe with me!*

At that point, Marnie popped back into the room. "I thought these might sweeten everyone up."

She placed a large tray of homemade creampuffs on the table.

Good old Marnie, Jack chuckled silently. *She can disarm even the most savage beast.*

It was true. Within seconds, all resistance in the room dissipated as they indulged in Marnie's mouth-watering specialty.

"So," Marnie finally said, looking at her husband, "have you brought Mr. D'Amato up to speed on your grand plan to vindicate Max?"

"We can't discuss this until Epi and Chief Snyder's crews arrive," Dave reminded her.

"That may be true, Dave," Sue said. "But surely you could give them a sketch of what you're thinking."

"Way to go, doll," Gus said. "An outline would be appreciated—and, I might add, necessary—if you want me to call my other three guys at the motel. Otherwise, it's a no-go! By the way, since when have you started calling your brother Max?"

"Max never did like Massimiliano," Sophia said. "Kids made fun of him. Too foreign sounding, too long, too sissy-like. He hated being called Mass or Mo."

Gus sighed. "I never heard him say that."

"He never said anything in front of Mamma or Pop. Didn't want to offend them. But once he got to college, he insisted on Max."

"Apparently he insisted on Max in prison, too," Dave added.

"So call him what you like, Gus," Tony said. "We're choosing to honor his wishes."

Jack nodded. "As you know, Max didn't commit the crime for which I sent him to prison. For justice to be served, his conviction must be overturned. There are two approaches we can take for this to happen. One is through the courts. The other is to find those who did commit the crime, and arrest and convict them."

"Well, that one won't happen," Gus growled.

"Actually, we think it's a strong possibility!" Dave replied.

Gus's eyes flashed angrily at Sophia and Tony. "Your fathers made a pact not to pursue that avenue. Need I remind you?"

"I wasn't part of that pact," Sophia retorted. "And it's a good thing."

Gus frowned. "You know who tried to murder Tony?"

"I do."

"Who?"

"We need your other surveillance crew here first, Gus… so motel and room number please."

Rocco and Al were totally captivated by the conversation. Without thinking, the information rolled off Al's tongue. Before Gus could react, Sophia had dialed the number and handed the phone to Gus.

"Be nice now," she charged.

Surprisingly, Gus complied. The truth was he was curious as to where this would lead. It wasn't long before three more "staff" of Frank Carron joined Al and Rocco on the floor. Gus had met them at the door and ordered them to disarm. Food again served as the ice breaker.

Dave cleared his throat. "Mr. D'Amato, Sophia agreed to look at Max's police reports and trial transcripts with Judge Walters. Our desire was to identify possible suspects, hoping they wouldn't be connected to either her family or Tony's. She was able to identify the culprits immediately from the police reports."

"And they are neither Sicilian nor Italian," Sophia declared triumphantly. The Leuzecki college scenario was then quickly unfolded to Gus and his men.

"So why are the Newark cops and FBI coming here?" Gus asked skeptically.

"These two brothers have been anything but sterling in their post-college activities," Dave explained. "They are suspect in multiple illicit dealings, international drug trafficking, and arms dealing to a European terrorist cell. The Bureau became involved, but someone blew the cover on the FBI agent and he was killed."

Gus nodded. "So the Bureau isn't happy."

"Right," Dave said. "They're also situated in Newark. A Newark officer stopped a car on a routine check. He was shot dead. It appears to have been done simply for the sport of it! The officer's gun was still in its holster."

"They seem like first-class idiots." Gus frowned. "But why are you telling the six of us this?"

Jack sighed. "The first reason is that nearly seven years ago both the Carron and Marconi families were victimized by the criminal activity of these two brothers."

"And now there's an even more personal reason for your involvement, Gus." Tony spoke slowly and deliberately, his eyes locked on Gus. "Lou is in Newark."

Gus laughed, his gold tooth glistening in the light. "They better not mess with Lou!"

"They already have," Sophia said, biting her lip.

Gus's eyes narrowed into slits. "What do you mean?"

Sophia hesitated. "They shot Uncle Tommy."

"That's bull," Gus scoffed. "Tommy's in a nursing home. Totally lost his mind, doesn't know where he is or even who he is." He looked at Marnie and Sue. "He's my wife's uncle. Nearly every month, she talks to Tommy's son, Lou. It's that Old Timer's disease or something like it. Pretty sad disease, that." He shook his head. "Sophia, Uncle Tommy's not with it. He never leaves the nursing home. Lou says it confuses his Pop to be taken outta his environment. Tommy's got nothing to do with the casino or any other of Lou's enterprises. That your idiots would have shot Tommy is a stupid rumor."

Dave shook his head. "I'm sorry, sir, it's not a rumor. Mr. Tomaso Bastaldi was in the locked area of the seniors' home. Somehow masked gunmen gained access, walked into the dining area and riddled your wife's uncle with bullets.

They killed him and another resident seated at his table. Both gunmen fled. They weren't apprehended, but suspicion points to the Leuzeckis."

Gus's jaw dropped. "Why kill an old geezer like Tommy?"

"Only the perps know the answer to your question. Police speculation is they were either trying to intimidate his son and cut in on his casino action, or simply enrage and provoke him to retaliate… possibly take a sucker punch, or at worst set up an all-out gang war."

Jack took a deep breath. "Sophia pulled you in here to see if it's possible to nail them on a crime they've long since forgotten."

"Sting them," Dave smiled. "With an alliance they're not suspecting."

"We get to work with the cops and feds?" Al asked in disbelief.

"That's the hope," Tony said softly. "That's the hope."

For the first time since he had entered the Walters' home, Gus was speechless. He thought for a minute and then suggested, "Let's call Lou."

This came as no surprise to Tony, though it did shock Dave and Jack. After some discussion, they agreed to do it—on the understanding that only Gus would do the talking, and he'd be discreet, not giving away their plans or saying anything that would cause Lou to alert Frank.

Gus was ushered into Jack's study, accompanied only by Tony. His own phone was returned temporarily to him, since Lou would recognize Gus' number. Gus agreed to put the phone on speaker so Tony could hear the full conversation. Gus pulled up Bastaldi's number and hit the green button.

Within seconds, a cheery male voice responded. "Hey, Gus, great to hear from you. Everything okay with Angel?"

"Yeah, Angel's busy getting a head start on her Christmas baking and I'm the official taster. But the reason I'm calling, Lou, is I have to be in Newark in a couple of days. In and out, purely personal matter. Any chance of dropping in on Tomaso for a short visit?"

There was a long pause before Lou spoke. "Gus, my father is dead."

"Gee, sorry to hear that. When did he die?"

An audible sigh was heard and then Lou softly said, "Look, Gus, I'll tell you what happened, but I'm asking you to keep it confidential. I just need time to sort things out and I don't need any bigger Family pressure, if you know what I mean."

"Yeah sure, Lou, mum's the word. What happened?"

"As you know, Pop was in a seniors' home. A couple of weeks ago, two masked gunmen burst in, shooting willy nilly. They killed Pop and another old guy, injured several and scared the hell out of a good number of folks."

"Lou, that's horrible. Did they get the guys? Where they disgruntled employees?"

"Answer is no to both those questions, Gus. But I have a pretty good idea…" Lou's voice trailed off. "Gus, you keep this to yourself. Tell no one, especially Angel! But there's two crazy—and trust me, very violent—brothers stirring the pot in Newark. I'm not sure yet how to handle them. Figure the best way is to lay low and be patient. The opportunity will arise."

"That's a good strategy, Lou. Rushing in hotheaded usually backfires. These yoyo's got a name?"

"Yeah, they're the Leuzecki brothers. Jon and Alex."

Tony clenched his fists, both thumbs up, and mouthed "Bingo."

"Look, Lou, I wasn't expecting to hear such difficulties," Gus said. "But of two things I'm certain: you got the brains and the balls to handle this rightly— your way, your timing! Trust me, I won't tell anyone in the Family. Likewise, can I ask a favor from you?"

"Sure, Gus, anything."

"Well, my little trip to Newark is private, has nothing to do with you. I just didn't want to come onto your turf without telling you. But I'd really appreciate you keeping this conversation to yourself. I don't want even Frank to know, at least for a month. Okay?"

"You got it, Gus, my lips are sealed. Gotta go, it's been nice talking… enjoy the rest of your day"

Click. The phone went dead.

Tony reached out and took the phone from Gus. The older man just sat there as if paralyzed. Without a word, he stood, turned, and walked slowly back to the others.

Standing in the living room doorway, Gus stared at Dave and murmured, "Everything you said about those creeps is true!"

Watching Gus' emotions was like watching a beach with the tide out— everything seemed drained away. But as the tide would return, and if there'd been a seismic shock a tsunami could hit. So it was for Gus. In the time it took to cross the room, a transformation had occurred.

He turned to his men and growled, "We're in on this sting!" He had only one reservation: "I never do nothing without first running it by Frank."

"Sorry, no can do this time, Gus," Tony said. "Be patient and trust us. You'll soon see why."

* * *

At four o'clock. Epi arrived with three other agents, one of whom was Brian. The other two, neither Jack nor Dave knew. Both sensed Epi was unusually relaxed and most cordial to Gus. His agents, on the other hand, appeared a little skeptical of the proposed alliance.

"Yet if it lets us take down the Leuzeckis, I'm for it," one of the agents said. "The agent they murdered was a close friend. He leaves a wife and two little kids."

Within ten minutes of the feds' arrival, Chief Snyder entered the home accompanied by four officers. It soon became evident that the slain police officer had been known by all the policemen. Consequently, everyone in the house was personally motivated to orchestrate the Leuzecki brothers' downfall.

Prodded by Marnie, Jack explained that he had married a couple earlier that morning. The couple was expected back at six, and at seven his wife had planned a wedding dinner. All were invited, but the meal would take place as scheduled. They would have to iron out any unfinished business following the meal.

"So, gentlemen, let's begin," Epi said. "This is a sting, meaning we aren't used to working with one another. I believe our willingness to do so will be the gauge of our success."

Jack began the discussion by detailing his involvement in Max's incarceration. Everyone gasped to hear that Max had been allowed to take Harvard law classes during his imprisonment.

"If we're able to clear his name," Jack declared, "Max will be eligible for the bar. He is a most promising candidate."

"In addition, he'll be most useful both to the Bureau and the State Department," Epi said, his eyes twinkling. "This will be obvious, I believe, when Mr. Carron arrives with his bride."

Epi observed the quizzical glances exchanged among the occupants of the room. He knew he had piqued their curiosity.

The Newark police pulled out diagrams of the automotive/electrical store that served as the Leuzecki's legal front. They were also able to delineate the brothers' covert operational space within the building, noting that their personal offices were located on the second level.

Epi outlined the basic strategy. "Sophia Marconi, Max's sister, is our key to luring the brothers into their trap." He went on to explain how she had met Tony at college in New York State. "The two of them were undergraduates, while Max was enrolled in a post graduate course. The Leuzeckis took a fancy to Sophia.

She was oblivious to their interests. To get their hands on Sophia, we believe the Luezeckis tried to lure Tony to a local motel room, intent on murdering him, making it appear like a drug deal gone wrong. Instead, Max ended up in the room. Caught off-guard, the brothers knocked Max out." Epi paused and turned to Chief Snyder. "As you well know, these two are very brazen, and apparently nothing has changed. The police report for the crime Max was convicted of states that had it not been for the actions of two civic-minded concerned students, this campus drug infiltration would have gone undetected. The report then names and praises these two upstanding young men. Anyone care to guess those names?"

Snyder grunted. "Jon and Alex Leuzecki."

"Right you are, Chief, and because of what we now know about those two, the Bureau has reopened an unsolved cold case regarding a missing coed who disappeared at that time. As for Sophia, Max, and Tony, all three left the campus unaware of the Leuzeckis' interference in their lives."

Epi looked at Sophia. "Later, we'll detail the decoy plan that's been formulated for you."

"Decoy? Sophia? There's no way! Her father would never stand for it!" Gus sputtered.

"But there's not a risk, Mr. D'Amato. That's where you and your men enter this sting. Our plan calls for five of you to be in the Leuzecki store when Sophia confronts the brothers. Your other man will be outside in your getaway van, ready to whisk you quickly out of the area. Again, we'll flesh out those details in subsequent meetings."

Epi leaned forward. "Gus, you and your men's roles are key. You'll enter the Leuzecki store as customers, before Sophia, and when she gets there you can't lose sight of her. However, you need to stay convincing as bona fide customers. You can't arouse suspicion or the whole thing will blow up in our faces. Now, these are the doors," Epi pointed to specific locations on the Newark Police diagram, "that their thugs will come through, and when they do you have to be prepared to stop them. You will be armed!"

"You mean we carry our guns?" Gus was incredulous at what he had heard.

"And knives?" Al added.

Epi smiled. "Guys, what you do in there is your business. The bottom line is Sophia must be protected. Just don't mistake the Leuzeckis' legit employees and customers for one of their goons and I'll guarantee you'll have no trouble with us or the Newark Police." He drew a deep breath. "Your game plan, Sophia, is to trap these two bozos into admitting their role in what happened to your brother in that motel room. You'll be wired, but we have a few props to help out your cause, which I'll detail later. The main thing is that you must keep yourself *always* at arm's length to those two."

Epi continued, "Our data on these two characters is that they possess phenomenal egos. While we actually will be recording her conversation with the Leuzeckis in our surveillance van, Sophia will have a dummy tape recorder. At some point, you'll expose your recorder to let them think you've pulled the wool over their eyes. Then you need to run like mad for the door. They will pursue you. This is where Gus and his men come in. You need to strategically position yourselves to slow her pursuers down… and you need to do it appearing as innocent, bumbling, dumb customers just long enough to allow Sophia to hit the street."

Epi gestured to the Newark Police. "When she does, you'll be there with an unmarked squad car. Pull her into it and take off!" He laid out a diagram of the street in front of the store. "See this little alley across the street? Your paddy wagon can be hidden there. The moment those two brothers hit the street, tackle them, cuff them, pull up the paddy wagon, and get them to the precinct."

"What about us?" Brian asked.

"You and I will be stationed at the front of the store." Epi gestured to his other two agents. "You two will be guarding the back door. As for you," Epi pointed to one of Gus' men, "Rocco, is it? You'll be in this van. Gus and his other men will make their way to this exit and into your van. As soon as they do, take off and head back here to Summerside."

Epi was smiling like the Grinch who stole Christmas.

"So what about me?" Tony demanded. "Where am I?"

"You'll be with Max in the surveillance van."

Tony started to protest, but Epi cut him off. "Neither of you can be out in the open. We can't risk Max's leg being reinjured. And as for you, it's too volatile a situation. You're Sophia's husband. This is going to be emotionally charged. We can't risk you reacting inappropriately. We need both you and Max at the precinct with Chiefs Snyder and Davidson, Judge Walters and myself. Although we'll have a wiretap admittance of their crime, our role in the precinct meeting is to convince these two brothers to sign a written confession of attempting to murder you and framing Max. Your identity and your Sicilian lineage is one card we need to play. If we're successful in this sting, Max will be exonerated and his conviction overturned."

Epi had barely finished outlining the plan when an unmarked car pulled into the open lane in Walters' driveway and entered the garage. It was Dave's car, and it carried Max and Kaye.

It was Jack's turn to issue the orders. "Max just got the metal brace off his left leg, and he is not to bear weight on it. Am I making myself clear? I'll bring him in here to meet you and inform him of our plans."

chapter twenty-three

A s the garage door closed, the women left the room, leaving seventeen men sprawled throughout the Walters' living room. The women's laughter wafted down the corridor as they greeted the new arrivals. Jack poked his head out into the hall.

"Hey, Jack, whose cars are those? It's not media, is it?" Max asked, concern registering in his tone.

Jack shook his head silently. Epi stood to make his presence known.

Gus's jaw dropped. Framed in the doorway was a very handsome, healthy-looking Massimiliano Carron, balanced on two crutches, left leg elevated.

Max spied Epi first, then Brian. "Why are you guys here?" Max's eyes swept the room. The two other agents and Newark cops were unknown to him. He furrowed his brow as his eyes met Tony's.

That was too much for Tony. He couldn't resist. He rose quickly, feigned a bow, and with a sweeping movement of his hand said simply, "Our stalkers, sir."

Tony stepped aside to reveal a glowering Gus.

Max angrily faced Jack. "Gus! Why are you here?" He looked furtively around the room. "Where's Pop?"

Gus became agitated. He chose to address the younger man in Italian. Although less than half the room could understand the language, none were in doubt that the older man was administering a severe tongue-lashing.

Max stepped into the center of the room while Gus continued his tirade, which from Gus's perspective wasn't unfair. After all, Gus knew full well the pain, worry, and outright grief experienced by Max's parents over their son's no-show following his release from prison. There had been no contact, no explanation given; he simply hadn't returned home. Good Italian boys weren't supposed to upset their parents, especially the Mamma, as Max had done. Given the fact that he appeared extremely fit, except for an apparently injured leg, his failure to contact his parents was without excuse.

Max, normally complacent and pleasant, appeared neither complacent nor pleasant. His brown eyes flashed with anger. Balancing on his right leg, the crutch supporting his left leg, he swung the right crutch up and jammed it firmly against Gus's chest. It caught the older man off-balance, driving him back into his chair.

Glowering, Max addressed the room in English. "Think what you want about me. Say what you will. I want four weeks by myself with Kaye, uninterrupted. Is that understood? I don't want family. I don't want press. I don't want FBI. And I don't want whoever the rest of you are!"

"Sometimes our wants and needs clash, Max," Epi said. "When that occurs, our needs must be given priority."

Max spied the diagrams on the coffee table and suddenly realized what was being orchestrated. He turned to vent his wrath at Jack. "Crap, Jack. You unfairly sentenced me to prison." He spun to face Tony and Gus. "I took that fall. I gave six years of my life so the family could make peace." He scowled at Dave and Epi. "I prevented a woman from being brutally murdered, a woman the two of you should have protected. Now, to satisfy all your guilt, you want to barge ahead to make everything right? With no thought to either Kaye's or my wishes? I don't care if I have a prison record! She and I know I'm innocent. That's all that matters."

"I know how this might seem to you," Jack said softly, "but the real reason we're pushing ahead is because of your needs."

Max opened his mouth, but before he could utter a word a gorgeous redhead entered behind him. Everyone's attention was instantly captivated by Kaye's beauty.

One of the FBI agents, a handsome man about Max's age, leapt to his feet to greet her. Bowing slightly, he took her hand and gallantly kissed it. "Why, Ms. McDonald, what a wonderful surprise!"

Despite being taken aback, Kaye responded politely. "Agent Warren, how nice to see you again. I didn't expect to see you here."

She looked to Jack and Epi for an explanation, both of whom appeared to be studying the ceiling. She then turned to Max, who was registering extreme interest in Agent Warren—or more explicitly, her explanation of the agent's apparent familiarity with her. Except for Dave, Matt, Brian, and Tony, she didn't recognize any of these men.

"Max, this is Special Agent Warren," Kaye said, looking bewildered. "He escorted me at one or two embassy dinners I was required to attend on behalf of Kayleen. As archaic as it may seem, some countries demand women be escorted by men. They apply their rules even when they host functions in America, and definitely when I travel internationally to those nations. Sometimes my escort is a board member or staff person, but often a CIA or Bureau agent accompanies me. A rather boring assignment for them, I'm afraid."

Max didn't think Agent Warren looked particularly bored.

"Mr. Warren, this is my husband." Kaye's hand took Max's. Leaning close to him, she smiled sweetly. "Now I have my own personal escort."

Warren looked stunned, and Gus looked like he might faint. Everyone else looked at Max with very green eyes… green with envy, that is!

"Actually, you don't," Epi said to her.

Kaye felt provoked. "Whatever do you mean?"

"Kaye, the fact is that Max has a criminal record. Until it is removed, it will interfere with him obtaining a passport for international travel. It will also make him ineligible to attend those state functions."

"You've got to be kidding!" Kaye said.

"You knew this all along?" Max said, his body language registering vexation.

"You need to get that conviction overturned," Jack replied firmly.

Epi spoke slowly but firmly. "Max, Sophia's identification of the Leuzecki brothers, coupled with their recent felonies in Newark, has garnered you a group of unlikely allies, all of whom are motivated to see these men behind bars." Epi paused, his jaw tightening. "However, we need to act now, even if the timing isn't optimal for the two of you. In your absence, we've outlined a strategy. We plan to move on Monday. Until then, everyone will remain sequestered here."

The others looked startled at Epi's pronouncement.

"Sorry, but I don't want a leak," Epi said. "I want these brothers corralled. I'm not prepared to risk an informant."

* * *

The caterer arrived at 6:30 and was busy in the Walters' kitchen and dining room. Marnie entered the room to give her wedding guests a head's up, leaving no doubt in anyone's mind that she expected all to heed her directives. At seven o'clock sharp, the wedding banquet would be served and everyone better be in attendance!

Max turned to Kaye. "Hon, go with Marnie. I need to go over plans with the guys."

The moment she left the room, Max's jaw tensed. "Show me the plan."

He watched intently as the details were laid out, periodically adding succinct instructions to Gus and his men.

When the full strategy had been divulged, Max turned to Epi. "If this is to take place, everyone needs to be fitted and issued bulletproof vests—including Tony, myself, and particularly Sophia!"

Gus and Tony began to protest that they weren't wussies.

Max shook his head. "This is not a debatable point. You *will* wear vests. My father is already upset with me. If I allowed any of you to go into this and you were killed or seriously hurt, my relationship with my father would be irreparably damaged."

Jack eyed Epi. "Well, this would certainly appear to fall into Chief Justice Malcolm Douglas's edict for us to ensure a happily-ever-after scenario."

"Done!" was all Epi said in reply.

"Time's up! Let's go eat," Dave enjoined. "Afterwards, Epi, you can size the men and Sophia, so appropriate vests can be secured."

Epi responded in the affirmative and added, "Jack's arranged for Snyder's and my men to stay at a Christian retreat outside of town. Any pertinent data Gus and Sophia need, we'll relay to them tomorrow. The whole group needs to meet both Saturday and Sunday afternoon to fine-tune this sting."

The die had been cast. The outcome was unknown, but the Luezecki brothers at last had a formidable foe.

At least temporarily, however, the gravity of the situation was forgotten, as the culinary skills of Vincenzo Catering buoyed everyone's spirits.

During the meal, Gus approached Max. Placing his hand on the younger man's shoulder, he murmured, "I'm sorry, Max. I had no idea what you were doing and what you had to accomplish to save her life."

Max clasped Gus's hand in his. "You're forgiven. You've always been like a second father to me. Believe me, I do respect you and my parents. I never imagined, let alone intended, that it would take so long for me to get back to Chicago." He grinned sheepishly, "But truthfully, I have no regrets. Kaye is a wonderful woman… a brilliant woman and a great joy to have as one's lifelong companion. She has been asked to speak at Our Lady of Mercies benefit dinner, about three weeks from now. It's important to us to keep our relationship secret until then. Kaye and I went through a very traumatic several weeks. We need time to balance ourselves and don't need media frenzy around us. Don't you think Mamma and Pop, when they know all the facts, will appreciate my reason for silence?"

Max continued, "I don't pretend to understand all the interest in unearthing Maxwell Kerr. However, Kaye's hint, in her New York speech, that he might appear at the fundraising event certainly increased the banquet's publicity. Hopefully that will translate into increased revenue for the hospital. If so, that would be my personal gift to Mamma."

Gus nodded and smiled, thinking to himself, *You may have left us as a young man, confident neither in yourself nor your role in life. However, you've returned a very wise man with the potential for a very prosperous future.* He laughed. "Yes, Max, I expect your parents will both understand. I'll definitely plead your case with Frank."

It was nearly ten before the festivities ended. Everyone had agreed to reconvene at the Walters' house on Saturday afternoon. The plan was for the FBI agents and Newark police to leave together. Gus, Rocco, and Luigi would room at Jack's. Tony and Sophia would stay with Max and Kaye. Al, Silvio, and Mario would bunk at Dave and Sue's.

All pitched in to clean up. The food was put away and dishes piled in the caterer's boxes when suddenly Kaye's infectious laughter commandeered the room.

"I believe speeches are made at weddings," she said. "So I'll begin. Our original plan was for Max and me to wed quietly here, returning later for a simple meal with the Walters and Davidsons. But our God has a most gracious sense of humor. Abruptly, our cozy party of seven mushroomed. I'm delighted that Sophia and Tony got to share this day with us. I'm really excited to meet Gus and all of your men. Chief Snyder, now I know some of Newark's finest." She smiled. "Epi, it's good to see you and Brian again, in much more pleasant circumstances, and to renew acquaintances with Agent Warren. Just think, Max and I will be able to tell our children how unique our wedding was. After all, not too many couples can say their dinner guests were seven policemen, four FBI agents, eight Sicilians, one judge, a nurse practitioner—and a school principal who, I might add, organized us all! I want to thank every last one of you for making this day so special for me. I also want you to know that this has been the happiest day of my life, for God has indeed blessed me with a soul mate!"

With that, she turned and kissed Max.

chapter twenty-four

When the wedding toasts and well wishes were completed, Kaye retrieved her car and drove Max, Tony, and Sophia down the street to her house. As the garage door opened, a second car was parked there. Tony gasped. "Max, that's your car!"

Kaye raised her eyebrows. "Max removed the plates so it wouldn't be easily recognized. How do you know it belongs to Max?"

Sophia sighed. "The moment they can afford it, they all drive the same make and model... a high-end black caddie with tinted windows."

Kaye couldn't resist. "No imagination."

"None," Sophia giggled.

Tony became defensive. "That's not it at all. We got imagination. It's just that if you get a flashy Porsche or a Beamer, you'll stand out like a sore thumb. Like a hooker, you're inviting to be picked up."

Kaye looked at him askance. "You're telling me that a black caddie with tinted windows blends into the scenery?"

Max laughed. "No matter what you say, Tone, you'll lose this one. Kaye isn't going to embrace a black car unless it's really a dark green. By the way, want a great deal on a barely used black caddie?"

"You serious?" Tony asked.

"Yep, with my leg I need to get something that will let me sit higher. I have a deuce of a time getting in and out of a car with these crutches."

"Can we leave the two of you to discuss cars?" Sophia interjected impatiently. "I'm anxious to see Kaye's house."

The two women set out on a tour, Kaye filling Sophia in on all the changes she'd made and why. Sophia instantly felt at home with her new sister-in-law. Kaye wasn't pretentious or aloof, nor were her tastes far beyond her own. The only truly luxurious element was the new pool. In Sophia's opinion, the best words to describe her sister-in-law's house would be "practical with modest elegance."

When the tour finished, the two women returned to the living room. Sophia saw Kaye's sofa and loveseat and expressed genuine astonishment that it was exactly like her mother's, except Mamma's set had a blue floral print whereas Kaye's was green.

"No way," Kaye said. "Max really struggled with the floral pattern. He says it's 'not for a guy.' And now you tell me your mother has the same set?" The two women began to laugh, tears rolling down their cheeks. "I got rid of the chair and bought Max this leather recliner. It was the first thing he noticed, when I brought him home this morning."

Sophia sniffled, regaining her composure. "When we were growing up, Pop had all leather. At the time, he was still ensconced in old-world thinking—namely, he pays, he chooses. However, around the time I headed off to college, my chaperone brother in tow, my parents moved into their new estate. Max purchased their Maple Grove Drive home. He got Bill and Lou to move into the two apartments, and the main house he left pretty much as Mamma had furnished it. Mamma had been in the process of furnishing her new home 'the American way.' In other words, he can pay, but she will choose. That's when Max got charged and sent off to prison. He never really saw my parents' new home décor."

Almost as an afterthought, Sophia added, "Mamma was devastated by Max's absence. Pop never imagined the impact his pact with Pepi would have on my mother." She sighed. "None of us even remotely anticipated the severity of the sentence he would receive."

As she talked, Sophia's voice became softer and softer. Kaye noted that Sophia was wringing her hands. For the first time, Kaye began to feel the depth of pain Sophia's family had experienced. In her heart, she wondered if Frank and Josephine Carron would ever gracefully accept Max's belief that the sentence was God's way of allowing him to save her. Would they ever be able to forgive Jack? More to the point, would they ever accept her, given the worry her seven months of silence had caused them?

"Anyway, I think Pop was feeling very guilty," Sophia said, her voice returning to a normal tone. "He'd never given Mamma a say in the pact, so he suddenly became more attentive to Mamma's wishes for their new home. He began to participate in her interior decorating schemes. I think he came to appreciate Mamma's artistic gifts. Gifts he'd never noticed before." She grinned. "Needless to say, their house clearly has a feminine touch to it. They've received many genuine compliments from guests, and as a result Pop is very proud of Mamma. When Max does return home, trust me, it'll be a big surprise for him, in more ways than one."

At that point, Tony and Max rejoined their wives. Max's tour of the house had focused solely on the new office area, pool, weight room, kitchen, and now his recliner.

"Hey, Sophia, maybe tomorrow you and Kaye could pick up some casual clothes for us and a bathing suit," Tony said. "I could help Max with his water exercises."

"Good plan, my dear brother-in-law, so how about we show you the upstairs? Sophia and I will go first." Kaye eyed her husband sternly. "Provided, Max, you promise not to show off and attempt something you can't yet accomplish with those crutches!"

"I shall humble myself appropriately and ascend the stairs bum first." Max sighed. "I have no desire to return to the hospital."

Sophia felt so comfortable in this house. It was like a deep peace enfolded everyone in its care. Tony and Sophia couldn't stop laughing at Kaye's description of how she and Max had survived three months of platonic living—the invisible line, the cold showers. Yet both sensed not only the horror of that night with Glaxton but also the terror at his early-morning phone calls. It was obvious that much healing still needed to occur in both Kaye and Max, healing that extended much deeper than a shattered leg.

I hope others can truly grasp how these two really do need one another, Sophia prayed, thinking specifically of her own family.

The two couples soon settled into their own rooms, each consumed with their own thoughts and concerns of the day's revelations. While sleep came mercifully quick to Sophia and Tony, it eluded the new bride and groom.

Kaye snuggled up to Max. She propped herself up on one elbow and stared into his eyes, her own twinkling mischievously.

"What's so funny?" he asked.

"You."

"I'm not feeling very funny."

"That's just the point. We've been married only half a day and I can read you like a book. You, sir, are worried!"

"You have indeed nailed it." He turned and faced her, propping himself up by his own elbow. "But don't be priding yourself on a new bride's intuition. Don't forget that for several months we lived with one another in pretty close quarters, and through some hair-raising situations."

He brushed her nose with his forefinger and flopped back down on the bed on his back.

"Kaye, did it ever occur to you that I wouldn't be able to travel with you, because I couldn't get a passport? That I couldn't escort you to those embassy dinners?"

Now it was her turn to flop down on her back. "No, not at all. I don't know why I never thought of it."

"Me neither. Professor Brown said I had a brilliant legal mind... not! I should have known... why didn't I see it?"

"Love maybe?"

"Love?"

"Yes, Max, love! You know the old saying, 'love is blind'? Well, we both know about passports and criminal records, yet neither of us thought of it. That's blind, isn't it?"

He shook his head. "I'm really sorry, Kaye, I mean it!"

"For what?"

"For screwing us up, for being so blind." Her hair brushed against his cheek and her arm fell across his chest.

"Well, I'm not the least sorry," she said.

"What?"

"I have no regrets whatsoever! In fact, I thank God for the blindness."

"You're joking?"

"Most definitely not! If either of us had recognized it, in all probability we would have walked away from each other. You especially, Mr. Carron!"

"Maybe that would have been the right thing to do, Kaye. When Agent Warren came to you and politely took your hand, he was being respectful of you. And me? I was so green with jealousy. I was greener than your little whatchamacallit."

Kaye laughed. "Leprechaun."

"That's not funny!" he protested.

"Being jealous? No. But calling a leprechaun a whatchamacallit is. Max, I knew you were upset, and that was precisely Epi's ploy."

"What?"

"Epi knows the agents who escort me. In fact, I suspect it's he who assigns them."

"But I thought Epi was my friend."

"He is, Max."

"He's no friend to pull that stunt on me! I just about lost it."

"So immediately you were willing to cooperate with his and Jack's plan, which I suspect you initially weren't. All I'm saying is that Epi planned that to get you on board quickly." She leaned forward on her elbow again. "Why do you think Epi sequestered his men with Chief Snyder's?"

"So they could fine-tune their strategy," he said. "Why? What do you think?"

"I think Epi might be worried about an informant, and I don't think he figures it will come from his own men. Brian was an obvious choice, because he knows about us. As for Agent Warren, well, I told you why he was selected. That third agent admitted he was a personal friend of the murdered agent."

"And as for Gus, his guys, Tony, and me—and for that matter, Jack Dave, and Matt—we didn't know the Leuzeckis. Or if we did, it was in the past."

"That's right, Max, and I believe Dave said it was Epi who contacted Snyder. That's why the two of them are concerned about an informant."

"It would make sense for the Leuzeckis to have a mole in the Newark Police Department," Max muttered. "After all, it's in Newark that the brothers are seeking to be a serious player on the crime scene. As if I didn't have enough to think about."

"What else are you thinking about, Max?"

"Just how risky this venture is. And that the people taking the biggest risk are the ones I care about most. I mean, if anything goes wrong, the whole thing could blow up in my face—and destroy my relationship with my family."

"But why do you need to place the burden of responsibility upon your shoulders? Gus is involved to get some justice for the brutal murder of his wife's uncle. His men are eager to participate. Sophia, it is true, is doing it for you. And everyone has safety in mind."

"That's just it. Tony and I won't be there!" Max said. "Epi sees me as too big a risk factor, because of my leg. Tony's too big an emotional risk. I mean, Kaye, look at how I reacted to Agent Warren. If Tony loses his cool, it could compromise the whole operation. Lastly, they want the two of us at the precinct to convince the Leuzeckis that we are who we say we are."

Kaye frowned. "I'm sorry, you've lost me."

"Well, these two dudes need to be pretty much convinced that their lives are over if they don't confess, plead guilty, and accept the plea bargain Epi is laying on the table, which is a six-year sentence like I got."

"How can Epi expect them to believe that?"

"Pepi is known as Mr. Italy in New York, and Pop has the same moniker in Chicago. Let's just say they've got friends in many places, including the mob. So look at what the Leuzeckis did. And look what they did to Lou's father! Mob justice is pretty straightforward. See, Kaye, that's how a sting works. If the underworld hates the guys and the cops hate the guys, if the cops signal the ballgame is over, we will step back. Cooperation becomes a matter of life and death. Look at it this way. The sentence for attempted murder is usually much more than six years. In fact, six years is a good deal! The issue is, will the brothers take the bait?"

"But couldn't they be found and killed in prison?" Kaye asked, intrigued.

"That's part of the deal. No one involved in the sting will be given access to where they're sent. And we'll all promise not to seek to discover it."

"But in six years, these men could be out again," Kaye objected. "In fact, what about parole?"

"Usually when guys like the Leuzeckis get busted, their whole ring of influence is shattered. They rule by terror. Their power will be undermined when others start coming forward. Those guys could end up being sent away for a very long time. That's why Epi's poking his nose back into the case of a missing coed. What really troubles me, Kaye, is what happens if Jack's non-court acquittal doesn't work."

Kaye sighed. "Well, then he could take it back to court."

"I can't have him go that route, Kaye. Not only would it smear Jack, it opens Pop up—even Pepi—to criminal charges, along with Scally and the prosecutor. I just can't do that."

Kaye leaned over and kissed him. "I know, and I wouldn't want you too. Your parents have been hurt enough."

"That's the problem, Kaye. I realized today that I won't be happy with you flying all over the world without me. It's not merely that other guys escort you to dinners. You're an attractive woman. Glaxton isn't the only deranged person on the planet stalking high-profile women. Not only that, you're an important American business executive and thus a feasible kidnapping target for terrorist groups. If something happened to you and I wasn't there to at least try and protect you, I couldn't live with myself."

"You want to know what I learned today?" She kissed her forefinger and placed it on his lips.

"What?"

"I learned that I can't fly around the world without you, or be escorted to any event by anyone other than you. So if this so-called sting doesn't materialize as planned, I'll step down as CEO of Kayleen."

"You can't!"

"I can and I must. Max, we vowed today to be faithful to one another, for better or for worse. When my life ends, what really matters will not be what I've done. What will matter is who I've loved and who loves me. My first relationship is with Jesus. As much as I love you, Max, I love Him more."

Max smiled.

"Why are you smiling?"

"Well, that's the one and only competitor I can take. In fact, He's the one I would hope you would love more than me. Truthfully, I also love Him more than I do you."

She smiled too. "So we're on the same page, Mr. Carron."

"Indeed we are, Mrs. Carron. Indeed we are."

"You, sir, are my next love. Should the sting fall through, I'm sure both of us can find meaningful employment to allow us both to live purposeful lives. Not only that, I know that if I make the honorable choice, Christ will see that Kayleen will have as its CEO a very wise person. I can trust Jesus to ensure that!"

Max folded his arms around her. "Their current CEO is indeed an extremely wise woman, whom I adore!"

"One moment, Casanova, we're not finished yet!"

"I am. You've set my mind at ease," he teased.

"Seriously, Max!"

"I don't want to be serious."

"Yes, you do! You really need to be."

"Okay, M.K. McDonald, I will be serious." He laughed. "Otherwise all my amorous intentions will fall short."

"Jesus said that we're to cast all our burdens on Him. I believe that in His great mercy, He brought you to me. I'm so grateful for that, and I want to thank Him for our first night in this house, as a married couple. I also know that we can talk and plan all we want, but unless we take our thoughts and our burdens to Him, everything will come to naught. In contrast, He promises that if we, acknowledge Him in all our ways, He will direct our paths. Max, we need to do that!"

Max reached out and caressed her hair. "You are so right. Let me begin our prayers by thanking Him for the helpmate He's given me to keep me grounded spiritually."

"Max, something else just occurred to me," she whispered softly. "Our God is a God of second chances."

"What do you mean, Kaye?"

"Think about what you just said: Jesus used me to ground you spiritually."

"Uh-huh," he said with a smile. "I sense there's a mighty revelation coming. I can tell by the look on your face."

"In the Garden of Eden, the woman didn't help the man spiritually. Instead she harmed him. The Bible promises that in Christ we become new creatures. When he used me to ground you, perhaps I was experiencing some of Jesus's redemptive work."

"Kaye, that is profound!"

"But it's not only me, Max. It's you, too!"

"How so?"

"We both believe that it was God who brought you to protect me. Yet in the Garden of Eden, the man stood by, saying and doing nothing to protect the woman from behavior that would bring about her death. So when you stepped in to protect me, it was you who experienced Jesus' redemptive work. "

"When you put it that way, He truly is the God of second chances, isn't He?" Max reached over and pulled her into his arms. He admitted that the future, even the next few days, was worrisome. Yet by faith, both of them were committing their ways to Him, trusting Jesus to guide and direct their steps.

Kaye added her gratefulness for all the many blessings He had showered upon them and asked that God would use them to point others to His love and redemptive work. Then together, in Jesus's name, power, and authority, they blocked any informant from endangering their lives. They prayed not only for themselves, but also for their enemies, asking God to protect the lives of all involved.

Kaye began to pray for Max's parents, that they would experience peace, even though he wasn't able to be present with them. She also asked that his father would be given wisdom to make the decision the Lord wanted regarding Kayleen.

They concluded by saying together the Lord's Prayer. When the final "Amen" was uttered, Kaye never moved her head from Max's chest. She found herself listening to the beat of his heart and realized she had lost all desire to live singly.

A few moments passed before she spoke again. "Max, are you awake?"

"Of course."

"Whatever possessed you to come up with that stupid idea of the invisible line?"

"The truth is, I took one look at M.K. McDonald and knew if I didn't stake out my share of the bed, I'd be left with no bed at all."

"Really?"

"Yes, really. Look where you are now!"

"Well, if you want, I'll move over."

"I don't want that," he said, passionately embracing her. His heart leaped for joy as she reciprocated.

chapter twenty-five

One person who didn't sleep well on the wedding night was Special Agent Bernard Epstein. He had secured the country retreat of Jack's church to sequester his and Chief Snyder's men. It was convenient for the privacy it afforded, but it had other benefits which were much higher on Epi's priority list. First and foremost, it was impossible for cell phones to connect. The retreat was situated deep in the middle of three converging reforestation areas. Second, there was only one land phone and it was located in his room—a room to which only he held a key.

Kaye had read the situation accurately. Epi was indeed concerned about the existence of an informant. He had read and reread both the Newark P.D. and Bureau reports on the murdered agent—Howard had been his name. Epi's gut told him that something was not right. But what?

The murdered agent was no novice. He was a seasoned undercover narc agent from the West Coast, totally unknown in the East. No way could his cover have been blown accidentally.

Howard's dossier reveals a meticulously cautious agent, Epi thought. *Yet neither the police nor our reports indicate the existence of a break-in or struggle. Furthermore, the position of his body is baffling. He was found sitting in his recliner, facing the TV.*

Epi pulled out the photos of Howard's studio apartment. It contained a sofa bed, coffee table, recliner, café style table with two matching chairs, small kitchenette, and of course the TV. The only other piece of furniture was an end table. On it sat one lamp. It was positioned at what appeared to be the foot of the sofa bed. The only other light in the apartment came from ceiling lights—one in the center of the sitting room, one each in the kitchenette and bathroom.

"Something's not right," Epi said to himself, shaking his head. "Why would Howard position his recliner with his back to the door? True, it was near the window, but he could have positioned the chair in a way that would have allowed street surveillance while still giving him visual access to the door. It also makes no sense that this table lamp was at the foot of the bed; it should have been at the head of the bed."

Epi picked up the written reports. Both sources reported two beer cans found in the room. One empty can was noted on the end table, on the other side of the room. It had Howard's prints on it—his left hand. The unopened can had been on the coffee table, in front of Howard's chair. Prints from Howard's right hand were found on it. Epi frowned and ran his hand through his dark hair. He set the reports down and turned to flip through the crime scene photos.

He sucked in his breath. "What's this, Agent Epstein?" He grabbed his magnifying glass to better examine one photo in particular.

The coroner's report had indicated that Howard was shot at close range. The bullet which had entered below the left nipple had penetrated his heart, shattering a rib on the right side as it exited his back below the right shoulder. In fact, the bullet had been found imbedded in the chair.

The police report had speculated that the killer somehow obtained a key and entered undetected by Howard. However, when the killer neared the chair, the report postulated that Howard was startled and turned towards the killer, who fired at point-blank range.

That's it! Epi thought. *That's what doesn't compute.*

If that had been the scenario, the bullet's trajectory would have been downward, not upwards as the coroner's report indicated. He furrowed his brow. To get the angle stated in the autopsy report, if Howard had been sitting, so would the killer have had to be seated.

Epi didn't like the direction his thoughts were leading him. According to the crime scene photos, there was no place to sit to the left of Howard. However, according to one photo, the carpet in front of the end table appeared flattened. *But by what?*

He reached for a couple of the photographs that showed close-ups of Howard's body in the recliner. One shot clearly exposed the base of the chair. It matched the flattened area seen on the carpet beside the end table.

Of course, he thought. Howard had used the table lamp for reading, both from the bed and the chair. So whoever had killed Howard had taken the time to move the chair, with the body in it, vacuum the carpet to eliminate the drag marks, and remake the bed to create the illusion of a surprise attack.

"Howard's killer was certainly no amateur," Epi muttered.

He turned out his light to try escaping the troubling thoughts that kept plaguing him. Unfortunately, the more he tried to sleep, the more sleep eluded him. One thought after another rammed his brain like a red-hot poker. Howard had apparently known his killer. But why should that thought be so upsetting?

He flopped onto his stomach and buried his face in the pillow. He knew the answer lay in the identity of the killer. If the killer had been one of the Leuzeckis' hired thugs, with whom Howard had been working, he wouldn't have let down his guard. They also would have ransacked the apartment, searching for any incriminating evidence.

Epi gave up chasing sleep. He sat up and grabbed the phone. His first call was to Washington, requesting a detailed report of all the agents and police officers assigned to the Leuzecki brothers' narcotics probe. The second call was to Dave Davidson.

"Epi! It's two in the morning. What on earth are you doing?" was the groggy response.

"I can't sleep."

Dave snorted. "You want to talk to me, or should I sing you a lullaby?"

"While I appreciate your musical talent, this is strictly business. Have your addled brain cells rearranged themselves into cop mode yet?"

"Epi, do you ever relax? You're at a retreat. It's the night following a wedding banquet, yet your head's into police business."

"Dave, I'm touched. I work with so many cops and you're the first one to actually ask about me." Epi's voice turned somber. "This police business involves the health and well-being of you and your friends."

As the two men talked, they arrived quickly at one consensus: the informant wouldn't be in the ranks of the sting coconspirators. The informant would reside in those sequestered with Epi.

"So what's my role?" Dave had moved into the bathroom so as not to disturb Sue. "And what's yours?"

Epi gave a hollow laugh. "My first role, I suspect, is to activate the eyes in the back of my head. You know, every agent's James Bond spy gadgetry. I had no idea Chief Douglas' assignment would take us down such a twisted road. My office is doing a check on all the officers and agents connected to the narc probe Howard was working on. They're cross-referencing the names to the ones sequestered here with me." He paused. "I need you to be my partner in this. Can you arrange for one of your savvy officers—you know, like Tom—to be on call, at the spur of the moment."

"To do what?"

That's when Epi revealed the real plan—they wouldn't go to Newark on Monday, but Tuesday. "Dave, I gave the earlier date to help people commit. The truth is that the Leuzecki brothers are never in their store on Mondays. This means we've got the weekend to flush out their mole. When we nab him, we've got to isolate him, allowing him no opportunity to transmit a warning of our impending sting. Failure to do that would spell disaster for Gus and his crew, especially Sophia."

"A most definite unhappy ending for Max," Dave muttered.

"Indeed," Epi echoed. "The third thing you can do is tap this line. Actually, more than tap, intercept any outgoing calls, especially if it should be to the Leuzeckis or their contacts. We really need to cover every base."

"I can do all three things, Ep," Dave replied reassuringly. "What's on your agenda for tomorrow?"

"Do you think we could bring everyone involved here tomorrow afternoon, instead of going to Jack's? It's important that we develop a level of trust."

Dave laughed. "Trust? I think that's feasible only through much prayer and divine intervention. By the way, will you have the bulletproof vests Max requested?"

"They're scheduled to arrive tomorrow morning, along with enough groceries to cover our forced three-day retreat. That's the major reason I've opted to meet here tomorrow. Do you think it's feasible to go to Jack's on Sunday afternoon?"

"Most definitely! But Epi, I need to warn you about something."

"What's that?"

"Don't discount any of your own agents as the mole. If the FBI van comes, make sure none of your guys is able to signal the sting to the outside. Get my drift?"

Epi sighed. "Yeah, Dave. I'll be honest: even entertaining that thought turns my stomach."

"I know, bud, but better a little nausea now than a lot of dead people later."

chapter twenty-six

"Good morning, Mr. Carron!" The rotund man shed his robe, but not his cigar, as he stepped into the pool. "How are you this fine weekend?"

The lone bather greeted his cheery newcomer with a scowl. "Scally, I don't want any smoke near me."

"No problem, Frank, it's not lit. I've renounced smoking as dangerous to my health. I simply hold onto the cigar as a comfort for my soul."

Frank's countenance softened slightly. "Really? You're finally acknowledging how bad smoking is in causing cancer, heart problems, and such. You impress me, Scally."

Scally grabbed a floater and allowed himself to sink into the warm water. He removed the cigar from his mouth and faced Francesco Carron. "No, none of that, my dear client. Just hazardous to my health when I'm around you!"

Frank's scowl returned. "I'm not amused."

"Somehow that doesn't seem newsworthy. You didn't look amused before I arrived, cigar in tow. So, why the funk? I'm not your shrink, just your lawyer, but sometimes litigation improves people's mood. By the way, where's Gus?"

"That's just it. Nobody's around when you need them," Frank growled.

"I'll ignore the insult of being dubbed a 'nobody.' Seriously, though, something's troubling you. Anything I can do to help?" Scallion's tone was conciliatory.

Frank sighed. "It's Max, or rather the absence of Max. It's more than six months since his release. No word. Absolutely no word! I got to thinking, if he's not dead, maybe he's lying low, waiting to hit that frigging judge when it's least expected. I sent Gus with a few young bucks to Pennsylvania to see if they could spot him."

"The judge?" Scally wasn't sure he wanted to be privy to this.

"How can someone so savvy legally be so stupid? No, not the judge. My son!"

"Oh," was the quiet retort. "Well, that would seem to be a wise move."

Frank stared at his counsel in disbelief.

"What did I say wrong now?" Scally asked.

"Why don't you try using the two ears and shutting the one mouth?" snapped Frank. "I'm upset because Gus phoned and said he'd contact me, not for me to call him. He's not sure if the hotel is being bugged. Obviously their presence has been noted and they're being watched. I suggested he give up and come home. He thought they should wait until the end of next week."

"So, you miss his counsel?" Scally said, delighted that for once his words seemed to verify what Frank was trying to communicate.

"Yeah, I do," Frank said glumly. "His counsel, his friendship, plus now I have Josie and Angel pumping me as to Gus's whereabouts. Angel is especially worried. She reminds me daily, 'Gus and you aren't the spring chickens you once were!'"

"True," Scally agreed, taking the cigar from his mouth. Seeing Frank's glare, he wished he'd left it there.

Frank leaned on his floater and raised a hand. "First, Max doesn't come home from prison." One finger went up. "Two, this upsets everyone, including me, but especially Josephine." A second finger was raised. "Third, every cotton-picking person is speculating as to the reason for our son's no-show. Some even question whether or not he's still alive. I get wind of all the rumors, and that isn't helping my sleep. In fact, I'm downright exhausted. Part of the time, I long to be able to embrace my son, and the next moment I want to strangle him!"

Scally gave a little cough, not certain if it was wise to interfere with this countdown. But he decided he must. "Frank, we all need to remember that we had a part in sending Max to prison. Unjustly!"

"Your point?"

"Well, just that whatever is behind Max's disappearance, maybe we all need to cut him some slack. Including you." There. He'd offered his counsel, and to his surprise no sarcastic response erupted.

"Yeah, thanks for the reminder."

Scally even thought he saw a tear in his client's eye. One thing was certain: he would never mention that observation to anyone!

"Fourthly," Frank said, resuming his count, "I'm involved with this hard-nosed Irish doll."

"Involved?" The word slipped out before Scally could stop it. "I assume you, uh, mean your business with Kayleen Enterprises?"

Frank blinked. "Of course I meant that, Scally!" The counting hand suddenly dropped, only to be raised again with the forefinger pointing directly at Scally. Frank's eyes were slits, his lips taunt. "For your information, never in my life have I been unfaithful to Josephine, and never will I be! Besides quitting smoking, you should also eliminate your other vice—chasing everyone who wears a skirt and hopping into bed with anyone who's willing!"

"Frank, you have your morals and I have mine!"

"You mean 'lack of,' don't you?"

"Look, I came down here at your invite," Scally responded hotly. "I've been willing to listen to your problems, but I didn't come to have you dissect mine. Why don't you elaborate on your business problems with Kayleen."

Frank paused a moment, as if reflecting. Finally, he returned his hand to the upright position, all four fingers pointing upwards. "Well, because of that Irish doll, I find myself torn."

He waited for Scally's interruption, but none came. Scally had surmised that discretion was the better part of valor.

"It's not just me that's torn," Frank continued. "The whole Italian community in Chicago is torn. The guys—including you, I might add—figure that brash chick insults me by refusing to offer me more money for my property. The dolls, on the other hand, are all abuzz with her kind and honoring words concerning Josephine. I have to agree that the broad's assessment of Josephine was accurate. Well, Josephine is naturally pleased with them. So this M.K. McDonald—"

"Walks on water, in the ladies' minds," Scally finished. After all, he himself had heard nothing but praise for this female CEO.

"Right, that's it. Not only that, but look at what's happening. She agreed to bail out Our Lady of Mercies Hospital's fundraiser by being the guest speaker. In her recent visit to the hospital, she displayed concern for the women and children. Chicago is beginning to view this broad as the best dish to hit the windy city in ages!"

"Maybe it would be wise for you to step back, take a gulp, and agree to her terms, given her genuine charitable interests." Scally cautiously put forth this idea, steeling himself for a blast which, to his surprise, never materialized.

Frank just nodded, pursed his lips. "That's what I was thinking, too, counselor. We can do that. You arrange for the parties to reconvene next week. But before we swim, let me finish my count."

"You're not done? There's more?"

Frank stared at his swimming partner. "I told you that I had a lot of problems."

"I know, but I couldn't imagine them all." Scally was once more visibly attentive.

Up went Frank's hand again. This time, his thumb joined the other digits. "Fifthly, I can't talk to Sophia, either."

"She's mad at you?"

"Naw, supposedly she and Tony are off on a romantic getaway. Won't be back for a week."

There was no way this very wary lawyer was going to venture another comment on either marital relations or sex. He was fully committed to using two ears and buttoning the one mouth.

"Josie and Lena are elated, of course," Frank continued. "They're counting on another grandchild being hatched. Pepi is ticked because Lena is babysitting the current brood of three. At seventy-two, he figures he shouldn't have to hear the pitter-patter of little feet for even a day, let alone a week." Frank chuckled. "Personally, I think it serves him right. After all, it was him who insisted the kids live in New York rather than Chicago. Pepi's discomfort isn't my problem. My problem is that Sophia and I have always seen eye to eye. I gave her a cell phone so we could talk whenever. So what does she do when I need her? She shuts it off! Which means I got this Irish chick making waves in my pond, and the only ones I can confide in aren't available." He jabbed his forefinger again at Scally. "By the way, I never did trust the Irish. With good reason, I might add!"

"Even if they're cute Irish?" Scally blurted, unable to help himself.

Frank's brow furrowed. "You think she's cute?"

Scally nodded. He wasn't going to reveal his true thoughts which were, *Now I know why you don't chase skirts, Frank Carron. You're myopic, perhaps even blind!*

"Well, cute or not, I have to deal with the turbulence she provokes on my turf," Frank said. "So here I sit. My always sensible, complacent son is a no-show. His sister is on a romantic week with her husband. Gus is unavailable, and my wife's comments are totally biased, as they pertain to the one who's my big problem."

"Indeed, Frank, you have a handful of problems," Scally intoned, hoping his facial features were registering concern. "But at least you made one decision this morning: to meet with Kayleen's representatives and agree not to demand more money for your property. I'd advise you to take their offer and redirect the extra money to a charity that would please the Italian community."

"Which would be?"

"One thought that crosses my mind is our need for a new sports complex in the inner city. You got some derelict eyesores there. You could tear them down and donate the land. They could use Kayleen money. I suspect others would chip in, and presto, it's a win-win for Chicago and us."

Scally smiled at the brilliance of the plan and noted that a faint smile crept across Frank's lips.

"Good idea, Counselor, good idea," Frank said. "Although I suspect M.K. McDonald's charity will equal your bill for this morning's legal advice. Regardless, it's time to get started on our laps, so let's go."

"Laps?" Scally's voice registered sheer terror.

"Yeah, I invited you to go swimming with me. I do fifty laps, length wise. It's good for your health."

"Maybe for your health, Frank, but not for mine! Here's the deal. I'll watch you do fifty laps. If you get in trouble, I'll push a life preserver to you. I'll even call for an ambulance. But no laps for me! My exercise is simply keeping you company. Hanging on to this floater will be my fee for the morning's consultation."

Scally was indeed desperate. The thought of even trying to swim one lap across the pool's width, never mind its length, caused near heart failure.

Frank narrowed his eyes. "You watch me. You count my laps… accurately! And no fee for today's consultation?" Up went his finger.

"For sure, accurately, and no fee," murmured Scally, nodding his head in agreement.

Frank nodded and reached across their floaters to shake Scally's hand. "Okay, it's a deal. No welching!"

"No welching," sighed a very relieved lawyer.

Frank held onto his hand. "But you know, Scally, you really do need the exercise. You've packed on too many pounds."

"I know." Scally paused. "Frank, you'd better start swimming. I have another appointment in two hours."

Scally breathed a sigh of relief as Frank started off.

"One!" he began to count.

chapter twenty-seven

All Independence Drive residents, both temporary and permanent, arrived at Jack's for breakfast. Marnie was in her glory as she orchestrated the meal—eggs, bacon, hot or cold cereal, crepes, omelets, and fruit. If you could name it, it was yours.

Her cuisine was slowly winning over Gus, and most definitely was improving his attitude. Al and Matt had fast become buds. The two were up early, jogging in the brisk fall morning, accompanied by Rufus. All three landed at Jack's with a hearty appetite. By the time they arrived, Gus's other four charges were already chowing down and appeared quite relaxed.

Jack earnestly dialogued with Sophia concerning her articling placement. He'd seen in her the same legal aptitude that was evident in her brother. He fully appreciated the bias she was encountering. More importantly, he was determined to help her overcome it.

Sue and Kaye pitched in to help Marnie. Tony cornered Max, curious to know more details of Kaye's rescue. He was astute enough to know that Max would only confide them in the absence of Kaye. Wisely, he appreciated that she was too traumatized and sensitive to relive the gory incident.

The only non-engaged resident was Dave, who simply toyed with his food. The others' preoccupations provided him his own personal space. Space he desperately needed in order to sort out Agent Epstein's early-morning revelation to him.

It was nearing noon when Dave decided the time had come to unveil the day's agenda.

"I got a call early this morning from Agent Epstein." Dave didn't bother to reveal how early. "He's inviting us out to the retreat. He'll have the bulletproof vests you requested, Max. Also, since the center has a good sport's facility, Epi thought it would be good for us to play some team sports, to help us develop some camaraderie for next week's venture." He turned to his son. "You have a question, Matt?"

"I was wondering if I could tag along, even though I'm not officially part of the plan."

Dave was about to say no when he recalled Epi's request. Matt might be useful to the Summerside sting component. "Yeah, I don't see any harm in it."

This obviously pleased not only Matt, but Al.

"As I was saying," Dave continued, "besides the three groups becoming familiar with one another, Epi is also inviting everyone to a steak barbecue courtesy of the Bureau."

"Does everyone include us?" piped up Sue.

"Absolutely, dear. I have just one request."

"Let me guess," his wife said dryly. "We girls bring the rest of the food."

"Nope, you got it all wrong!" He grinned at having the opportunity to gain a rare one-upmanship over the Independence Drive Organizational Committee, as he affectionately called Marnie and Sue. "I'd like the four ladies to get bathing suits for all the guys. That way, when we return, we can all enjoy Kaye and Max's new pool."

"That's it?" Marnie asked. "We get the afternoon off to shop?"

"Well, only partially. Have fun shopping, but then come to the retreat to join us for the barbecue. That way, we'll be able to fit Sophia for her vest."

Now it was Tony's turn to interrupt. "Wait a minute. Sophia's an integral part of the team. She needs to be in sync with everyone else."

This was the moment Dave had secretly hoped would arrive. It was an opportunity to score big with Gus, who by his body language had displayed disdain at the improving camaraderie between his crew and law enforcement.

"Actually, Sophia is really on Gus's team," Dave said slowly, choosing his words carefully, allowing them to register with everyone in the room. "He's the captain. Her coordination will need to be with you, Gus."

It worked. Suddenly, Gus was all ears. He was being given authority and jurisdiction over one important area of the sting. He wasn't simply being used. He was an integral part of the team.

Gus nodded his approval to Dave's plan. "We can work on it here together, Sophia."

Dave cleared his throat. "Agent Epstein shared some additional information with me that I feel is wise to convey." All eyes focused on him. "Our sting must take place Tuesday, not Monday."

"Why?" Max asked.

"Because Epi discovered that the Leuzeckis usually aren't at the store on Monday. However, they're always there Tuesday morning. This is actually better for us, as it allows us an extra day to prepare."

Silently, Dave thought, *At least I hope it's better for us!*

"I expect Epi will have already told the others about the change," Dave said. "Or maybe he'll do so when we're all together. I just wanted to give you fellows a head's up. I know Max isn't into surprises." He grinned at Max. "But I'd appreciate it if everyone handled my info with discretion. Meaning, if the others know, simply acknowledge that Epi gave me the information to share with you."

"If they don't and he reveals it when we're all together, act surprised," injected Gus. "Don't behave as know-it-alls. That doesn't build team spirit."

Way to go, Gus, Dave thought, *Way to go!*

"And if Epi doesn't reveal it today, hold your tongues," Max cautioned. "Trust Epi. He does nothing without finding the most advantageous scenario—and the most advantageous scenario for us guys is to clean up the kitchen to encourage Marnie. After all, we have two more days of needing her to be a cheerful hostess with the mostest."

This delighted the four women. Armed with the men's sizes for their bathing suits, they decided to get a head start at shopping.

Utilizing Dave's van and Jack's SUV, every one of the guys, including Rufus, descended upon the retreat center for their 2:00 p.m. Camaraderie Day—or CD Day, as they were jokingly calling it.

Epi had secured a layout of the store. He and Snyder went over the details with Gus. The large retail section encompassed most of the downstairs area. The remaining space housed six mechanical garage bays to service customers' vehicles. Adjacent to this was the service office. Cashier checkouts were located at the front of the store, alongside a customer service desk. Snyder pointed to a stairway, leading to the upstairs offices. The upstairs contained an open hall which extended the width of the building. A steel railing allowed visibility from the office area to the floor downstairs, and likewise the offices were visible from below. The office wall was made of glass.

"One-way glass or two?" Gus demanded.

Snyder looked at Epi, then at Gus. "At the top of the stairs, it's two-way. At the far end, it's one way. I also need to tell you that there's a connection between the offices. The brothers appear to have an open office at the head of the stairs, visible for all to see. Their real office is at the far end. We also know there's a hidden stairway from that office to the lower level and to a back exit. The stair also leads to the basement, which supposedly is used for storage."

"Where do you propose Sophia should meet these characters?" asked Gus. As far as he was concerned, there was only one plausible place.

Snyder, it seemed, had read his mind. "There's only one place she can go, Gus: at the bottom of the stairs. At no time must she get drawn into those offices, though."

"What happens if these characters get suspicious and make a grab for her?" Gus asked.

Epi spoke up quickly. "Then you'll need to get her out of there asap."

Gus looked Epi in the eye. "At what cost?"

"This is a sting," Epi replied. "If someone attempts to stop you by force, retaliate with discretion."

"Meaning?"

"Meaning we know the Leuzeckis have legitimate employees of a legitimate store," Snyder replied. "But that store is a front for all their illicit activity. Shoot the ones with weapons and exit via the main door. An unmarked van will pick you up, driven by one of my men, whom you'll know. We'll get you safely out of Newark."

"And we'll smokescreen you," Epi added. "Our spin will be that the Bureau has evidence of an interstate automotive theft ring. Fortunately, the Leuzeckis foiled the thievery. Those two are so egotistical that they may embrace a story they know is false, just for the publicity."

"Where does a failure leave Max?" Gus asked.

"Back at square one," Epi said. "He'll need to be cleared in court."

"Not desirable," muttered Gus. "And it leaves the Leuzeckis at large and unaccountable for Uncle Tommy's murder. Even more undesirable!"

"And unaccountable for our officer's murder," Snyder added.

Epi nodded. "And our agent's murder."

"Timing is crucial, gentlemen," Snyder stated bluntly. "Epi, I didn't say anything yesterday, but the Leuzeckis are never in the store on Mondays. Our sting needs to take place Tuesday, sometime shortly after eleven and before noon."

"Thanks for the information, Doug," Epi said, choosing to address the chief by his first name. "My sources gave me that same data today."

Gus was no fool. "So this means the sting is pushed ahead one more day?" he asked, acting convincingly surprised. "What's the reason for the one hour window, Chief Snyder?"

"If I can call you Gus, Mr. D'Amato, please call me Doug."

Gus was starting to warm to this initially unwelcomed drama. He and Frank had had their share of intrigue in days gone by, but they'd always managed to keep their noses clean. Gus had to admit that he had reveled in the suspense. This sting was especially appealing, though, because this time he was clearly on the "good guy" side.

Snyder went on to explain that Tuesday was dependable, because the Leuzeckis always did an on-the-spot TV ad for their upcoming weekend specials that day. The brothers dressed impeccably and were on their best behavior. Customers and curiosity-seekers would invariably be there. The Leuzeckis basked in the limelight.

Snyder smiled. "They characteristically end with the line. 'It has been so much fun getting to know you, our customers, but we do have a business to run. Please excuse us while we go take care of your needs.' Then they beat a hasty retreat, until the following Tuesday. It's not that they can't be spotted throughout the week. They can, but the timing cannot be predicted."

* * *

While Epi, Gus, and Snyder were meeting, the other team members engaged in a basketball game in the retreat's gym. Everyone except Max, whose leg had sidelined him, and Jack, who had chosen to keep Max company.

When Marnie told Jack how beautifully Max had sung in the shower, Jack asked him if he'd like to make their Independence Drive trio a quartet. Max had agreed, and now was the perfect opportunity for Jack to coach Max on a gospel piece they could sing the next day in church. Not only did Max love to sing, he was equally excited about publicly attending church for the first time with his wife. In fact, he was ecstatic in being able to go anywhere. He'd been cooped up for nearly seven years—six years in prison, three and a half months in Kaye's house, and another three and a half months in a hospital bed. Furthermore, he was enjoying all this male companionship. For the moment, the burden of the sting had faded from his mind.

Not so for Dave. He kept a close watch on the whereabouts of each person throughout the game. All were present and accounted for, but when the game ended one agent indicated he wanted to take a run on the retreat trails before supper.

"Great idea!" Dave enthused. "The woods are lovely this time of year."

Al and two Newark cops also indicated they'd like to go, and Dave volunteered Matt to lead them, since Matt knew the trails. Pulling his son aside, Dave instructed him to make sure he knew where each one was at all times and to have them back by four-thirty.

"Under no circumstance are you to allow anyone to go off by himself," Dave said.

As the five set out, Dave wondered if it was just his imagination or if one of those men hadn't seemed to relish the concept of an organized run.

Prefer a solo, old boy? Dave thought to himself. *I wonder why.*

Everyone was back and accounted for at four-thirty, including the four women. The barbeque went off without a hitch, and by seven o'clock the Independence Drive crew was on their way home for a much-anticipated swim.

Dave elected to ride with Gus, Jack, Tony, and Max. The conversation between the latter three was animated and jovial. Dave and Gus, on the other hand, were unusually silent, each lost in their own thoughts.

They were almost home before Dave realized that Gus, like himself, hadn't uttered one word.

He seems troubled about something, Dave mused. *Dare I risk asking him? Will he confide or resent my intrusion?*

Dave's opportunity arose later when Sophia and Tony called home to speak to their children. Dave and Gus were alone in the change room.

He began tentatively. "Gus, I noticed you've been particularly quiet. Is something troubling you?"

To Dave's surprise, Gus opened up. "It's one of the FBI agents. Something's bugging me about him, but I can't put my finger on it."

"Which one?"

"The guy who claims to have been the murdered agent's friend."

"That would be Talbot. He's the one who went jogging with Matt, Al, and the two Newark officers."

"Yeah, that's the one. I can't help but think I know him, only my mind's drawn a blank."

"Well, if it's important, I'm sure you'll remember. Did you ever tangle with the FBI?"

"No." Gus paused for a laugh. "We were too smart!"

Dave had to admit he appreciated Gus's wit. In fact, he was even getting to like Gus.

Marnie apprehended both as they headed for the pool. "The two of you are needed immediately in the living room."

The two men exchanged quizzical glances but headed directly there. Even before entering the room, Dave could hear Max, and it was obvious he was very upset.

"There's just no way we can go through with this, Sophia. I can't have you do it!" Max stated adamantly.

"What's going on?" Dave asked.

"Tony and I called the children, and now Max is all freaked out about my involvement in the sting," Sophia said angrily. "It's okay for you to martyr yourself, Max, but when anyone else steps up to the plate, you try and snatch their bat and refuse to play!"

"Sophia, listen to reason," Max pleaded. "When I went to prison, I was single. It was just me. You're a mother. You have three little kids. They were on the phone crying because they miss you. You've been gone only three days. If anything happens to you, those little guys will be devastated!"

"Nothing is going to happen to me. Quit hanging out the black crepe. You're such a pessimist, Max. You always were," she snapped at her brother. "There are nearly twenty people involved in this venture, all working as a team. Get on board! This is not a one-man band!"

"Excuse me, but remember when you, Miss Know-It-All, said there'd be no harm in dating him seven years ago?" Max jabbed at Tony and said, "I went along with you and nearly got killed. Then you two, Pop, Pepi—and yes, Gus—said, 'No problem. Just plead guilty. Nobody will ask any questions and you'll get a year and a half, maximum, Maybe even probation.' And you dare accuse me of being a pessimist, of always looking on the dark side? Maybe it's time someone listened to me! I know what I can't live with—my nephew and two nieces having a dead mother because of a harebrained scheme to clear me of something I never did."

Gus started to speak, but Max wheeled around. Max's eyes were black with determination. "I'm not finished yet, thank you! Sophia, you cannot do this for me! I'm calling Pop. This nonsense is ended!"

He yanked the phone off the receiver and began to dial, but as he did Gus stepped forward and yanked the cord from the wall.

"Sit down," he ordered Max. "Now!"

The decisiveness in Gus's action stunned everyone in the room. Max sat. It appeared he was about to speak again, when Gus barked at him.

"Shut up! No one speak for ten minutes, and I'll time it!"

Jack and Dave exchanged glances and sat down. Everyone sat silent for ten minutes. When the ten minutes were up, Gus started to chuckle. "It appears you're more like your father than anyone, including you, ever imagined."

Max looked puzzled. Everyone else's eyebrows raised. This revelation didn't amuse Sophia, since everyone had likened her to their father, not Max. She stood with arms folded and toe quietly tapping. She eyed Gus, unsure as to how she should challenge the man.

"What do you mean?" Max asked.

Gus sighed. "In any venture, your father weighs the risk to everyone around him. If he senses a great risk, a risk greater than he wants a person to take, he can be depended upon to try and abort the mission. He'd consult with his lieutenants, and their consensus would prevail. Your father chooses his confidants deliberately to ensure they won't be yes men. In a crunch, all are expected to convey their own sense of risk." Gus paused. "And we do. Sometimes it takes us three or four days to hash it out. I tell you the truth, the correct decision always follows, even if the outcome isn't what we expect initially."

"Like the decision seven years ago," Tony quietly spoke up. "You said it yourself, Max. It was a necessary decision. It saved Kaye's life!" He bit his lip and looked at his wife. "I love Sophia more than my own life, and I know the risk is real. Very real, Max! But so far my gut says we should carry on with the sting, and that's what I hear Sophia trying to say." He paused and looked at everyone else in the room. "And I think that's what we all believe, too. Am I right?"

"We hear your concern," Gus said to Max. We acknowledge that the danger is real. But the consensus, at least for the moment, is that we remain on track. Now it's your turn, Max, to look the rest of us in the eye and affirm or reject your trust in us."

Max found himself gazing into the eyes of those he'd come to trust. He nodded his head. "I honor your opinions. The sting can remain on course."

Sophia ran to her brother and kissed him. "Max, thank you so much for caring, for me and for Jo, Micki, and Rici."

"Personally, I think it was a sly diversionary tact to avoid exercising your leg," Tony said. "It's about time we head to the pool and ensure you do just that!"

chapter twenty-eight

Kaye woke early Sunday morning feeling as giddy as a teenager on her first date. Going to church this morning would be her first time in public with Max. Her heart's desire was that he would feel welcome and at home.

She lay quietly in bed, praying. *"Lord, this sting is so beyond me. I sense it could be very dangerous, especially for Sophia. Please send Your ministering angels to protect her and give her success in her task. I also pray that You would keep Gus and his men, the police, and the FBI agents safe."*

Kaye paused before continuing. *"I also ask You to guard our hearts and minds in this venture. We hate the evil the Leuzecki brothers have done, but we cannot hate them. Protect all of us, particularly Max and his family, from any seeds of bitterness taking root in our hearts. Wow! It's so easy to get angry and blame others, isn't it? But You came to forgive us and call Your followers to forgive our enemies. Vengeance belongs to You, our God, not to us. Grant us grace to let go and let You handle everything! Protect Max and his leg. Please don't let him reinjure it. Look after Tony. It will be hard for him not to be there to protect Sophia."*

She let out a deep sigh and bit her lip. *"Heavenly Father, I can't imagine how I can ever have a good relationship with Max's parents—well, maybe with his mother. She seems like she might be a very forgiving person. But his father? That's something else! All I can do is trust Your word, which promises that with You all things are possible. I give to you my relationship with Frank Carron. Only through you could I ever hope to find favor with that man."*

She rolled over onto her side. *"Thanks, Jesus, for Your invitation to cast all my burdens unto you. I wish somehow that You could use me to help others see the peace knowing You brings."* Curled up like a child on the side of her bed, Kaye couldn't help adding, *"You're right, Holy Spirit. Even though I'm so excited about my first public appearance with Max, I do have a foreboding today that I can't explain. Your word instructs me to be anxious about nothing but to offer up all my concerns to You. So here is this nebulous dark cloud that I don't understand. I surrender it to you. Thank You, Lord God, that all things are under Your control. I have absolute trust that you will work all things to the good of Your kingdom. Amen!"*

As she rolled out of bed and headed for the shower. "You certainly keep Your word, Jesus," she whispered to herself. "Yours is the peace that passes all understanding."

The final touches of her make-up completed, Kaye opened the door to discover Max dressed in his dark pinstriped suit, balancing on one leg as he adjusted his tie. So accustomed to seeing him in casual clothes, she found herself staring. He really was a strikingly handsome man!

Satisfied with his tie, Max glanced again at his reflection in the mirror and realized she was standing behind him. He broke into a smile, put his weight on his crutches, and turned to greet her.

"How long you been there?" he asked.

"Long enough to note how handsome the husband I picked is," she teased.

He laughed. "The husband you picked? If I recall correctly, it was I who found you."

"But I let you stay," she murmured as their lips touched. "And I'm so glad I did."

A knock on the bedroom door abruptly ended their reverie.

"Hey, lovebirds," Tony shouted. "It's half past eight. If the groom has to be at the church in an hour to practice, you'd better come for breakfast. Coffee's poured and Sophia's dishing out the eggs."

Max gently kissed his wife on her forehead as he opened the door. "After you, Mrs. Carron. The day awaits us!"

"Very nice!" Tony offered as he eyed the couple. "Very nice, indeed."

"I'm sure you're referring to my suit and the deftness with which I knotted my tie," quipped Max.

Tony watched his new sister-in-law head down the stairs in front of him, admiring her svelte figure. "Of course, my dear brother-in-law... yeah, my remark was all about you!"

They arrived at Summerside Community Church at 9:30. Max, Tony, and Sophia were astonished at the size of the complex. They later commented that they were equally surprised at the friendliness of the people. For their part, Gus and his crew noted with pleasure that free coffee was served in the lobby. Not only that, they were even invited to take their cup into the service.

Sophia's real joy came when Max sang four-part harmony with Jack, Dave, and Matt. Everyone was shocked by the fact that Al accompanied them on the baby grand.

Gus sat with his mouth agape. "I never knew he could play. He's good!"

For his part, Al was in his glory, *"Wow! I never played like that before, and never in church! I hope I get the chance to do it again."*

Afterward, Kaye treated everyone to brunch at Grandma's Country Kitchen, a literal smorgasbord of all you'd ever want to eat. Consequently, the Independence Drive group arrived at Jack's only twenty minutes before two o'clock. Everyone had time to change into casual clothes while Marnie got the large coffee percolator up and running.

"It's a good thing," Gus commented. "I for one could easily fall asleep after all that food."

Sitting in the large family room, Epi elected to begin with some "fun mixtures," as he called them. Snyder and Dave—and of course Max and Gus—elected to observe the games. Everyone else, including Jack and the women, leapt into the fray.

"Everyone whose birthday is between January and June, stand by the fireplace," Epi said. "Everyone whose birthday is between July and December, stand by the sliding doors."

He went on to organize them by the state in which they attended school, how many siblings they had, and whether they were married or unmarried.

Soon most everyone was laughing and making wise cracks. All except one; Gus' countenance darkened, almost in direct contrast to the increasing levity of the rest of the room. His eyes followed Talbot as he moved from one area to another. Gus' memories were returning to him. A single flashback recurred over and over again.

At first, he tried to dismiss it. However, the more he fought to suppress the imagery, the clearer it burned into his mind.

Why now? Gus wondered. *Why this memory? And how can this agent possibly be connected to my memory?*

Placing his hand in front of his eyes, he began to massage his temples. That did nothing to stop the violent replay assaulting him.

Suddenly, Talbot announced that he had to take a pee break. The guy had been fully involved in all the frivolities. As the agent left for the washroom, he appeared accidentally to bump into Sophia. He squeezed her hand.

"This is going to be fun!" he said to her.

Gus's blood went cold. He waited a moment, then quietly left the room in the opposite direction, but headed for the same washroom.

Going down the hall, Gus froze. The portable phone was no longer in its stand!

Seconds later, Talbot emerged from the washroom, still laughing. He slapped Gus on the back. "Hey, Gus, this is going to be fun!" he said, then sauntered back to the family room.

Gus' heart pounded as he made the fastest bathroom break in history.

Talbot was still hamming it up when Gus returned. Gus noted the man was starting to perspire.

Not surprising, Gus mused, *considering what he dropped in the basket in the bathroom.*

Gus found himself becoming enraged. They were being set up! Of this he was certain, beyond a shadow of a doubt. But to whom could he share his fears? Was Talbot acting alone? Were Max's friends really his friends? These suspicions tormented Gus' mind.

Gus wished he was anywhere but here, just as he had wished he had been somewhere else thirty years ago.

Thirty years ago! Gus gave a start. *This guy only looks to be in his late twenties. It can't be the same guy... What am I thinking?*

He had just about argued himself out of his torments, when Talbot doubled-over laughing. When he finally stood up, he exclaimed, "Wow, Epi, I'm really sweating. Mind if I step out back for a few gulps of fresh air?"

Without even thinking, Epi nodded. "Sure, just make it quick. We need to settle down and fine-tune our plan for Tuesday morning."

Gus watched Talbot head to the front door. Rocco was standing there.

The results of indecision thirty years ago flooded Gus's mind. He abruptly stood and, in Italian, barked a command to Rocco, who instinctively exploded into action. He landed a solid left into Talbot's midsection, doubling him over. As Talbot's head went down, Rocco's right connected with Talbot's chin and drove the man back into the family room, sprawling flat on his back. Out cold!

The room went immediately silent. All camaraderie, if it had ever existed, evaporated. Gus was livid, ranting in Italian at both Max and Tony. He strode over to Talbot and yanked at his jacket. Out fell the mobile phone.

Gus spun around to face Epi, who by now realized he'd been outwitted.

"This is your friend, Max," Gus exploded, pointing his finger at Epi. "He was setting us up to be murdered."

Tears flowed down Gus' face—tears of rage.

Max stood. Using his crutches, he moved to get a better look at the other side of the comatose Talbot.

"Not so, Gus," Max said. "Epi didn't set us up."

Expletives flew from Gus's mouth.

"Gus, sit down!" Max spoke, more forcefully. "I knew there was an informant. Epi did, too, and I suspect Dave did."

Dave nodded in the affirmative. "We just didn't know who."

Gus's eyes still blazed fire, but he was now at least silent. He sat back down.

All that went through Jack Walters' mind was, *Thank God everyone was disarmed. Otherwise it would have been a massacre.*

Max settled down on a stool behind the prone Talbot.

"Someone might like to cuff him before he comes to," Max said matter-of-factly. When nobody moved, he looked up with a grin on his face. "All these cops and no handcuffs?"

Matt tore home and returned within minutes with a pair of cuffs.

"Roll him over and cuff him behind," Max commanded. "Marnie, have you got a pair of scissors?"

"For what?" Jack asked, wide eyed.

"Just be patient, Your Honor. You'll see." Now Max had the attention of the whole room, including Gus. Max cocked his head to the side and motioned to Tony. "Take one of Marnie's table napkins, pull down his pants. I'm betting there's a glock right about there." He indicated the location with one of his crutches. He turned out to be right! "Take it with the napkin and give it to Epi. I'm a bit suspicious that the prints on the gun won't match Agent Talbot's prints."

"Whatever do you mean?" queried Epi.

"Chief Snyder, would you mind taking the scissors and cutting this man's turtleneck from the neck down to the belly button?" Max looked across the room at the Newark police and two FBI agents. "I'd have one of us do that, but it might make some of you nervous."

Snyder did as instructed. The whole room let out a collective gasp. Just below Talbot's collar line was a strange, skin-like flap.

"Good Lord!" Brian yelped.

Max motioned to a couple of the Newark officers. "Maybe you fellows could prop him up, as he's starting to wake. Brian, you might be interested in yanking up on that little flap there." He pointed with his crutch to the flap.

Brian dashed to obey. In a second, the man's mask had been stripped away and everyone came to understand why the real agent Talbot's prints were unlikely to match the ones on the gun.

Gus stood, his eyes wide with disbelief. He began to tremble, overcome with emotion. "It *is* him," he snarled. "Get him outta here before I kill him!"

Epi looked at the older man. Tears were moistening his face—no longer tears of rage but of great sorrow.

Dave had already summoned Sergeant Tom, and Epi had contacted the Bureau with instructions for two very specific agents to be sent immediately to Summerside. These new agents were well-known by him.

"Gus," Max spoke very quietly, "can you tell us who you think he is?"

"Please," Epi said, almost begging. "We need all the information we can get. If you know anything, share it. I assure you, nothing will be held against you."

Gus spoke slowly and deliberately. "It was over thirty years ago in L.A. Frank and I had been invited to go to the Rose Bowl. Frank had made some good investments for a few Italian businessmen, and this was their way of saying thank you. We were even told we could take our wives. Both Angel and Josephine were pretty excited. During the game, the girls went shopping. We were to meet some people our Italian businessmen friends thought might make good new clients for Frank. We ended up meeting Big Eddie."

"Eddie Fortunato?" Epi asked in amazement. "The man who was killed in that L.A. massacre?"

Gus shook his head sadly. "Yep, same Eddie."

"You were there?"

"If I were there, Agent Epstein, you'd be talking to a dead man, thanks to that creep over there!" Gus sighed. "Anyway, Big Eddie was definitely posturing that day. Also present were business friends from Miami and Vegas, and some other places I can't recall. Eddie introduced us all to your so-called Agent Talbot, only he called him Officer Giovanni Pavanti with the LAPD. Eddie called him a 'smart cop,' his mole on the force. Eddie gave a sinister laugh and said the guy was going to take some other smart cops and surprise some 'good friends' on the other side of town. Eddie patted the guy on the face. 'Right, Gio?' Eddie said, and you know what Gio said back?"

Everyone shook their heads.

Gus looked Sophia in the eye. "He said, 'Yep, Mr. Fortunato, this is going to be fun!'"

Sophia blanched, remembering Agent Talbot's words to her moments earlier.

"Eddie planned a party for around six that night. Already he had some Hollywood starlet types starting to show. Not bad-looking dolls, but considering the way they were dressed, this didn't seem to Frank and I like the sort of party we'd want to take our wives to. We began to be a little uneasy about the whole thing. However, one of our Chicago friends was going to go with his wife. I think it was his third missus, and he was pressuring us to go, too. I remember his wife, a young chick about six months pregnant. Anyway, we left to meet our wives." He looked at Max and Sophia. "Your father was grumbling all the way, like he always does when he has to do something he really doesn't want to. I remember saying to Frank that I had a bad gut feeling about that Giovanni kid. A kid? I mean, at the time, we were only six or eight years older.

"I told Frank that I had considered sharing my concerns with our Chicago friend, but I hesitated to do so because he was all pumped about being part of this bash. Anyway, our wives got held up as usual. They saw some movie star, got his autograph. That torqued Frank and me. Needless to say, we were about fifteen minutes late in getting back to Big Eddie's—and not on particularly good terms with our wives. As we were coming down the hall to the banquet room, we heard several shots fired. We ducked behind a row of planters as five or seven guys dressed as cops, including our Gio character, ran past us carrying semi-automatics. They went out the front door and hopped into two waiting cars.

"Within seconds, people were rushing into the banquet room. Frank and I left the girls standing there and pushed forward with the crowd." Gus drew a deep breath and put his hand over his mouth, as if even the memory nauseated him. "Blood was everywhere. A few people were still moving, one or two guys crying in pain, a few moans. That's when I saw our Chicago client lying dead in a pool of blood, his missus beside him riddled with bullets. Dead—and along with her, the unborn child. She wasn't the only woman killed, either."

Gus buried his face in his hands.

"The final count: eleven guys, six dolls dead, seventeen in all and another fifteen wounded. Needless to say, we left L.A. on the next flight we could get. I haven't thought of that scene in years. I blocked it out, but it just kept coming to me all afternoon, over and over again. I tried to dismiss it, to excuse it, but nothing seemed to stop it! When I heard that creep say to Sophia, 'This is going to be fun,' I couldn't believe my ears. My mouth went dry. I followed him to the john and realized the portable phone was missing. I knew he hadn't used the phone in the john. When he came out, he repeated that phrase to me: 'This is going to be fun.' Then, Epi, you were going to let him go outside alone. The flashback of that Chicago businessman's dead, pregnant Mrs. Number Three overwhelmed me. I kept thinking, if only I'd said something, maybe she and her kid would still be alive."

Gus stopped, overcome with emotion.

"This time round, I thought, 'Buddy, I'm not giving you a chance to call in your other coppers.' So I told Rocco to level him. But I kept thinking this couldn't be the same guy, because your Agent Talbot looked like he was maybe thirty."

Max moved over to sit beside Gus. He put his arm around him. "Thanks, Gus. Thanks ever so much!"

It wasn't long before the Summerside police van removed the former Agent Talbot under strict security. Those remaining at the Walters' house sat silent for over a quarter of an hour.

Chief Snyder was the first to speak. "Ethnic gangs seem very violent today. It doesn't seem to matter if women and children get hurt. But thirty years ago, I thought it was different. Like, wasn't there a code with the mafia? Women, children weren't to be touched?"

"Exactly," Gus said. "That's why it made no sense to Frank and me. After all, Eddie Fortunato had introduced the guy as Giovanni Pavanti. That's Italian. We gave the name to our friends in Chicago, but no one was ever able to locate him."

"As I recall, the police investigation concluded the murderers weren't cops," Epi said. "But all the eyewitness accounts agreed that the killers looked like uniformed officers carrying heavy artillery, running and jumping into unmarked cars and fleeing. Ironically, even in the street scuttlebutt, no gang took credit for what proved to be L.A.'s bloodiest massacre."

Brian spoke up. "Ep, didn't the police conclude that the perps were simply bloodthirsty thrill seekers?"

Sue couldn't remain silent any longer. "If Talbot, or Giovanni, or whoever, has resurfaced, could there be another six or seven on the loose with him?"

"My guess is no, Sue," Epi said confidently. "Over the next three or four years, police apprehended who they believed were five of the massacre suspects. Two were killed in botched robberies dressed as—"

"Let me guess," Marnie chimed in. "Police officers."

"You got it, Marnie," Epi said. "Of the three in custody, two confessed and incriminated the third."

"Which leaves one, possibly two unaccounted for, and one of these includes this Gio dude," Tony snapped. "He obviously tired of imitating ordinary cops. Perhaps it was more challenging to infiltrate the FBI?"

Epi nodded. "This could be a key breakthrough for us. What a bonus, if we can discover his true identity and link the Leuzeckis to this impersonator." At this, Epi shared his earlier concerns about the existence of an informant. "I had hoped we could flush him out in these three days. If we couldn't, I knew it would be necessary to cancel the sting. Thanks to you, Gus, I think we found our mole. Nonetheless, given the circumstances, I believe it only fair to give everyone the opportunity to remove themselves from the operation, if they want. I'm going to give each of you a piece of paper. Write your name on it and simply state 'in' or 'out.' I will honor your wish."

As the papers were counted, everyone was unanimous. All were in! The sting was on!

chapter twenty-nine

"Brain freeze, and I haven't even eaten ice cream," Kaye grumbled to herself as she strove to mentally process her 6:00 a.m. phone call. "Why now, Lord?"

"What's up?" Max mumbled.

"Does your father lie awake at night planning how he can be most disruptive to other people's lives?"

Max was now very wide awake. "That was my father?"

"No, it was Alice. Apparently, Vesuvius Enterprises informed us late last night that they've accepted our offer of equal recompense for their property. They also apparently very much appreciate Kayleen's offer of a charitable donation. They are willing to contribute land, in the city's inner core, to kick off the building of a large recreational center to benefit all Chicago's citizens—especially the young, seniors, and impoverished residents—"

"That's bad?" Max interrupted. "I thought you were all for helping those less fortunate, especially kids?"

Kaye stared at him in desperation. "Max, they want me in Chicago to finalize the deal! I have to leave by noon today. I probably won't get back until very late Tuesday evening."

Max flipped on his bedside lamp and couldn't help but grin at his wife. Even when she scowled, she was beautiful!

"I don't see anything funny in this," she snapped, bopping him with a pillow. That only got him laughing.

"Hon, I'm smiling because you're so beautiful, tousled hair, pout, and all! But Kaye, I think I can cope with a two-day separation, even though it's on our honeymoon. After all, I expect to be preoccupied myself those days."

She sat up on the bed, legs crossed, hands on her hips. "Max, this is no joke! Today, you're going over the final plans for this… this sting." She paused, concern showing on her face and in her voice. "Sophia, Gus, and the others are taking a tremendous risk. Furthermore, the outcome impacts you and me tremendously!"

Those words had the desired sobering effect. "I'm sorry, Kaye. But it's probably good for you to have Kayleen demands over the next forty-eight hours. If you're preoccupied, you won't worry so much about what's going on here."

"That's just the point." She looked at him in disbelief. "I can't focus on the Kayleen situation without worrying about Newark. Except for Sue and Marnie, everyone I care deeply for is going to be there. After yesterday, I have no illusions about how violent and dangerous it will be."

Max pulled her close to him, holding her tightly. "Kaye, either way, you cannot be in Newark with us. Everyone needs to focus. I need to focus."

"Are you saying that I'm a distraction?"

"Indeed you are. Remember what I needed you to do in the Glaxton case? Your role was to get away safely. The cops, the FBI, Gus's crew, and the rest of us all know the high level of risk we face on Tuesday. None of us are naïve."

"Even Sophia?" Kaye queried.

"Even Sophia! She grew up meeting some very tough characters. In New York, in her legal work, she's had to face some horrendous realities. Bottom line: everyone who's involved in this sting have specialized training or experience, and you haven't." Max stated these facts firmly but gently. "On the other hand, my dear, you've accomplished something few others have managed."

"What's that?"

"You got Pop to capitulate." He gave her a playful hug. "That is no mean feat, trust me!"

"Why do you think he gave in? Do you think he knows about us?"

"Of that, I can assure you. No!"

"How can you be so sure?"

"If Pop knew about us, he would be here. Yelling at me, in all probability," Max responded ruefully. "And one more thing: the sting would be off. He would never allow Sophia to go through with it."

Kaye sighed as she snuggled deeper into Max's arms. "I don't know if I can do what I must."

He kissed her on the forehead. "Let's ask for God's strength and protection for you and us, trusting that He promises to provide abundantly more than we can imagine."

They heard a sharp knock on the bedroom door.

"Kaye, Max, are you awake?" a muffled voice inquired. It was Sophia.

"Yes," Kaye said. "Come in, we're awake."

Sophia opened the door. "I heard the phone ring. Is there a problem?"

Tony followed his wife into the room and both plunked themselves down on the bed.

Isn't this cozy? Max thought to himself. *What every groom needs on his honeymoon: his baby sister and her husband in bed with him and his bride.* Out loud, he said, "Actually, it's good news. Well, good news, but difficult for Kaye."

Before Tony or Sophia could respond, Kaye explained. "Your father agreed to Kayleen's terms of sale. I'm needed later today in Chicago, and then tomorrow I have to do some publicity."

"You are really good at that publicity stuff, Kaye. What's the difficulty?" Tony asked, genuinely unable to conceptualize a problem. After all, had not his new sister-in-law just bested Frank Carron? That in itself was cause for celebration in his books.

"Don't you get it, Tony?" Sophia said. "Kaye will be in Chicago when we're in Newark. She'll have to act like all is A-okay while wondering what's going on with the sting."

"My point exactly," Kaye said jubilantly. She gave Sophia a high-five. "I'm glad someone appreciates my dilemma."

"Seriously, Kaye, do you know how very few people ever get Frank to back down on anything?" Tony asked. "You're the first one outside of family. Actually, you *are* family, but he doesn't know that yet, so your one-upmanship scores big!"

"So why do you think he changed his mind this time?" Kaye demanded.

Sophia's dark eyes sparkled. "Every community is made up of he's and she's, and our Italian community is no different. Good leaders pay attention nowadays to the vibes emanating from both sexes. Let's face it: as a successful business executive, you're a role model to many younger women. Your accidental yet honoring encounter with Mamma at the hospital strengthened your appeal with older community members, including Pop."

Sophia grinned. "Mamma is a very sweet, caring person, greatly loved by a lot of people in Chicago. Pop's decision to yield to your offer, particularly with the charity carrot, is political savvy, pure and simple."

"Hon, if the papers are any indication," Max said, "it looks like everyone views Kayleen's arrival in the windy city as a positive. You gave Pop a graceful out. He's a wily old codger, so he took it. Go to Chicago with all our blessings,

Ms. McDonald!" He bent over and kissed her. "Sophia will help you pack while Tone and I prepare breakfast."

* * *

It seemed to take only minutes for Lewis to pick her up and whisk her to the airport, though in fact it was nearly five hours later. Tony, Sophia, and Max elected to hang out in the pool so as to be invisible when Lewis arrived.

Max had remained faithful to his leg exercises. The warm water was helping his joint mobility. That, and the positive outcome in Chicago, had Max in good spirits when he arrived at Jack's for the next big sting meeting. He was hopeful that the next day's venture, though daring, would prove equally fruitful.

The atmosphere had definitely altered. An aura of mutual respect had settled over the group. Epi had secured a dossier on the L.A. massacre for his and Snyder's men to peruse. It didn't take a whiz kid to recognize that many of those killed had died simply because they'd been in the wrong place at the wrong time.

The Bureau was still trying to identify "Talbot," who as expected was anything but cooperative. Evidence was mounting, however, that he may have emigrated from the same eastern European country as the Leuzeckis' father. Fortunately, both Dave and Epi were able to report that he was secured and wouldn't interfere.

"Thanks primarily to a very astute Gus," Dave said.

The stature of Frank's lieutenant had definitely increased, not only among his own men but also with the police.

The principal focus of Monday's meeting was to coach Sophia. Dave and Jack likened it to a quarterback being grilled for a bowl game. No detail was overlooked as they described the Leuzecki brothers' strengths and the chinks in their armor. The biggest assets the sting had going for it was the brothers' egomaniac temperament and their insatiable lust for the opposite sex.

Epi had secured a house on the outskirts of Newark. They would arrive there at 7:30 Tuesday morning, in two vans, two cars, and a station wagon. They would appear as a work crew arriving to renovate the house. At nine o'clock, Rocco would travel in one of the vans with Epi, Agent Warren, and the new replacement agent, and two Newark police to the parking garage opposite the Leuzeckis' store.

Once there, the two agents and policemen would deploy with rifles to the rooftops of the adjacent buildings. All would be disguised as construction workers. Thus, both the front entrance and all side and rear exits of the building would be covered. Rocco, around 10:30, would move his van down the side alley towards the rear of the building, where he would wait for Gus and his crew to exit.

Epi would leave the parking garage dressed as a business executive, walk down the street, and rendezvous with Brian in the little diner located on the street opposite the store. They would keep vigil there until eleven, at which time they'd head to the unmarked car that Brian had parked opposite the store's entrance.

Snyder and his remaining officers would take the second van with Sophia, Tony, and Max. The latter two would be dressed as city construction workers. They would meet up with a Newark City Works truck—the Newark P.D. surveillance vehicle in disguise. That truck would proceed to a "work project" located in the street outside the store.

Snyder's van would position officers in uniform to patrol the street on foot, one approaching from the north and the other from the south. The van itself would park in the garage opposite the store.

As for Jack and Dave, Matt would drop them off at the Central Newark precinct to await the Leuzeckis. Matt would remain there until the police brought in Sophia. He would then take her directly back to Summerside. Once the Operation had secured the Leuzeckis, the surveillance truck would transfer Max and Tony to the precinct. The game plan was to have Epi, Snyder, Dave, and Jack all take part in the interrogation, using Max and Tony only if needed.

Gus's group would leave the house in the remaining car and station wagon. Gus, Luigi, and Silvio would use the station wagon; it had a handicap license and would park in the reserved space right outside the store's entrance. Al and Mario, to their delight, got the souped-up car. They could park on the street or in the parking garage. The plan was for them to get into the store around 10:30 to 10:45.

"Gus's crew should be the first group to enter. He'll move slower, being old and handicapped," Epi said with a laugh. "He's going to be slower to make his purchases. Both groups need to be in that store and comfortable with their surroundings before eleven, because that's when the Leuzeckis will stop fraternizing with the customers and head upstairs. It is then that Sophia will enter the store."

All attention turned to Sophia.

"Hopefully, you'll be able to connect with the Leuzeckis in the open," Snyder said, "yet still be private enough to get them to acknowledge their involvement in the frame job. Remember, Sophia, you don't have to activate the electronic recorder. The surveillance truck will handle it. But you've got to pull it out to get them to chase you. When you do, girl, make a bee line for the front door. Don't stop and don't look back. The moment you step into the street, I'll grab you and pull you into an unmarked car and get you out of there."

Snyder turned to the others. "If we're lucky, those two brothers will give chase and follow her onto the street, and that's when you nab them! Gus, your role is to ensure Sophia gets out that door without blocking the Leuzeckis' pursuit. Once she's out, get yourselves out of the building, through the back exit if you can. If it's too dangerous, use the front." He turned to the two officers who would be in uniform. "Steve, you two are responsible to ensure that no one interferes with Gus and his men hightailing it to Rocco." Next, he pointed to Rocco. "Be alert! While we prefer Gus to exit at the back, should you see them running from the front, get the van to them as quickly as you can, and take off!"

Epi motioned to the ones who would be stationed on the rooftops. "Meanwhile, you be alert. Where necessary, give the coverage needed."

As the debriefing wound down, Jack put his head in his hands. Finally he straightened up. "I feel like we're reaching into a bear's den to snatch her cub. I know everyone agreed to this, but I need to be reassured. Is it worth the risk you're all taking? There's still time to abort."

Snyder was the first to respond. "Jack, the Leuzeckis' operation poses the biggest threat to law and order in our city. This is the first tangible opportunity we've had to dismantle their organization. If this blows up in our faces, while I may not lose my life, I likely will lose my job. Also, I can be pretty sure the Leuzeckis will be gunning for me later. You're absolutely right that it's risky, especially for Gus and his crew. They need to speak for themselves. As for myself and my men, we've already buried one fine officer. We want to prevent the deaths of others, and this is our best chance. We're on board!"

All his men nodded their agreement.

"Jack, I know this all began with your desire to reverse the injustice done to Max," Epi said, "some of which admittedly was your fault. Even though you're my friend, I want you to know that I'm in this because of the Bureau, not to help you out. Somehow the Leuzeckis hold a clue to Howard's murder. I want justice for our agent."

Gus spoke quietly and calmly. "Yes, there are big risks. Personally, I see it more like stepping into a rattler's den, Jack. But these guys have shown only disdain for us Italians. Anybody who thinks they can walk into an old folks' home and shoot whoever they like needs to be stopped. Furthermore, yesterday was pretty shocking. I want to know how Talbot's impersonator connects to them, and maybe even the L.A. massacre." He looked at the younger men. "What about it? Are you still in?"

He received overwhelming affirmation.

Sophia's usually warm and lively eyes were as hard as flint. "These two men, with no provocation, attempted to murder the man I love, and then they framed my brother. They benefited from our ignorance and were responsible for bringing great pain to my mother and father. Going the court route would be devastating to both my parents and Tony's. I know it would harm you, too, Jack, even though I know that's not your motivation for wanting to avoid it." Tears sprung to her eyes. "I also know that if we abort this plan neither Max nor Kaye will support a court route, which means they'll suffer. I believe the Leuzeckis' ruthlessness needs to stop. It's time they suffer the consequences of their own actions, and this sting offers us a pretty good weapon to ensure that it happens—now!"

Max closed his eyes. "I need to thank you all for your willingness to take such risks. I know your motivations go far beyond helping me. Yet undeniably I'll be a great beneficiary of your efforts. So thank you, and may I also add that it would be a great comfort to me if we could once more lift this venture up to my Savior and Lord. Would everyone agree to that?"

Murmurs of assent made their way around the room.

Max looked at Jack, "Would you please do so?"

At the conclusion of Jack's prayer, a chorus of "Amens" filled the home.

212

chapter thirty

The normally unflappable M.K. McDonald was taken aback by the reception she received when her plane landed at O'Hare. She was used to press attention and was definitely media savvy. However, in the past that attention had been centered in *The Wall Street Journal*, the business section of local newspapers, magazines, and TV or radio reports. Now she found herself being treated akin to a celebrity. Much to her personal amusement, her no-nonsense directors seemed to relish the increased public interest in the business world. So did investors! Kayleen's stock had risen appreciably.

Arriving at her hotel suite, Kaye was pleasantly surprised by the response of her two aides. Looking at Philippe and Alice, she couldn't help think, *The two of you are almost purring. You certainly are in your element! Thank goodness, for I definitely need your sensitivity to people and attention to detail right now.*

She paused in front of the gilded mirror that graced her suite's lavish foyer. In her mind's eye, she imagined her father, R.K., smiling at her and saying, "That's my girl! Go get 'em, Tiger! I'm so proud of you!"

She closed her eyes as a tear trickled down her cheek. *Oh, Daddy, how I miss you, both you and Mummy!*

Kaye sighed and beat a hasty retreat to the washroom, where the trickle erupted into a raging torrent. She stuffed a towel over her mouth to deaden the sobs that were convulsing her.

Why now? At their funeral and in the days that had followed, no tears had sprung. She had been the epitome of stoicism. Now, sadness overwhelmed her. She leaned against the wall for support and slid to the floor. Her shoulders heaved as pent-up grief exploded. Minutes passed as she vented her heartache into the towel.

How I wish the two of you could have met Max. She gasped for breath, painfully aware, that at least in this world, that could never happen.

Gradually, her breathing became more controlled. The tsunami of tears receded and slowly a deep abiding peace encompassed her.

A quiet thought swept over her being. *"If those who believe in Me are with Me when they die, then through Me you are much closer to your parents than you may appreciate."* In response, Kaye took a deep breath and murmured. *"Right now, Jesus, I do feel so close to you!"*

This had a calming effect on her and a smile stole across her face. "Please, Jesus," she said softly. "Tell them how much I love them, and let them know how much I cherish Your gift of Max to me."

She sighed, rolled onto her knees, and rose once again to face herself in the mirror.

"Oh my," she gasped. "A major overhaul is needed here!"

Kaye had just finished washing her face with cold water and reapplying her makeup when Alice tapped softly on the bathroom door.

"M.K., are you all right?" Alice asked. Receiving a muffled reply to the affirmative, she continued, "Mr. Carron and Mr. Scallion are here, along with the other property owners. The mayor has arrived, too." Alice laughed. "They all await your presence, Your Majesty."

Seconds later, a rejuvenated M.K. McDonald emerged from the bathroom, eyes sparkling. All signs of her meltdown had been obliterated.

As she entered the suite's large reception area, it was apparent that one white-haired individual held everyone's attention. No one had yet noticed her arrival, so for a brief moment Kaye was afforded the rare opportunity of actually observing Chicago's so-called Mr. Italy.

Kaye's lips curved into a faint smile. *You really do have the gift of standing next to a person while simultaneously distancing yourself. No wonder Max found it hard to relate to you. Yet your daughter appears to have cracked your reserve.* She paused in her thoughts. *And I think I know how she did it!*

With that, she glided into the room, heading straight for Frank Carron. Extending her hand in greeting, she flashed a most provocative smile.

"Mr. Carron, I was surprised yet delighted to hear that you had agreed to sell your property to Kayleen."

Clasping his hand in hers, she looked directly into his eyes. His control completely evaporated. She had thrown him off-balance—something both he and she knew, yet a fact that Kaye, with both skill and wit, discreetly concealed from the rest of the room.

Gotcha, Mr. Carron. You no longer intimidate me.

214

The photo shoot, with all the dignitaries signing the transfer of property ownership to Kayleen, went off without a hitch. It had been agreed that all would meet the next morning at the building site, where Kayleen would unveil a model of the building soon to be erected. Further historic photos could then be taken. Following the site visit, all would gather for a simple lunch back at Kayleen's hotel suite. There, they would fine-tune the details of turning over ownership of the properties. Later in the day, Kayleen would host a dinner party for all the dignitaries and their guests. The dinner would provide the strategic opportunity to unveil plans for the city's new recreational center.

As for the day at hand, Omar, the Relocation Committee co-chair representing the board, had requested a meeting of key members of Kayleen's board of directors and management staff. At Kaye's suggestion, dinner would be served in the suite to maximize their time. Her real motivation was to provide herself a distraction from her mounting anxieties over Tuesday's Newark activities. It proved to be a wise decision. Omar was thrilled at the sudden turnaround in Vesuvius Enterprises' decision to sell.

"Building always creates enthusiasm and rejuvenates people," he commented exuberantly.

In the midst of all the optimism, Kaye realized that Clarin, the other Relocation Committee co-chair who represented management, was unusually quiet. "Something's troubling you, Clarin. What is it?"

"Well, M.K., you're right. I am troubled." Clarin glanced nervously at board member George Cantarro, who sat savoring his port. "Perhaps you can relieve my fears, George?"

Cradling the wine goblet in his hand, George eyed Clarin, not hiding the puzzlement the man's question had evoked.

Leo Solanger, Vice-President of Marketing, interrupted. "Whatever concerns could you have, Clarin? Everything's going so well. M.K. has become the darling of Chicago—single handedly overpowering the old boys' club, I might add." He chuckled. "Furthermore, the local newspapers are alluding, tongue-in-cheek, of course, to Chicago's roaring twenties and the thirties mob clashes between the Italians and the Irish. The Tribune said, 'Does the last hurrah belong to the Irish?' Things are going our way, Clarin, my boy. You need to learn to savor the moment!"

Clarin pursed his lips. "What you consider favorable press, I consider unfavorable. I don't know anything personal about Carron, but I do know that there's a powerful Italian influence in this city through the labor unions." He eyed George. "You have Italian connections. Do you know Carron? How do you read the situation? It seems to me that in some circles, there's a subtle putdown of this man. How is he likely to react?"

All attention now turned to George. Clarin's questions had caught him totally off-guard.

Kaye looked hard at George. George had just been placed squarely between a rock and a hard place. He had always been a hundred percent aboveboard. She wondered how he would respond. Certainly, his next words could determine his future usefulness to both herself and the company.

George's mouth went dry. He had dreaded a situation like this. He drew a deep breath. *Well, George, this is where the rubber meets the road. "Dear God, give me the wisdom and grace to speak the truth."*

Then he began, speaking slowly to accentuate each word. "Yes, I know Frank Carron. Not well, but I do know him. As you know, Italian Catholics often have large family connections. My wife's father, it turns out, was a second cousin to Josephine Carron."

This admission drew startled responses from the others. For Kaye, it evoked a quiet sigh of relief. George had chosen to remain transparent, in keeping with the trustworthiness Kaye always believed he had.

"Did you influence his decision?" Clarin asked incredulously.

"No, I didn't. I honestly can't tell you why he reversed his position. And yes, it does concern me about the spin that some media representatives are placing on his decision." George ran a hand through his hair. "Frank has lived most of his life in the States, but he was born and raised in the old country. For men his age, there is a certain pride or level of respect that's both desired and expected. I also agree that some parties seem intent on undermining him."

"When Kayleen begins construction, are you suggesting he might perceive it as an opportunity to retaliate?" Clarin queried bluntly.

George shook his head as a smile tugged at the corner of his lips. "While I can't be certain, I don't think so. Frank is too smart a cookie to ever be so obvious."

George paused, studying the faces around the room, especially M.K. McDonald's. His heart was with Kayleen, yet how much could he—*should* he— say? He threw his head back against his chair and sighed.

"I don't know how much you are aware, but Frank Carron's oldest child and only son, Massimiliano, was charged with drug trafficking seven years ago." George proceeded to share how out of character that behavior had seemed for everyone who knew the younger Carron. He had no previous record, and from all the family gossip, as far as George could tell, no one had ever seen him crossing the line. Regardless, in court he'd had the book thrown at him.

"That sentence was never appealed," George said. "Why? I haven't a clue. All I know is that Frank's son was released in April, and for all intents and purposes, he seems to have fallen off the planet."

By now everyone in the room was leaning forward, captivated by George's story. Kaye hoped that she looked equally intrigued.

"The one thing I can say for certain is that Massimiliano's failure to return home devastated his mother. Although Frank is a closed book emotionally, I sense that his son's disappearance is tearing him up, too."

George turned to face Kaye. "M.K., all I can speculate is that with all those personal pressures on him, coupled with your genuinely complimentary words concerning his wife, Frank didn't have the energy or passion to fight. Consequently, he capitulated to Kayleen's terms." Here, George's voice became firm and directive. "But I do think it would be prudent, as Kayleen's leaders, to strive not to demean Frank Carron. Both through our words and actions, we ought to afford him the respect he is due. This would benefit not only Carron and the Italian community, but Chicago as well. Frank has earned respect in both segments of the Italian community."

Clarin cut in. "George, please clarify your last remark. Do you mean that Carron holds respect both in the legitimate Italian circles and the mafia?"

"Yes," George replied curtly. "It is a delicate balance to maintain, but Frank appears to have been able to walk that fine line."

At last Kaye spoke. "I wish to thank you, George, for your candor and insight. Your frankness is most helpful. I'll personally take your advice to heart. I also request that the rest of you be attentive to any perceived demeaning comments concerning Mr. Carron. Should any be discovered, let us seek creative ways to counteract them."

When she finally retired to her private quarters, Kaye was emotionally drained. On the one hand, she was elated at the stance George had taken. From her perspective, his honesty had assured his advancement up Kayleen's corporate ladder. Though none of the others were privy to all the knowledge she possessed, including George, when everything was revealed they would all realize that tonight George had proven himself totally loyal to Kayleen.

On the other hand, Chicago wasn't her primary focus; it was Newark! She had hoped to speak with Max. Unfortunately, aware of the early start he would have to make to Newark, when she was free to call, the time zone difference made it too late to do so.

Lastly, although she couldn't put her finger on why, George's talk about the Carrons heightened her own nagging concern for Frank.

chapter thirty-one

For most people, getting up at 5:00 a.m. isn't the most enjoyable way to begin a day. In November, in Pennsylvania, it definitely sucked—at least that was Max's assessment of the situation. He dressed in blue jeans, a turtleneck pullover, and fleece-lined denim jacket. In Kaye's absence, he elected not to shave. Riding down the highway, his every thought was a prayer: for his parents, for Kaye, for Sophia, and for the sting. He took each thought to the Lord.

One thing he couldn't seem to shake was the foreboding he felt for his father. At last, he decided to pull out his pocket Bible. Using a small flashlight, he began to read from the Psalms. They always seemed to comfort him, especially the ones written by King David. In Max's opinion, David was an okay guy who knew all about being misunderstood. David never minced words about his troubles and his despair. Yet no matter what David was experiencing or feeling, even considering the mistakes he made, in the end he always turned to the Lord for the strength and hope he needed to carry on.

That's what I'm doing with my father. Max prayed, *"Lord, please keep him safe, and please look after Sophia. Let us all come together as a family and, dear Jesus, please let my family welcome Kaye."*

After that, he figured he must have dozed off, because as they pulled into the rendezvous site, he suddenly realized it was daylight.

Epi greeted them as they stepped from their vehicles. He took one look at Jack and quipped, "A tad tense are we, Your Honor?"

"Small wonder," Jack replied. "What we're doing isn't even remotely in my job description."

Everyone began dressing for their respective roles. Epi instructed Max and his crew on the proper positioning of their bulletproof vests. Snyder and Brian distributed the electronic communication devices, reminding each member of the team that they would be monitored by the surveillance truck. Gus wore an earpiece that resembled an ordinary hearing aid. He would be in direct contact with the van. If there was any need to abort the mission and get his men out quickly, he would be alerted. Visual cues had been established for him to alert Mario and Al, and all five men had the procedure for doing so down pat.

"We're not going to abort the mission," Gus growled. "Take my word for it!"

Sophia was fascinated by the minuteness of the hidden mikes and cameras, all of which were wireless. One appeared as a gold pendant, another as her earring. In her stylish, fur-lined jacket, she carried the tiny portable decoy recorder. Epi went over the logistics with her, warning that she didn't have to be close to the Leuzeckis to capture their conversation.

"These mikes will clearly pick up voices ten to fifteen feet away," Epi said. "Our equipment in the van is able to differentiate speakers and match voices."

It seemed like no time before Epi began to deploy the various teams. Max gave Sophia a hug, his eyes registering deep concern. Tony took his wife's hand and they walked off to the back porch.

He cupped her face in his hands. "Hey babe, no heroics. Promise? You got three kids who need you. If those guys ever did anything to you, I couldn't stand idly by, and I mean that!"

She melted into his arms. "I know, and I promise—no heroics. Tony, you do know that when I speak to those brothers, I'm going to have to put you down, don't you?"

"What do you mean?"

"If I'm going to flirt with them, I have to dismiss you." She gazed intently into his eyes. "You need to know that I don't mean anything derogatory I say about you. You need to tell me now that you understand."

"What am I supposed to say?" Tony asked blankly.

"That you know anything I say about you and your sexual abilities is phony," she replied tersely. "I need to know that you trust my love for you."

"Yeah, hon, I know you love me and nobody else." He gave her a bear hug and a passionate kiss. "There, is that proof enough?"

Sophia tossed her head back and laughed. "Yes indeed."

* * *

Tony and Max rode silently in the unmarked police van with Chief Snyder and his officers. The sting had begun in deadly earnest.

Max reached under his jacket, his hand closing on his gun. *J.D. is my pacifier today,* he thought. *Its presence brings me both confidence and peace. I really enjoy target shooting, sure, but even the thought of using it on people is distressing.*

He looked at Tony and mouthed, "You got a gun?" and received a glance that spelled 'Duh, yeah!' as if Max somehow had three heads.

It wasn't long before Snyder pulled into a secluded laneway and parked beside a large white surveillance van boldly marked "Newark P.U.C." Two men dressed in city work coveralls, complete with safety vests and hard hats, sat in the cab. They nodded to Snyder, looking with interest as Max, aided by Tony, hobbled over on his crutches.

"Here's your passengers, boys. The one with the crutches is Max. Tony is his brother-in-law." Snyder opened the door to the back of the van, holding it open for Tony and Max. "Your fellow camper is Charlie."

"Hi, guys, come on in," Charlie's cheerful voice called out from the front. "I've been expecting you." Charlie was a huge, freckle-faced cop with a mop of red hair pulled back in a ponytail.

Tony hopped into the surveillance van and reached back to help Max up. No sooner were they in than Snyder slammed the door shut. Both heard a distinct click.

"What's that?" Tony asked in alarm, looking at Max, who obviously shared his concern. Max grabbed the handle.

"No use, guys," Charlie said amiably. "You and me is roomies for the next few hours. As you heard, my name's Charlie. I take it you're Max." He nodded towards his crutches. "Better sit down, we'll be moving soon. You, big guy. You must be Tony." He extended his hand to the two of them. "Don't look so shocked about the locked door. The Bureau said that under no circumstances were we to let either of you loose until this is all over." He gestured toward Max. "So you don't further injure your leg, and you," he jabbed at Tony with a beefy hand, "so you don't lose it when you hear your wife and blow our cover."

"What do you mean, hear my wife?" Tony asked.

"Hey, everything that happens with her, we hear it too. And see some of it." Charlie began turning switches and dials. Suddenly, the inside of the vehicle came alive.

"Sheesh! This looks like something out of a spy movie," Tony said.

Both men were captivated by all the technology. Their anxiety levels diminished as their curiosity piqued. "You've got to be older than you look," ventured Max.

"Uh-huh." Charlie laughed. "Likely the same vintage as you, if I've correctly pegged it. You in your thirties?"

His easygoing nature disarmed both Tony and Max. For a brief time, they were so intrigued by all the bells and whistles that they forgot all about their mission and about being locked in the truck.

Abruptly, the van came to a stop.

"Fifteen minutes to show time," Charlie chimed. Images soon emerged on the instrumentation panels.

"Wow!" Tony exclaimed, sucking in his breath. They could see the entrance to the store. They were also able to see the street in both directions. Way down, they could make out a patrolman slowly walking his beat.

"How's the weather, Steve?" Charlie said into his mike.

"Top of the morning to you, Charlie," came the chipper response.

"That's one of our guys," Max blurted. "I mean, one of your Newark officers."

"You were correct the first time," Charlie chortled. "We're in this together, dudes!"

It wasn't long before the old Chevy station wagon drew into one of the handicap parking spaces in front of the store. The driver and another young man got out of the car. One went to the passenger side and opened the door, helping out a gimpy older man with a cane.

"There's Gus." Tony gulped as he watched the three men move slowly toward the store's entrance. He started to laugh. "Man, Gus looks like a dotty old geezer. Didn't know he could act so good!"

The trio entered the store.

"So we lose visual now?" Max asked.

"Nope. All we need is a flip of the switch."

Soon the screen had the three in full view. A clerk came up and they could hear Luigi outlining his quest to find spare parts for his uncle's wagon. The clerk pointed them towards the back of the store. Charlie, Max, and Tony watched Gus' antics with amusement as the clerk alerted him to the TV crew and requested customers to be quiet until the advertising taping was over.

Tony stifled a laugh. "Look at the old codger asking that clerk all about the TV camera, as if he's really fascinated by it."

"He's pretty convincing," Charlie acknowledged, stroking his chin.

"You can say that again." Tony snorted. "Sly as a fox!"

About five minutes later, Al and Mario entered. Both looked like well-heeled car buffs. Mario clearly knew his stuff. The clerk directed them to the opposite side of the center aisle from Gus. Several other customers were present in the store, obviously delighting to be near the video shoot.

"They pay them," Charlie commented.

"You're joking," Max said in surprise.

"No," Charlie said. "It's the truth."

At that moment, the brothers came into full view of the surveillance camera.

Tony leapt to his feet. "They were slimy creeps then and nothing's changed, except they're older and paunchier. You'd have to pay a dame to look at them."

Totally missing Tony's figure of speech, Charlie simply nodded. "Right, and that's exactly what they do. Unfortunately, any gal who thinks it's easy money will soon discover otherwise."

The TV crew exited the building as the brothers issued their farewell to their devoted customers and turned to head up the stairs. Right on cue, Sophia burst through the door—provocatively dressed, sexually alluring, and oozing wealth. In the surveillance van, three pairs of eyes stared at the monitor as she waltzed towards the information desk demanding to see the Leuzeckis.

Halfway up the stairs, the men turned, eyebrows raised. "What can we do for you, miss—"

"Ms. Carron," Sophia interrupted. "I can see now that my attraction for you two was misappropriated."

"Pardon?" stammered one of the brothers.

Max smiled. "She's caught them both off-guard. Way to go, sis!"

Feigning a Marilyn Monroe pout, Sophia purred, "All along, I thought you two had eyes for me. Now I see you can't even remember."

"Ms. Carron? Oh-ho, do I remember!" Jon Leuzecki said, drooling. "I went to great trouble to get your attention, babe!"

"Really?" she asked.

"Yes, really!"

Both brothers were now coming back down the stairs. Sophia positioned a large display box between herself and the advancing Leuzeckis. She struck a sultry pose.

"Just what trouble did you exert to win my attention?" she asked.

The brothers waved staff away from the immediate vicinity. Alex Leuzecki reached across to touch her open blouse. "Nice locket, dear. Did your blockhead boyfriend give you that?"

Tony was on his feet, fists clenched.

"Don't lose your cool, bud," Charlie warned. "Our equipment is sensitive. A wrong move could interfere with our transmission."

It was a good thing Charlie had uttered his word of caution, because the subsequent dialogue had Tony literally beside himself. He felt like taking a crow bar and smashing everything in sight. Sophia hadn't lied to him. She was putting him down in every way, especially his sexual prowess.

Suddenly, Jon Leuzecki could contain himself no longer. Sophia had successfully stoked his pride. He was as puffed-up as a peacock. "Listen, doll, we went to great expense and risk to bed you."

The younger brother chimed in. "We succeeded in conning your stupid goon of a boyfriend to come to the hotel room, on the premise of completing his course project. We even paid his classmate a thousand bucks to lure him."

Jon began to laugh. "Naturally, when the idiot was a no-show and we had to deal with your nosy brother, we managed to get a refund on our deal." He looked at his brother. "He wasn't going to give back our hard-earned cash initially, but let's just say Alex's persuasiveness finally paid off."

"Hey, gorgeous," Alex said with a chuckle, "at least we took care of your babysitter. With the drugs we dumped on the floor, those stupid cops were sure they'd nailed a major drug pusher!"

The older Leuzecki sneered. "I hope he woke with a good headache. No brother should interfere in his sister's pleasure. I'm all for women's lib!"

Sophia heart was racing. She could smell the garlic on the men's breath as they leaned across the box. Jon frowned. "We went looking for you the next day but you were gone."

"Gone? What did you expect?" She snapped. "You blew it when my boyfriend heard you'd fired a shot at the bed to kill him. He grabbed me and ran!"

This prompted the older Leuzecki to explode at his younger brother. "I told you not to fire that shot, Alex, but no, you were all for killing him. To make it look like a drug deal gone bad, you said. Idiot!"

How convenient is sibling rivalry, Sophia mused.

In the split second the brothers focused on each other, she backed off. About five feet away, boxes expediently placed between herself and them, she pulled out the decoy recorder. She held it high.

"Thanks so much, boys, for the confession," she drawled sweetly. With that, she turned and headed for the door.

It took a moment for the men to register that they had just been taken. Then, in rage, they charged after her, bursting through the boxes and uttering every vulgar expletive known.

When Sophia was about six feet from the door, Tony saw one of the Leuzeckis' goons race to cut her off. Just as suddenly, the man was careening out of control, thanks to Al dropping a box of ball bearings in his path. The man sprawled into another display, sending even more boxes flying and enabling Sophia to exit onto the street, both brothers in hot pursuit.

Jon Leuzecki grabbed Sophia's coat, yanking her toward him. He raised his fist to smash her face. In fact, the microphone captured the explicit threat.

The street erupted with the finest of Newark's P.D., both in plainclothes and uniforms. In the surveillance truck, Max and Tony held their breath only to let out a whoop when they saw Snyder pull Sophia into his squad car.

Another unmarked cruiser tore from the alley across the street. It stopped at the front of the Leuzecki store, ready to retrieve the now-handcuffed brothers. With the Leuzeckis on their way to the precinct, Tony figured the sting was over, but then something totally unexpected happened.

The Leuzeckis' staff began setting the store's computer towers out on the street. It caught the cops by surprise, but it didn't take Epi long to capitalize on this turn of events.

"Warrants aren't needed for anything placed on public sidewalks," he yelled to the police, and soon the remaining cruisers were filled with nearly twenty towers.

Scrutinized later, most were found to contain routine business inventory and sales information. These were, of course, returned to the store after the IRS performed a thorough and incriminating audit.

The really interesting data, however, was found on two specific computers. To say the two brothers were psychopaths would have been a major understatement. They had documented all their recent criminal activities, including the murders of Tommy Bastaldi, the Newark police officer, and their complicity in Agent Howard's death. They had even catalogued the identity of the Talbot impersonator.

Much to the Bureau's delight and surprise, the sting unearthed a previously unrecognized international drug and arms cartel in Eastern Europe. It turned out the Leuzeckis could be linked to the L.A. massacre culprits, after all. The Talbot impersonator had been an older cousin. He had operated in the west for many years on behalf of that European cartel as it sought to slice into organized crime profits. Skilled in theatrical makeup, the man had relished impersonating police officers, thereby catching his victims off guard. He had done this in L.A. thirty years before. He had done it with Agent Howard, and he'd been attempting to do it again with the sting. His downfall had been his cousins' massive egotism and Gus's recall. The latter had succeeded in getting him arrested. The former would provide the evidence needed to convict.

While all this would prove useful to the state's case against the brothers and their cousin, it did nothing to strike down Max's conviction. The sting's original purpose was still unfulfilled. That's why Max and Tony ended up with Charlie in the Newark precinct, awaiting the outcome of the Leuzeckis' interrogation.

chapter thirty-two

Kaye found herself tossing and turning all night. Sleep came in fits and
starts. Each time she awoke, a prayer was on her lips. Her mind flitted
constantly between the two time zones. Rising to shower at seven, she
knew it would be eight in Newark.

They should be there now. "*Oh Lord, please keep everyone safe and help me
function as I must today.*"

She found herself singing spontaneously. "What a friend we have in Jesus,
all our sins and griefs to bear. What a privilege to carry everything to Him in
prayer."

Kaye slipped the gold chain that carried her wedding ring around her neck
and tucked it underneath her turtleneck sweater.

"Very soon, I'll have the honor of displaying you publicly," she said to herself
with a sigh. "And oh, how proud I will be to do so!"

Dressed in a sky-blue weekender outfit—slacks, turtleneck, and knee-length
cardigan jacket—Kaye was indeed a very striking woman. Joining Philippe
and Alice for breakfast, she was briefed on all the dignitaries she would be
encountering that day.

"By the way, M.K.," Alice said, "far be it from me to interfere in your dating
selections, but I'd be remiss if I didn't note one individual."

"Surely, you're not turning matchmaker?" Philippe chided.

"Definitely not," Alice replied wryly. "The correct designation is non-
matchmaker! There's a lawyer in town who somehow weaseled his way onto the
city's payroll. At one time, he was on staff at the district attorney's office. He
appears to fancy himself as God's gift to women, though I note there's a gold
band on his ring finger."

Philippe smirked. "Dear Alice, don't tell me he's womanizing you."

"No, Philippe, he isn't 'womanizing me.' If he tried, I'd deck him. As it is, I have to restrain myself every time I'm near the man. He's so patronizing and demeaning." She began to mimic the sound of his voice. "Oh, dear, would you be so sweet to…" She paused and added in Kaye's direction, "I also note that he seems particularly derogatory to your Mr. Carron."

Kaye smiled. "My Mr. Carron? I don't think that he's a member of my fan club, Alice. But tell me, dear, what is the name of your sleazy lawyer?" She grinned, her green eyes twinkling. "Sorry, Alice, I just couldn't resist!"

Alice feigned a pout, "Kayleen should pay me a huge bonus for having to endure meal time with the two of you! His name is Gavin… Gavin McLeod, I believe."

"McLeod?" Kaye chewed on her lip. "Why does that name sound familiar?"

Philippe grunted. "It's fortunate that some of Kayleen's staff have good memory retention. It's small wonder that you sensed him putting down Carron, Alice. He was the prosecutor who sent Carron's son to prison."

Kaye nearly spilled the juice she was about to pour. "McLeod sent his son to prison, and he has the nerve to taunt Carron?"

"From my observations of him, he only does so when he has an audience," Alice chirped. "I suspect if anything happened to dear Mr. McLeod, Carron would be the prime suspect. Like Mr. Cantarro said, Mr. Carron is too smart for that. I guess McLeod thinks he's safe to play the big shot."

Kaye sighed. "Nonetheless, McLeod's putdowns, in the midst of an elite audience, will be all the more hurtful to Mr. Carron, particularly given his son's disappearance."

Their conversation was interrupted by Clarin's arrival and his admonition that they should dress warmly. The limo was waiting to carry them to the construction site.

Onsite, Kaye gritted her teeth and groaned inwardly. *More photo ops!* Good-naturedly, she donned her white hardhat, picked up the gold-plated spade, and shoveled the first dirt. *Fortunately, winter has been a bit slow arriving. The ground is still soft enough that it doesn't scratch our precious spade.*

To her dismay, the group chose to linger in the area, recounting folklore about the site—from the great Chicago fire to prohibition gangsters and musings about gangland burial grounds. From Kaye's read of Chicago history, none of those events appeared to be situated anywhere remotely near their site. And given her preoccupation with Newark, it took all her resolve to appear cheerful and upbeat.

At one point, Gavin McLeod baited Carron. Gesturing toward the warehouse Kaye herself had once visited, he said, "Hey Frank, they say that when Kayleen begins to dig here, they can expect to uncover several graves."

What an ass, Kaye thought.

Frank raised an eyebrow. "During the time period in question, I wasn't even a glint in my mother's eye."

Kaye couldn't help smiling. *Way to go, Frank. Way to go!*

Because of all the discussion, everyone was delayed in arriving back at Kayleen's hospitality suite, not returning until 1:00 p.m. Chicago time—which meant 2:00 p.m. Newark time. Kaye was beside herself. She had asked Epi to notify her as soon as he had any word. It disappointed her to arrive and discover no such message.

In a sense, she felt as if she existed in slow motion. She was conscious of both movement and voices around her, yet emotionally she was detached. It was nearly an hour later when her eye caught a man approaching one of the security guards. She saw the man flash his credentials. The guard then pointed towards Kaye.

She stood as the man approached and motioned for him to step aside and speak privately with her. The man was smiling.

Kaye's heart was pounding hard. *If he's smiling, that has to be a good sign.*

"Ms. McDonald, our agent in Washington, Bernard Epstein," the man said, "asked us to convey a message to you. Mr. Epstein said simply, 'Tell Ms. McDonald that the harvest was successful, and no fruit was damaged in the process.'" He paused and looked quizzically at Kaye. "He said you would understand the message."

If this agent had expected Kaye to do anything more than nod, agree that it was good news, and thank him, he would have been disappointed, for that was all she did. However, the moment the man left, she took a deep breath. Her eyes moistened and she discreetly buried her face in her hands. Quickly excusing herself, she hurried to the washroom—her private prayer chamber. There, in the privacy of a cubicle, she gave thanks to her Lord for His mercy, grace, and providence.

In Kaye's absence, Gavin McLeod had also received a message. His messenger carried a little portable radio and whispered something in McLeod's ear. Philippe, who happened to be standing nearby, witnessed the whole event. He heard McLeod say, "Really?" Then McLeod raised his eyebrows and momentarily paled. He seemed to recover, check his watch, then swagger over to where Frank

Carron sat talking with Mr. Scallion and one of the mayor's officials about the proposed recreational complex.

At that point, Kaye returned to the room. She was shocked to hear how McLeod was addressing Carron.

"Apparently, Frank, they've found your son," McLeod said, stone-faced.

One could have heard a pin drop. All eyes riveted on Gavin McLeod, a situation the man obviously reveled in.

Frank simply blinked and swallowed hard. His eyes locked onto McLeod's, not daring to ask the question whose answer he dreaded.

"Is he alive?" Scallion asked.

McLeod just grunted, as if to imply, *How should I know?*

"Apparently," McLeod said after a moment of hesitation. "And apparently I owe you an apology."

"Why?" Frank asked.

McLeod paused to ensure that he had captured the attention of everyone in the room. "Apparently he didn't do what he was sent down for. It looks like he was framed. The feds have the real culprits. Good news, Frank?" He clapped the older man on the back, allowing his hand to linger. "Of course, it will be interesting to learn why the defense made no appeal, won't it? My assistant brought me a portable radio and said more details should be forthcoming in the next hour." Gavin shrugged. "That is, if anyone wants to listen."

Frank turned to his lawyer. "Scally, I need to get Josephine."

With that, he stood and strode to the coat room.

He was halfway there when McLeod bellowed, "Hey Frank, I expected at least a thank you for my news." He burst out laughing.

Kaye couldn't believe what she had just witnessed. Anger surged within her, but above the rage she heard a quiet whisper within her: *"Go to Frank."* She wheeled around to exit the room on the far side, to avoid the crowd which now blocked the exit Frank had used. All were glued to McLeod's radio. No one saw Kaye either enter or leave the room.

By the time Kaye reached the multi-tiered parking garage, Carron was nowhere to be seen.

"Oh Lord, where is he?" she whispered.

Within her heart, Kaye swore she heard a single word: *"Up."*

She ran up a flight of stairs. On the second level from the top, she saw him, though he had not seen her. She slowed to catch her breath, noting that he was on the passenger side of the car.

Why? she wondered.

She saw him reach into the car and retrieve something from the glove compartment. He was oblivious to her presence as he closed the passenger door and walked around the car to the driver's side. But instead of entering the car, he simply leaned against it and rested his arms on its roof, his head buried in his arms.

Kaye stopped, unsure whether she should interrupt him. He seemed preoccupied with something, but the quiet voice within her heart urged, *"Go to Frank."*

About sixty feet away, she had an overwhelming urge to remove her shoes. Not only would he have heard her coming, but her heels, even though they were low, would have slowed her pace.

About forty feet from Frank, she suddenly realized what it was he had retrieved from the car. Now she wanted to run—not *to* him, but *from* him. In his hand, he held a gun!

"Oh, Jesus, help!"

Her eyes were opened wide in terror, yet that still small voice persisted: *"Go to Frank."*

Trembling both in fear and from the cold that seeped into her body through her shoeless feet, Kaye inched slowly toward him. His lips were moving, but no sound could be heard. Within twenty feet of the man, she saw him cross himself, then turn so that his back was to her.

She finally understood what he was about to do.

"Oh, God, no!"

She tried to scream, but nothing came out. As he raised the gun to his temple, she raced towards him. Hurtling herself full-force, she made contact and drove him toward the pavement. As they both went down, she heard a sickening click, and then a loud bang!

chapter thirty-three

By the time Max and Tony arrived at the precinct, the interrogation of the Leuzeckis had begun. Jack and Dave were sequestered in the observation room as Epi and Snyder confronted the brothers about their involvement in the attempt on Tony's life and Max's subsequent frame job. The brothers demanded the presence of their lawyer, who was one slippery, unscrupulous character.

Charlie escorted Tony and Max to a large, glassed-in lounge area located down the hall from the interrogation room.

"You guys play cards?" Charlie pointed to a table at the back of the room.

Tony's countenance brightened. "How about penny poker?"

Tony found the mere thought of playing cards with cops, in a precinct, entertaining. The thought of playing poker and winning? His father would never believe it, and Tony relished any and all one-upmanships on Pepi.

In contrast, Max merely raised an eyebrow, shook his head, and offered a polite and quiet, "No thanks." He anticipated the discussion with the Leuzeckis to go rather quickly. His optimism slowly ebbed, however, when after two hours no one had emerged.

At 1:30, coffee and subs were brought into the precinct.

Great, Max thought bitterly. *They rob me of six years of my life, and in just two hours those creeps are handed lunch so as not to inconvenience them!*

Tony, on the other hand, was thoroughly enjoying the interlude. Over lunch, another couple of cops joined Charlie's poker game. The men were exchanging friendly banter. The other officers mistakenly assumed Tony was an undercover New York cop, and Tony was doing nothing to correct their error. He simply insisted that a New York boy would be no match for Newark guys.

"Wait for a few more hands," Charlie smiled amiably. "Don't forget, it's not over until the fat lady sings."

Max gave up staring down the hall waiting for Jack to emerge with the Leuzeckis' confession in hand. He looked out the lounge door, glumly thinking, *I had to be a first-class idiot to think this scheme would work. Maybe I need to let go my desire to escort Kaye around the world.*

He began to surrender all his rights and expectations to God. He was feeling pretty miserable when the words of King David sprang to mind: *"Oh, my soul, why are you so downcast? Yet will I trust and praise the Lord."*

It caused him to take the focus off his own situation and back onto God's promises and blessings. At that point, to Max's utter surprise, Warden Blackmore walked into the lounge.

Max's shock at seeing the warden of the penitentiary in which he had been incarcerated was mirrored on Blackmore's own face.

"Max, what are you doing here?" Blackmore asked. He checked Max's wrists, further amazed to discover the absence of cuffs.

Max stood, aided by his crutches. Hesitantly, he extended his hand to the warden, prompting more questions to flood Blackmore's mind. He knew of Max's disappearance. It had, in fact, been as much an enigma to him as to others.

As Blackmore reached out to shake Max's hand, a sinking thought hit him. *If Max has slipped back into crime, there goes the new educational opportunities about to be launched in our prison.*

Max had just begun to explain his presence when he heard a muffled *pop-pop* from down the hall. A man in a trench coat entered the hall. The glass walls of the lounge afforded Max an excellent view. In astonishment, he watched the man race towards them. He half-expected the fellow to be one of the Leuzeckis' henchmen.

Max was the only one in the room aware of the intruder. A chill went down his spine as he glimpsed the crazed look in the man's eyes.

Lord, he's on crack, Max thought. Then he spied the gun barrel protruding from beneath the trench coat—Blackmore's back was the obvious target! Max had only a split second to react. Balancing on his good leg, he shoved the warden with all his might. Caught off-guard, Blackmore tumbled to the floor.

Max dove to the floor as the first shot was fired. As he fell, he secured J.D. firmly in his hand. Even with a semiautomatic, the assailant was no match for Max's agility. Max fired fast and the man crumpled in the doorway before he could let loose another shot.

Max turned to see where the man's first bullet had struck. His heart went cold. His brother-in-law had toppled off his chair and lay sprawled on the floor.

Instinctively, Max rolled over. Using his good leg, he propelled himself to the prone Tony.

Straddling his brother-in-law, all Max could think of was his sister's grief. He saw the gaping tear in Tony's shirt where the bullet had blasted into him.

Max was simultaneously yelling and crying. "Tony! Tony! Tony!" He shook his brother-in-law. To his shock, Tony's eyes fluttered open.

Charlie was trying to pull Max off Tony while one of the other officers yelled for a medic. The room quickly filled with police.

What happened next stunned everyone. Tony began to laugh.

Max stared at him in horror. "You faked the whole thing! This isn't funny!"

Except for Charlie's intervention, Max would have slugged Tony in the face.

On hearing the shot, Jack exited the observation room and raced down the corridor to the lounge. The scene greeting his eyes was an apparent dead man, lying at the entrance to the lounge. Max was straddling Tony, ready to pummel him, all the while screaming, "This isn't funny!"

The only thing Jack could think of was Max's leg and the need to protect it. He charged into the fray.

"Watch his leg!" Jack yelled.

Fortunately, Charlie knew the situation with Max and was already ensuring that Max got to his feet without bearing weight on the injured leg. Max was quickly given his crutches.

Max was furious at Tony. He wasn't thinking of the bullet wound in Tony's chest; he figured Tony had just fallen over to play a practical joke on him.

Jack, however, was sure Tony had shot the man on the floor.

In the midst of the melee, Chief Snyder quietly posted guards at the interrogation room. He left the Leuzeckis alone with their lawyer, on the pretext that they could converse privately with him. This allowed Dave, Epi, and himself to come to grips with what would soon be referred to as the "lounge incident."

As Tony was helped to his feet, he began to share the reason for his laughter. "Sheesh, Max, I was laughing because I realized I was still alive. All I saw was you knock over that guy." He gestured toward Blackmore, then to the still body lying face-down in the doorway, surrounded by a pool of blood. "And that creep. I saw a gun pointed directly at me, then the gun flashed. I felt the impact, and the next thing I know you're on top of me screaming. I mean, I figured I was dead, and whoa, here I am, back in the land of the living." He looked around at everyone. "You, guys, would all be laughing, too!"

With Jack beside him, Max regained emotional control.

Epi was the first to act decisively. "Tony, give me your jacket," he commanded. "Let's get your shirt off and see what damage has been done."

"You want me to undress here?" Tony yelped, eyeing the onlookers.

"Now is not the time for modesty," Epi barked. "We need to see how badly you're hurt."

His jacket and shirt were soon removed, and the reason for Tony's survival was unmasked. The bulletproof vest he had so vehemently protested against wearing had saved his life. Tony was shocked at the damage inflicted both on his clothes and the vest. He was even more astounded at the massive bruise now developing over his chest.

Tony went white. "Gee, Max, thanks for insisting we wear these. Thanks for loaning them to us, Epi!"

With all the focus on Tony, nobody saw a new arrival, dressed to the nines, stomp into the lounge. The man just stepped over the body in the doorway like he didn't even see it, but he stopped dead in his tracks when he spied Tony and Max.

"Tony! Max!" the man roared in utter disbelief.

They both looked up. "Lou!" they replied in unison.

"Bastaldi, what are you doing here?" Snyder demanded

That brought Lou abruptly back to his reason for the precinct visit. "One of the hazards of being an Italian father is siring precocious teenage sons. My junior's been making a nuisance of himself, not only with the cops but also with some of my trusted clientele. I had a dinner theater date with my wife. But Junior got into yet another altercation with the local constabulary."

The precinct officers in the room confirmed the story. They'd summoned Lou earlier in the day to come get his kid.

"I gotta pick up the missus in forty-five minutes," Lou said. "She'll be mad if I arrive late or fail to show. She'll blame it on me, not the brat."

Dave joined them from the observation room. Together with Jack, he shared their difficulty in securing the Leuzeckis' cooperation. Their money-grabbing lawyer knew a lengthy trial would bring him revenue, while a confession wouldn't. Consequently, he was urging them not to capitulate.

At this point, Snyder offered a suggestion in the hopes of breaking the impasse. "We need to convince these two of who you are and of your connections," he said bluntly to Max and Tony. "And we need to assure them that if they don't cooperate, we won't protect them when they hit the street. We'll be hands-off. On the other hand, if they confess and agree to the plea bargain Epi has presented, we'll ensure that nobody learns the place of their incarceration or their identities in prison."

Max was incredulous. "They won't believe who we are?"

"You got it," Dave said.

"Lou, would you go with Agent Epstein and Chief Snyder into the interrogation room?" Max asked. "They've got the two dudes who tried to kill Tony and framed me on a drug trafficking charge. That's why I spent six years in prison. Now, if they'll confess they did it and sign a confession, I'll get a full acquittal." Max grimaced. "And it's of great importance to me to get it now rather than later."

Lou looked at Max, then at Tony. "How can I be of assistance?"

"Well," Max said, "if you go in there and tell them Tony and I are who we are, that would be really appreciated."

Lou was puzzled by the unusual request. "What do you mean, who you are?"

Epi said softly but firmly, "Tell them that Tony Marconi is the son of Giuseppe Marconi of New York, and that Max is really Massimiliano Carron, son of Francesco Carron of Chicago."

"Yeah, they are," Lou said, still perplexed. "That's all you want me to do? Who are these two idiots anyway?"

All eyes turned to Chief Snyder. He sighed, rubbed his neck, and pondered whether the lounge could survive another eruption. "Lou, before I tell you, can we hold your gun until you're ready to leave?"

Lou shrugged and complied. Apparently this was standard operating procedure. Snyder handed the gun to Charlie, who stepped away quickly from the group.

Snyder looked Lou in the eye. "The Luezecki brothers."

Lou went as white as a Sicilian was capable. His eyes hardened and his jaw tightened. "They killed my father!" he hissed in Snyder's face.

"You know, we know," Snyder said. "But neither of us has proof. However, we *do* have proof of their involvement in this crime seven years ago. Lou, you're grieving your father's death. We're grieving our officer's death. The Bureau is grieving their agent's death. If we nail them on this case, maybe we can get them on the others. At least they'll be out of commission for a while."

Lou looked at Max. "Gus called me the other day and said he had some brief business in Newark. Said he'd be in and out. This was the business?"

Max nodded. "We're real sorry to hear of Uncle Tommy." he stepped forward and surprised Lou by giving him a hug. "Lou, the trial judge," he gestured toward

Jack, "realizes there was a miscarriage of justice. He could go the court route, but that would incriminate Pop and Pepi. They agreed for me to take the fall. A feud existed between the two of them back then. When Tony and Sophia fell in love and married, Pop and Pepi wanted to bury the hatchet."

Tony stepped in. "They figured that someone tried to rub me out. Pep knew it wasn't Frank, so they figured the truce was the best way to let sleeping dogs lie."

"Which means," Lou said, catching on, "that a court route wouldn't be healthy for your fathers."

"Correct!"

Lou jabbed a finger at Max. "And if these yahoos confess, you're clear?"

"Absolutely," Max replied.

Lou turned to Snyder. "Can I say whatever I want to them?"

"Yes, provided you don't touch them and are careful not to utter death threats. Choose your words wisely, Lou."

"Fine," Lou muttered. "Let me at them. It's a good thing you have my gun."

Lou started down the hall with Snyder, then stopped and turned back to point at Tony, who by now was wearing a regulation Newark Police Department T-shirt.

"Tone, you can do me a huge favor," Lou smiled slyly. "I'd ask Max, but it would be a bit difficult for him on crutches. My bratty kid is in the precinct's receiving room, sitting smugly with two of my guys. I don't want him back here." He motioned to Snyder. "They don't want to see him again. Can you get that point across to the brat?"

"Here?" Tony asked in astonishment.

"Yep. And whatever the damage, I'll be happy to pay it." Lou bowed low and chuckled, obviously delighted by something. With that, he turned and accompanied the others to the interrogation room.

chapter thirty-four

The earsplitting noise that erupted as Kaye slammed Frank Carron to the ground momentarily stunned her. The sound came from twenty feet to the left, not near her head as she had anticipated. The gun had squirted from his hand as he hit the pavement. Both the force of her tackle and his own body hitting the pavement temporarily had paralyzed Frank. Kaye had collided with him just as he pulled the trigger. The impact had jolted his arm, forcing the bullet off its deadly trajectory. It grazed his scalp, causing him to bleed profusely.

Although dazed, bleeding, and winded, Frank was certain of one thing: he wasn't dead. Yet it felt like a deadweight was on top of him. He began to curse.

Kaye was also winded. Initially she was terrified that she'd been too late. As she felt him move, she was furious at what he had tried to do. So was he when he realized who was on top of him.

Fortunately for Kaye, at the moment of recognition, she was less groggy than Frank. She held the upper hand.

"How could you try such a stupid thing?" she yelled, grabbing his coat lapel in her fists.

Frank's eyes filled with rage. "Stupid? What did I do to you that you're so intent on undermining my every move?"

He had rolled over and was lying flat on his back on the damp pavement. She lay on top of him, their faces inches apart.

"Me, destroying you?" she said. "The gun, sir, was in your hand. Not mine! How stupid can you be to let that Gavin McLeod get to you like this? Yes, I heard what he said to you, and yes, I heard him laugh at you. Well, guess what, Frank, that old adage is correct: he who laughs last laughs best. You wimp! If it was up to you, you'd never be around for the last laugh."

She propped herself up on his chest, giving his shoulder a cuff with her fist.

Now it was his turn to vent. He couldn't believe his ears. She had called him a wimp! He glared at her.

"You stupid, stupid…" He managed to check his tongue. "You don't know a damn thing about anything. This was not about Gavin McLeod."

She was still a little more alert than he, and she realized he was beginning to think about his gun again. Fortunately, she spied it before he did. She was about to make a leap for it when a car from the upper ramp drove by. It screeched to a halt—something neither Frank nor Kaye desired. This was their private war.

Two concerned young men jumped from the car, looking anxiously at Kaye and the bleeding man.

"Lady, are you okay?" one of the young men asked.

Before Frank could react, Kaye smiled sweetly. "Oh, thank you for stopping. I think both my father and I are fine, but we are shaken up. I'm afraid I slipped on a small oil spill. I knocked him off-balance. We both fell and he hit his head." She glowered at Frank. Her look spoke volumes: *Play along! Be nice and thank them!*

Frank scowled back, but he did play along. He allowed the young men to help lift him to his feet. All the while Kaye chatted pleasantly.

"Are you sure nothing's broken, Daddy?" Kaye asked before turning back to the men. "Would you be so kind as to help him into the passenger seat?"

As they were doing so, Kaye managed to sidle up to Frank's gun and slip it into her jacket pocket undetected.

"Thank you so much!" Kaye said to them. "How can we repay you? I'm going to take him right away to our doctor. I think he'll need stitches."

She waved politely to the young men.

As they headed to their car, she hissed at Frank, "Give me the keys, so they think I'm doing what I said I would. Or do you want them to bring someone else up here?"

Frank complied and the young men drove away.

"Where do you think you're going?" he growled as she started the car.

"To get my shoes."

Frank was certain he hadn't heard correctly. "Your what?"

"I'm getting my shoes." Kaye stopped the car sixty feet down the ramp, opened the door, and snatched up her shoes.

"My gun is back there," he snapped. "That happens to be a little more significant to retrieve than your shoes."

"Not to me," she countered. "Furthermore, I know where your gun is. You don't!"

"What? Tell me."

She just stared at him. "After what we've just been through, I think not. You and I need to have a long talk before I turn over your gun. Do you have a clean handkerchief?"

"What for?"

"Do you have it?"

His jaw tightened. He glared at her, then slowly reached into his breast pocket, snapped out the handkerchief, and gave it to her. To his surprise, she reached over and gently touched his head, dabbing away the blood.

"Is there some place we can go? Where you can be stitched up, no questions asked?" she asked softly. "I can drive you there, and we can talk on the way."

Kaye began to back up slowly.

"By the way, Frank, I know more than you think. Perhaps you should call somebody to come quickly and change the front tire on that Lincoln SUV. Again, someone who won't ask any questions."

Startled, Frank turned to look out the car window. Sure enough, a big SUV sat lopsided, its left front tire as flat as a pancake.

"Fortunately, it took the bullet you intended for your head." Her whole demeanor suddenly changed. Near tears, she demanded, "How could you do that, Frank? How could you do that to your wife, to Sophia, and yes, to your son? It would have devastated them!"

The truth of her words hit home. Frank swallowed hard. "It was for them." With those words, his anger towards her flared again. "For your information, seven years ago someone tried to kill my son-in-law. They framed my son. However, my daughter had fallen in love with the son of my most bitter foe."

"A Romeo and Juliet scenario," she interjected.

"Yeah, only neither his father nor I wanted the Romeo and Juliet outcome, so we decided to bury the hatchet. We agreed not to pursue who was responsible, which meant my son had to take the fall in order for us to keep the peace in our circle of acquaintances." He grimaced. "In my world, Ms. McDonald, you don't welch on those deals."

It dawned on Kaye that Frank was close to an emotional meltdown. She saw a parking space and pulled over, then reached out and touched his hand.

Frank stared ahead, lost in his thoughts. "When that ass hole McLeod laughed, I recalled a horrid memory. I was an eight-year-old kid." He closed his eyes and slumped forward against the dash, his head buried in his hands. "It was in Sicily. Some guy made a pact, just like me, but he welched on it. Unfortunately, he happened to look like my father. It was a case of mistaken identity." Frank moaned and shook his head sadly. "We'd gotten off school early. I was so excited that I ran home, otherwise I never would have been there."

Frank threw his head back, his face stained with both tears and blood.

"These goons were beating my father terribly. He kept yelling over and over that he didn't know what they were talking about, but they wouldn't stop. When he saw me, Pop screamed at me to run. Before I could, they grabbed me. I watched as they began to shoot him in different parts of his body." Frank's voice was now barely a whisper, his face twisted in agony. "They toyed with him like a cat with a mouse. A one point, the guy holding me took a knife as if to slash my face. Through his own agony, Pop pleaded with them not to harm me." Frank shuddered. "He suffered terribly. Finally, right in front of me, they killed him. My tormentor grabbed me by the hair and pushed my face into my father's blood. They threatened to kill me if I ever revealed their identity."

Frank turned and looked at Kaye, his eyes racked in pain, his voice hoarse.

"How could I?" he said. "I never saw them again."

The memory long hidden, now exposed, sliced through his emotions. The child within cried out in anguish. Frank slumped forward, sobbing uncontrollably.

Kaye crawled over the console between the two seats, folded her arms around his shoulders, and held him gently. Slowly, the cries began to ebb.

"Frank," she whispered into his ear, "the men who tried to kill Tony, who set up your son, they weren't Sicilian. They weren't Italian."

"What?"

"I suspect they're as brutal and psychopathic as those who murdered your father, though."

Frank sat bolt upright stunned. Her words had succeeded in yanking him from the pain of his past into his present angst.

"Frank, McLeod's laughter was a trigger that caused your flashback. Post-traumatic flashbacks are emotional hotbeds that can erupt and damage us in the present and cloud our reasoning. Please trust what I'm saying. I meant it when I said you can have the last laugh when everything settles and the full truth is revealed. I beg of you, please be patient and don't do anything rash. Give time a chance."

Frank sat very still. Kaye wondered if anything she said had registered.

In fact, it had. His rational control was returning.

She's right about one thing, he thought, staring at her blankly. *That memory was certainly an emotional hotbed! I'm totally drained.*

Somehow he found himself drawn to her. He couldn't explain it. It wasn't sexual, he didn't think, because when he looked at her he saw Sophia.

He drew a deep breath. "Well, Ms. McDonald, thanks to you I'm still alive, but—"

"But what, Frank?"

"But if what you said is true, then I'm destined to live out my life with my own son hating me." Remorse filled his voice. "My stupid pledge cost him six years of his life. I doubt that travesty will ever be rectified."

Kaye started to laugh. "Wrong again, Frank. Do me a favor. Stop thinking and simply give me directions to your doctor. If you cooperate there, I have something for you."

She reached up under her sweater and pulled out a handwritten envelope addressed to him and Josie.

He recognized his son's handwriting immediately.

"As soon as I had definite word about what was happening in Newark, I planned to give this to you," she said. "But not with quite as much drama as you chose to initiate!"

As he reached for it, she smiled and pulled it back to herself.

"Oh no, sir. Not until after you've seen the doctor. Otherwise you might take the letter and run."

Frank's eyes narrowed, but this time there was a hint of a twinkle.

He complied with her wish and was in and out of the clinic he had selected in less than twenty minutes—stitched, patched, and cleaned. Their clothes were anything but clean, though. Both were streaked with dirt from the parking garage and his blood.

Back in the car, he held out his hand. "Okay, Ms. McDonald, I've kept my end of the bargain. Give me my son's letter."

She glanced at her watch. "I most definitely will, but first things first. Direct me to the hotel. We have a half-hour to make the dinner."

His mouth dropped. "You can't be serious! We can't go in looking like this."

"Oh yes, we can," she said, smiling demurely. "I've already thought of my line. On the way there, you can choose yours. After you've read the letter! Then your thoughts will be more positive about the day."

He read the letter in total disbelief. In it, his son shared how much he loved both Josephine and himself. Far from being upset about the prison term,

Massimiliano was positive about "his blessings," as he termed it—a free education both formal and informal. He went on to say that he had met a wonderful woman. He really loved her and, God-willing, he hoped he might be able to marry her. He said her name was Kaye. He also closed by saying that he hoped they didn't mind, but he didn't like being called Massimiliano. His preference was Max. They could still call him Massimiliano, if they wanted, but for everyone else it would be Max.

When he finished the letter, Frank turned to Kaye. "My son gave this letter to you?"

"Yep."

"It sounds like he's dying."

"He could have, but fortunately he didn't. He's fine. You and your wife can decide what you'd like to do. If you want, I can take you to him tonight."

"He's in Chicago?" Frank was dumbfounded. One glance at her, however, told him it had been a bad guess.

"No, he's not. I'm flying out tonight and will return next week for the hospital benefit. You could travel with me tonight, if you'd like, and I could take you to him or you could wait here. It's your choice. I was informed that your son most likely would return to your house later next week, possibly Wednesday or Thursday."

"Can I think on my answer?"

"By all means."

Frank hesitated, then decided he'd risk his next question. "Our son said he'd fallen in love with a wonderful woman and wanted to marry her, if she'd have him. He said her name was Kaye. Do you know her?"

Kaye was caught off-guard. "He said that in the letter?" She hoped her voice didn't give away her surprise.

Fortunately for her, Frank was more preoccupied with the letter and missed both the verbal and visual clues.

"Yeah," he said, glancing up from the letter. "Have you met her?"

Now composed, Kaye smiled sweetly. "Yes, I have." As she wheeled his car into the hotel parking lot, she couldn't help but add, tongue-in-cheek, "She's very nice, extremely quiet, and very, very shy."

"Well, that probably will work. He's kinda quiet and reserved himself," Frank commented absentmindedly.

"Not to change the subject," Kaye said, though that was precisely what she intended, "but do you care on which level I park?"

"No, here's fine."

Kaye wheeled into a space, shut off the engine, and handed Frank's keys back to him. "You will find your gun under the driver's seat, Mr. Carron."

Frank simply nodded as he got out of the car. He walked around the car to open the door for her. "Thank you, Ms. McDonald, I'm indebted to you."

"And I to you, for agreeing to Kayleen's terms of sale." She grinned. "You could tuck in your shirttail, though."

He bowed and did so. "Does that meet with your approval, Ms. McDonald?"

"Most definitely."

"Then shall we go to dinner?" He extended his arm to her, and that's exactly how they entered the banquet hall—clothes disheveled, damp, and stained with dirt, grease, and blood. If nothing else, it was an-eye catching entrance.

The room went silent, and into that silence Kaye said, "You'll be glad to know that we have settled our differences!"

He headed for his table. "She knows martial arts," he added.

chapter thirty-five

When Snyder returned to the interrogation room, the Leuzecki brothers greeted him with a sneer. Ensconced behind a large table, their lawyer by their side, they sat scowling.

"You wanna charge us with this college crime, go ahead," Jon Leuzecki spat disdainfully.

Their lawyer added quickly, "We'll drag you through the courts so badly, the whole town will mock you, Chief. What an amateur ploy! Bringing in that dame, who my clients allegedly liked in college, to eke out a so-called confession." He scoffed as he rocked back on his chair, thumbs tucked in his suspenders.

Epi entered the room and stood at the end of the table. "I question, gentlemen, that your solicitor has adequately informed you of the gravity of your situation. Let me reiterate our offer again. The police records clearly support Mr. Carron's testimony that a shot was fired into the head of the bed. He had, in fact, placed pillows in that bed to simulate a sleeping person. The ballistic report indicates that a bullet was found imbedded in the wall above the baseboard. That is the exact trajectory one would anticipate if the gun had been fired from the door adjoining the next room. In addition, the doctor at the hospital corroborates that Carron suffered a concussion from a blow to the left temple. This is consistent with someone from the adjacent room stepping into Carron's room and striking him on the head as he slept in the chair next to the door." Epi paused for effect. "And you, gentlemen, are recorded in our surveillance van as admitting to being in that room and confessing that Alex fired the shot."

"Whadda ya mean, surveillance van?" Alex asked. "The bitch had a tape recorder."

"A dupe," Epi said with a smile. "The 'bitch' you referred to, gentlemen, happens to be the wife of Antonio Marconi. He happened to be in the surveillance van, hearing not only how you described him, but also that you had intended to eliminate him."

"Hey, that bitch was baiting us," Alex Leuzecki protested.

"Alex, please refrain from commenting," their lawyer pleaded.

"Absolutely, Mr. Leuzecki, listen to your counsel," Epi snapped. "Because I'm not finished. Antonio Marconi is the son of Giuseppe Marconi, New York's Mr. Italy, with a huge number of friends he could call on for a favor."

Jon Leuzecki glared at Epi with utter contempt.

"Let me also inform you that Mrs. Marconi's maiden name is Carron. Her father is Francesco Carron, Chicago's Mr. Italy. Both Frank and Pepi hail from Sicily. Am I painting a clearer picture here, boys?" Epi glimpsed a flicker of hesitation in their eyes. "So, guess whose son you framed? Right! A rather painful experience, especially for the Carrons."

"Bull! Pure bull," their lawyer shouted. "If those guys are who you claim they are, no way would Carron's father let his son go down."

"Oh, how wrong you are," Epi said, speaking softly. "You see, until their kids fell in love, the elder Carron and Marconi were decidedly not on friendly terms. With their kids acting as a modern-day Romeo and Juliet, neither wanted it to end in tragedy. They elected to bury the hatchet and not pursue who attempted to kill Antonio."

"You stupid dick, now you want us to believe they care?" Jon Leuzecki spat.

"Most definitely, most definitely. You see, up until a week ago, the Carrons and Marconis figured the perps were Italian, even Sicilian. That's why the fathers were content to live and let live, to let bygones be bygones. Unfortunately, the trial judge took another peek at the transcripts and recognized that a major travesty of justice had occurred. He got Mrs. Marconi, who, by the way, is now articling herself for the bar, to go over the transcript. And guess whose names appear there?"

"Ours," Alex replied sullenly.

"Right on! And you know what? You boys aren't Sicilian, let alone Italian. You two have caused the Carrons and Marconis, now on very friendly terms, a great deal of grief."

"Your point?" snarled their sleaze ball lawyer.

"My point is that justice is justice. You two fine gentlemen can make official your confession. In return, the deal we are offering is for you to receive the same sentence Mr. Carron received—six years. In my book, six years for attempted murder, interference of justice, and the framing of an innocent person is a very light sentence indeed."

Alex Leuzecki glowered. "Then we get locked up and those wops kill us in prison!"

Epi smiled gallantly. "Oh no. No, no. Absolutely not, gentlemen. Our deal also includes what the Carrons and Marconis have agreed to—in fact, it's a deal all of us involved in this endeavor have agreed to. Your place of incarceration will not be revealed and your identity will be concealed—all this, in return for your cooperation in officially admitting your guilt."

Their lawyer pounded the table with his fist. "Jon and Alex, this is nothing but a cock and bull story. Don't be duped! You've got your rights."

"Absolutely, guys, you have your rights," Snyder said. "But we have some rights, too. One is that we're under no obligation to babysit the two of you. Spurn our offer, and in terms of protection, you two are on your own. Protect your own hides." He turned to the lawyer. "By the way, while in jail they're still your clients. In a coffin, your solicitations are of no value. It's your call, gentlemen… it *is* your call!" He punctuated his remarks by slapping the table.

Epi studied their eyes and felt he could detect a slight wavering of confidence.

"Don't listen to them, boys," chortled their lawyer. "That dame, those guys aren't who they say they are. They're trying to freak you out."

Epi looked askance. "Isn't it amazing? That's exactly what I thought you'd say. That's why I asked Chief Snyder to arrange for someone with better credentials than I to convince you that Mr. Carron and the Marconis are exactly who we have declared them to be. Please, excuse me for a moment."

Epi left the room and headed for the viewing room where Dave and Jack had been sitting with Lou Bastaldi.

"Am I correct that you heard everything that was said?" Epi asked.

Jack and Dave nodded.

Lou was visibly enraged. "You're going to give them only six years, then secret them away so none of us knows where they are?"

Epi got right in Lou's face. "Lou, look at me. Yes! A hundred percent yes. For that college crime, none of us, including you, will know where they are imprisoned." He smiled. "But I believe you, myself, and Chief Snyder are aware that there are quite a few other infractions in which those two can be implicated. Am I correct?"

"Of course," Leo fumed.

Epi raised his eyebrow. "With them incarcerated, it will be a whole lot easier to gain evidence and testimonies, don't you think?"

Lou was starting to relax. "What you're saying is that you aren't going to sweep my father's murder under the carpet."

"You got it, Lou," Epi said. He extended his hand. "That's a promise."

"So what do you want me to do?" Bastaldi asked.

"Go in there, look as angry as you can, and scare the pants off them. Just—"

"I know, I know. Don't threaten them!"

"Correct." Epi winked. "Leave it to us to imply that as a possibility, after you're gone. What's most important is that you let them know Max and Sophia are who we said they are, that Tony is who we said he is."

And that's precisely what happened. When the Leuzeckis saw Lou enter— what with them handcuffed and all—they started squealing like stuck pigs, shouting police brutality.

Without cracking a smile, Snyder informed the brothers and Mr. Sleaze Ball, as he had nicknamed their lawyer, "Mr. Bastaldi is definitely not a member of the Newark constabulary. He's both a friend and family member of Mr. and Mrs. Marconi and Mr. Carron. Since your lawyer demanded that the identity of the three be verified, we trust Mr. Bastaldi's testimony will suffice."

Lou never even sat down. He leaned across the table and glared at the brothers. "You tried to kill my friend Tony, and you framed my cousin Massimiliano, robbing him of six years of his life." He turned to the lawyer. "Six years for six years. You don't think that's fair?" He jabbed a finger at the lawyer, then slammed his fist on the table. "I gotta leave. I'm allergic to the present company."

With that, he exited with Epi and returned to the observation room.

Lou's presence worked magic! The brothers and their lawyer had a radical attitude adjustment and agreed to the proposed deal. Jack had the legal documents ready for signing. Willing signatures went on the confession and the terms as outlined. FBI agents appeared on the scene. The Leuzeckis were whisked out of Newark immediately.

Jack rejoined Dave in the observation room.

"It worked!" Jack said. "It actually worked! Praise God! Max will get his full acquittal!"

Jack leapt forward to embrace Dave. Noticing Dave's apparent reticence, Jack realized to his embarrassment that Lou was still there.

"Sorry," he said sheepishly. "I got carried away. As a former college football quarterback, I'm used to celebrating big wins." Jack laughed and unashamedly reached to grab Lou's hand in a firm grip. He looked the man square in the eye. "Mr. Bastaldi, thanks ever so much. You stepped up to the plate and tipped the scales of justice in our favor. This is incredibly big for Max, and he is a very special man! Thank you!"

As Jack shook Lou's hand in gratitude, it was obvious to Lou that something major had happened. Something for which he was being credited, the significance of which appeared to be more than simply exonerating Max, yet for the life of him he couldn't imagine what that could possibly be.

Snyder at last joined them. "Thanks, Lou, we greatly appreciate your help on this one." He checked his watch. "Looks like you've got about five minutes, Lou. Just enough time to gather up Junior and make your dinner date with the missus."

As the four men walked down the hall to the lounge area, three of them were surprised to find the lounge vacant.

"Where did Tony and Max go?" Dave asked.

"Hopefully to your reception area, Chief Snyder," Lou said dryly.

"Where's that?" Jack questioned.

Snyder pointed. "Just around the corner."

They had just come to the doorway to reception when a teenage boy hurtled through it and landed on a table, which splintered under his weight. Chief Snyder looked like he might crap his pants.

"Whose kid is that?" Dave asked, wide-eyed.

Snyder started to move forward into the fray, but Lou put up his hand to block him.

"The kid's mine," Lou said, "and I'll pay for any damages incurred."

Neither Jack nor Dave nor Snyder could believe the sight that greeted them in the reception area. Max and Charlie were standing off to the side. Max with an amused grin on his face. The officers in the room looked totally shocked at what was going on. If the truth be known, there also seemed a sense of satisfaction on their faces. Two of Lou's men stood in place, sort of staring at the ceiling. And as for Tony, he was grabbing the kid, throwing him, kicking him in the pants… Obviously he'd bloodied the boy's nose.

They heard the kid yell, "Police brutality!" Tony only smacked him harder, simultaneously dressing the kid down in both English and Italian.

Tony grabbed the lad by the shirt collar and yanked him up to his face. "Do I look like a cop, you little punk?" He jerked the kid by the scruff of his neck, pointing him at the desk sergeant. "The sergeant is sick of your face! Do you understand?" By now, all the kid's swagger had evaporated. "I said, do you understand?"

"Yes, sir! Yes, sir!"

Tony swung the boy around by his hair, gesturing to all the police in the room. "They never, ever want to deal with your shenanigans again. Do you get that? They never want to deal with your sorry ass again. Never, ever! So tell them they'll never have to."

The kid was sniveling now. "You won't! You won't! You won't!"

Tony jerked the kid around to face Lou's men. "You're not a big boy!" he screamed at the kid. "Repeat that back to me."

"I–I–I'm not a big boy," the kid stammered.

"Then don't mess with the big boys ever, you little punk. Start acting your age. Put your nose into your books and smarten up!" He slid the kid across the floor to Lou's men. "Take him outta here!"

"Our pleasure, sir," they replied, yanking the boy up by his jacket and dragging him whimpering out the door.

"Look, here's the truth," Lou said. "His mother has pleaded with him to apply himself in school. I reasoned with him, not once but several times. Your guys have picked him up not once, not twice..." He held up his hand. "Five times. Each time, he got a warning. Yet each time he grew bolder and saucier. He started to swagger with some of my..." Lou paused to find the right word. "...clientele."

Tony emerged from the washroom, having washed his hands literally of Junior's blood.

"Thanks, Tone," Lou said, extending his hand.

"No problem. Glad to be of assistance," Tony replied nonchalantly.

Lou turned back to Snyder. "Look, I'm the brat's father. I don't want him killing someone. You certainly don't want him killing one of yours. Nor do I want to come in and identify him in your morgue. Yet at least one of those unpleasantries was bound to happen soon, the way he was careening out of control. This would really make the missus very unhappy. We Italian fathers have got this little game plan where, when needed, we help each other out. Kinda a brotherhood deal."

"No kidding," was all Snyder could muster.

"Figure out what Tone busted and let me know. I'll gladly pay. I'm glad this happened in November," Lou added absentmindedly. "Junior should have a good crack at the honor roll by June and entrance eligibility to a decent college. Anyway, glad you're not dead, Massimiliano. Take care, guys. I have to go. As it is, I'll barely get to my dinner date."

250

With that, Lou Bastaldi left the precinct.

"So?" Max said.

Dave, Jack, and Snyder stared back at him, still in shock.

"What happened with the Leuzeckis?" Max prodded.

The question yanked Jack back to the reason he had come to Newark in the first place. "It worked! It really worked!" he exclaimed.

"No kidding?" Tony said.

"Absolutely. Max, you'll have a full acquittal," Jack said, poking Max in the ribs. "Praise God!"

Max stood silent for a moment, stunned. "Wow! It really worked? I get to travel?" A smile stole across his face.

"You get to travel and escort your wife," Epi stated as he came into the room. He stopped dead in his tracks, observing the carnage—the broken table, spilled pencils, and scattered papers. His mouth dropped open.

"They'll explain it on the way home," Dave said, motioning to Tony and Max. "It's time we were getting back to Summerside, before the others start to worry."

chapter thirty-six

Angel rushed breathless into Josephine's bedroom as she was dressing for the Kayleen supper. "Massimiliano didn't do what he was sent to jail for," Angel blurted. "The feds have just announced that two men in Newark confessed to framing him."

"Who?" Josephine asked, acutely aware of her friend's connection to the Bastaldi family.

Angel stopped dead in her tracks, her hand covering her mouth as she suddenly realized what Josephine was thinking.

"Oh, Jo, I'm sure Lou would never do anything to hurt Massimiliano, or even Tony for that matter. Lou is too straightforward a guy. Trust me. If he's upset with someone, they would know it. He would never shoot someone who was sleeping!"

"I'm sure you're right Angel," Josephine said reassuringly. "Of more importance to me is whether there was any mention of Massimiliano. Did they indicate if he's alive?" Tears came to her eyes. "I've been worried about him. Every night I pray for his safety."

Angel clasped her friend's hands. "Oh, Josie, I can't recall if Massimiliano was said to be there. One thing I'm certain of is that they didn't say he was dead. You know the old saying… no news is good news!"

Josephine sighed deeply. "Frank was going to pick me up for this dinner, but with the announcement on the news about Massimiliano, he may get waylaid. Angel, would you please go with me? You know how I hate traveling alone."

"You get a driver and I'll be ready in fifteen minutes," Angel said. "Chances are that Frank may not even have heard the news. It would be good if we tell him."

The two arrived at the hotel lobby shortly after three in the afternoon. They made their way to the Kayleen hospitality suite, and would have been turned back by the security guards had not Alice spied Josephine.

Knowing M.K.'s affection for Mrs. Carron, Alice called out a cheerful welcome. "You must be so pleased at the news concerning your son, Mrs. Carron."

Josephine smiled shyly. "Oh, I am indeed!" She turned to Angel. "Actually, it was my friend Angel D'Amato who heard the announcement. That's why we came right down. I was unsure if Frank would have heard the news. I was hoping to talk with him."

Josephine peered into the room, which by now was empty of everyone except hotel staff busily setting up for the dinner.

"I believe Mr. Carron left around an hour ago," Alice ventured. "Someone heard him say he was going to pick you up."

"Oh dear, I always seem to muddle things up," Josephine replied apologetically.

Angel turned to her. "Josie, there's no point in us going back home. You left word at the gatehouse where we were going. So when Frank gets there, he'll turn around and come back."

"Mrs. Carron," Alice offered, "why don't you and your friend rest in our suite for a half-hour or so until everything is set up for our evening meal?"

"Oh, I couldn't impose, and Mrs. D'Amato hasn't been invited for dinner," Josephine said. "But I do thank you for your kind invitation."

"Nonsense," said Alice. "You will not be imposing, and Mrs. D'Amato has just received a dinner invitation." She checked her clipboard, noted the Carrons' table number, and called out to the steward, "Please, set up one more setting at table eight. Thank you!" She returned her attention to the two women. "Now, please, won't you both come with me? With Kayleen moving here, I need to familiarize myself with Chicago, its history, things to see and do…"

Josephine had a most delightful time with Alice and Angel. Around four o'clock, they returned to the banquet hall. Many of the other guests had arrived by now. In fact, Scallion came in with his wife just as Angel and Josephine showed up. He looked disapprovingly at Angel.

"Oh, it's all right," Josephine beamed. "Alice invited her."

Scallion rolled his eyes. "So already you're on a first-name basis with M.K. McDonald's senior staff? Frank should have had you negotiating for him. By the way, where is he?"

"Someone said he left to pick up Josephine, but obviously we left before he returned home," Angel said. "Josie thought that perhaps Frank hadn't heard the news about Massimiliano."

"He heard," Scally said, perturbed both by Frank's absence and the necessity that he would need to host not only his wife, but now these two women. Truthfully, had it been three single, younger women, Scally would have relished the opportunity.

"It is wonderful news about your son, isn't it, Josephine?" beamed Scallion's wife.

Scally checked his watch. "Frank's been gone over two hours. If you left word at the gatehouse, he should be back by now."

Kayleen's people began to be concerned about the absence of M.K. McDonald. Both Alice and Philippe assumed she had retired to her room to rest. However, when they checked her room, it was obvious that no one had been there. General alarm soon gave way to panic when it became apparent that Frank Carron was also absent.

Poor Josephine couldn't avoid the innuendos circulating in the room concerning her husband. The mere fact that others thought Frank capable of harming this young woman, who had been so kind to her, was devastating. In fact, Clarin, Kayleen's senior vice-president, announced that if M.K. didn't appear within the next half-hour, he would notify the police.

The room was filled with a mixture of relief and utter disbelief when, twenty-five minutes later, Frank and Kaye made their dramatic entrance together. Each looked like they had emerged from a major automobile crash. Mouths gaped and eye brows raised as Kaye made what shortly would become one of her most famous quips: "You'll be glad to know that we have settled our differences!"

Frank Carron only heightened everyone's curiosity, stating, "She knows martial arts."

Once in the room, the two separated. They created the impression that it was perfectly normal to arrive at a banquet battered, bruised, bloodied, dirty, and disheveled.

Frank went to his table—with a slight limp, some thought. He politely kissed his wife. "I'm so glad you came on your own, Josie. Thanks, Angel, for accompanying her. Glad you could make it, Mrs. Scallion. You, too, Scally."

He sat down, rather gingerly.

Josephine had long since learned not to react publicly to Frank. In private, she could let loose with questions. She tried not to look closely at her husband.

Tonight, I will indeed be letting loose with my questions! she thought to herself.

There was one question she did not wait until the privacy of their room to ask. "Frank, did you hear what's being reported about Massimiliano?"

He nodded. "Yes, dear. Wonderful, isn't it? Your prayers have definitely been answered. In a very big way, I might add!"

A really big way, he thought silently.

"Is he alive?"

Frank reached over, took her hand, and squeezed it. "Most definitely, dear!"

Tears of relief flooded over her. She knew Frank hated public displays of emotion, but she couldn't help it. To her surprise, he turned to her and held her in his arms, comforting, soothing, and reassuring her.

"It's been a long haul, love," he said. "A real long haul, but for us it's ending well!" He kissed her on the forehead.

Frank's behavior was definitely out of character. Besides Josephine, no one knew it better than Angel and Scally.

When Josephine finally composed herself Frank confided, "Ms. McDonald gave us a letter from Massimiliano. You can read it when we get home." He gave her a warm smile. "I can tell you it's very honoring to you, and also to me."

"Did Massimiliano say when he'll be home?"

"We can expect him possibly next Wednesday, but definitely by Thursday." Frank had unilaterally decided to decline M.K.'s travel invitation. The day's events had overwhelmed him. His body had definitely been battered, and already he showed the consequences. The next few days would be physically trying. In addition, nearly forty years of marriage told him that this day hadn't yet ended.

Alone with Josephine, he would face big questions which would demand big answers. Transparent answers! He must be honest and face the fears that had hounded him for seven years.

At the conclusion of the banquet, Kaye crossed the floor to the Carron table. "Mrs. Carron, I'm so happy for your good news today."

Josephine smiled demurely. "Thank you, my dear. My heart will go to bed peacefully tonight, for the first time in a long while."

"We look forward to seeing you again." Frank added, "At the charity dinner, a week this Friday."

Kaye smiled pleasantly. "I'm looking forward to the charity dinner." To herself, she added, *And you, Frank, are in for even bigger surprises!*

As the Carrons headed for their coats, Frank turned and took Kaye's hand. "Have a safe trip."

She leaned forward, her green eyes twinkling. "And you... you be sure to stay alive," she whispered.

He simply grinned.

Josephine caught the exchange out of the corner of her eye. Never had she seen her husband so open to anyone. Something had happened to him, but what? She was certain of one thing: before she went to sleep tonight, she would know the answer.

Scally kept close to Frank, expecting and hoping the man would open up to him, but to no avail. "Shall I see you in the morning, Frank?"

Frank shook his head. "Scally, I'm going to rest for the next few days. It's been a long haul for Josie and me. We need some time for ourselves."

"Sure you don't want me to pursue this fed announcement?" Scally pressured.

"Nope. We'll get the full details when Massimiliano gets home."

"So he's coming home soon?" Angel couldn't refrain from asking.

Frank sighed. "Yeah, probably late next week. Then maybe some semblance of normality can hit us."

The drive home was unusually quiet. Frank was hurting. It was all he could do to drag himself up the stairs to the bedroom. He told Josephine that he wanted to shower. As he began to undress, Josephine was shocked at the bruises on his body. He even requested a shower cap, so as not to wet the bandage on his head. However, before he headed to the shower, he pulled out their son's letter and handed it to his wife.

"You can read what Massimilano wrote to us, dear, while I shower. Afterwards we can discuss it in the hot tub. If I don't let that water massage my muscles, tomorrow I'll be like the tin man in the Wizard of Oz... totally seized up!"

As he showered, she eagerly read and reread Massimiliano's letter, pondering each word. He had expressed a love for them far greater than she had ever imagined. At last, she set the letter down and climbed into the whirlpool. She was already enjoying the warmth when he gingerly lowered himself into the water.

"All right, Frank," she said, finally beginning her cross-examination. "What about you and Ms. McDonald?"

She had steeled her heart, preparing to hear him admit to being unfaithful, even that he loved the young woman more than she. She was unprepared for the real story.

"I want to be totally open with you," he began. "Jo, I'm alive now because of Ms. McDonald. The blood you saw on us was mine." He tapped his bandaged head and then poured out all the details, including his terrifying childhood flashback. He told her the truth about their son's prison stint and the fact that he, Sophia, Tony, Pepi, Gus, Scally, and Massimiliano had all known of Massimiliano's innocence.

The more Frank shared, the bigger Josephine's eyes grew. It was hard for her to fully comprehend all that was said. He explained that they hadn't been able to appeal Massimiliano's sentence for fear that it would reveal who had really tried to kill Tony, thereby starting yet another family feud.

Finally, he arrived at the point of his greatest dread. "Josephine, I realize you needed to know the whole truth, even if it means that you'll hate me forever. I can't keep trying to hide the truth from you. Eventually you'd find out anyway, and then what?"

Josephine now knew for certain that she never needed to fear Frank being unfaithful. In fact, for the first time she understood that the real fear in the room belonged to him, to the man who seemed to exude fearlessness. His fear all along had been that she would reject him when she discovered the truth. As she watched her husband struggle to openly communicate his heart, her love for him didn't diminish… it increased! In fact, her love for Frank seemed to grow in leaps and bounds.

Experiencing dread beyond what he had ever felt before, Frank closed his eyes, not wanting to witness his wife's rejection of him.

He sighed deeply. "Josie, Ms. McDonald told me that the two guys who tried to kill Tony and framed our son aren't part of the family network at all. They aren't Sicilian, and they aren't even Italian. They're just brutal, violent men like the guys who tortured and killed my papa." Tears streamed down his face. "Jo, when we married, I told you that I'd protect you and our kids. I promised I'd stay out of jail and keep our kids out. Josie, I failed you!"

There, it was out in the open where she could see it. This was the moment of truth he had agonized over for seven years—seven very long years. To his surprise, he felt her brush against him and heard her laughing softly. He opened his eyes, startled to find her next to him in the tub, staring intently into his eyes.

"Oh, Frank, whatever am I to do with you? I've been sitting here waiting for you to open your eyes and look at me." She shook her head. "I agree with M.K. McDonald, that what you attempted to pull this afternoon really was very stupid!" She leaned her head against his. "And I am so grateful that she…"

Josephine paused, for she suddenly realized the double meaning of what she was about to say.

"She what?"

Josephine laughed. "That she knocked you up!"

Frank looked at his very genteel wife and saw the humor she had already appreciated in her speech. Both started to laugh. The laughter was healing. Indeed, the truth had set them free.

"Frank, I loved you when I married you. I've loved you all these years, and I love you now. You are far from perfect, and so am I. Imperfect people disappoint others all the time. But if we choose to love one another, despite those imperfections, God promises that He will work all things to the good. Today, I believe God has allowed us to glimpse His redeeming work in our family."

She put her arms around him and kissed him, tears flowing freely.

"Frank, there's one promise I do need to hear you make. It is that never again will you attempt what you tried this afternoon. I love you too much!"

"I promise, Jo," he whispered, embracing her. "I really do!"

As the two stepped from the spa, Josephine again looked closely at her husband. "You, sir, are going to be a one sore and stiff man these next few days. You may need more X-rays."

"I'll recover just fine if you continue to join me in the hot tub," he said with a laugh. "Truthfully, Josie, I feel like a new person. Fears have lifted off me that I wasn't even aware I carried until today—the fear of your rejection, the fear of losing both Massimiliano's and your love, the fear of failure, the fear of a family member seeing the mob kill me like I saw them kill my father."

She smiled. "God is good."

He kissed her gently on the cheek. "Yeah, all the time."

"Josie, I feel that our family can start afresh. Tomorrow we'll call Sophia. I'm surprised she hasn't called us. I'll also ask Gus to come home."

"Where is Gus?"

"I sent him to watch that judge's place to intercept Massimiliano, just in case he had any idea of revenge up his sleeve. I didn't want him doing anything foolish."

"Frank, I can hardly wait to see him again. I'm so relieved that he loves us." She snuggled closer to her husband. "I wonder who the young woman is," she said, giggling softly. "Maybe he'll come home with our new daughter-in-law in tow. Well, it's possible, isn't it?"

"After today, I'd say just about anything is possible except one thing,"

"What's that?"

"That I won't be extremely stiff and sore when I wake up in the morning!"

chapter thirty-seven

With Sue's help, Marnie had organized a celebration feast at her home for when the sting crew arrived back in Summerside. The first to show was Matt, driving Sophia. Sophia was clearly drained emotionally. Immediately, the two women bundled Sophia off with them to Kaye's pool. To unwind, Matt took Rufie for a long walk in the woods. When he returned an hour later, Gus and his crew were pulling their van into Jack's driveway. Their major concern was Mario's arm, though he kept insisting it was only a flesh wound.

Matt headed for his mother, who overruled Mario's protests and insisted he visit her health clinic. There, X-rays confirmed there was no fracture. The wound was cleaned and sutured, allowing Mario to return to Independence Drive with his arm in a sling.

"The conquering hero returns," Sue quipped as they entered the Walters' house.

This prompted Sophia to ask what exactly had happened after she'd run out of the store.

The four younger men eyed Gus.

"So what did you see?" Gus asked them

"Not a thing, Gus," Al said, speaking for the group. "Not a thing!"

Gus burst out laughing. "Good answer, Al. Good answer!"

Sophia planted herself in front of Gus, hands on her hips. "Wrong answer! Excuse us, but we're part of the team, remember?" She pointed to Matt. "He was my chauffeur." She gestured to Sue and Marnie. "They're our operation's canteen and medic brigade."

At that point, everyone burst into laughter and the storytelling of the initial stages of the sting began in earnest as Sophia, Gus, and his men described what they had encountered.

Sophia shared how Jon Leuzecki had grabbed her coat as she exited the store. Fortunately Chief Snyder had yanked her into his car. By then, both brothers had been on the street and the Newark officer had pounced on them with Epi and Brian.

Al chuckled. "Did you see the computers?"

"Computers?" Sophia shook her head. "As soon as I was in the car, Snyder told the officer to get me to the precinct. What computers?"

"As soon as you and the two Leuzeckis exited the store, Gus blocked the door," Al recounted. "He pulled out his semi and demanded that everyone freeze."

Mario nodded. "The two of us covered the downstairs, which was full of mostly legit customers and staff."

"Yeah, except Leuzecki's henchman, who knocked himself out sliding on those ball bearings you accidentally dropped," Silvio said to Al. "I frisked him and eliminated his hardware. Gus told the old doll at the cash register to give me a bag, and we dumped his gun in it. Gus had us frisk the other two bozos who were obediently standing there, hands behind their heads. We added their hardware to our bag. Gus had us give the bag to the old girl and he told her to put the bag outside on the sidewalk. She did, but boy was she ever freaked!"

"She calmed down when Gus promised nobody would get hurt," Al chimed in. "That is, as long as everyone cooperated and kept their hands visible. Of course, we cuffed the two conscious dudes and one unconscious guy. We didn't trust them."

Sue's eyes were wide. "Where on earth did you get handcuffs?"

"We sort of borrowed them from various police agencies," Gus said with a grin. "We did make sure that none belonged to the Summerside or Newark P.D."

"Why?" Marnie asked him.

"I didn't want to incriminate the Newark cops in any way, neither Dave's jurisdiction nor the Bureau—"

"Oh hey, you forgot the first thing we did," Al interrupted. "Remember? I figure that's what got everyone's attention and helped them listen up."

"Which was?" Sophia questioned.

"We shot out all their video cameras. Gus had us check out their locations when we entered the store. As soon as you left, they went out. Ping, pang, pop." Al demonstrated with his fingers.

"Right," Silvio said. "That's what Mario was doing as he headed up the stairs. Then that guy came out of the back office and started firing. The first one hit Mario in the gut. Of course, he had on the vest, but the second shot is what winged his arm. I'd just passed that door, so I wheeled around and yanked it open, exposing the shooter. Gus nailed the man's leg, and I kicked his gun over the railing. The other two yo-yos came out, hands up high. It was pretty cool, I'd say!" Silvio leaned back against the couch. "Most excitement I've seen in a long while."

"Then what?" Matt asked, intrigued.

"I flushed one more henchie from the front office, along with a bona fide secretary," Mario declared. "And then we got to work."

"Doing what?" Sue asked, not certain that she really wanted to know.

"Gus primed us to grab all the computers," Mario said. "The towers, that is, along with laptops and cell phones."

"Whatever for?" Marnie asked, directing her question directly to Gus

"Well," Gus said, "what's usually on computers and cell phones?"

"Everyone's business." Sophia smiled wisely. "And you put the computers out on the street?"

"Of course not, Sophia, I'd never do anything that stupid. A guy could get accused of stealing if he did that," Gus chortled. "We simply invited their toughies to carry them out and set them down on the street."

Silvio hooted. "Yeah, they'd open the door and when they saw the street packed with cops, they'd set down their package and hop back inside quick."

"We also requested the videotapes and had them set outside," Gus added. "All that took about fifteen or twenty minutes. We cuffed the wounded guy to the upstairs railing. I suggested to the old doll that she might like to call for an ambulance. By now, the out-cold guy was awake, so we herded him upstairs, along with the others. They seemed a little anxious about what might be coming."

Mario began to laugh. "Their faces were chalk white. Gus told them it's a good thing I was only winged, otherwise he couldn't be so nice. Then Gus said, 'As it is if you fellas can run real fast, you might wanna get outta here real quick, before I change my mind and before the cops bust you.'"

"Boy, did they ever high-tail it out of there," Al commented. "Then we left."

"Wait a minute," Rocco said. "You didn't come out for a minute or two after they left? Let me tell my story,"

"Your story?" Gus asked, surprised there even was one.

"Those guys bust through that door like the building was on fire," Rocco said. "One of them saw me with the van. He grabbed a tire iron, yelling at me to open the doors. I mean, I'd locked them all. You can't be too careful in alleyways, you know. Anyway, as he gets ready to smash my window—and my head, I suspect—I simply look up and point to the rooftop with my finger. There were our FBI and police guys, all in their SWAT gear, pointing their automatics at them." Rocco laughed so hard that tears rolled down his cheeks. "I thought the guy with the tire iron would crap his pants. He dropped it like a hot potato and ran, like he was in a hundred-yard dash."

After the sharing session ended, the participants settled in to wait for news from the rest of the sting crew—Tony, Max, Jack, and Dave—to learn whether the final events of the day had been successful.

The wait proved to last another four hours. During this time, the younger men enjoyed Kaye's pool. At Jack's, Gus went to his room and napped. Mario played solitaire in the family room while Sophia pumped the women for all the details about her brother's romance with Kaye as the three of them bustled about the kitchen preparing the evening meal.

As time dragged on, everyone started to become anxious.

"There's no point in any of us speculating as to what's taking them so long," Marnie declared after a while. "All that does is increase our anxiety level. Dinner is ready, so I suggest we eat."

They had already begun the meal when Dave drove up to Jack's alone.

"Where are the others?" Sophia asked him worriedly, when he came into the house.

"They're okay. I thought it best that Max and Tony be checked out first, so I took them to Sue's clinic." Dave paused, groping for the right choice of words. "The doctor thought it best to be on the safe side, so he called in Dr. Chandra. She scheduled Max for an X-ray to make sure his leg was okay."

Sue furrowed her brow. "Why would his leg not be okay? He was supposed to be in the surveillance van, wasn't he?"

"Well, yes, that's correct, Sue." Dave paused. "Before I explain, I thought everyone might want to know about Tony."

It was Marnie's turn to become alarmed. "What about Jack?"

"Jack? Oh he's fine. He's simply their babysitter," Dave said absent mindedly. "With the bruising to Tony's chest, the doctor ordered an X-ray, an EKG, and some other tests—to be on the safe side."

Sue leaned against the doorway, simultaneously crossing her feet and her arms and glowered at her husband. She could read him like a book. "Okay, Dave, what went wrong?"

Those words grabbed everyone's attention.

"First things first," Dave said emphatically. "The guys will be okay. I'll give you a full update in a minute. The good news is that the sting was successful! Thanks to all of you, I might add. Sophia, you conducted yourself like a real pro." He grinned at her. "Epi told me to tell you that you'd make a good undercover agent. As for you, Gus, I don't know whatever possessed you to dump the weapons and computer hard drives onto the street, but that was absolutely brilliant!"

"Oh, but Chief Davidson," Gus said absolutely deadpan, "we didn't dump anything onto the street. We wouldn't do that. After all, that could be construed as stealing. That, sir, was the work of the Leuzeckis' own employees."

Dave burst out laughing. "Indeed, Mr. D'Amato, I did word it wrongly. It happened exactly as you said. The one older lady testified that some men in the store invited the Leuzeckis' men to do so and they did. Double brilliant!" He then noticed Mario's sling. "You okay?"

Mario nodded.

"You wouldn't believe it," Gus said to Dave. "Here we were in that store, minding our own business, and men with guns started chasing Sophia. Shook us up so much that Al dropped a box of ball bearings, and one of those thugs skidded and fell, knocking himself out. Another character opened fire on Mario here." He turned to Mario. "Show the chief what he did to your brand-new bulletproof vest. Fortunately, Silvio yanked the door open, exposing the shooter. I mean, what was I to do except knock the gun out of his hand and ensure he didn't pick it up again? After all, with so many people in the store, it could have been really dangerous to have that man continue shooting. Don't you think?"

Dave responded equally serious. "That is scary indeed, Gus. It's also amazing that you and Chief Snyder think so much alike. I was told that Snyder informed that older woman that it was a good thing someone else was in the store with a gun to ensure nobody got seriously hurt. The paramedics figured that the man who was shot had a broken wrist and tibia, both reparable. Too bad for him, though, it was discovered he has a record a mile long, as well as several outstanding charges." Dave cocked his head. "There's another point that might be of interest to you. The older lady, along with several other staff and customers who witnessed the whole thing, were shocked that the five armed men in the store didn't rob the store. They actually commented that when those gunmen let the Leuzeckis' hired thugs go—yep, *thugs* was the actual word several witnesses used—it looked like everything they'd witnessed had been a staged publicity stunt!"

Gus's jaw dropped. "You've got to be kidding!"

"No," Dave said, stone-faced. "In fact, Chief Snyder acknowledged that it was an interesting theory, as well as a good possibility. He apologized for any anxieties the staff or customers might have experienced and added that, if their theory was correct, the stunt had backfired for the brothers." Dave paused. "It might interest you to know that Snyder also reassured the employees that the police were documenting each piece of equipment found on the sidewalk. They would identify the owner of each piece found. Everything that legally belonged to the store would be returned. Terrific job! Very well executed. I said it before, but it needs repeating... brilliant!"

Dave acknowledge everyone's smiles.

"Incidentally, Epi is certain those computers will reveal the identity of our FBI impersonator and his connection to the Leuzecki's," Dave added.

He then described how Epi and Chief Snyder had come to a standstill in the interrogation room, when he and Jack in the observation room heard a gunshot in the building. He conveyed how Tony had been shot at close range and how Max had prevented further carnage by shooting the gunman.

"The issue for Max is whether or not he bore weight on his broken leg, and if he did, what damage he did," Dave said. "We think he managed his acrobatics on one leg. At least, that's the hope. Dr. Chandra is checking it out. As for Tony, it appears he lost consciousness momentarily. Was he simply winded or did the blow shock his heart?" Dave paused and stroked his chin, establishing eye contact with each person. "The truth is, without those vests Max insisted we wear, we would have had a funeral!"

"If Tony is all right, why is he in the hospital?" Sophia cried.

"Well, when he took the vest off, everyone realized the bruising his chest had taken," Dave said. "We were going to send him for tests straight away, but that's when we got the big break in the interrogation." Dave motioned to Gus. "Lou happened to be in the precinct for another matter, at just the right time. He became our trump card. The Leuzeckis and their lawyer thought we were bluffing concerning Tony, Sophia, and Max's family connections. The brothers, however, had no delusions about who Lou was. When Lou authenticated the situation, they quickly opted for the deal Epi offered."

Gus scowled, unaware that there were to be deals. "Which was what?"

"The deal concerned the crime of attempted murder on Tony and obstruction of justice in Max's case," Dave said. "If they would confess, in writing, to those charges, and accept the same sentence as Max received, they would be incarcerated immediately. Furthermore, the location of their prison wouldn't be revealed to anyone connected to the sting."

Gus's countenance darkened "No way!"

"Gus, please understand," Dave said quietly. "Their confession means that Max has an immediate acquittal, which is what we were striving for. That's why the sting was organized in the first place, and that's why it's a success."

"But what about Uncle Tommy's murder, the FBI agent, and the Newark policeman's murder?" Sophia asked.

"No deal there, Sophia." Dave smiled. "Fortunately, neither their lawyer nor the Leuzeckis were aware of the computer street snatch. If evidence of any criminal activity is revealed, they'll get nailed further."

"On the other hand," Gus mused, "it's to our advantage not to know where they go. Guys like them are quite capable of making their own enemies and should anything happen to them, we are in the clear—above suspicion." He paused and looked at the others. "We need to focus on healing and rebuilding our own lives."

Dave clapped him on the back. "Exactly, Gus. Wisely spoken!"

Sophia bit her lip. "Can I go to the hospital now, please? I really need to see Tony and be with him."

"Matt, you take her in the van," Dave said. "Al, would you go with him? If Max has been sedated, Jack will need your help with him. It would probably be a good idea for the rest of us to set up the hospital bed in Jack's study. That way, when Max returns from the hospital he can safely sleep it off."

Marnie smiled. "While the rest of us relax and celebrate a job well done!"

Shortly after nine, all the Independence Drive sting team members had returned safely. The groggy Max was taken to his bed in Jack's study, but it was Tony who received most of the attention.

"You are so fortunate, my man, that you're in the land of the living, relatively unscathed," Sue said to him sternly.

The flamboyant, jovial Tony was unduly subdued. "Believe me, Sue, I realize how blessed and fortunate I've been today. It's pretty sobering to think I might not have seen my kids grow up."

"It's amazing you didn't break a rib," added Jack, "and that the rhythm of your heart has begun to regulate."

Dave shook his head. "It's a wonder you didn't have a heart attack throwing that kid around."

That served to open a whole new discussion with a barrage of additional questions. The ensuing conversation was so intense and animated that no one heard the front door open and close.

chapter thirty-eight

A s the solitary figure entered the foyer of the Walters' home, a soft light peeped through the cracked door to the judge's study. Tiptoeing quietly to the door and peaking in, Kaye was startled to discover Max sleeping soundly in his old hospital bed.

Kaye draped her coat over the high-back chair and gently lowered the guardrail. She curled up beside him. Every part of her body ached. Emotionally, she was bankrupt. Her mind was numb, yet her heart sang with gratitude.

"Thank you, Jesus. Thank you, thank you, thank you," she murmured

Though dimly aware of conversation elsewhere in the house, Kaye collapsed into a deep sleep.

Eventually, everyone began to drift to their respective sleeping quarters, whether at Kaye's, the Davidsons', or the Walters'. That was when Marnie popped in for a final check on Max. She was surprised to discover Kaye snuggled beside Max. Since both were sleeping soundly, she gently pulled the blanket up and quietly secured the guardrail. Closing the shades, Marnie turned off the small table lamp and tiptoed from the room. With a sigh of relief, she headed upstairs to her room.

As Max's mind struggled to awaken in the darkest part of night just before dawn, his hand reached out and found itself grasping a bar. He could see the man with the gun, saw the spark as the weapon fired, felt himself falling, taking aim, firing back. He saw the strike and the man sinking to his knees, collapsing facedown. Max tried to move and instantly realized he was confined.

Panic swept over him. He broke out in a cold sweat. As he struggled to regain consciousness, the what, why, and where all eluded him. Breathing heavily, he forced his eyes to open. He gasped. The bar wasn't that of a cell but of a bed. Turning his head, he soon saw the reason for his sense of confinement; he was not alone in bed.

He rubbed his hand over his face. He sighed, his panic beginning to recede.

"Kaye." Gingerly, he turned his body to face her. He gently stroked her hair. She stirred, her eyes briefly fluttering open.

As his recall returned, he remembered the reason for his grogginess. They'd sedated him to reexamine his broken leg. They had wanted to ensure no further damage had occurred during that precinct scuffle.

The precinct scuffle? Oh no! I shot someone...

Still in a daze, he gently shook his wife's shoulders. "Kaye, Kaye."

Her eyes opened momentarily.

"I'm so sorry," he whispered. "I didn't intend to, but I ended up shooting a guy."

"That's nice," she mumbled and was sound asleep again.

Max blinked his eyes. "He's dead," he added.

"Mmmhmm."

Somehow, his wife's reaction defused his own anxiety and he drifted back to sleep.

Sometime later, he awoke fully refreshed. He checked his watch: 7:30 a.m.

The light of day squeezed beneath the blinds. Max glanced at Kaye to see she was still sleeping soundly. He touched her hand, then noticed her clothes. He sat up slowly, so as not to awaken her, and stared. Her clothes were stained with what looked like a mixture of grit and grease. The hand he had touched was bruised. Her forehead had a red welt on it and a crimson streak went down her sleeve. Although she lay partly covered, he could see that the front of her blouse had those same crimson blotches.

Gently he called her name, and she finally opened her eyes.

"Hon, you're covered in blood."

Before he could comment about the bruises, her eyes closed again.

"It's your father's," she said simply.

Max blinked. He couldn't believe he had heard her correctly. "How did you get Pop's blood all over you?" he asked tentatively.

"He shot himself," she said, rolling over.

Max hadn't been prepared for that.

Then, just before she dozed off again, she added, almost as an afterthought, "He's okay."

Maybe she's dreaming, he thought. *That must be it. Like I thought the bedrail was a prison bar.* He managed to quietly put down the guardrail on his side of the bed, slide out, and on one leg retrieved his crutches. *The only problem with that theory is that she looks like she's come from a war zone—bruised, battered, and that sure looks like blood, not ketchup!*

He closed the study door and hobbled down the hall toward the kitchen. There, he found Jack drinking his coffee, morning paper in hand.

"Ah-ha, our sleeping prince has roused himself. Where's the princess?" Marnie sang out cheerfully. "Here's a cup of coffee. Would you like some toast?"

Max couldn't speak. He just stared at Jack, who peered over his glasses at him,

"For heaven's sake, Max, how can anything be wrong this morning?" Jack asked. "Wasn't everything settled yesterday?"

"Have you seen, Kaye?" Max managed to croak.

"She wasn't in bed with you, in Jack's study?" Marnie suddenly sounded alarmed. "She was there when I went to bed. You both were sleeping so soundly, I threw another cover over you."

Max screwed up his face. "Sorry, I worded my question wrong. I guess the sedative hasn't worn off completely. I know where she is. I meant, have you seen how she looks?"

Jack shook his head and looked at Marnie quizzically.

"Max, we only had a night light in the room," Marnie said. "I didn't want to disturb either of you. I took a spare comforter, threw it over you, and actually removed the night light. Is something wrong?"

Jack pursed his lips. "Marn, he's not going to look like that if nothing's wrong." He turned to Max. "So, what *is* the problem?"

"She's bruised, battered, and has blood stains all over her clothes. It looks like she's rolled in dirt and grime," Max rasped. "But that's not all."

Jack set down his coffee. "There's more?" He rolled his eyes to the ceiling. "Why, Lord, was I not content to stay in the law firm?"

"It's not funny, Jack," Max snapped.

"Do I look like I'm laughing?"

"Stop it, the two of you," Marnie implored. "Max, you are obviously distraught. Please, tell us what's wrong."

"She says it's Pop's blood!"

Jack gasped. "Your father beat her up?"

"Oh no!" Marnie exclaimed. "What happened?"

"I can't get her to wake up. All she gives me is half-sentences. When I asked about the blood, she mumbled, 'It's your father's.' When I asked what happened, she said 'He shot himself.' Then she said, 'He's okay,' and went back to sleep."

The two followed Max back to Jack's study and the sleeping Kaye. He was definitely correct. Her clothes were a mess and covered in blood. All three stared in disbelief at what they saw, trying to make sense of it.

"Good morning, Mr. Carron," Gus's voice called out from behind them. "I gather all is well with you and your leg?"

Max turned, mouth open. "Gus!"

Gus took one look at Max and assessed the situation, just as Marnie and Jack had done. "Now what's wrong?"

The three stepped aside, giving Gus a good view of the sleeping damsel.

"Good grief!" Gus said. "What on earth happened to her?"

"Come, get a cup of coffee and some cinnamon buns," Marnie said, quietly walking back to the kitchen.

They had just sat down again at the kitchen table, prepared to tell Gus everything, when Tony and Sophia joined them. Tony's arm was around his wife, who had obviously been crying.

Max's heart sank. "Did you talk to Mamma?" he whispered, not really wanting her response.

"Not to your Mamma, but mine," Tony said grimly. He kissed Sophia on the head, sat down on the chair, and pulled his wife into his lap.

"And?" Jack said.

Sophia sniffed. "Do you know of anyone I could article with?"

"What do you mean?" Jack asked. "I thought you only had five months to go?"

"She did," Tony said, hugging Sophia. "But ever since she started, they've looked for any excuse to bag her—just because she's my wife. She took more razzing and was given more crummy assignments than anyone. All of which she endured stoically and efficiently, putting in extra, long hours, but when we took off last week with you, that proved to be just what they needed to justify canning her. The office called my mom yesterday and told her that Sophia was finished. Mamma said that she was sure Sophia would be at work this Thursday and asked if Sophia couldn't use this past week as her holiday time. 'No!' was the emphatic reply. 'She's not barrister material!' With that, they hung up."

Jack rose, grabbed a tissue box, and walked over to Sophia. "Look at me!"

She did, tears in her eyes.

"Have a tissue," Jack said. "You, Sophia, are most definitely barrister material, of that I can assure you! I could get you an articling position in a snap, but there's no point in wasting seven months, provided you feel you can tough out the next five."

"Jack, didn't you hear?" Sophia cried. "I don't have five more months. They fired me!"

"Trust me, Sophia, you'll have five more months," Jack said grimly. He grabbed the phone and spoke into the receiver. "Epi, we've got a problem here."

Jack proceeded to detail Sophia's situation. A smile broke out on his face as he listened to the agent's response.

"That's what I thought, too," Jack said, laughing. "Thanks, I'll tell Sophia."

After hanging up, Jack turned to Sophia.

"Not to get rid of the two of you, but Epi said that if you'll meet him at the airport by noon, you can fly with him to New York," Jack said. "Can you get home on your own from LaGuardia?"

"Yeah," Tony responded. "We can arrange that."

"Epi plans to pay your workplace a visit," Jack said. "He suggests you go into work tomorrow as usual, Sophia. Should they make you pick up your stuff and exit, simply do so and step outside and call this number." Jack handed her a slip of paper. "Epi plans to do some work in the Bureau's New York office tomorrow. If Tony has no objection, he'll drop by and have lunch with you. Sound like a plan?"

Sophia's tears had dried. "Epi honestly thinks I can have my job back?" Relief and shock registered in her voice.

Tony grinned. "Looks like it, babe. Hey, dial him back, Jack, and ask him if he can get me another vest."

"Don't have to. He already told me he was bringing one on the plane," Jack said, chuckling. "He figured you'd want one. He's also bringing the old one. Thought you might like a souvenir. They retrieved the bullet, to ascertain it was from the same gun as the one that killed the parking lot attendant and wounded the others. The vest would be garbage, but for you it has historical significance."

"How come they're being so generous?" Gus asked suspiciously.

"Two reasons," Jack answered. "The police are relieved the bullet that downed that guy didn't come from a police weapon. In other words, no bleeding heart inquiry—but the big reason, I suspect, is that the Bureau is surprised that the vest held at such close range given the strength of the gun. Epi wants Tony to test out a few more jackets."

Everyone but Tony laughed. "I don't think that's funny at all," he grumped.

Sophia gave him a big kiss. "At least you impressed them, dear!" Then she added, "Thanks, Jack, for everything you've done for us. I really mean it! Yes, we'll definitely catch that plane."

"Woah! Hold on, not so fast," Max yelled. "Sophia, you've got to phone Pop. I want to know how he is."

"You want to talk with him?"

"No, don't tell him about me, not just yet. Dr. Chandra said if the X-rays indicate significant progress, I can be driven to Chicago early next week. I'd like to get a day or two in with them before the hospital fundraiser. But I need to know he's okay."

"Why?"

"Never mind why. Just call, sis!" Max snapped. "It's nearly eight, their time. They should be up."

"Fine," she pouted. "I see we're back to normal family life once more. You're in your bossy, big brother mode! I'd almost forgotten what normal was with you."

"Please just call, Sophia," Jack pleaded. "We'll explain why after you hang up."

"Can you put the phone on speaker," Max asked. "I'd like to hear his voice. The rest of us will all be very quiet."

Sophia flipped out her cell, pushed one button, and waited.

"Hello, is that you, Sophia?" a distinctly female voice asked.

"Mamma? Where's Pop?"

"Can't you speak to me, dear? Your father's still sleeping."

"Of course, Mamma, I want to talk to you. I was surprised, because normally it's Pop who answers. Is he all right? He never sleeps past seven!"

"Sophia, is everything okay with you? I'm surprised to hear your voice. I thought you and Tony were having a few days off together?"

"Well, that's why I'm calling. We're about to get on a plane and fly home. I wouldn't be able to speak to you until later and I didn't want Pop to worry if he couldn't reach me."

"Hold on a moment, dear. I'll see if your father can speak with you."

Max massaged his forehead. His whole body was tense. *"Please, dear Lord, let him be okay,"* he prayed.

It took nearly three minutes before Sophia heard her father's familiar voice.

"Tony and you are all right, Sophia?"

"Yes, Pop, everything is just fine with Tony and me." She crossed her fingers. "We really did have a restful week. How was yours?"

"Yesterday was a little more stressful than most, I'm afraid." Her father sighed. "I had an…" He cleared his throat and continued, "I had an accident, nearly died. In fact, if it weren't for M.K. McDonald, I would be dead."

Sophia's eyes began to widen. "Really? You're kidding! Are you all right now? I mean, aside from being rather sore and bruised?

"Yes, Sophia, I'll be okay."

"But what did you mean, if it weren't for M.K. McDonald you'd be dead?"

Sophia by now was pacing back and forth in the kitchen, in a very intense dialogue with her father.

"Sophia, Mamma said Tony and you and the Marconis are all coming to the charity banquet next week. I'll give you all the details then. Right now, I need to lie down again. Oh, by the way, we expect Max home late next week, too."

"Wait, Pop, how do you know Max will be home next week?"

"Ms. McDonald has contacts with the Bureau, Sophia. They gave her a letter from Max to give to your mother and me. Apparently, they told her he might be home next Thursday."

"Am I to assume your animosity with her has diminished, Pop?"

"Yes, Sophia. Now, dear, I really must go. Here's your mother again. She can tell you what happened at Kayleen's dinner last night."

Tony and Gus eyed each other, the same thought flashing through both their minds: *When did Frank never have time to talk with Sophia?*

"Mamma," Sophia said, "Pop said that you'd tell me what happened yesterday at the Kayleen dinner with the city dignitaries and those selling their properties to Kayleen."

Josephine started to laugh. "My dear, I'm afraid you might not believe me, but just before the dinner was to begin, your father and Ms. McDonald came in at the last minute, arm in arm, both covered in dirt and blood."

Sophia's face simultaneously registered shock and disbelief. The same expression was mirrored on the faces of the other five people in Marnie's kitchen.

"Then Ms. McDonald said simply, 'We've settled our differences.' And your father added, 'She knows martial art.' With that, they both went to their respective seats and the rest of the evening was business as usual." Her mother paused. "There is more, Sophia, but it will have to wait until you're here in person. I'm very excited that finally we'll have Massimiliano and you and your family home at the same time. Please give Micki, Jo, and Ricci a kiss from us, and call when you get home. Love you."

"Love you too, Mamma. Bye."

Sophia closed the phone and spun around, her eyes like saucers. Shaking her head, she said, "If it wasn't Mamma telling me what my father and Kaye did, I wouldn't believe it. Would you?"

Tony looked blankly at his wife. Jack, Marnie, Max, and Gus on the other hand just stared at one another. Josephine's description of M.K. McDonald certainly agreed with the one they had witnessed sleeping in Max's bed.

But before anyone could utter a word, Kaye staggered into the kitchen, eyes half-closed.

"Can I please have a cup of coffee?" Kaye plunked down in the nearest chair.

Marnie quickly gave her one, folding Kaye's hands around the mug. To put it mildly, Kaye looked like a walking disaster.

"What on earth happened?" Sophia squeaked.

"I don't know if I have the strength to tell you. I'm so stiff and sore," Kaye said apologetically. "Please, give me a few moments."

"We will," Jack said tersely.

Sophia cleared her throat. "Kaye, I was talking to my mother just now on the phone. She said at last night's dinner you said my father and you resolved your differences."

Kaye looked up, her coffee mug clenched in both her hands, and nodded. "She's right. I did say last night that we resolved our differences."

"How did you resolve your differences?" Max asked.

Kaye yawned. "Oh, Max, let me tell you later. It's so dramatic! I can't do it right now." She looked at him, adding, "Hon, it was really stressful."

"Pop said you saved his life." Sophia looked at her sister-in-law, who simply sat there nodding, eyes closed. "And that you gave him a letter Max wrote."

Kaye's nods continued.

"You told him you were his daughter-in-law?" Tony asked.

Her eyes snapped open. "Absolutely not! That's for the charity dinner, but I had to let him know Max was alive and that you didn't hate him." She looked at her husband. "Not only that, he needed to know that it wasn't Italians who tried to kill Tony and framed you."

"You told him all that?" Gus queried.

"Of course, I had no choice. If I hadn't, he could have hurt himself. Badly! As it is, we're both sore and stiff, but we're alive." She glanced down at herself and frowned. "Boy, am I ever a mess!"

"You can say that again," Gus agreed.

"Do you mind if I shower and clean up first," Kaye pleaded. "But first tell me, on the News it said those brothers confessed to framing you. Is it true?"

Max took her hands in his. "Yes, Kaye, they did."

"So you and I can travel together?" The others nodded affirmatively. A smile crept across her face. "God is so good!"

chapter thirty-nine

The Our Lady of Mercies fundraising banquet was emerging as Chicago's social event of the year. In part, this was sparked by the shocking appearance of Frank and Kaye at the Kayleen dinner, where the announcement had been made that all was in order for the company to relocate. This, coupled with the speculation that the private investigator from Indiana credited with saving Kaye's life might also attend, had the whole town abuzz. The simultaneous revelation concerning the false imprisonment of the Carron's son and the expectation that he would accompany his parents further fueled public curiosity. Consequently, the hospital foundation found itself deluged with request for tickets.

In an unprecedented move, the banquet relocated to a large convention center. Kayleen's board of directors voted to cover the costs of the larger facility. Meanwhile, the national and international media clamored for interviews with Ms. McDonald and Private Investigator Maxwell Kerr.

Bishop Masseroti confessed that this banquet had exceeded all expectations of support. It appeared that the hospital's dream of a new pediatric and obstetric wing would become a reality.

The Carrons' extended family was as eager as anyone else to be present. Josephine soon realized that a family reunion was in the making. People from Miami, Las Vegas, New York, New Orleans, Dallas, Los Angeles, Newark, San Francisco, Boston, and Chicago itself all sent in hefty donations to the foundation. Angel was thrilled that Lou had called and said that the Bastaldis would be coming. In addition to her hospital commitments, Josephine and Angel were kept busy securing appropriate accommodations. Frank had insisted that they host their guests for at least one meal and a social hour.

Josephine Carron was the happiest she could ever remember. She was indeed thankful for the financial boost the hospital was receiving. However, her real gratitude focused not on the charity banquet, but rather the coming Wednesday—or, as she periodically reminded herself, "maybe Thursday." That's when she expected her son to once more be under her roof.

Tears came to her eyes every time she thought of him, and that was frequent. She was thankful for his letter. It had removed her gnawing fears that he would return to the house bitter, broken, even resentful of Frank and herself. Though she tried not to show it, she was elated over the news that, in truth, Massimiliano had done nothing wrong. She had always believed her son had a good heart, and the thought that he had capitulated to crime had devastated her. Over the past seven years, she had quietly agonized as to how she had failed as a mother to raise a good boy. Now, she had been vindicated!

Although the demands of the week allowed her few moments of quiet, she found two regular times of solitude every day—in the stillness before she slept at night and before she rose in the morning. In those times, Josephine thought of Mary, Jesus's mother. Somehow the past eight months had allowed her to identify better with Mary's grief over Christ's death. But now—oh yes, now—Josephine could sense the awe, the joy Mary must have experienced on that first resurrection morning!

In the hymn "Amazing Grace," one line said, "I once was lost but now am found." She knew it referred to humanity's sinful state, but the song, for her, also encompassed and embraced maternal grief. She and Mary had lost their sons, but now God's amazing grace had returned them back to their mothers' hearts. The more she dwelt on those thoughts, the more profound became her personal experience of God's gift of the resurrection of His Son.

She knew Mary had literally experienced the death of her son and his rising from the dead, whereas Josephine's experience was only figurative. Yet emotionally, Josephine had felt the separation from her son. She had experienced a "death" in their relationship. Mother and son had been unable to share their lives these past seven years, but now their relationship would have new life! In fact, when he had failed to return home following his release from prison, she had begun to fear he might even have been killed.

Josephine bit her tongue as tears filled her eyes. *And I have even more for which to be grateful. My family could just as easy have been gathering to help me bury Frank.* This prompted her to gaze at her sleeping husband and further ponder the reality of God's grace. *Grace—undeserved, unmerited favor. That's what the word means. Simply put, it's God doing for us what we cannot do for ourselves. Nothing Frank or I did merit him receiving his life back, no more than any other person whose loved one has died deserves their grief. This is the mystery of life, Lord Jesus. All we can do, in any scenario, is trust Your love for us and believe that You will use both our joys and sorrows to bring us closer to You!*

For his part, by mid-week Frank was beginning to navigate with a little less tenderness and stiffness. His scalp wound was healing nicely. He devoted most of his time to the pool and hot tub. These activities not only provided relief to his bruised body, they also offered him time to catch up with his comrade in arms—Gus. He had asked Gus to bring the guys home, then related how M.K. had given him the letter from Max, how the letter had relieved his personal angst that Massimiliano might reject him.

Frank chuckled. "Guess I'll have to train myself to say Max."

He showed Gus the letter, which Gus could now read with an even deeper understanding of the meaning behind each word. Gus's guilt of not being one hundred percent open with his friend dissipated as he realized that remaining mute now would only heighten the honor and joy Frank would receive later.

As for the other members of Gus' entourage, they were equally desirous to remain silent. They had all been invited to the charity dinner, with their spouse or date. Needless to say, those four young bucks, as Gus called them, were anxious to busy themselves in any work that kept them physically distant from either Mr. or Mrs. C.

It was Monday before Frank realized he had not seen Al.

"Oh," Gus casually commented. "Back east, Al followed up with a distant relative his mother had told him lived in Summerside. He found the old couple, but because of our surveillance he didn't have any time to spend with them. I figured we likely wouldn't need him for a few days, so I let him stay behind."

Since he was spinning a yarn, Gus figured he might as well embellish it. "Seems the couple has a grandson Al's age. He's athletic, like Al. They should have a good time together. I expect him home later this week."

Frank listened with interest. "That's fine. I like Al. He's a good kid. Sort of quiet, so it's nice if he can get chummy with someone."

Yep, Frank, really nice he can get a chum, Gus thought to himself. *Especially one who's a cop.*

* * *

Al was set to be home soon. Tuesday morning in Summerside dawned sunny and crisp. Dr. Chandra had given her permission and blessing for Max to drive to Chicago. Matt and Al were his designated drivers. The two alternated driving responsibilities while Max sat in the back with his leg propped up. They took Jack's van and loaded it up with the luggage of the other Independence Drive residents, including Rufie's bowls and bedding.

Late Thursday night, the others (Rufie included) would fly to Chicago. The plan was for them all to stay in the convention center's top floor suites.

By now, Max knew the reason for Kaye's bumps and bruises and he, too, was heading to Chicago with a happy, grateful heart.

The trio heeded Dr. Chandra's instructions to stop frequently—every two to three hours—to allow Max to move around. The mood in the van was jovial. The two younger men had fast become buds. Nonetheless, Max found himself dozing on and off. The past eight months, he had to admit, had been stressful.

* * *

Wednesday found both Frank and Josephine anxiously looking forward to their son's return, though Frank was careful to conceal his eagerness.

"Josie's exuberance was all the household could contain," he commented.

Even the news that Aunt Louisa would arrive Friday morning "expecting to have her usual room ready," in her words, so she could nap before the evening's festivities failed to dampen Josephine's spirit. She chose to ignore the insinuations in the rest of Aunt Louisa's message. The old dowager had demanded that Frank purchase her dinner ticket, made it clear she expected Massimiliano to have an audience with her, and asked if he had enrolled in the seminary. When the evening came and still no Max, Josephine admitted she felt a little disappointed. She sat in the bedroom window staring at the gatehouse well past eleven o'clock.

Frank walked over to his wife and put his arms around her. "Josie, your watching isn't going to speed his arrival. Better go to bed and get some rest." He kissed her gently on the cheek.

"Frank, what if he doesn't come?"

"Jo, we'll deal with that if it happens." He paused. "But my impression of M.K. McDonald is that she's not very fluffy."

"Meaning?"

278

"Meaning that when she states something will take place, she expects it to happen." He turned his wife around and hugged her. "In all her business dealings with us, what she meant she said!"

It was nearly 3:00 a.m. when Al pulled the van up to the gatehouse. The guard recognized him immediately and opened the gate.

Al leaned out the window. "I don't have the automatic garage opener in this van. Mind lifting the door for me from your controls? Thanks!" He guided the van into the underground parking garage. "The eagle has landed! I suggest, Matt, that we only take in our overnight bags. Tomorrow, you and I can take the rest of the luggage to the hotel."

"Hey, Max!" Matt yelled. "You made it! You're home!"

Max opened his eyes and yawned. All he wanted was his bed.

"Over here," Al said, directing them towards the elevator.

"You have an elevator?" Matt asked in surprise.

"Please be quiet, guys," Max urged. "I prefer my reunion with my parents to occur when I'm a tad more awake and a lot less sore."

Max stepped inside his bedroom door, grabbed his bag from Matt, motioned goodbye, and quickly closed the door behind him.

He took a deep breath. "Not like I actually used this room that much," he said to himself. "The real out of control feelings are going to hit when I get to my own house."

Even as he sank into the bed, he found himself burying his head in the pillow to silence his sobs.

Sheesh, where did that come from? he thought, gasping. *If this happens in an empty room I barely used, what's in store for me when I actually see Pop, Mamma, and the others?* He shuddered. *What am I in for Friday night?*

He hobbled to a mirror.

Boy, Maxie you look really rough. Puffy red eyes, unshaven... better get some sleep quick!

He sat on the bed, glanced at his left leg, and winced. Muscle loss had definitely occurred, though since he had started his pool exercise he thought there had been a slight gain. The incision was a long purple red welt from his groin to his knee.

Not very pretty, he thought with a chuckle. It was a good thing he didn't have to wear a bathing suit Friday evening. On the other hand, he had the leg and he was alive! He grinned and flopped back on the bed. *Yep. Alive and the husband of a much-admired gal, and on Friday night everyone will know she's mine!*

He fell asleep with a smile spread across his face.

* * *

Frank opened one eye and was greeted by a big red 7:00 on his alarm clock. He glanced over his shoulder and was pleased to discover Josephine still beside him. He turned carefully so as not to waken her.

She's as beautiful as the day I first saw her, and just as feisty! To everyone else, she may appear gentle and mild, but when we're alone she never fails to let me know her mind on all family decisions and concerns.

The more he stared at her, the more gratitude filled his heart. He really hadn't deserved her, yet she loved him.

Love? Love is amazing and certainly more of a mystery the older I get.

He reached out and tickled her nose. She raised her hand to swat the imagined fly, and instead found her hand gently held. Opening her eyes, she discovered Frank staring at her.

"Good morning," he said. "I didn't think you'd want to miss a moment of your day of vigil."

"This is the day, isn't it?" She awoke with a start. "What time is it?"

"After seven, love!"

"Has he come home?"

"Josie, I just woke up. I don't know, but my guess is we're supposed to watch and wait." Frank gave her a playful poke. "And since it's already after seven, I suppose we should be up and watching."

Gus and Angel had already started breakfast by the time Frank and Josephine arrived in the dining room.

"Are you excited, Josephine?" Angel whispered as she poured the coffee.

"Personally, I don't know how I'll survive the day," Josephine confided.

Luigi poked his head around the door. "Mr. C., the gatehouse just let us know that Mr. Scallion should be here shortly."

"Were you expecting him, Frank?" Gus asked.

"No!" was the emphatic reply.

"Then why is he here?" questioned Angel.

"Because he's nosey," Josephine said frankly. The others stared at her in amazement. Rarely was Josephine so outspoken. "I'm sorry, Frank, but it's the truth. Scally has a need to feel he's one up on everyone else. You told everybody that Ms. McDonald said Max would be here today. So Scally has come to check it out, to be the first to analyze Massimiliano and us. Quite frankly, that doesn't amuse me."

"That's obvious, dear," Frank replied with a twinkle in his eye. "I can tell him Massimiliano—I mean, Max—isn't here, but when he does show I'll let him know. There, how's that?"

Josephine sat ramrod straight in her chair, eying Frank. "That would be fine, except I know you won't do it."

"Won't do what?" Scally said as entered the room and walked over to pour himself a cup of coffee, simultaneously helping himself to one of Angel's Danish pastries.

"Please, do help yourself to a coffee and something to eat," Josephine invited coolly.

"Thanks, I will." Scally sat down next to Frank. "What won't you do, Frank?"

"Tell you to take a hike and leave us alone today," Josephine retorted.

"Oh, I see Massimiliano hasn't returned yet. Well, Josie, maybe he won't," Scally said bluntly. "You have to prepare yourself for that letdown. After all, tomorrow is the big charity dinner, and your presence is necessary there, son or no son."

"But Ms. McDonald told Frank that Massimiliano would be here by Thursday," Angel protested. "That's today."

"Angel, Ms. McDonald is a businesswoman," Scally replied. "She'd say whatever she has to just to get her way."

"You're saying that she lied to Frank?" Josephine snapped.

Scally looked at Josephine patronizingly. "All I'm doing is attempting to prepare the two of you for a letdown, should it occur. Then at tomorrow night's festivities, you'll be able to keep your angst to yourself, put on a cheery face, and behave like all that really matters to you is a successful fundraiser. After all, that's what the public will expect."

Before Josephine could retaliate, a tall and solidly built young man stepped into the dining room. The muscular blonde was unshaven and wore only a T-shirt, jogging pants, and socks. He appeared totally oblivious to the Carrons' dress code.

"Hi," he greeted cheerily as he sauntered over to the coffee. He looked under the warming tray and proceeded to serve himself a very hearty breakfast. He sat down with the other five, bowed his head, said a silent grace, looked up, and politely asked for the ketchup.

So taken aback at his brashness, Angel simply complied. Frank was set to explode at the young man's impudence.

"What time did you get in last night, Matt?" Gus asked, trying his best not to laugh. "How was the drive?"

The young man paused to swallow his food.

At least he shows some manners, Josephine thought.

Before answering, Matt chose to look at his watch. Perhaps his pause hadn't been related to manners after all.

Matt furrowed his brow. "I think it was about three, your time."

"You're doing well to be up by nine o'clock then," Scally replied sarcastically.

The insult was either missed or ignored. "Not really. That's actually ten my time and my stomach is used to eating no later than nine. So I'm really hungry."

"So we noticed!" said Frank.

Then to everyone's shock, Matt stood up and said, "Oh, wow! You must be Mr. Carron." He extended his hand toward Frank. "Pleased to meet you."

The whole thing took Frank so off-guard that he actually returned the handshake.

Matt sat down and began eating again. He looked over at Angel and broke into a wide smile. "I bet you're Angel." He turned to Gus. "You're right. She really does look like one. Your hair is very pretty, ma'am."

Again he stood and extended his hand to a now very blushing Angel.

Then Matt noticed Josephine. He flashed a warm smile at her. "I can see they're right. You are a special lady. I'm real pleased to meet you."

Josephine, too, found herself automatically reaching out and accepting his hand.

Turning to Scallion, Matt said, "I'm sorry, sir, I can't place you." And again he extended his hand.

"Scallion is the name." He shook Matt's hand as well.

"This is my husband Mr. D'Amato," Angel said, gesturing to Gus.

This elicited a laugh from Matt. "Oh, I know him, ma'am."

Gus couldn't help himself. He glanced at his watch and calculated that by now Max should have had a good six hours of sleep. He cleared his throat. "You actually interrupted our conversation, Matt."

Never mind that you shouldn't be eating at my personal table, and certainly not dressed the way you are, Frank grumbled to himself.

Matt looked sincerely apologetic. "Oh gee, Gus, I'm sorry. I didn't mean to interrupt. I thought it was a buffet breakfast."

"Well, it is breakfast, dear," Josephine said kindly. "I'm glad you like it."

"Mr. Scallion came out here because he was concerned Mr. and Mrs. Carron might have a terrible letdown."

"Oh, I'm sorry, is there a problem?" Matt asked. "Anything I can do that might help?"

Frank stared at Gus in disbelief. He wasn't sure if it was because of the young man's cornball attitude or because Gus had dared share family concerns with a total stranger.

Gus chose to ignore the figurative daggers Frank was throwing at him. "Maybe you *can* help, Matt. You see, Mr. Scallion was telling the Carrons that he doubts M.K. McDonald's word that their son Max would be home today." To Gus's delight, he saw indignation rising in Matt. He chose to throw a few more logs on the fire. "Just before Matt came in, Scally, I believe you were telling Mrs. Carron that Ms. McDonald is a businesswoman and she would say anything to get what she wants."

Yes! Gus snickered to himself. *Oh yes!*

Matt's smiling demeanor suddenly changed. He glowered at Scallion. "That may be how you do business, sir, but that's not how M.K. McDonald does it." He turned to Josephine. "Ma'am, don't listen to this character! He doesn't know what he's talking about."

Gus thought he'd bust a gut. Scally's mouth dropped. Nobody put Scally down; he put others down!

But oh Buddy, it's happening now! Gus thought.

Before either Frank or Scallion could reply, Matt pulled up a chair beside Josephine. Scowling at the lawyer, Matt took her hand and quietly said, "I don't know whether you call 3:00 a.m. yesterday or today, ma'am, but that's when Max arrived."

Frank had a rapid attitude adjustment, from desiring to throw this bum out of his house to sudden attentiveness to the young man's every word.

"What did you say?" Frank demanded.

"I said that this guy's an idiot to smear M.K. She'd never say anything mean to mislead another person. Max is here, just like she said he would be!"

"Max is here?" Josephine's eyes were wide in amazement. "Here? In this house?"

Matt frowned. "Yeah. That's what I said, ma'am."

"Where?" Frank challenged.

"In bed, I guess." Matt looked at Gus in desperation.

Gus could contain himself no longer. "Did Max go to the second room to the left, at the top of the stairs?"

Matt nodded. "Yeah, I think that was the room we helped him to."

"How'd you get in here in the first place?" Frank asked, dumbfounded.

Matt shrugged. "Al just said hi to the guy at the gate, and he let us in."

"You came with Al?" Frank was clearly flabbergasted.

All at once, Josephine rose. "I don't care how he got in, when he got here, or who he came with, Frank Carron. I want to see our son now, with or without you!"

Josephine stormed up the stairs. Frank wasn't long following her.

Gus looked at Scally. "You owe this young guy an apology. He's rather fond of M.K. McDonald.

chapter forty

"Josephine, for heaven's sake, at least knock before you enter! He's not your little boy anymore." Frank chased after his wife, who was sprinting up the stairs to their son's room.

His words jarred Josephine back to reality. She stopped with her hand on the doorknob, her lip trembling. "No, he's not, is he?" she whispered as she turned to face him. She blinked back tears. "Maria LaRosa said her Mickey went into prison a decent young man and came out a horrid scumbag."

"Josie, Mickey LaRosa went into prison a scumbag and came out a scumbag," Frank stated firmly. "While Max may not be your little boy, I remind you that he wasn't your little boy when he went to prison. My point, dear, is that you don't go barging into a grown man's bedroom, even if he is your son. Don't worry, Massimiliano will still be your Massimiliano, only remember to call him Max."

He gave her a gentle kiss and rapped on the door. There was no reply. Frank turned the knob and slowly opened the door.

The two stared at an empty room. "He's not here!" Josephine cried.

Frank gave a low chuckle. "He was here, dear. Look at the bed. With pants over there, shirt over here, a bag on the chair, and shoes at the end of the bed… this looks like Massimiliano's room always looked. Your Max is back."

"Why would you say that?"

"You have a short memory, my dear. Our son was challenged when it came to keeping a neat room, and it looks like prison didn't alter that handicap," Frank grumped. "As for where he is, I'm afraid you'll have to wait for his shower to finish. In the meantime, you and I can sit here and let him serenade us." Frank sat on the side of the bed and pulled his wife towards him. He grinned. "One more thing prison didn't change was his tenor voice."

"Frank, his singing was one thing I missed terribly." She leaned against her husband. "When he was here, the house swelled with music."

The sound of running water stopped.

"Well, Jo, since he isn't your little boy anymore, and since he may have forgotten that two sexes exist on the planet, I think I should alert him to your presence." Frank strode to the bathroom door and knocked. "Max, be forewarned your mother is here. Clothes would be advisable."

A muffled "Pop? Mamma?" emanated from behind the closed door. The door cracked open and Max popped his face from behind the door. Spying his parents, he broke into a wide grin. "Missed ya! I'll be out in a second."

Frank turned to his wife. "At least from the neck up, he looks like your Max!"

"Oh, Frank, he looks so much like you. Much more than before, don't you think?"

Neither were prepared to see him emerge in his bathrobe with crutches.

Josephine's hand went up to her mouth in shock. "Massimiliano."

Frank's face clouded with concern. "What happened?"

"This isn't bad," Max said. "Trust me, it's much better than before, but can we sit on the bed and hug? I don't want to bear any weight on my left leg."

Sitting between his parents, Max reached out and put his arms around them both, closing his eyes.

"I really, really missed you," he said softly. He turned and kissed them—first his mother, and then his father. Soon all three were sobbing.

Frank tried clearing his throat several times. He finally grabbed the tissue box, had a good blow, and managed to choke out, "Except for the leg, you seem okay. Are you?"

Max sighed. "When I was released, I'd have to say, in hindsight of course, that I was very bitter." He gently bumped foreheads with his mother. "But I have to say, it really didn't last long."

Frank hesitated, unsure whether he should bring up the next topic in front of Josephine. Finally, he decided to bite the bullet. "Lou and Bill said that when you left them, you said you'd promised to do something. You had a job to finish?"

"Is that a question, or are you making a statement?"

Frank thought of snarling, *Don't get smart with me!* But one look at Josephine softened him.

"A question," he said instead. He was glad, because Max's response revealed that he honestly hadn't understood what Frank had meant.

"It's true," Max began. "I did tell them that. But I had no idea what those words would end up meaning. You know, Mamma, I've been learning what I think you've known all along, which is that God talks to us. Not in ways like we're talking now, but He does communicate, and at times we miss it. Then, all of a sudden, the Holy Spirit taps us on the shoulder and points to something in our life we've totally overlooked." Max pointed a finger at his father's chest. "Like right now, God used you, Pop, by your question, to help me see how in those words I spoke to Lou and Bill, the Holy Spirit was actually showing me that He had a job for me." Max exhaled deeply. "And boy, it was some job! Over the next few days, I'll share more. It's just that right now everything is so overwhelming!"

His mother put her hand to his cheek. "We understand, son. We understand." She smiled at Frank. "When we woke this morning, your father reminded me that I needed to be patient and wait."

Frank looked at Josephine and decided that since she was giving him good press, it would be prudent to remain quiet. He coughed. "Jo, Max needs to dress. Why don't you go make sure there's some breakfast left. I'll wait with him."

"Do you still have your pool?" he asked before his mom left. "I have to do several strengthening exercises in the water. I'd like to go to the pool before I eat. Maybe you'll swim with me, Pop? Anyway my femur was badly shattered. I was lucky a military-trained orthopedic surgeon happened to be at the hospital when I was brought in. Even though it looks real bad, let me assure you a lot of healing has taken place, and there will be much more. I don't want you freaking. Especially you, Mamma." He playfully tapped her nose with his forefinger. "Promise?"

"Of course," Josephine said, staring intently at him. However, when he opened the housecoat and pulled up the leg of his swimsuit, both parents gasped at the extent of the purple red welt.

"My dear boy." Josephine's eyes filled with tears. "Does it hurt?'

"Not now, Mamma," he said softly. "But let me tell you, at the time, it sure did!"

The shock treatment worked just as planned. Father and Mother, for the moment, were satisfied with the past; they wanted to move quickly into the now. Josephine left to put aside breakfast for her son while Frank got into his trunks and led the way to the pool. Gus declined to join them, but let them know that Al had taken Matt jogging.

This left Frank alone with Max, just as the elder Carron had hoped. He had something he needed to discuss with his son, but first things first.

"Max, Gus said that this Matt guy was a lost relative of Al's."

His son nodded. "Seems like I heard something like that."

"Did they drive you home?"

Max nodded again. "I saw Gus in the airport before he left and he suggested Al could help drive me home." Max rolled his eyes to the ceiling. *"Not a lie, Lord. Both of those things did happen."*

"I don't know how to say this, son, but the guy dresses and acts like a bum. I mean, he walked into our dining room and helped himself to breakfast like he owned the place." Frank was clearly dismayed. "All he wore were socks, sweatpants, and a T-shirt."

As his father spoke, Max recalled the old-world formality that had existed in his father's household. In some respects, it had helped him adapt to the rigid routines of the pen. Since his release, however, he'd come to enjoy the Independence Drive residents' informality. He heard his father, though; he understood this serious dress code concern, but quite honestly it was all he could do to smother the bubbles of laughter that threatened to erupt from within him.

When his father finished speaking, Max chose to assume a very pensive look. "Hmm," he said, "Yes, I can see why you might think Matt a bum. But I know he isn't. He has—" Max caught himself, then paused and coughed. "He has a, er, good job. It's probably my fault, Pop."

"Your fault?" Frank looked puzzled.

"Well, yeah. You see, with my leg like this, for a long while it was in a steel frame."

"Uh-huh." Frank tried to imagine where his son was going with this.

"And all I could wear was track pants. I mean, they're cheap. A seamstress could cut one leg off and zipper the side, so I could put the pant on. Also, for a long time I could only wear socks. Everyone around me just adapted to my dress. You know, to make me feel comfortable."

Frank frowned pensively. "I never thought of that possibility. That would be different, like the people would be considerate, not lazy or sloppy. Interesting!"

"That's right, Pop. Everybody was most considerate and caring," Max said emphatically. To himself he added, *"And that, Lord, is the whole truth. Big time."*

Apparently, Max had adequately covered Frank's concerns, for now the elder Carron turned to the subject most on his heart. "Max, when you were recovering from your accident, did M.K. McDonald track you down?"

"Yes, I guess that's one way of phrasing it." All the while he was wondering, *Where on earth are we going to go with this one?* He opted for a diversion tactic, asking his father to help him with his water leg exercises. It proved a temporary stopgap only.

With the exercises completed, the two men hung on a floatie, relaxing in the warm waters of the pool. That's when Max recognized an answer to his prayer. His father was growing very fond of Kaye—even if it was in a grudgingly sort of way.

From his father's perspective, Kaye had utilized the resources at her disposal to discover where Max was. As a result, Max had given her his letter. Consequently, Frank felt comfortable revealing to his son how she had also helped him.

Frank began to unburden himself to Max.

"Son, something horrible happened to me when I was a little kid." Frank closed his eyes. He'd discovered that each time he shared this memory, it seemed to take on a life of its own—drudging up more pain and hurt than he'd ever imagined existed within him. Yet he also realized that when he had opened up and shared, it was as if an unknown hand had yanked some of the terror from his heart, flinging it away from him like one would discard a dreadful weed.

A tear began to trickle down his cheek. Frank's voice trembled, as he continued. "When I heard the news that the feds were saying you were innocent and had been set up, all I could think about was we'd welched on the deal we'd made with Pepi not to pursue who'd tried to kill Tony. My whole vision flooded with the memory of those vicious men mercilessly beating and torturing my father, finally killing him and pushing my face into his blood—all because those men mistook my pop as someone who'd welched on a deal with their mob boss."

Frank's face contorted with anguish. Max had never seen his father so open and raw. In his wildest imagination, he would never have dreamt his father could have had such a terrifying experience and be so wounded. He remained still, almost afraid to breathe for fear it would block the older man from continuing his story.

At last, Frank opened his eyes, locking them on his son. "So, Max, two things hit me. One was that I didn't want any of my family forced to watch either of us being murdered, like I had been forced to witness my father's murder. Second, I didn't want you blamed for welching on the deal. I thought that if I killed myself, it would look like I had been the one who tipped off the feds."

Max could see his father was both ashamed and embarrassed at his attempted suicide. Given the fact that the mob wasn't even involved, it would have been a useless act, and one that brought great grief to his family. Max knew his father now appreciated how devastated Josephine would have been, and this only deepened his guilt all the more.

"So, Max," Frank concluded, "this McDonald broad really did save me from killing myself. She spied me with the gun to my head and ran and tackled me." He buried his face in his hands. "God, Max, it was so stupid. I would have brought so much pain to your mother. Thank God that woman came when she did, and had the courage to do so!" He paused and added, almost as an afterthought, "Not everyone would have the guts to run toward someone with a gun."

Max hesitated and then decided to risk a comment. "So in some ways, you really are indebted to Ms. McDonald."

"Yeah, I guess I am. I figure I need to do all I can to help her succeed in Chicago." Frank paused and looked at his son. "But truthfully, Max, at first I really didn't like her at all."

"I know the feeling, Pop. Believe me, I do!"

"Yeah, I guess you might, after all you've been through." Frank sighed. "Anyway, in my books, son, a man is one who will admit he was wrong."

"And you're telling me that you're admitting you were wrong on your initial assessment of McDonald?" Max was careful to allow only a faint smile to grace his face. Fortunately, it went unnoticed by his father.

"Absolutely, son, absolutely. Maybe you'll get the chance tomorrow to thank her for tracking you down, taking your letter, and giving it to me. If you do, let me know, okay?"

As they headed to their rooms to change, Max replied, "Pop, I'd be happy to do so. Trust me, that would make me feel good, too!"

By the time they got downstairs, Josephine and Angel were all atwitter. Their relatives from L.A. had just landed at O'Hare.

Josephine sighed. "I feel so sorry for Lucinda Verqussi, my cousin's daughter."

"Why?" Max asked.

"I don't think it can be very pleasant for her."

"Now, Josephine," Frank cautioned. "Be careful what you say and how."

"Frank, I'm only saying what everyone can see. Her husband and oldest son are terrible womanizers. I feel so sorry for Lucinda's daughter-in-law. Their son is so disrespectful of his wife, even when she's in the room. If he pulls those stunts in my house—"

"He will get your evil eye," Frank said with a chuckle.

"Absolutely! And Lucinda's other son is so—"

"So gay, Josie?" Frank completed her sentence.

"Well, maybe not. Maybe he's simply very creative."

"Maybe, dear." Frank smiled. "We'll leave it at that."

A few hours later, the Verquzzi family arrived at the Carrons' place. Max had no trouble understanding his parents' conversation. He wished he'd gone with Al and Matt when they skipped out to take the luggage to the convention center's hotel, but he realized that his was to be the command performance. So he remained and tried to be as vague as possible about his accident. In some ways, his parents' focus on the following evening's charity dinner and M.K. McDonald made it easy for him.

Max couldn't believe his ears. The older married son, like his mother had said, right in the presence of his own wife and mother, implied that all M.K. needed was to be laid, and he would be glad to oblige.

Buddy, the last one who tried is dead, Max thought. *And family or no family, attempt to hurt Kaye and you'll answer to me!*

Father and son were clearly members of Pop's questionable family clientele. The father wanted to discuss investments with Frank, and when Gus accompanied them and Frank into Frank's study, Max declined. "I really need to rest my leg," he offered.

Instead he headed into the parlor to pay his respects to the ladies. The Verqussis' younger son—a grown man in his own right—had spread out some drawings. From what Max could make out, they seemed to be of women. His curiosity piqued, Max opted to join the conversation.

"Ever since I can remember," Lucinda was saying, "Roland has always enjoyed drawing women and clothing them."

"I wonder about you, Rollie," twittered the daughter-in-law.

Max glanced at Roland. He appeared both frustrated and hurt by their remarks. However, when the young man started to speak, Max was blown away.

"Auntie Josephine," Roland stammered, "it's not a joke. It's not what they say. M—my dra—drawings are clothes for women. I always wanted to design clothes. No one at home seems to understand."

Lucinda stood up. "I wonder, Angel. We don't have much time, and our husbands will soon want to get back to our hotel. Would you share with me and my daughter-in-law some of your pastry recipes?"

"I'd be delighted." Angel led them out of the room, abandoning Roland with Josephine and Max.

Roland looked up, relieved to be left behind. "As you can see, no one in my family takes me seriously. That's why I left to go to the East Coast, to see if anyone there might be interested in my work. In a nutshell, Aunt Josephine, I literally was starving. All my funds were gone and I had but one last hope. Do you know what it was?"

Josephine looked at Max and shook her head.

"Your friend!" Roland beamed.

"My friend?" Josephine asked, dumbfounded. She was about to add, *Angel?*

"Yes, M.K. McDonald," Roland said. "The lady who's speaking at your charity dinner tomorrow night."

"Really?" Josephine said.

"Really?" Max echoed.

When Roland realized he had their attention, he became like a little boy in a candy store. Gone was the stammering, and with great passion he explained himself. "I ran into her somewhat coincidently, mind you. It was so unreal!" He went on to share that she had liked his work and had been willing to give him a chance. "I thought I was dreaming, but I wasn't!" Tears flowed freely down his face. "I'm actually having my very first show in two weeks. I'm so excited!" By now, he was fairly bouncing in his chair. "When I heard my family was coming here, I decided to join them and surprise M.K. I've designed a gown especially for her. Would you like to see it?"

"Of course, dear," Josephine kindly said.

"Definitely!" Max added, hoping he hadn't sounded over-interested.

Roland produced his drawing.

Max's jaw dropped. "You drew this?"

Roland simply nodded and grinned.

"It's stunning!" Max looked at Roland in disbelief.

Roland suddenly looked very serious. "It really would suit her. I designed the dress for her frame, hair color, and skin tone."

"But it's just a picture, dear," Josephine said gently, thinking the lad was probably a bit unbalanced.

"Right," he said with a grin. "Of course, we had to bring the sketches to life. M.K. set me up with Mrs. Baxter."

"Stephanie's mother?" Max asked before he could catch himself.

"Yes, absolutely. She's a very gifted seamstress. You obviously read about that horrid man and what he tried to do to M.K. and how he used Steph."

Max breathed easier, knowing Roland had inadvertently covered for him.

"Would you like to see the dress?" Roland asked.

Both mother and son, for totally different reasons, had lost their tongues. All either could do was nod and look wide-eyed at each other.

Roland slipped into the hall and retrieved a small suitcase. He brought it to the parlor, opened it, and out came the most gorgeous gown Max had ever seen. The green would perfectly complement the emeralds in Kaye's wedding and engagement rings—rings only he knew she had... rings she would wear tomorrow evening.

"Roland, this is a work of art," he sputtered. "Ms. McDonald will look gorgeous in it!"

"It is amazingly beautiful," Josephine added. "But how will you get it to her?"

"I have the cell phone numbers of her personal aides, Alice and Philippe," Roland replied matter-of-factly. "I plan to contact them tomorrow."

At that point, Max heard Al and Matt in the hall. Excusing himself from Roland and his mother, Max made a beeline for the two young men.

"I need you to do something for me," Max whispered. "Al, do you know a really good florist?"

Al gave him a look. "Hey, man, I'm back in my town. We have lots of good Italian florists."

"I need you to take this young man, his name's Roland, to the florist shop," Max said. "I want him to design a wrist corsage for Kaye to match the dress he's made for her. Then I want you to take him to the hotel and check him into one of our suites. Kaye is going to want to see what he's designed for her."

When Max returned to the room, Roland was carefully packing away the dress and his drawings. He had just finished telling Josephine that he wanted to dedicate any proceeds he received from his first ever fashion show to a fund to support the victims of sexual violence.

"You are one of the most caring young men I've ever met," Josephine told him.

"Roland, can I see you for a moment?" Max inquired.

"Sure, but can I call a cab first?" Roland said. "Also, I need to book a hotel. Could you advise me of a reasonable and safe one?"

"Roland, look at me," Max demanded. "You have no need of either a cab or a hotel. Al and Matt will take you to the convention center hotel. There's a room there for you. It's all taken care of. You might have to share it with another guy, though."

"Like who?" Roland asked cautiously.

"Maybe Matt and Al here. Or you may end up with your own space. But this is what I want you to do for me. If Al takes you to a florist, can you, with

293

the florist's help, design a special wrist corsage for M.K., to go with the dress?"

Roland looked like he'd just scored the winning goal in the World Cup. "No sweat!" he said, beaming.

"M.K. will be at the suite tonight and you need to tell her your plans." Max smiled. "Buddy, you're part of her troupe and you need to be housed with them." He next turned to Matt. "Make sure you register him at the hotel. See that he gets the special code, and you, Roland, enjoy yourself. You deserve it! Al, here's a blank check. Use it to pay for the corsage, and write on the card the words 'from Mrs. Josephine Carron. Also, here's a list of several other corsages I'd like them to make up for me. I've listed the colors. No need for cards. I intend to distribute them myself."

"Oh, that's so sweet!" Roland exclaimed.

Matt took Max aside. "Is he… you know?"

"Gay? Don't know," Max said. "Wear pajamas and get over it!"

chapter forty-one

When the 5:30 commuter train pulled into the station, Dave was there to pick up Jack. By six o'clock, they had joined their wives, and of course, Rufie. Shortly thereafter, Lewis arrived and drove the entourage to the airport.

As he settled into his seat on the private jet, Jack loosened his belt, undid his tie, and let out a deep sigh.

"That sigh probably sums up how we're all feeling," Sue said.

As the jet roared down the runway, Marnie added her perspective. "Sometimes just organizing the itinerary exhausts me."

"I know what you're saying," Jack said, "but it's more than that. All the hype around Glaxton's murders, coupled with what will explode when the media becomes aware of Max's involvement, and his connection with Kaye… it's like our private lives are on a collision course for a very public display. The thought of it stresses me out!"

Marnie patted her husband's arm. "Well, dear, perhaps you'd be less stressed if you thought of all this like a football game."

"What on earth do you mean?" Dave said.

"You fellows played before thousands of cheering fans. You got attention both if you won and if you made mistakes, but that attention was very transient, wasn't it?"

"I see what you mean," Sue chimed in. "Yes, we can expect the public's and the media's attention, but that doesn't need to define who we are or our relationships with one another."

"Exactly!" Marnie laughed. "The key is we should all take our cue from Rufie."

Everyone looked at the big dog sprawled on the large sofa.

Jack grinned. "That's right. A couch is a couch, whether in one of our houses or thousands of feet up in the air."

"He's had his bath," Sue added. "He got his hair trimmed and nails cut to look real pedigreed, but he's still just our Rufie!" As if in response, the big dog wiggled his stubby tail.

Al and Matt met them at the airport with Luigi. They had already deposited the luggage in the hotel suite.

"Gus had us take Angel and his luggage, along with Mr. and Mrs. C.'s, to their rooms," Al shared. "But Gus said that Kaye and Max's relationship is still a secret. He's made sure that neither Angel nor the Carrons know they're staying at the hotel. Chicago's hype level for tomorrow's hospital fundraiser is off the wall!" He grinned. "The money coming in for that old hospital is unprecedented, which has Mrs. C. absolutely thrilled!"

"Yeah," Luigi added. "With that and now having Max home, Mrs. C.'s zest for life has finally returned.

"Do any of you have information as to when Kaye's flight is expected to arrive in from England?" Jack asked. "I simply don't know how she manages to keep up with the demands of Kayleen. Their London corporate office called on Tuesday insisting that it was imperative she attend some sort of celebration for the Queen's diamond jubilee. So, off she treks."

"Personally, I think the British were hoping to get a sneak preview as to Max Kerr's identity." Dave chuckled. "It's amazing the interest all this has caused, even overseas."

Matt checked his watch. "Her plane is scheduled to touch down in a half-hour."

"Well, let's wait," Marnie suggested and received unanimous consent.

The downside to that choice was that they didn't arrive at the hotel until 1:00 a.m. The upside was that everything was quiet there. The media hadn't anticipated Kaye's arrival in the middle of the night. Thus, all managed to slip in under the radar.

Nonetheless, as a precaution, Kaye drove with her "family" while her staff traveled on their own, arriving before she did.

It turned out to be fortunate that Al and Matt had previously taken the Independence Drive luggage to the hotel, because when Kaye's plane arrived, she had three special parcels. One was extremely large. The other two were bulky, but not as big.

Kaye had a big grin on her face. "They're for my new nieces and nephew. I wonder, Al, could you take them directly to the Carrons? I think Sophia's having the children remain at her parents' on Friday evening. The presents might be a pleasant diversion for them."

"Bribing the family already, Ms. McDonald?" Jack piped up.

"Guilty as charged, Your Honor." Kaye smiled. "I can't wait to see them. I always dreamed of having twins, and to have twin girls and then a little boy? That's very special."

"This is off-topic, Kaye, but do you know a guy by the name of Roland?" Matt asked.

Kaye looked alarmed. "Why, yes, is anything the matter with him?"

"Nah," Al replied. "It's just that he was at the Carrons' house. He made a dress for you or something. Max liked it and thought you would, too. He had us deliver him to the hotel. We put him up in our room." Al deliberately left out the corsage detail, as Max had clearly indicated he wanted that to be a surprise.

"Who is Roland?" asked Sue.

"He's a brilliant young designer who has the potential to impact the fashion world internationally, and I had the good fortune to discover him," Kaye said triumphantly. "My board was so impressed with him that Kayleen has waded into the fashion market for the first time in our history. But why would he be at the Carrons' place?"

Al shrugged. "Same reason all the others are showing up. The family is arriving on the pretense of supporting Mrs. C.'s hospital charity. Actually, they're just as curious as everyone else about your Mr. Kerr."

Kaye's eyes were like saucers. "Roland's related to the Carrons? No way!"

"Yes way," Luigi said, laughing. "His mother is the daughter of Mrs. C.'s cousin. The family lives in L.A. Get used to it, Kaye. Sicilians have big families."

"They flew all the way from L.A. for a charity dinner?" Marnie was clearly astonished.

"Actually, there's more to it," Luigi said. "When you told Mr. C. that Max would be home this week, it went around our circles like wildfire. Everybody's curious as to what took him so long to show." He looked at Kaye with a mischievous grin. "Personally, I suspect you had a lot to do with Roland's father and older brother showing up."

Kaye appeared puzzled. "You mean Roland would have told them about his business relationship with Kayleen?"

"Not likely, would be my guess," Al interjected. "Didn't look like they gave Roland the time of day, much less the time to even listen to him for anything."

Marnie frowned. "But Luigi said they would have come because of Kaye."

Al looked at Luigi in desperation. "That's because they're probably the worst womanizers on the planet," Al scoffed. "They want to see Kaye in person. They're here for the chase."

"Well, won't they be in for a surprise tomorrow night." Kaye laughed. "Thanks for the head's up, Luigi, but I'm curious: couldn't Roland's father have helped him financially to get started?"

"His father's non-support won't be for lack of dough. Don't quote me, but I suspect he's into the rackets big time. It's likely because…" Luigi paused, searching for the right words.

"You mean because they think he might be gay," Kaye said sharply.

"You pretty much hit the nail on the head, I figure."

"Is he?" asked Dave.

"I really don't know," Kaye said. "He is an exceptionally gifted young man when it comes to women's fashions." She smiled. "And you say he made a special gown for me?"

"But Kaye, you already have your outfit selected for tomorrow evening," Sue protested.

"Yes, but I'll set it aside for Roland's. It will allow Rolando Designs some free publicity!"

After dropping off his passengers, Luigi decided to head back to the Carrons' house. Matt and Al chose to stay at the hotel.

"Max wants me to bring Jack and Dave to the Carrons' tomorrow," Matt said, "so we can practice our songs for the charity dinner and the church concert, at the cathedral on Sunday." He paused. "The Carrons have a grand piano, and does Al ever make those keys dance!"

chapter forty-two

It was mid-morning before Jack, Dave, Matt, and Al went to the convention hall. Jack wanted to get a sense of the acoustics and familiarize himself with the sound system. They had arranged for the sound technician to be there so Jack could outline their routine to him. The tech tested each man's voice, designating specific mikes to each. They promised they would have the fourth member of the quartet at the hall an hour and a half before the dinner, for the tech to assess his voice.

Preparations were in high-gear at the Carron house. A tailor had arrived to outfit Max.

Aunt Louisa had landed and was demanding to see him. Perched in her wheelchair, dressed all in black, complete with pillbox hat and veil, Louisa leaned forward, her hands firmly clasping a gold-headed black cane.

"She looks like she's here for his funeral," muttered Frank. "We just got rid of the Verquzzi family yesterday, and now she descends on us. Some people seem personally gifted at throwing cold water on what otherwise should be a great celebration."

Josephine tried placating Louisa by offering her tea and some of Angel's special pastry. Pepi and Lena had arrived the night before, and they joined the others in trying to humor the old dowager. Yet everyone knew Louisa was totally fixated on arranging a marriage for Max. She referred to it as her "M" mission.

"M mission," Frank mumbled to his wife as he made his way to the parlor to greet Louisa. "The 'make Max miserable mission' is her real agenda."

Josephine raised an eyebrow. "Did marriage make you miserable, Frank?"

"She didn't pick you for me," he retorted sharply.

Josephine gave him a playful poke in the ribs, then smiled sweetly at Aunt Louisa. "Frank's here, Aunt Louisa."

"Don't you think it's high-time your son settles down?" Louisa demanded.

Josephine ignored the old woman's caustic query. "Yes, Aunt Louisa, it is nice when a person is able to find someone they love and who loves them back."

However, neither the Carrons, Marconis, nor D'Amatos quite expected the prince in question to appear before Louisa attired as he did. Max hobbled into the room on his crutches, wearing faded jeans and a white T-shirt, with his denim shirt open, its tails out as if masquerading as a dinner jacket. He wore sneakers on his feet, and horrors, he was unshaven!

"Good morning, Aunt Louisa," he said, bending over to kiss her. "How good it is to see you again."

"Are those your prison clothes?" Louisa squeaked, aghast at his appearance.

Max smiled innocently. "Yes, we wore denims. I kind of got used to it after six years." He ignored his father's nonverbal communiqué, which roughly could be translated, *What on earth do you think you are doing?*

One thing could be said of Louisa. Even though she was taken aback by his appearance, like a good trooper she pressed on to achieve her goal.

"At my house, this attire would not be acceptable." Louisa cleared her throat. "However, I'm sure you will be dressed more like a gentleman on Sunday, and of course be shaven, dear!"

Max pulled up a chair next to her wheelchair. She reached out and patted his hand. Her wrinkled face broke into a broad smile.

"I'm arranging a party for you, Massimiliano," she said. "I have invited some very, let us say, *pretty* guests to meet you."

Max appeared genuinely touched by her invitation and horrified that he would have to decline. "Oh, Aunt Louisa, I'd love to come, but I can't on Sunday afternoon. I'm already committed. And we have to be at the cathedral at six."

This news not only surprised Aunt Louisa. It caught everyone else in the room off-guard, too—except Gus.

"You're going to church both in the morning *and* the evening?" Pepi blurted.

"Oh yes, and Saturday evening Mass," Max intoned solemnly. He knew that if he looked at Gus, he'd lose it. Gus coughed and quickly excused himself to go to the washroom.

Max turned to his mother. "Mamma, when do you expect Sophia and her family?"

"She said she'd be here for lunch," Josephine said. "I'm planning lunch for one o'clock, to give them time to arrive."

"Wonderful. I'm so looking forward to seeing my nieces and nephew. But if you'll excuse me, Al and Matt are bringing over two special friends." Max took his aunt's hand and kissed it. "You're so kind to think of me."

He deftly exited the room on his crutches, passing Gus in the hallway.

"You have a date?" Gus asked. "What exactly was all that about?"

"Just fighting fire with fire," Max deadpanned and went on his way.

Sophia and her family arrived earlier than expected. Her children were excited to be at Grandma and Grandpa Carron's.

"And even Nonno and Nana are here!" little Ricci squealed. Those were the children's names for Tony's parents.

Josephine busied herself by occupying her grandchildren with a special video she had bought just for them. The ladies sat visiting in the room next to the children. Aunt Louisa, however, had gone back to the parlor, with the full intent of accosting her brother and Frank about their need to help poor Max "shape up," as she put it, and learn to adjust to "normal society."

By this time, the quartet and Al had worked out their repertoire both for the fundraising dinner and the Sunday evening service at the King's Cathedral, a large nondenominational church associated with Jack's home congregation in Summerside. The cathedral's pastor was well aware of Jack and his friends' musical talents. He'd been after Jack for years to come sing in their church. Knowing the publicity the Friday evening banquet revelation would garner, Jack figured now was as good a time as any to fulfill the request. He had arranged with the pastor for the quartet to practice Sunday afternoon at the cathedral. The Sunday evening service had been billed as a Gospel concert with the *For Him Four* quartet from Pennsylvania.

"You realize, guys," Jack remarked, "that at this point in time, the only ones interested in our concert will be the cathedral's parishioners, who love Gospel music."

"But after tonight's Max and Kaye show, a lot more could show up simply out of curiosity," Dave commented. "God's giving us an opportunity to share His Son, perhaps to some who've never met Jesus."

The four men gathered around Al at the piano and began to pray for the presence of the Holy Spirit to anoint their music on both evenings. "Lord Jesus, I just ask that if there is anyone who comes to either event and has never experienced the reality of your love, that You will reveal yourself to them," Max quietly prayed.

Afterwards, the five simply enjoyed jamming together. At one point, Max left the room only to reappear about five minutes later. He leaned towards Jack.

"My Aunt Louisa would like to meet you," Max said. "Actually, she's Tony's aunt, too. She's going to be ninety-four next April."

"Ninety-four? Does she have all her faculties?"

"Oh yeah!"

And then some, Max added to himself.

"That's wonderful!" Jack replied amiably. "Sure, I'd love to meet her."

"She uses a wheelchair and she's sharp as a tack," Max volunteered as they walked down the hallway.

While Max hadn't met Aunt Louisa and his family's dress code, he had met the Independence Drive dress code. He knew exactly how Jack would dress this morning. He'd have reasoned, "Why shave twice? I'll be wearing a tux tonight, so to balance the day I'll begin it in my comfortable old Harvard jogging suit."

"Hey," Tony boomed down the hall when he saw them. "Max, did you know Aunt Louisa's in the parlor with our fathers?" Tony, on the other hand, was dressed appropriately, in the old Italian code that both his father and father-in-law approved—sports coat, slacks, and turtleneck. And of course he had shaved.

Max smiled ever so innocently. "Yep, I was just taking Jack to meet her."

Max entered the parlor on crutches, Jack in tow.

"Aunt Louisa," Max said sweetly, "I want you to meet my friend, Jack."

Now Jack will do what any gentleman of his stature and upbringing does, Max thought. *Or at least, that's what I'm counting on.*

To Max's delight, Jack squatted down in front of Aunt Louisa's wheelchair to establish eye contact. He conversed gentlemanly with her, being entirely pleasant. The problem was that Aunt Louisa had never met a Harvard WASP-type before.

"Jack and I have a Sunday afternoon date," Max told Louisa. "We'll be going to the Cathedral for six o'clock, otherwise we'd love to be at your party."

Jack smiled in polite agreement.

This kind of overwhelmed Aunt Louisa. She stared wide-eyed at Pepi and my father, then quickly excused herself.

"I need to talk with the ladies," she said hurriedly and left.

After she was gone, Max introduced Jack to his father and Pepi. Jack stood up and shook their hands in a very manly fashion.

Jack simply nodded at Gus. "Good to see you again."

This surprised Pepi and Frank and got their curiosity juices flowing. It was at that point that Tony, Al, Dave, and Matt joined them. That meant the two dress codes were pretty evenly balanced.

Apart from Max, the only other guy in the room who grasped the big picture was Gus. As for Max, he chatted away as if everybody knew everything. As a result, Gus was exceedingly relaxed, while Frank and Pepi, both of whom usually ensured that they did know everything, grew increasingly tense.

In the middle of it, Sophia flew into the room, arms folded and toe tapping. She stopped in front of Tony.

"What did you tell Aunt Louisa?" she demanded, eyes flashing.

Tony's facial expression was that of surprise. It was as though he held a bomb in his hand and hadn't a clue how he had gotten it.

"Aunt Louisa is in the kitchen horrifying Mamma and Lena," Sophia continued, "telling them that Max is gay and Jack is his partner."

That bombshell brought a similar look of horror to Dave, Al, and Matt's faces. Jack, on the other hand, was in utter shock, wondering how on earth the old lady had ever concocted such a tale.

Frank intervened and came to his son-in-law's defense. "Sophia, Tony wasn't even in the room when Max brought Jack in and introduced him to Aunt Louisa."

Sophia swung around to Max, who tried to conjure up a look of innocence. Unfortunately for him, Gus could contain himself no longer. He let out a whoop and started to laugh. He laughed so hard that tears flowed down his face.

Fortunately for Josephine, her large decorative pillow was closer to Sophia's hands than her mother's antique Roman vase. Sophia grabbed the pillow and started belting Max with it, screaming in Italian something that roughly translated meant, *How could you dare do such a thing!*

Surprisingly, despite Max's shenanigans the evening's big surprise managed to remain secret. "The date I spoke of," Max clarified, "was an afternoon practice session at King's Cathedral in preparation for a concert we're giving at their Sunday service." He looked at his father. "Pop, I also wanted our quartet to sing a number or two tonight to both surprise and honor Mamma. That's why we were practicing this morning." He added, "I hope you'll keep this quiet, please."

With that, Max quickly ushered the quartet out of the room, saying that they had to go home to rest and dress for the evening.

As the men got into the van, Max had to placate Jack, who by now clearly realized that Max had set him up.

"You know my little black book?" Max asked. "Well, I just ripped up three of the six years you owed me! Come on, Jack, how'd you feel if you knew that woman was lying awake at night plotting for years how she could marry you off to somebody you could care less about, all so she could get a groom's fee? I finally got even in a nice way."

"At my expense," Jack groused. "But she really did that? Match-make, I mean? And the girl would pay your Aunt Louisa if a guy married her?"

"That's what I was told, scout's honor!"

"So what about your Aunt Louisa? Is she out of your black book?"

"You think she should be?"

"She's ninety-four years old," Jack retorted as he extended his hand to Max.

"Okay, deal," Max said as the two shook hands.

"Which means that I have no more pages in your book!"

"How do you figure that?"

"Two years for the times I nursed you," Jack said, "and one year for arranging the sting, and the three today. We're even, Mr. Carron!"

"I'm glad that's settled," Dave snorted. "I want to get back to the hotel for a late lunch and a nap. See you at four, Max."

By the time Max joined his own family for lunch, everyone's ruffled feathers had been smoothed and Max got to meet his little nieces and nephew. It was instant mutual attraction, and the gifts Kaye had brought for him to give them sealed their relationship.

chapter forty-three

Max elected to go to the convention center earlier than planned. He called Jack and asked to schedule their practice for three o'clock rather than four.

"That will allow us to dress later, yet still ensure that I can be on the banquet floor by five," Max said. "I told Bill, Lou, and my friend Rob that I'd be there early to greet them. I kinda thought it would be nice to have a few moments with each of them before the crowd arrives. It'll also give me time to mingle with others who I haven't seen for nearly seven years."

That decision, however, generated alarm with the elder Carrons, particularly when their son, still unshaven and still in his denims, announced he was departing with Al for the convention center.

Aunt Louisa, in fact, was very vocal. "How dare you dishonor your family by appearing like that!" she said, waggling her boney finger at him.

Max diffused her tirade by hobbling on his crutches to Aunt Louisa and kissing her on the forehead. "No need to worry, Aunt Louisa," he reassured her. "I'm simply going early so I can practice the hymn I want to sing for Mamma. Afterwards, both Al and I will dress in the hotel room I've reserved."

"Why waste your money renting a room when you could just as easy dress here?" the old lady objected.

"Aunt Louisa," Max replied gently but firmly, "I had six years of forced saving, where I had no opportunity to spend my money!"

This remark had the desired effect and served to silence further objections.

The quartet's practice went off without a hitch. The sound technician needed little time to blend their voices.

"You guys sound like you've been singing together for a long time. You do this professionally, right?" he enthused as he fine-tuned his settings both for when the men were close together and when they were singing in separate areas of the hall.

His compliment particularly impressed Matt and Al. Dave, on the other hand, merely laughed.

"Actually, as a full group, it's been only a month or two," Dave said. "Trust me, we're anything but professional singers. But we love the Lord Jesus and we love to sing. I've discovered that whatever anyone does to honor Him, He blesses."

"Which reminds me," Jack said. "It's our practice to ask God's provision and anointing on this ministry. As our sound technician for the evening, you are part of us. Would you care to join us as we pray? Perhaps you have something specific you'd like us to include?"

The young man looked stunned. "Actually there is. My two-year-old is very sick. The docs can't seem to figure it out. They're even considering cancer, which has my wife and me terrified."

Max nodded. "That is pretty scary."

The six of them formed a little circle—a "prayer huddle," Dave called it. They thanked Jesus for Our Lady of Mercies Hospital; prayed for all who would attend the charity dinner to somehow be blessed by God; prayed for everyone involved in the evening, whether they were volunteering or getting paid, to do their job well; and asked the Holy Spirit to be all He wanted to be through each one of them. Jack specifically prayed for their sound technician, not just for his work but for his family, that Jesus's healing presence would be with his little child, restoring the toddler to full health. He prayed that the doctors might be given full understanding of the child's illness. At the end of their prayer, there was a resounding Amen. Even the young technician raised his voice in agreement.

Max's timing was perfect. He was showered, shaved, and in his tuxedo by a quarter to five. He met Jack on the way to the elevator.

"Do you think my Aunt Louisa will approve?" Max quipped.

"I'm not sure your aunt would consider my opinion adequate validation of your appearance." Jack laughed. "But for what it's worth, you do cut a mean figure, sir!"

Jack stopped, turned around, and firmly grabbed Max's hand.

"God bless, Max! I pray this will be a very special night for you and Kaye."

Max gripped Jack's hand, his eyes moistening, "Thanks, Jack, and thanks for all your help and support."

Their handshake gave way to a full embrace just as the elevator door opened.

"Whew!" Jack said. "Lucky for us no one was on board, or there would have been another misunderstanding."

Bill and Lou and their wives, Rosa and Anna, did arrive early, as Max had anticipated. In fact, they were entering the hall as he stepped off the elevator. It was impossible to tell who was more pleased to see whom.

"Oh Max," Rosa gushed. "Aren't you the dapper one? All the girls will be after you!"

Max blushed. "Thanks, Rosa." He gave her a peck on the cheek.

"No, it's us who need to thank you, boss! We could never pay for these tickets," Lou said.

"Or for the duds," Bill chimed in.

"That reminds me, come here." Max motioned for the four to follow him. Off to one side was a table staffed by a young woman from the florist shop where Al had placed Max's order. "Excuse me, could I have the corsages set aside for Anna and Rosa?"

"And you are, sir?" the young woman asked, giving Max an appreciative onceover.

"Mr. M. Carron."

"Oh, of course, sir." Immediately the young lady handed him two beautiful corsages.

Bill and Lou began to pull out their wallets.

"They're already paid for, gentlemen," the young woman said, smiling.

Rosa and Anna stood there, beaming. "They match our dresses perfectly," Rosa exclaimed.

"They should." Max grinned. "I asked Bill and Lou to tell me the color of the dresses you chose."

"Max?" Lou said worriedly.

"Is something wrong?"

"Well, yeah," Bill spoke up. "We've never been to anything as posh as this before. What do we do?"

"He means, how should we behave?" Anna said anxiously.

Max looked at the four of them with love. "Just be yourselves. Come, let's find your table."

Together they went to the large seating display at the hall entrance, found their table number, and then located the table. Max gave them a quick overview of the cutlery—which fork was meant for which item of food, and so on—and soon the four were at ease again.

Max gave the two men a computerized passkey. "When the festivities here are ended, go to that elevator." He pointed to the one on the left side of the hall. "There will be a security guard there. He'll ask you to swipe your keys. This will allow you access to the penthouse and my reception. Do not give your key to anyone, and don't invite anyone else to come with you. Okay?"

The four nodded in agreement.

At that moment, Max heard his name being called from across the hall. Excusing himself, he turned and demonstrated how well he had mastered his crutches as he literally sprinted towards the voice.

"Wow! Look at you," Max called to his friend. "All decked out in Chicago's men of blue finery. Good evening, Captain Rob! Or should I say Captain Robert?"

Max shook the policeman's hand warmly.

"Just plain Rob is fine," Rob said. "And Max, thanks so much for the dinner tickets. Normally we're not allowed to accept such favors, but since you noted 'for your many visits to me in prison and your encouragement for me to attend the prison Alpha course offered there,' my superior okayed it."

Rob's petite wife beside him added, "Don't forget to tell Max that the announcement of his wrongful conviction also influenced the decision."

"That's true, Max. I was glad to hear the news. Somehow, all along, I couldn't believe that you'd do something so brazenly amateurish and—"

"Stupid," Max finished his sentence, laughing.

"Exactly," Rob said. "All I could think about was that incident at school when I accidentally hit the ball through the cathedral window. You grabbed my bat and told me to run, then took the fall for me."

Max grinned. "Hey, Rob, it turned out okay, for you and for me."

"Not so good for you. You got a licking and a school suspension."

"True, but aside from that, it earned my father's attention, even if briefly, which was good for me and for him. I think it gave him hope that I might not be the wussie he feared I was."

"Are you implying good arose out of your wrongful imprisonment?" Rob's wife expressed shock at the thought.

Max looked at her and winked. "Most definitely! You'll be able to see how, both at the dinner and at the private reception afterward. But, please, come with me." He then pulled out another electronic passkey, as he had done for Lou and Bill. He also took them to the florist's table.

"Didn't you say that you attend the King's Cathedral?" Max asked as he placed a corsage on Rob's wife.

"Yes, we do," Rob replied, curious as to why Max should bring up the matter of his church attendance.

"I'm in a singing group and we're singing there on Sunday night. Hope you two can make it. It's both comforting and encouraging to look out and see a friendly face."

No sooner had Rob and his wife sat down at their table than others Max knew arrived. He greeted each one with delight. Family members also began to arrive. Max was careful to acknowledge everyone and thank them for coming and supporting Our Lady of Mercies Hospital.

Sophia floated up to her brother. "Better not let Lou Bastaldi get too close to you. He wants to know who shot the dead guy in the Newark precinct. He was shocked to find Tony at Pop's."

Max chuckled. "You mean he figured Tony shot him?"

"You got it, brother dear," said Sophia, clearly not amused.

"Your warning's too late, sis," Max replied with a grin. He glimpsed Lou heading directly for him. He extended his hand to the man. "Nice to see you again, Lou."

Lou glowered as he took it. "Who?"

Max pulled him close, whispering something in the man's ear.

Lou looked surprised. "Yeah, sure, Max." He then followed Max towards an empty part of the hall, away from the crowd. Once there, Lou leaned into Max. "Your father doesn't know you killed a guy?"

"Correct."

"So how did you get here?"

"I drove."

Lou frowned. "Stop with the smart stuff! I meant that was a cop station. If you shot that guy, how come they let you leave the state?"

"Lou, the man went on a shooting rampage. Before he entered the station, he seriously wounded a couple of people and killed the parking attendant. If Tony hadn't been wearing a bulletproof vest, he would have been killed. The guy was set on firing off more rounds. It's called self-defense. When it takes place in the midst of people more interested in being witnesses than victims, accolades follow, not accusations."

Max's words and tone left no doubt that as far as he was concerned that shooting was a non-issue. Yet Lou recognized something clearly *was* an issue, and his expression indicated that whatever it might be, he hadn't a clue. He stared at Max, helpless.

Max put his arm around the man's shoulder. "Lou, neither Pop nor Pepi know that Tony was with me in Newark. Nor do they know Gus was there."

"Oh, okay," Lou said, his countenance clearly revealing it wasn't okay.

Max simply smiled, looked at his watch, and pulled out another passkey. "All I'm asking, Lou, is that you don't say anything to anybody until after tonight's banquet. Then you can say whatever to whomever. Here's a key for you and your family to join us upstairs after the festivities have ended." He looked Lou in the eye. "Promise? Do I have your word?"

"The reason for your request is honorable, right?" Lou asked intently.

"Absolutely, Lou."

"Okay, Max, it's a deal. Until after the charity stuff is over, I'll keep quiet."

Max shook Lou's hand, repositioned his crutches, and headed towards his parents' table. The elder Carrons had just sat down when he arrived.

It didn't take long for his mother to come to her son's side. "I see you and Lou had a nice reunion," she said, smiling sweetly.

"We did indeed, Mamma. We did indeed."

"Max, Ms. McDonald should arrive shortly. Did you meet her personally?"

"Yes. Mamma, I did." He tried to sound indifferent.

Josephine pushed a little deeper. "Don't you think she's beautiful? I know I do. I just wondered what you thought."

Max looked at his mother and chuckled. "I'm not blind, Mother, if that's what you're getting at." He took her hand and gave it an affectionate squeeze.

And so the gala event began. Bishop Masseroti thanked everyone for supporting Our Lady of Mercies and offered the blessing. The cuisine for the five-course meal was exquisite. However, it was very clear that everyone's focus was not on the food; all eyes were on the five-foot-eight redhead with the charming smile and winsome laughter.

Roland's clinging emerald gown accentuated Kaye's dancing green eyes, clear ivory skin, and rosy cheeks. Stunning was too mild an adjective to describe Our Lady of Mercies after-dinner speaker.

Equally on the mind of the dinner guests was the empty seat at the head table. Many had come hoping to catch a glimpse of Indiana's mysterious private investigator, who the police had credited with saving Ms. McDonald's life. It appeared that her hopes of him being healed sufficiently to attend had been dashed. Nonetheless, the air was filled with anticipation that tonight she would at least divulge his identity.

As the meal concluded, the chairman of the Hospital's foundation announced a fifteen-minute recess for the caterers to clear the tables, allowing the guests an opportunity to stretch their legs and visit the washroom.

At their respective tables, Max, Roland, and Al excused themselves. The absence of the latter two bothered no one. In fact, in Roland's case, his brother caustically sneered, "Glad to have you leave, brother dearest."

In Max's case, Josephine not only noted her son's absence, she began to fret when he didn't return. "I so want him to hear Ms. McDonald's speech," she said to Frank and Sophia.

To keep Frank from setting out to haul in his wayward son, Tony quickly made a point of getting up to go find Max. He returned a few moments later and pointed to the back of the hall. "Max is at the back, standing up. His leg was starting to cramp, but he can see and hear clearly."

This explanation appeased Josephine and diverted everyone else's attention from Max.

The chairman requested that everyone take their seats. Shortly thereafter, the lights were dimmed. A spotlight illuminated Ms. McDonald at the back of the hall. It then followed her as she walked up to the podium, arm in arm with a beaming Roland. Around the room, many began to stand and applaud, obviously assuming this handsome blond man was from Indiana. Not so in the Carrons' section of the room, especially where the Verquzzis sat. If father and brother were in shock at seeing Ms. McDonald on Roland's arm, they were even more surprised when she introduced him.

"This is Kayleen's commercial for the evening," she said. She went on to share how her company was in partnership with Rolando Designs. She touted Roland as a young American whose designs would soon be recognized alongside the works of Europe's great fashion icons. Then she revealed how he had designed the dress she was wearing specifically for this occasion. At that point, she invited Roland to tell the audience about Rolando Designs and his upcoming fashion show.

To say that Roland did a good job would be an understatement. He was superb! He began by saying that he took great delight in talking about women's clothing and the people he cared about. He went on to describe how he'd met Ms. McDonald and her receptionist, Ms. Stephanie Baxter. He credited Stephanie's mother as being instrumental in bringing his designs to life through her creative seamstress abilities.

Referring to the trauma Ms. McDonald and Ms. Baxter suffered, Roland stated emphatically that he wanted to do something to highlight the problem of violence against women.

"Consequently," he concluded, "the proceeds of Rolando Designs' first fashion show will go to assist such women in their recovery. The event is to be held in New York, two weeks from now."

Kaye then asked the audience to welcome her receptionist, Stephanie Baxter. She, too, wore a gown designed by Roland. Her flowing pale blue gown proved equally flattering to her figure.

"It should be obvious to all that Ms. McDonald and I have two distinctly different body types," Stephanie said confidently. "We women come in many sizes, shapes, and skin tones. A good designer respects our differences and works to dress us in clothes that complement who we are. This way, each woman can be positive about herself." She beamed and took Roland's hand. "Roland has that ability."

The convention center erupted in applause as Roland escorted Stephanie from the platform.

Kaye thanked the audience for their reception of the two young people. "I'm encouraged that you received my commercial so well!" As the laughter died down, she continued. "Before I speak, I'd like you to welcome the *For Him Four* quartet from Pennsylvania. I'm trusting in the old adage that says music calms the savage heart. My hope is that this special music may soften the media's reception of my speech."

Her remark elicited further laughter throughout the hall.

"In a few short weeks, we will celebrate Christmas," she said. "Christians, at this time, reflect on God's gift to us of His Son, Jesus Christ. Jesus came to open the door to forgiveness and reconciliation, both between us and God and us with one another."

Kaye paused and sighed. "Throughout history, I'm afraid that we Christians often failed to live lives that proclaimed the power of God's reconciliation to others. Our quartet is living proof that through Jesus, not only is forgiveness possible, so also is reconciliation." She smiled. "Forgiveness and reconciliation allow new life to spring forth and bless others. Tonight, as you listen to the music, you will be privileged to be witnesses of God's reconciling love!"

With that, the music began. From different areas in the hall, the men began to sing. The hall was darkened, the singers invisible; their rich melodic voices cascaded like a waterfall into the audience's soul.

The first in their repertoire was "Ava Maria," honoring the many Italian Catholics present. Max dominated that piece. Josephine recognized her son's deep rich tenor and was moved to tears. "O Holy Night" followed, each man

312

having a solo, yet voices intertwining throughout, in perfect harmony as each moved slowly towards the center of the hall, where the podium was situated. Indeed, the venue was ideally suited to convey their theme of reconciliation.

As they converged at center stage, they switched from Christmas carol to southern Gospel: "Lead Me to the Rock that Is Higher than I," based on Psalm 61:2. By now, the four were bathed in the spotlight. At Jack's direction, the spotlight swung to their sound technician. Jack asked the young man to take a bow.

The piano was to the right of center and all four gathered around Al, who played "When the Saints Come Marching In." The quartet encouraged everyone to clap and sing along with them. Even Frank joined in, stunned at what he was experiencing.

They then concluded with a rousing rendition of "A New Name in Glory," after which the room erupted in spontaneous applause.

When the applause at last subsided, Kaye said softly, "I'd like to introduce my friends. If you'd like to applaud them further, would you please refrain from doing so until all have been introduced?"

She began with Al, commenting that he was a young man on Frank Carron's staff. Next, she introduced Matt and Dave, explaining they were a father and son team, both members of the police force in Summerside, Pennsylvania.

When she did that, Sophia noticed that both Pepi and her father's jaws dropped.

Then Kaye introduced Max. "Our Tenor is Massimiliano Carron of Chicago, who recently had his name cleared after serving a six-year prison term."

At this, murmurs were heard throughout the banquet room.

Josephine leaned over to Frank and Sophia. "No wonder Max said he knew her. Isn't Ms. McDonald being gracious, acknowledging him this way?"

Sophia nodded and smiled, trying hard not to look at her father, who by now was shell-shocked. She made a mental note of where his personal physician was seated, in case they soon needed him.

Finally, Kaye turned to the very tall, distinguished, bespectacled man standing between her and Max. She slipped her arm into his and beamed. "And now I'd like to introduce you to the quartet's leader and baritone, Justice Jack Walters, who happens to be the trial judge who sentenced Mr. Carron to prison." Audible gasps were heard throughout the audience. "Would you please refrain from applause for a few more moments? Mr. Carron would like to say a few words."

She probably hadn't needed to make that request, as everyone was literally too shocked to respond.

So Max finally appeared publicly, in Chicago. "Forgiveness releases bitterness and opens the door for one to begin to heal," he shared. "Carrying resentment, on the other hand, causes anger to fester and leads to hatred. Hatred will only destroy the person harboring it. I know that feeling, for it ate away at me for six years. But I was fortunate that in prison God used several people to point me to Jesus. As a result, there came a time, following my release, when I knew both that I had to get rid of my hatred, and that on my own I was powerless to do so. In desperation, I yielded all of myself to Christ."

He paused and softly declared, "The words of our last song, 'A New Name in Glory,' are real to me. When in your heart you experience Jesus's forgiveness and pardon, God starts to make you whole. Jesus gives you the power to forgive others. I actually forgave Jack before I even met him. It wasn't Jack's or my ability that allowed us to become friends. It was Jesus working in both of us."

"Initially, neither of us trusted the other," Jack added. "I was bound by my bias against him. He was bound by his anger and bitterness at the injustice I was responsible for."

"But each of us chose to trust Jesus rather than our own thoughts or feelings," Max said. "That's why Jack looked again at the trial transcripts and recognized a problem. The details aren't important. What is important is that an amazing alliance happened. That alliance allowed those responsible for framing me to be found, resulting in their arrest and subsequent confession. Consequently, I was cleared of wrongdoing!"

Max acknowledged the help of the FBI, the Newark and Summerside police departments, and his own family, particularly Tony, Sophia, Gus, and his men. He said that he felt they deserved a round of applause. To his surprise, the audience rose and gave a standing ovation that lasted several minutes.

Sophia noticed tears trickling down Aunt Louisa's wrinkled face.

"Are you okay?" Sophia asked softly.

"Oh dear," Louisa cried. "I thought so badly of Massimiliano and his friend, that he was dishonoring his family. That they were bums!"

Sophia knelt down beside Louisa's chair and gave the old lady a hug. "Aunt Louisa, none of us are perfect. That's why Jesus's forgiveness is so important. Once we've received His forgiveness, we're able to share that forgiveness with those who've offended us. I know both Max and Jack forgive you!"

Louisa sniffed, dabbing her eyes. "You're sure?"

"Absolutely, Auntie, absolutely!"

Kaye then stood alone at the center of the podium. The round stage allowed her to walk as she talked, continually moving, continually connecting and reconnecting with each area of the convention floor.

"I knew one day I would need to publicly acknowledge the ordeal I experienced earlier this year." She paused. "Thus, when Ms. Marconi asked if I would speak at this benefit, I accepted for these two reasons. First, I saw it as a way to honor Mr. Maxwell Kerr near his home. Second, I knew this charity would especially benefit women and children in need."

Kaye inhaled deeply. "There are several approaches I could have taken to deliver this address." She closed her eyes. "However, I soon discovered there are areas I am still unable to deal with. I cannot recount the details of Mr. Glaxton's horrific middle-of-the-night calls, other than to say they were very graphic." She stopped, shook her head sadly, and bit her lip. "Emotionally, I simply cannot go there. I cannot because of his victims. These were precious women, one as young as twelve! They were cherished daughters, wives, mothers, and sisters. Both they and their families need to be respected."

Tears streamed down her face. "I can say that every night, Mr. Kerr and I had to detail the specifics we heard from that evening's call. We anonymously sent that information to the FBI. Through the papers, the Bureau authenticated those cases in an agreed code. Thus, I knew my caller wasn't a disturbed prankster but a dangerous psychopathic serial killer. That's all I can and will say about that aspect of my ordeal."

She appeared to regain her composure, but another tear began to fall as she started to speak again. "The other area I cannot bear to discuss in detail is what happened the night Mr. Glaxton invaded my home. I cannot speak about how badly Mr. Kerr was injured that night." Her voice broke. "I just can't! To do so would force me to relive that night all over again. Emotionally, I am unable to do that."

Her eyes closed as she shook her head sadly.

"I pray you will understand." She paused. "What I realized that I can talk about briefly—and I emphasize the word *briefly*—is how Mr. Kerr and I began to work together. I can speak about his recovery process and our current relationship."

As she paused, applause began to resonate throughout the building.

Her infectious laughter broke out. "Yes, I thought that might be a good choice, too! I figured there might be people here interested in gossip."

And so Kaye set the tone for her fifteen-minute disclosure.

While everyone was laughing, Max Carron hobbled back onto the stage unnoticed.

"First things first, there is no Maxwell Kerr from Indiana!" Ripples of gasps could be heard throughout the auditorium. Kaye smiled, and that smile was captured for all to see on the large overhead screens throughout the hall. "But there *is* a Massimiliano Carron, from Illinois, who prefers to be called Max!"

Those sitting near Josephine and Frank thought the two would collapse. It seemed to take five minutes before they could breathe again.

By now, Max had come to stand beside Kaye, arm around her waist, looking most handsome and debonair.

Kaye suddenly became very serious. "We need to talk about God's great love for a moment."

"Yes," Max interjected. "I always knew that my mother would hold me in her prayers, and my awareness of that sustained me."

Kaye added, "Many people were also praying for me. They knew I had received disturbing phone calls several months before. Initially, when the police began to investigate, those calls stopped, throwing doubt as to whether those calls ever occurred. This was very traumatic for me. My friends stood by me. Concerned for my wellbeing, they kept me in their prayers."

She glanced at Max and chuckled. "Some people prayed for my sanity because they had a financial investment in Kayleen and didn't want its CEO going off the deep end. Bad for business!"

Laughter again echoed throughout the building.

"In all seriousness, though," Kaye continued, "God always answers our prayers. It's just that how He chooses to do so can catch us off-guard. His ways often don't fit our expectations."

She sighed. "Perhaps I should confess that initially I felt very guilty about Max helping me and his family not knowing where he was. Then one day I stopped to consider how he had gotten involved in the first place. I mean, I hadn't sent for him. Invited him. Asked him. He just showed up one night in my bedroom." She paused, caught the eye of a person sitting at a table closest to the stage, and quipped, "Yes, the doors were locked!"

Kaye smiled. "So maybe he spent six years in jail for something he didn't do, but I figure three months in my house is pretty lenient for break and entry! Anyway, the reason he got stuck in my house is that the moment he entered my room, the phone rang. Well, naturally he wanted to know to whom I might be talking. He listened in on the conversation and became the first person to authenticate Glaxton's awful calls."

Kaye screwed up her face. "I'm sure you can appreciate my dilemma, however. Someone who breaks and enters has a bit of a credibility gap as a witness! This meant we had to devise a less than straightforward strategy."

That's when Max began to tell what had happened to him in prison—how he'd been allowed to take law courses from Harvard, how Professor Brown had encouraged him, and how one of those courses had required the student to investigate and research a specific avenue of crime. He had chosen to do a paper on psychopathic criminals, because their prison had a psychiatric wing that housed such persons. He had designed his protocol, had the prison ethics board and the graduate school ratify his proposal, and secured the voluntary participation of each inmate interviewed.

"That formal education proved helpful in this case," Max said. "Informally, I was incarcerated with several of this country's most skilled cat burglars. I simply listened as they described both how to enter an electronically wired home, as well as how to set up your own system to alert you to a break-in. This, too, was useful in apprehending Glaxton."

Both Kaye and Max then shared openly and honestly how their own relationship began to blossom, ending with the revelation that, in fact, they had become husband and wife.

Josephine covered her mouth in utter shock. Frank let out a very deep sigh and breathed two audible words, "Thank God!" He realized the damper his rash action in the parking garage would have had on this joyous celebration had not Kaye dramatically intervened on his behalf.

At that point, Professor Brown emerged, dressed in academic regalia to bestow on Max, on behalf of the Dean of Law, the Harvard law degree.

Warden Blackmore then stepped forward with a certificate honoring Max for forging the way for the development of a new program that would allow qualified inmates opportunities to further their education.

Max started to laugh when Jack stepped forward and said that his own punishment for missing the irregularities in the original trial and erroneously convicting Max was to spend a year supervising Max, as he articled for the Bar.

Needless to say, in the days that followed, radio, TV, magazines, newspapers, and the Internet were all atwitter. In the end, Marnie's prediction came true. Just like it does for the big sports game heroes, life does go on. Other stories happen, and normalcy returns to the lives of yesterday's headliners. Thus it was for Kaye, Max, the other residents of Independence Drive, the Carrons, and the Marconis.

Reflecting on their situation months later, Jack grumped, "And that is exactly how it would have remained, had Max never been attacked and knifed!" He took off his glasses, absentmindedly chewing on one of the stems. He shrugged and pensively commented, "But then, that's a whole other story! Perhaps someday it, too, may be told."